THE END OF EVERYTHING

ESME CARMICHAEL

Copyright © 2021 Esme Carmichael
All rights reserved.

The characters and events portrayed in this book are fictitious. Any similarity to real persons, living or dead, is coincidental and not intended by the author.

No part of this book may be reproduced, or stored in a retrieval system, or transmitted in any form or by any means, electronic, mechanical, photocopying, recording, or otherwise, without express written permission of the publisher.

~ ABOUT THIS BOOK~

Can you hear the music? Listen to it sing...

It has been 183 years since Mason destroyed the Old World, terraforming it into a beautiful, frozen tundra which he claims with tyrannical sovereignty.

In the midst of this New World, Alira is a wanted woman, running from Mason and his sadistic minions. Forced to hide her true identity, Alira must survive the darkest, cruellest forms of humanity as she searches for the truth of who, and what she is. Why is she prophesied to destroy the world, why is she known as The End of Everything? And why, when Mason can kill with a single stare, does she want to look into his eyes?

Filled with murder, mystery and dark suspense, *The End of Everything* is the first in a brutal tetralogy of emotion and survival. Each part twists Alira's personality, turning her from a naïve, immature girl into a relentless survivor who straddles the boundary between heroine and villain.

Please note, the "The End of Everything" is a dark fantasy and contains material that is unsuitable for young readers. A full list of content themes can be found on Page 373.

For those who never stop dreaming

1

SPRING

It started with a conversation.
You understand, of course, that the interior of a longhouse was full of conversation. A perpetual buzz of laughter, chatter and drunken revelry. An intoxicating mix that all but drowned the whizz of the outside blizzard.

Gusts of wind fought through gaps in the walls, the grand fire flickered in response. Sparks from cracking wood struggled to rise, only to disperse throughout air choked with smoke. Strings of dried fish hung from the rafters; their strong, salty scents diminished by hanging herbs, like strings of dull emeralds.

Sitting at a corner table, I sipped my tankard of mead, and observed.

Opposite was an old woman, tapping a crooked finger against the ruts in the table. To my left sat a man with a black eye patch, his blond hair and beard braided and decorated with turquoise beads. To my right, a thirteen-year-old girl, sprawled and comatose on the table after a few pints of beer.

My own curiosity – the range of human interactions before me – spread until every man, woman and child were known to me. The old man in the corner; the pregnant lady sitting by herself; the group of young men huddled over their bread and lamb shanks. I studied their mannerisms, their appearances; the way their teeth gleamed in the orange firelight from the central hearth.

Most were fisherman, for they had homemade, intricate bait hooks hanging from their trousers. Prized possessions, coveted like money. Others were blacksmiths, their faces blackened from soot, their hands calloused and scarred. The Traders were also obvious, more from their charismatic smiles than the enormous rucksacks hanging from their shoulders.

Then there were the Roamers, such as myself. Aimlessly wandering the wintry tundra, we only sought shelter when the outside world threatened to kill us.

My attention fell to the collection of antlers, dotting the walls. Huge, marvellous structures, stretching out like tributaries from a river. Many were still attached to the stuffed heads of wild beasts: elk, moose, reindeer, pronghorn… They were next to heads of bears, mountain lions, snow leopards… A whole host of dead, lifeless eyes that gazed forever at the bustling scene below.

Did they know what fate lay before them? When they were slaughtered – whether by arrow, bullet or knife – did they know they'd be hung up on the wall? Doomed for all eternity to watch cruel and idle humans eat their fellow kind?

My thoughts were squashed beneath the harsh, hoarse tone of a man at the table beside me.

"Forget it, Thorik!" Each word was a hiss through clenched teeth. "T'is no good coming out with nonsense like that!"

The second voice belonged to a man who shared my twenty-or-so years. It was a little slurred as it snapped, "But it's odd though, innit? After all, she's the End of Everything!"

My interest piqued, rising into a singular, moving point.

"Exactly!" the old man snapped. "Which means it's a bloody good job he's found her."

"Then why hasn't he killed her?"

"It's none of our concern, Thorik – stay out of it!"

I suddenly found myself standing before that table. The two men stopped and stared at me with questioning eyes.

Nerves choking me, I cleared my throat and placed a grubby, long-fingered hand upon the back of a spare chair.

The elderly man raised an intrigued eyebrow. Thorik's attention started on my face, and then strayed down, admiring my slim figure with a glimmer in his eye. I wished I still wore my coat – a long, tatty thing that was made of brown leather, and significantly covered all parts which I deemed fit to cover before strangers, which was all of me.

I shuffled my feet. "I couldn't help but overhear. You're talking about Alira, right?"

The old man continued to observe me with suspicion, his stained fingers playing with his grey beard. I swallowed hard, concentrating on an eye that was marred by a long scar, clouding what would have been an electric blue iris.

"Girl, eavesdropping is not a trait that is perceived highly," he said.

"Forgive me. I'm afraid my curiosity got the better of me."

"Why are you so curious? Can't a father and son have a conversation in peace?"

"Of course you can. Please, feel free to tell me to bugger off." That earned me a quick chuckle. "But, with all due respect, this *is* Alira we're talking about. I have the right to know about her just as much as you do."

"Bit late, though," Thorik said. He leant back in his chair, the orange firelight illuminating sharp features that were not dissimilar from his father. Those same electric blue irises persisted, scanning my body up and down with a carnal gleam that gave me gooseflesh. "As you say, this *is* Alira. Surely the End of Everything is a topic that's on everybody's lips, particularly now."

I shrugged, crossing my arms high, trying to cover my breasts from his penetrating stare.

"But I'm a Roamer," I said, as if that explained everything. "The Fjordlands are a long way from here, and you know how it is. We don't hear the best news until six months after the fact. Remember when that train derailed in Maelstrom?" I paused, recalling the disaster that occurred on the outskirts of the New World's capital, killing over two hundred Aristocrats and injuring countless more. "Well, I didn't hear about that until months later."

"Point taken," the old man said. He nodded towards the vacant chair. "Take a seat. We'll fill you in."

Without a second thought, I obliged.

"So, tell us what you know about Alira," Thorik said, his eyes still wandering. The sheathed hunting dagger weighed heavy on my thigh.

"I know that she's the End of Everything, and that Mason's looking for her, but other than that..." I shrugged. "I don't really keep up to date with Mason's vendettas."

"Ha, I don't blame you."

Mason. The New World's dictator, a mass murderer, sitting up in his grand Palace and enslaving and butchering every innocent being who didn't bow down and accept his sadistic ways.

"But," Thorik continued, "you know he's been after her, right?"

"Of course I know that. The whole of the New World knows that."

After all, Masonians were roaming the wintry tundra, questioning and torturing anyone for even a whisper of Alira's movements. All information led down a winding, dried up riverbed. This only angered Mason, leading to the deaths of countless. Mostly Roamers, like myself.

At my somewhat snappy outburst, Thorik smiled. A cold knot of anxiety settled in my gut.

"What's your name, girl?"

I stared at him. Hard.

"Maya." The word rolled easily off my tongue, encompassing the space between us. "What's it to you?"

Thorik shrugged, then took a leisurely sip of mead. "Just wondering."

Anger bubbled up with me, replacing the cold fear with an insatiable heat. I turned my burning gaze back to the old man. "Sorry mate, what were you saying?"

I pushed a strand of thick, chestnut hair behind my ear, boasting an ear shell that was home to eight rings, of varying size. Each ring spoke to onlookers. They were a golden warning that spat in the eyes of any attacker: *Back off!*

Rings on the curling cartilage of a Roamer's ear were a sign of defiance: one ring for each failed assault, each attempt upon my life. Over my twenty years, five unlucky men and three equally unlucky women thought they could have a go at me, only to end with bullets in their brains.

I was always a good shot.

Thorik's wandering eyes quickly found the rings, and he counted each and every one of them. Gold glinted at each lost life.

Too bad for them.

Thorik turned very pale. Then he swallowed hard and disappeared into his tankard while his father spoke.

"So, you've been wandering the wilds, have you?"

"That's what us Roamers do best."

"Indeed." From within his pocket, he produced a long pipe. Striking a match, his wrinkled face glowed orange as his cheeks hollowed, inhaling in short, abrupt bursts. "But what about before that?"

"How d'you mean?"

"Your accent," he said, pointing the stem of his pipe towards me. "Though your English is impeccable, you can't hide your accent. You're a Herder."

I bowed my head, my teeth scraping against my lower lip. "That was a long time ago."

"Perhaps, but the past gets in your bones, girl. You can't escape it."

"I'm not trying to escape my past."

"Then why are you being evasive?"

I squeezed my eyes shut, seeing remnants of the snow and fur tents surrounded by reindeer. My accent reminded me of my Papa. He spoke slow and steady, almost like a melody, and rolled his 'r's like his very voice was wind flowing down a mountain. He once told me that his language – the language of all Herders – was carried down from the Ancestors, and our accent helped to tell the old tales to the next generation. It was my heritage, I spoke with pride.

"So," the old man continued, bringing me out of my reverie. "Obviously the ways of the reindeer are behind you, and you've been Roaming ever since. So, I trust you know that Mason's been looking for this Alira for... How long is it now?"

"Twenty years," I said. My throat was dry. I missed my mead.

"Yes, twenty *long*, frozen years..." Another inhale of smoke. Another smirk that the firelight was able to distinguish. "She's the End of Everything, y'know."

"Yes, I'm aware."

"Do you know why?"

"No one knows why."

"But you still believe she is?"

"Yes." I swallowed hard, fighting the thick ball of nerves in my throat.

"Mason's an intelligent man. If she wasn't a threat to him – or to his New World – then why would he be so obsessed with finding her?"

"You make a good point." A quick inhale of smoke into old lungs, followed by a smoke ring that floated off into the rafters. "Strange though, innit?"

"Not really. Mason sees her as a threat, so he wants her dead."

"That's New World mentality."

"I don't know any different."

This time, the man stared with a mix of incredulity, and maybe a smidge of pity.

"You don't know anything about the Old World, do you." It wasn't a question. It was a fact. A fact I didn't deem fit to answer.

The old man shuffled in his seat, rearranging his arthritic bones.

"Can't blame you there, girl. Ragnarök occurred over one-hundred-and-eighty years ago. I suppose young'uns like you find such a place hard to believe. To most of us, the Old World remains a mystery – other than to Mason, that is. All that's left is the truthful barbarity of this world."

Yes, it was barbaric. Yes, it was cruel and harsh and unyielding.

But it was also beautiful.

During Ragnarök, Mason slaughtered almost two billion people, destroying the Old World in a calamitous display of power that rendered all buildings and mountains to the ground. But when he created his New World, he did make it beautiful.

Yet, evil still clung to its wintry veins. Like a disease, Slavery infected the snowy world, poisoning its ethereal lustre with torture and blood. Those who were lucky enough to avoid Slavery had to contend with the unforgiving act of survival. Starvation, disease, murder – all were prevalent.

Should one survive that, Masonians were everywhere. Why did they kill in Mason's name? Most of the time, it was simply for fun.

"Do you agree that Alira needs to die?"

The question punched me in the stomach, knocking all essence of reply. Before me, the old man's patience grew as thin as the tobacco in his pipe.

"Depends," I said, carefully. "She's the End of Everything – whatever *that* means. I know she's *somehow* meant to destroy everything, but…"

"But what?"

I licked my lips, the skin cracked and rough from the cold outside air. "But she's also a living, breathing person."

"Even if it's said she will destroy the world, and all of us in it?" The old man took a laboured drag of his pipe.

"If we kill her, then we're no better than Mason."

"But you've killed." He gestured to the rings on my ear. "You've killed plenty."

"To protect myself," I stated, bristling in my seat. "It was kill or be killed, or worse. Trust me, they didn't leave me much choice."

That seemed to settle the old man. He dug deep into the pockets of his tatty trousers and emerged with a handful of loose tobacco. Thick fibres fell to the table as he pressed them in his pipe.

"Well then, girl, seems you're in luck."

Luck? What was he on about?

"I don't understand," I said.

"Mason's found her."

The entire world stopped. The voices, the crackle of the fire, my own heartbeat... It had all just stopped beneath the weight of those three, impossible words. Crushed beyond recognition.

Mason's found her.

My lips curved on their own, bewildered accord. "I don't believe you," I said.

"Oh, believe it, girl," Thorik grumbled. "Whole damn Territory's singing it."

Words failed me. I sank back in the chair.

Thorik slammed his hand on the table, making it quake. "She's the End of Everything and what does he do? Sod all, I tell you!"

Dazed and weary, my eyes slid sideways, fixing on his crooked nose. "What d'you mean he's done *nothing*?"

"Well, this is where the confusion arises," the old man said. "Word is, Alira's alive and well and living in Mason's Palace."

"*What?*"

The old man bobbed his bushy grey eyebrows.

"But," I began, my mind fogging with unsavoury possibilities. "Why? Is he waiting to kill her or –"

"Far from it. She's living the high life, going to all his dinner parties, socialising and just generally being a fucking Aristocrat."

Aristocrats. Descendants of those who profited exceptionally well from Ragnarök.

"But she's meant to destroy him, to destroy the world and all of us in it!" Now it was my turn to laugh – a horrible, feeble sound that could barely be called a laugh at all. "Why keep her alive?"

"Only Odin Allfather knows that."

My chest expanded on a deep inhale, my lungs burning with smoke. The more I considered this strange and incredulous tale, the more ludicrous it seemed to become.

"Wait." I slammed my hand upon the table, donned with cheap rings and bangles. "Are you absolutely sure this girl is Alira? Like, *the* Alira?"

A thick cloud of pipe smoke covered the old man's features, yet I could still sense his scowl. "Maya, don't doubt the truth we tell."

"I'm not doubting," I said, exasperated. "I'm just confused."

Huffing, the old man delved crooked fingers into his nest of a beard. "You know the stories of Mason, don't you? The way he can shape the land with a flick of his wrist, or change the weather with a wink of an eye?"

I scoffed quietly beneath my breath. "Of course," I said.

"Well then, I suppose you've also heard about his eyes."

"Of course I've heard about his eyes." Gooseflesh ran across my skin. "His eyes are the most infamous things about him."

"Yes…" His stare fell to his knuckles, disfigured from arthritis. "I suppose having eyes that look like diamonds are infamous indeed."

"Even more infamous knowing they can kill with a single stare," Thorik mumbled.

All children heard these stories. It was a barbaric truth carved into the brains of all young'uns: *Don't look Mason in the eye.*

No one knew exactly *what* Mason was. He resembled a normal man, after all. He slept in the same beds as we did, he ate and drank to merry fulfilment with the rest of the Aristocrats. And yet, he didn't bleed, he didn't age. It was said he could pull entire mountains from the ground with little more than a grimace, and that his deadly eyes sparkled with the lustre of a thousand diamonds.

"What's your point?" I asked, with a mild scowl.

"My point is that Alira also has eyes made of diamond."

"Yes, yes – I know that."

"Well then." The old man sat back in his chair, which creaked ominously. "There you have it. Mason knows that he's found Alira, because she has the same diamond-coloured eyes. If she was not Alira, then she would have eyes like you or me or Thorik, wouldn't she?"

I forced a nervous smile.

"So what happens now?" I asked, some moments later. My voice was small, my accent prominent.

The old man simply shrugged, then boasted his yellowed, cracked teeth.

"We pray he kills her."

I jumped at the sharp slap on my shoulder. "Come on, girl. Storm's passed."

I accepted my long tatty coat from a hairy hand. At over six-foot-three, Campbell Anders was a broad-shouldered machine who had seen his fair share of violence. Thick scars decorated his cheeks, yet his smile shone bright and proud through a layer of dense stubble. "I'm not dead just yet, so stop looking like you've seen a ghost."

"Well, look'ee what we have here then." Thorik laughed low and menacing, and more than a little slurred. "Another *bloody* Aristocrat!"

Indeed, Campbell's posh accent and straight spine did little to prove his rough living. Not that his prized sword and revolver did anything to help, that is. Though covered with oxidised grime, they shone against his faded black leather jacket like the expensive relics they were.

"I stopped being an Aristocrat a long time ago," Campbell said. The smile was gone, his blue eyes carved directly from glacial ice. He wrapped long fingers around his revolver, just peeking from its sheath on his right hip.

The old man, obviously sensing Campbell's agitation, leant forward and whacked his son over his head. Thorik yelped like a puppy and sank back into his hole.

"S'cuze my son, Sir. Boy's got no manners."

"I'm not a *Sir*," Campbell snapped, then dulled his snarky tone with a heavy sigh. "But I appreciate the apology."

He turned to me, blue eyes sparkling. "Come on, girl. We've got a long walk ahead of us."

And just like that, we left the smoke of the longhouse and escaped into the icy wilderness.

* * *

To say it was cold would be an insult to my aching bones.

The entire world was enveloped with snow. A thick, untouched layer of white, smothering all but the most persistent logs, rendering everything else to a snowy grave. The trees could not even escape, for their woody skeletons were encased in winter, their frosty skin the only clue to the blizzard's breath. But, despite the cold and a chill seeped into your very bones, the world was strangely beautiful.

Following Campbell through the snow, my mind kept drifting. Like a snow flurry rolling down the mountain before us, all thoughts I had raced back to that longhouse, and a curious conversation between father and son.

Mason's found Alira. Why were those words so hard to comprehend?

"Ah, here will do." Campbell's words were muffled by the thick black fabric over his mouth.

Quickening my pace and carving deep gutters in the snow, I caught a glimpse of his affections.

A cave. A dark, dank cave, framed with snow and icicles. Its aura was plagued with foreboding malice.

"Campbell, there's probably a bear in there." My own mask trapped my breath, warming my cheeks with moist heat before the cold set in, chapping cracked lips.

Campbell's glacial-blue eyes stared at me from behind his goggles. Made from brown leather and glass, they were impractical things that always fogged up or frosted over. I disliked them. No, it was far better to let your own natural warmth thaw your eyeballs.

Although, sometimes that was easier said than done. My amber contact lenses made such things difficult.

"I highly doubt there's a bear." He pointed a gloved finger to the ground. "Look, no droppings."

"Hibernation though, innit?"

"It's spring."

"Doesn't bloody feel like it."

"Well it is, and you know as well as I do that hibernation season ended weeks ago. If there was a bear, there would be signs."

With a sarcastic spread of my arms, I bowed low, curtaining my face with frozen chestnut curls. "Then after you, my good Sir…"

"Piss off," he snapped, plucking out his revolver and marching into the cave.

Sure enough, the cave was empty. No bears, no deer, no people.

The entrance of the cave formed a narrow passage that erosion had long since crafted, eventually opening out into a cavern, sealed from the elements. That was not to say it was any less cold, for the walls sparkled with frost. A frozen stream crisscrossed the base of the cave, creating a line of white against an otherwise black background.

A fire soon fixed that. Soon enough, the slow trickle of water filled the silence between Campbell and I, both wrapped in our fur bedrolls with the fire's soft glow illuminating our features. I remained staring into that fire, watching as each flame raced up to the rocky ceiling, at each crackle of wood or the sparks that floated aimlessly above. Fire was strangely beautiful against a white world.

"Something on your mind, girl?" Campbell asked. Leaning against the wall and half encased in fur, Campbell was cleaning his revolver. It was a large black thing that had certainly seen is fair share of violence, just like Campbell himself.

I just shrugged, transfixed by the fire.

"Go on," he pressed.

"I'm fine."

A small smile tickled his lips. "Y'know, for a girl of your limitless talents, lying is something you've never quite grasped."

"Well what if I don't want to tell you?"

"Then don't."

"I won't."

The weight of that curious conversation eventually got the better of me. Sighing, I heaved myself up, leaning against the wall with my knees pressed into my chest. Opposite me, Campbell continued cleaning his gun, only observing me with the occasional glimpse from those glacial-blue eyes.

"Have you heard about the rumours?" I asked.

"No." He spat on his revolver, working the saliva into the grooves with his thumb. "What rumours?"

"Well, it's not even a rumour. More fact."

Campbell remained quiet, waiting for me. My stomach twisted inside itself, dread curling around every muscle.

"People are saying that Mason's found Alira."

Campbell stopped. He remained staring at his gun, his limbs stilled, his eyes unmoving. He was a statue, frozen by the fearful chill embedded in my voice.

Eventually, as my words absorbed into his black leather jacket, those eyes flicked up to mine. "That's impossible."

"Well, that's what people are saying. Word is, he's found her and she's living life as an Aristocrat."

Campbell did not bat an eye. Becoming impatient, I said, "She's the End of Everything – or so we're meant to believe – and he hasn't killed her. Don't you think that's a bit strange?"

Shaking away his stupor, Campbell puffed up his shoulders. "I'm still having trouble comprehending that he's found her at all. Girl, you know how *ludicrous* that is."

"Then why are people saying it?" My voice echoed in the small space, only drowned by the crackling from the fire. "Look," I said, a little more gently. "I know how crazy all of this sounds, but people wouldn't be saying it if it wasn't true! Something like that is just so big… Campbell, people just wouldn't make shit like this up."

Campbell ran two hairy hands down his face. They came to rest vertically against his lips, only framed by the thick black stubble of his jaw.

He did not say a word.

"Is it… I mean…" I cleared my throat. "Is it possible that Mason's just got it wrong?"

Campbell just looked at me. "She has diamond eyes, girl. As you know, they're pretty damn hard to miss."

I groaned beneath my breath, my head falling to my knees. My heart raced past my ears, each deafening thump intensified by my own trepidation. Fear shook my bones like a blizzard.

Alira was the End of Everything. That was a fact, plain and simple, and although the exact reason *why* or *how* she was meant to destroy the New World remained a mystery, Mason had been exceptionally eager to find her. To put an end to her destiny, once and for all. But now, Mason's apparent agenda had been turned on its head, encircling an entire mountain of uncertainty.

"It mustn't be true," Campbell said, after some time. "There's only one of you."

Yes, there was only one of me. Only one Alira. Only one with diamond eyes.

Only one End of Everything.

"So, who do you think Mason's found? Since it's clearly not me."

I knew my diamond eyes glittered in the light of the fire. It must have been such a contrast from my amber contact lenses. I probably didn't look like the girl who called herself Maya: the girl who has been running from Mason since that fateful winter's night twenty years ago, when she was pulled from her dying mother's womb.

Each iris resembled a flawless diamond. Like he often did, Campbell watched in awe.

"I don't know who he's found, but you're Alira and –"

"Don't call me that," I snapped. Alira wasn't my name. It wasn't the name my Papa called me or the name chosen by a dying mother for her baby girl.

My name was Maya.

Campbell formed a heavy sigh. "Look," he said, treading on eggshells as lightly as he was able. "I know you're scared, but you have to look at the bright side."

"*Pfft,* what bright side?"

"If Mason's found *her*, he's stopped looking for you. Think about it."

I did think about it. It only made me angrier. "But he's not found *her*, has he? He's found someone *pretending* to be me."

Neither one of us, of course, had mentioned the possibility of this *Pretender*, but it was still present. Like some deformed mammoth lingering in the corner of the cave.

Campbell deflated, sinking into his thoughts. His stare fell to the gun cradled within his fingers.

"And when he kills this Pretender," – I leant forwards – "and he *will* kill her, he'll start looking for me again."

"You don't know that –"

"Yes I do, Campbell. How many girls with diamond eyes have been born since Ragnarök, hm? A hundred? *Two* hundred?" I huffed bitterly to the fire. "You know that if an *Alira* dies by any hand other than Mason's, she's just reborn anew, in a different body, then left to be hunted or killed, and then she's reborn again and again until Mason finally kills her and breaks this cycle of rebirth. I'm the last of them, the only one who's made it into adulthood, and he's been sensing my heartbeat for twenty goddamn years."

A bitter laugh escaped me. "When he kills this *Pretender*, he'll know she's not me because he'll sense that *I'm* still alive. And then they'll start coming after me again. So, Campbell – please tell me, in all of this shit, how am I supposed to see the bright side?"

"Because," he said, before spitting into the grooves of his gun. "I'm here to protect you. I won't let him get you, girl. I promise."

2

My Papa was a good man. He never considered hindsight. He never considered me as a bad thing.

What went through his head, when I opened my eyes. When they glinted in the light of the fire, sparkling with the same lustre as the twinkling stars above, did my Papa regret his decision to cut my mother open? To get me out before we both succumbed to Death's grip?

If he did, then he never showed it. He loved me dearly. Perhaps my facial characteristics had just enough echo of my Mama that he saw through the negativity of hindsight, and simply saw me as his little girl, his daughter.

He called me Maya, as was the name decided by them, many moons ago. Alira, my *destined* name, was only told to me by Campbell, many moons later. My Pa was dead by then, slaughtered by monsters in blue coats and glinting swords. Killed because of the very eyes he was so determined to protect.

I was lucky to be born to him. Very lucky.

He taught me how to hunt. How to craft a bow from a fallen branch, or to skin a reindeer and tan its hide. He taught me how to fire an arrow, how to track predators and prey alike through the blanket of snow.

I missed those lessons.

Walking through the mountains always reminded me of my Papa. After all, I grew up in the mountains. They were my home.

Oh, and what a home they were. They spread ahead of Campbell and me, row upon row, disappearing into the horizon like a sea of jagged teeth. Puncturing the unblemished sky above with their snowy points, where nothing but the odd wisp of cloud or the bravest eagle dared tread, the mountains reminded us that we were nothing but a blip upon their snowy skin. A blip that could be blown away like specks of dust upon a table.

"You're losing your strength, girl." Campbell smiled, his breaths strained, his brow doused with sweat. "You're flagging."

I was flagging because the sight of South Seal Glacier had grabbed me, sinking its claws through my toes and grounding me to the mountain's treacherous slope. So, stationary I remained, squinting in the cold wind.

"Oi!" Campbell called, stomping ahead. The wooden paddles attached to his shoes gave him some stability, but deep ruts still remained in the snow.

"I'll catch you up," I called back. The view of the glacier was just so...*magnificent.*

Meandering its way through the mountains, South Seal Glacier was a natural marvel. Its skin was scarred and rugged, its inner ice glowing a glorious shade of turquoise blue. Snow powdered the glacier's surface, but even so, a thick line of dirty rubble ran through its centre, following its movements. Two separate glaciers had merged further up the mountain, forming the current icy beast.

At its front, the glacier flowed into a fjord, where its glacial dust clouded the turquoise hue of the water. A colony of seals inhabited the ice rafts that floated on the surface, originating from the glacier as the spring sun warmed it just enough to calve.

As I watched with silent awe, large chunks of ice broke off and crashed into the water. A bang resonated down the fjord, echoing, rumbling like thunder.

Campbell always liked South Seal Glacier. He stood upon those snowy slopes, gazing at the icy beast with such awe, utterly beguiled by the sight. He closed his eyes, inhaling the cold air deep into his lungs in some silent meditation. Those eyes reopened, glossed with some unknown emotion. Sadness, maybe? It was difficult to tell.

"C'mon," Campbell eventually said, having trudged back down to join me. "You know the drill – we stick together."

I just looked at him, eyebrows raised. "You kidding? I'm not nine years old anymore."

Campbell returned my raised eyebrow. "I like to keep my eye on you."

"Oh, is that so? Race you to the top!"

The wind was my aid, pushing me up the slope. The summit was in my sights, its pointed peak shining like a beacon in the sun. My lungs burned with the altitude, inhaling ice crystals.

Campbell was laughing behind me, his heavy footsteps muffled by the snow clinging to his calves. His laughter was contagious, reverberating into my lungs, making them burn with suppressed amusement.

"I'm gaining on you, girl!"

"No!" I half-screamed, half-laughed, my matted chestnut hair blowing all around me.

As the wind whipped passed my ears, I heard him coming closer, gaining ground with every second.

But I was almost at the finish line: the peak at the top of the mountain.

In three enormous leaps, I made it to the summit. Throwing my hands up to the air, I shouted my victory to Asgard itself. The mountains rejoiced in the form of snow flurries – light as feathers – that drifted from the peaks and disappeared into the frosty air. Glaciers curved below me, sliding and creaking their way through the mountainous valleys.

All around, the splendour of this icy world shone.

"You've still got it, girl." Campbell panted his way beside me, his mouth open as he gasped for air, his expression both proud and pained.

"Damn right," I replied, grinning.

We were left with silence, listening to nothing but the howl of the frigid wind. Somewhere below, an eagle screeched, soaring gracefully through the air as it absorbed the sights of this wondrous world.

"Come on," Campbell said, bringing me out of my reverie. "Drunk's Redoubt is still a two-day hike away, and Joe stipulated we get there quickly. The sooner we reach the pass down into the valley, the better."

Indeed, the moment Campbell received Joe Matheson's letter, detailing with urgent clarity that the scrupulous Trader required a meeting with us, Campbell's stride had been long and focussed. Only the sight of the glaciers slowed his perpetual march, for they were truly marvellous.

Absorbing the sights one last time, I nodded and stepped down from the top of the world.

* * *

DARKNESS HAD DESCENDED.

The stars had come out to play, sparkling against a pure black sky. The moon caressed mountains with silver.

But, in the wake of this beauty, the bitter cold had returned. Traversing a pass through the mountains, the steep slopes acted as a wind tunnel. Specks of ice whipped our skin, froze our blood. Even with Campbell's goggles and my protective hand, it was treacherous.

Campbell stopped, his hand raised, poised in mid-air.

"What?" I asked through my fabric mask.

His attention fixed to the blanket of snow. Slowly, I followed his gaze.

There, squinting through the cold, I saw the frozen mounds. So many of them: some big, some small. Some had antlers that grew icicles. Others had arrows sticking out of their torsos, their fur matted and bloodied. Eyes stared lifelessly at the mountains, shining like frosted black marbles. The reindeers' fur was mottled, speckled with thick layers of frost.

Bodies were numerous. The Herd had been large.

As Campbell and I stepped forward, we saw more bodies. Not reindeer, this time. Instead, the dark familiarity of human fingers peeked from the snow, frozen in a state of perpetual convulsion. Limbs were sticking outwards, the glorious designs of Herder robes easily recognisable in the moonlight. Their fur blankets were stained with blood, the remainder of fur tents smouldering.

The Tribe had been decimated, smattered with blood and violence on the side of that mountain.

Silent, I just stared at them, and imagined the stories that once tickled their lips, the songs that used to decorate that small, frozen corner. The Herd would have been content, their muzzles sniffing through the snow, their low groans echoing up the mountain pass. The Tribe would have been happy. So, so happy.

Who killed them? It was difficult to say, though the sheer brutality of such a scene speculated that Masonians were responsible. Clear enjoyment was taken with each cut, each butcher. I was reminded of my own Tribe, my own Herd.

Guilt grew, like it so often did at such sights. Tears licked my eyeballs, then numbed in the freezing air.

Campbell was still as I took slow, careful steps forward. He knew my heritage, my history. He knew that such sights were not new to my eyes.

I fell to my knees, sinking in the snow.

There, as the bitter cold whipped my skin, I closed my eyes and prayed to the Old Gods. My words, spoken in my native tongue, rippled in the air of the mountainside. I prayed and wished for these innocent people to walk feely in Freya's fields, to hunt in peace, to feast in the grandeur of Odin's Hall.

A single tear slipped down my cheek, blown away by the wind.

Diamond eyes opened. I imagined them catching the light from the moon and glowing a full, unadulterated silver, becoming bright and forceful as I marched passed Campbell.

"We'll go the long way," I said, wiping my cheek on my sleeve.

* * *

BY NOON THE NEXT DAY, we had cleared the majority of the mountains. Now they were few and far between, their roots smothered with dense forests and rocky plateaus of nothing but pure, untouched snow. The sky was blue and the air was calm, and other than the gentle rustle of coniferous needles, it was silent.

As evening fell, we reached a small village, only housing half a dozen grass-roofed huts and a small market. A few villagers crowded around a well centred in the town, their shadows cast long by tall torches, blazing orange into the night.

Once the sun disappeared entirely, the snow started falling. It trickled in small waves from the black sky, slow at first, and then intensified into a great veil of impenetrable white. Visibility was severely reduced in such conditions. Roaming at night was dangerous, at best. In a snowstorm, it was damn near impossible.

So, as a brief reprise, Campbell and I took refuge in the inn. Old and musty, it was only large enough for five tables. The bar was miserable and simply stocked with mead and water. We took the latter, simply because it was free. The bartender – a skinny chap with a vacant expression – wondered if we'd like to try the daily special of smoked rabbit liver. Campbell politely declined.

For the next hour, we remained at that table, sipping our tankards of water and allowing the fire's warmth to evaporate the memories of that mountainside. Yet, despite the cleansing heat, those memories assaulted us from all corners.

I could still see the remains of that Tribe.

Seconds wore on, and my Pa's piercing scream echoed through my memories...

"You alright there, girl?"

This was the first thing Campbell had said to me in almost two days. The sound caught me by surprise.

"Hmm? Oh, yeah, I'm fine."

Hoping that was the end of our conversation, I continued to tap my fingers against the table. Each brass ring caught some essence of the fire's light, and I wondered if my amber contacts had the same warm glow.

Before me, Campbell sighed. "You've never been one for lying, girl."

"Then what do you want me to say?" I snapped. "I'm *fine*, Campbell."

We remained in awkward silence. Campbell kept staring at me, slowly placing the tankard to his mouth, and then back to the table. Metal clinked against wood.

"It's difficult, y'know?" I said, eventually. Campbell, though silent, studied me intently. "When I see my people – my *culture* – being butchered with such...*enjoyment*."

Tears threatened. I swallowed hard, blinking towards the ceiling. If I cried, I risked dislodging the lenses.

"I understand that," Campbell said.

Memories flooded. I remembered my Pa's hushed voice as he wrapped his arms around me, squeezing firmly as the Masonians marched closer. He told me to run. He told me not to look back...

"Do you think they were looking for me?" I asked, quietly. "Back there, on the mountainside, I mean."

"I don't know, but Mason's already found his Alira – or so they claim. There would be no reason to look for you now."

I huffed bitterly. "Oh, so sport then?"

Did that make it better? Not for them, they were dead regardless.

Visions of my Pa threatened to push more tears from my eyes. The fear embedded in that last, longing look...

Guilt ballooned inside my belly. The knowledge that *I* was responsible for my Tribe's destruction – and the deaths of so many other innocent people – was still so raw to think about.

"It wasn't your fault," Campbell constantly said, when he could see the flutter of painful memories. "Never blame yourself for what happened."

But how could I not? I was born with diamond eyes. I was born to be hunted, to be found by the men in blue coats and long, glinting swords.

I remembered running, the snow crunching beneath my boots, unable to stamp out the shrieks of our slaughtered Herd. I remembered my Pa's dying breath, his screams piercing my eardrums. They went on for so long. Hours, it seemed, did his screams ring through the trees. Then, as the flames roared and the entire forest became bathed in an angry, red haze, I didn't look back. I just raced through the labyrinth of trees with the rest of the animals, as we escaped the hungry fire.

That fire was my Tribe, deforming into smouldering ashes.

Months later, Campbell caught my thieving hand in his coat pocket. He was angry at first, as one would be, but then he saw my eyes. He knew the danger I brought, but he still nestled me beneath his wing. He taught me English, and how to read and write. He taught me how to fire a gun, how to protect myself.

Sometimes I wondered why he saved me, why he suddenly dedicated his life to protecting me. Perhaps I reminded him of someone he'd lost. A daughter, perhaps? I'd never asked.

Regardless of his reasons, Campbell turned a lonely, lost little girl into a survivor. For that, I was eternally grateful. Even if, sometimes, I was bad at showing it.

"How can I not blame myself, Campbell? They came for *me*, they were trying to find *me*."

"You don't know that –"

"Yes, I do. That's why he screamed, why they..." I couldn't bring myself to finish.

Eleven years later, the memories of what they did to my Tribe still stung deep.

"I'm sorry, girl," Campbell said, after some time.

I smiled tightly and disappeared into my water. It was lukewarm and tasted stale, yet I needed something to preoccupy myself. I forced its metallic taste down my throat.

Less than an hour passed and the snowstorm merely intensified. It howled outside the inn, blowing away all essence of Roaming. Campbell exhaled a stream of frustrated air, for we had Joe's appointment to keep and were losing time.

A blast of chilly air rushed in as the door opened. In stumbled three men, their fur hats speckled with snow, their blue coats long and flowing with each step of a black boot.

I'd seen those uniforms before. Dread sank heavy in my gut, the warning shining with glistening revolvers, hanging from their hips.

"Masonians," I whispered to Campbell, lowering my gaze. I teased the dagger strapped to my thigh.

They were laughing to themselves, evidently drunk. Their sheathed swords clattered against the tables as they each stumbled to the bar, summoning the innkeeper with a smooth curl of their fingers.

"Sweetheart, your best three rooms, if you'd be so kind," one of them crooned. He leaned far over the counter, until he could pinch her chin. She doubled back, her eyes wide and terrified, and quickly sped around the counter to prepare their rooms. One of them slapped her hard on her buttocks. She squealed loudly, then scurried away from their cackles.

"And *you!*" He removed his fur hat and threw it on the counter, knocking over a lone tankard. "Get us some mead!"

The bartender poured them each a free drink, then scurried off to the cellar.

Campbell and I were alone with three Masonians. The odds did not look good.

"Should we go?" I whispered, barely audible. A subtle shake of Campbell's head, his muscles stiff and rigid as he listened, intently.

The Masonians continued to laugh and joke, their drunken amusement spinning around the room. As they grew bored with their own conversation, they noticed Campbell and I.

"Eh-up," one of them said, grinning. He was a few years older than I was, his nose already crooked and his brown eyes reeking of foul intent. "We have company, gents!"

Cradling his tankard of mead, one of them sat next to Campbell. Another sat beside me with a coy smirk on his lips.

The third Masonian was little more than a teenager. His patchy stubble tried to cover a mess of acne spots, his large eyes unable to fully grasp the job he had signed up for. He remained sitting furthest away from us, his limbs tightly tucked to his side, the tankard almost constantly pressed to his lips.

"So, what brings you out this way, mate?" the lead Masonian asked.

Campbell forced a toothless smile, his cracked lips stretching.

"Just seeking refuge from the storm, boys. We'll be on our way soon."

Two Masonians laughed loudly, slapping each other on the arms. The third – the teen – remained on the outskirts and forced a small chuckle.

"An Aristocrat, hey? What brings you all the way up here then? You're far away from the Fjordlands."

The Masonian beside me continued to leer, puckering his lips. "And what about you, sweetheart? You his Pleasure Slave?"

I grimaced around the notion, shaking my head.

"Don't speak, huh? What he cut your out tongue for?

"She's not my Slave," Campbell said. "She's my niece."

"I wouldn't care if she was my sister, I'd still bang her." He leant close to me and sniffed. I recoiled back, disgusted. "Oh, I think she likes me!"

"Boys, I think we're going to call it an evening." Campbell pushed his chair back, so it screeched loudly against the floor. "Allfather Guide You, and all that."

A sharp slap on Campbell's shoulder pressed him back down to his seat.

"Oh, but mate, the party's only just getting started. Isn't it, sweetheart?" He grinned to me, boasting his yellowed teeth.

I smiled tightly, lowering my gaze.

"Awful quiet, is your little *niece*. I do hope she livens up later."

He gestured to the teenager, sat behind him. "This one hasn't been with a woman yet, would you believe? We're looking for someone to pop his cherry."

My eyes widened in horror.

"She will do no such thing," Campbell's said, slow and stern.

"Not your choice though, is it mate?" The Masonian took a lengthy sip of mead and winked at me. "Not your choice either, darlin'."

Campbell and I exchanged a fleeting glance, our weapons cool against the tips of our fingers.

"Well," Campbell said. "I'm afraid I have a problem with that."

"Don't bloody care." The Masonian's hand caressed the tip of his revolver, still secured in the belt around his hips. "Y'see, we've already had a spate of bad luck. The other night, we tried to get this little Herder slut to come and have a party with us, but then her Tribe got all riled up. Ruined the mood, it did. I hate party-poopers."

I saw the bodies of those poor people, buried beneath mounds of fresh snow. Bile rose to my throat, mixing with the first wave of heated rage. My hands balled beneath the table, my inner temperature rising. I bit my tongue, hard, to stave the flood of profanities just *itching* to be released.

"Oh yes?" Campbell said, glowering. "We discovered the remains of your *party*. Not what I would call *fun*."

"Well you better get on it, mate! I mean, what are you? Forty-five? Fifty? You're running out of lead in your pencil."

The Masonian lifted his finger to touch me. I slapped it away, before it could get close. "You should utilise this one while you can. I sure will, when I've finished my drink."

Another sip of mead, a wink of a leering green eye.

The rage came bubbling. Hot and fast, and without mercy.

The Masonian swallowed his mouthful just as my dagger sank straight into his throat.

Herdinese curses spat from my gullet, my eyes burning behind the lenses, and I willed that Masonian to see the power, the *hate* behind my glare. As his blood trickled down my hand, as his entire body trembled around the knife and his tankard clattered to the floor, I ensured my anger was the last thing he witnessed.

I ripped the knife out as Campbell unsheathed his sword. The other

Masonian doubled back, his drunken eyes wide with panic. He stumbled, falling to the ground with a breathless thud. He clambered back across the floor, desperately gaining distance from Campbell, but he was too quick. With an enraged yell, Campbell jumped forwards and stabbed his sword straight through the heart.

"Fucking *animal*..." Campbell hissed through gritted teeth. A large bubble of blood rose from his Masonian mouth, seeping down his throat. It mingled with the pool of red, spreading across the floor.

As the last breath of life left his lungs, Campbell retracted his sword with a sickening squelch. He was sure to wipe the bloody blade on the Masonian's coat, marring its rich blue lustre.

I did the same, before tucking my dagger back against my thigh. Only then did I notice the teenager. He cowered in the corner of the inn, tears streaking his cheeks, his limbs trembling. He looked far younger than his adolescent years.

We locked eyes. I saw his fear, his pure unmitigated terror.

"I don't think you're cut out for the Masonian life," I said. "Get out of here."

The boy didn't need to be told twice. He ran from that inn like his life depended on it. In his exit, we noticed it had stopped snowing.

"C'mon, girl," Campbell said, picking up his bag and throwing the strap across his shoulder. I gathered my hunting rifle, still leaning against the wall. It weighed heavy on my shoulder as I marched towards Campbell.

I shot an angered look at the two corpses, their eyes still open and staring lifelessly around the inn. The pool of blood, thick and glossy, shimmered in the light of the fire. It would probably stain the wood. I suggested we leave a tip for the damage, or at least bribe their silence. The last thing we needed was retaliatory Masonians, thirsting for vengeance.

"No need," Campbell said, opening the door. "I daresay we did them a favour."

3

There was something so undeniably satisfying about filling an empty belly with hot stew.

From that first delectable mouthful, then to the spectacular swallow, and finally the cosy warmth growing in a satisfied stomach. Sheer bliss.

Between the mouthfuls of stew, I took large, lengthy gulps of mead. Some might say I was trying to drown the memories of murder, to forget the Masonian life I'd snuffed out merely two days previously. That couldn't be far from the truth: I ate because I was hungry, I drank mead because I enjoyed its sweet buzz. As far as I was concerned, those two Masonians could rot in Hel's fiery grip. I didn't care that I put them there. After all the suffering they'd caused, why should I?

So, I took another slurp of stew.

"Girl, as much as I love to see a healthy appetite, would you please show some manners and at least attempt to use a spoon."

Campbell's words fell on deaf ears. I continued to tip the wooden bowl to my mouth, slurping. Meaty juices spilled down my chin, covering my collar bones in the stew I guzzled with a speed verging on desperate.

Spoons? I had no need for spoons.

But some of Campbell's Aristocratic upbringing was still engraved into his psyche. His glare could cut ice when I finally lowered the bowl, and wiped my mouth on the sleeve of my jumper. Although moth-eaten and partially reverted to maroon threads, it still mopped up food pretty well.

"Better?" I grinned.

"Much." His mood had not improved. "It's refreshing to see that absolutely zero manners reside within those veins."

"Oh pipe down – this is Drunk's Redoubt, not some high-mannered establishment in the middle of Maelstrom."

"No," he agreed, drowning a piece of mutton with his spoon. "But there has to be something said for the bits of meat stuck to your neck dissuading my appetite."

Wiping myself more thoroughly, I debated whether I should remind him of the time I shot a buck elk, sliced open his belly, and then ate the animal's liver, still warm and bloody. But noticing the thick lines of agitation in Campbell's dirty scalp, I merely shrugged my shoulders.

The Drunken Stag Inn was a relatively new establishment, having only been built within the last twenty years. As the times would allow, the interior reflected its youth. Runes and symbols, representing the Old Gods, were carved into the wood. Originally only worshipped by Herders, the Old Gods – Odin, Freya, Hel and all the rest – had gained popularity in recent decades. Now, their runes and symbols could often be found decorating inns, especially in the more northern Territories. The Drunken Stag Inn was no exception, and those same elaborate patterns disappeared up into the rafters, supporting long strings of grain: barley, rye, even hops.

Herbs were situated high over the fire, allowing the perfumed scents of rosemary and lavender to disperse around the room. Yet, they did little to penetrate the heavy cloud of smoke that the state-of-the-art chimney failed to alleviate. Still, the fire was cosy and the atmosphere was pleasant, despite the ripe stench of debauchery. Indeed, it overpowered whatever concoctions the owners had smouldering in the back room.

As one of only three taverns residing in a town with no brothels, which was in itself an achievement, the drunken residents of the aptly named Drunk's Redoubt had to get their fun elsewhere. The Drunken Stag Inn, being a place for merry banter and excessive mead, was as good a place as any, and had many of its customers sneaking off to the back corners. Indeed, customers paid for the drink rather than the flesh, but the essence of a seedy establishment still flourished. The only difference was the presence of children, and the strict rule that all genitalia remain safety tucked away until owners of such attributes were in private.

"You alright?" I asked, when Campbell's mood continued to sour.

Campbell's eyes met mine for the briefest of moments. A flick of the candle's flame, and his stare fixed back to his sad piece of mutton, bobbing about in his stew.

"I just want to eat," he replied.

"You've been staring at that piece of meat like it's going to jump out and smack you."

"Well you never know."

I smiled broadly as the tankard touched my lips, cracked and scabbed from the bitter cold. Swallowing a large mouthful, I sighed out the scent of alcohol. The tankard returned to the table with a dull *clank*.

I remained staring at the other people in the inn. So many different varieties of men and women, or children who would grow up into men and women. Each vastly different, yet in some way, all the same. Different hair colours, body shapes, demeanours, genders... But take all manner of change and variety away, and the human race was simply left with three distinct drives, shared with every species that ever existed: to eat, sleep and shag. In that respect, we were no different than rodents.

"What time is it?" I asked.

"It's five minutes since you asked me last, on this day: the *Whatever-th Day of the Whatever-thieth Month*. There, does that satisfy your curiosity?"

"There was no need to be snarky about it, Campbell. I only asked you a question." I frowned my way into my tankard, avoiding the guilt that now spread like a stain across Campbell's usually stony features.

More silence. More mead. More staring into oblivion.

"Joe's almost twelve hours late," I finally blurted out, the smoke making my head fuzzy, and my dry eyes sting and itch behind the contacts. "I don't see why we can't meet him tomorrow morning. As far as I'm concerned, his window of opportunity has passed for this hour, and I'm not prepared to wait however many *more* hours before he decides to grace us with his presence."

Given the urgency of his letter, Joe's tardiness was immensely frustrating.

Now, given the late hour and the warmth in my belly, I saw no reason why we couldn't just meet him in the morning.

When I voiced this to Campbell, he just looked at me.

"Joe Matheson is a Trader, girl," he said, as if that answered everything.

"Yes, I know. But he's still going to have to stay the night, isn't he? I mean, Spring's upon us – or so you claim – but the cold outside could still freeze balls off. Besides, you know Joe – he's got a reputation here. Young Missy Baloo won't want to spend this cold and stormy night alone once she sees her handsome boy."

I chanced a look at *Missy Baloo*, flaunting her sizeable assets to one of the wealthier members of the inn's rabble. Blond, full-bodied and with lips redder than bloody elk's liver, Missy Baloo had a reputation that spanned an entire Territory.

Campbell audibly sighed. "Whether he spends the night with Missy Baloo – "

"Which he will –"

"Doesn't mean he'll stay here past dawn–"

"Which he will – "

"As opposed to being on the far side of Glacier Territory come sundown –"

"Probably will –"

"Dammit girl, will you stop interrupting me!"

"Sorry. Please, continue my good Sir." I motioned my hand to a graceful bow, hiding a stubborn smirk.

Campbell glared knives for a few seconds, before he composed the flush in his cheeks.

"Traders aren't Merchants," he said. "They move about from one town to another, living off the grid and selling their wares to whomever has the highest price or offers the best deal. You know as well as I do that much of Joe's merchandise isn't exactly legal tender. Not to mention he's helped you several times, not least by giving you those contacts. He has to stay off the grid."

"Look, Campbell," I said, leaning back in the chair with a loud creak. "I appreciate all that Joe's done for me over the years, and I've no doubt of his illegal deals with the Mulch Gang, but couldn't he find the time – just an inch of time – to let us get some sleep in an actual bed? That's all I ask."

"I'll do my best," said a brazen, cocky voice behind me.

As soon as that pretentious voice from that *infuriating* man found my ears, all annoyances were forgotten. One glimpse at those bright green eyes, and I flung my arms around Joe Matheson's skinny neck.

"I've missed you too, girl." He smiled into my chestnut locks. "Hmm, you smell good this time, a bit less sweaty."

I punched him hard in his pectoral. Annoyingly, it did little but turn his insufferable laugh into a guttural little hiccough.

"Oww," he groaned, clearly amused and certainly not in pain.

"Oh suck it up big boy."

"Wish you'd suck it."

I leant around the table to smack him again, but Campbell caught my hand with a stern, disapproving stare.

Joe boasted a wide, boyish grin, surrounded by a dark mass of stubble. Still, that grin was electric, his teeth whiter than a virgin's wedding dress. But, above everything, his eyes were the most defining trait on his handsome face. Green and cloudy, like seafoam, they resembled something akin to intelligence, if they were not obscured by immense immaturity.

Campbell's deep voice rose up, quelling Joe's inappropriate response that no doubt hung on the very tip of his tongue. "We're here at your behest, Joe. In your letter, you said to hurry, but we've been waiting here for the best part of the day."

"Ah yes," Joe said, unzipping his leather jacket, covering a hideous mix of cashmere and wool, dyed to extravagance and yet resulting in a garment Joe Matheson seemed, by all accounts, to pull off rather well. "Firstly, I do apologise for my delay. That was rude of me."

"Why are you so late anyway?" I growled under my breath.

"Eh?"

"I want to know why I'm not curled up in a nice feather bed."

"Girl – "

"No Campbell that's a fair question. I've kept you and the good Lady waiting." Joe puffed up his narrow shoulders and cleared his throat. "I trust you know that I am involved in occasional dealings with a...*shady* bunch of characters at best."

Referring to the most dangerous illegal gang, run by the insane drug lord Mike the Mulch, as a *shady bunch of characters* was a definite understatement.

"And?" I pressed.

"And, they had a job for me."

"Dare I ask what job?"

"Let's just say, I had to make a quick detour and deliver the goods, otherwise Mike the Mulch would roast my balls on a stick and eat them. And I like my balls. Both of them."

"*Anyway.*" Campbell strenuously cleared his throat. "Returning to the matter at hand, your letter said you had urgent information."

Something shifted in Joe. His usual, immature demeanour suddenly switched into something far wiser than his thirty-three years. He leant two skinny elbows on the table, his entire being turning hushed and subdued, like a mountain lion prowling in the snowy undergrowth.

"Something's afoot," he said. "Entire Territories are bristling."

"Why?" Campbell asked. "What's happening?"

Joe licked his lips, then took a strained look at our surroundings. "Word is, a new Rebellion's on the rise."

I startled, then took a quick glance at Campbell. His throat convulsed on a large swallow, but he remained unreadable. No doubt he was remembering last Rebellion to grace the New World. He barely survived its defeat.

"Whose is it?" he asked, quietly.

"Dunno, some *boy*, barely old enough to grow a beard. His name's Ashtree, or similar."

"Ashworth?" Campbell's eyes grew wide.

"You know him?" I asked.

Campbell avoided my eye. "Perhaps."

"Well, whoever he is," Joe said, leaning back in the chair, "he's got every town from here to Asgard singing his name, rejoicing in his dream to become free of Mason's dictatorship."

"Mason's not gonna like that," I muttered.

"Not half. But the diamond-eyed bastard's been rather late to the party on this one. Been too preoccupied."

Missy Baloo spotted Joe from the corner of her eye, and was sure to parade over, her wide hips swinging from side to side. Joe, rather annoyed, simply waved her away and snapped that he had important business to discuss. Missy Baloo served Joe nothing but a spitting curse and then finally left us in private. Her evident annoyance dragged a triumphant little smirk out of me.

"Look," Joe continued, slightly flustered. "I don't know if you've heard, but some weird shit is going down in Mason's Palace."

"Such as?"

Joe licked his lips again and shuffled in his seat, as though sitting on glowing embers.

"Girl, Mason's found Alira."

A small smile tickled my lips, those words still sounding so bitter.

"Yes, I've heard. But I don't understand it at all. I mean, is it true that he hasn't killed her?"

Joe immediately avoided my gaze. Instead, there was a brief glimpse between him and Campbell, the exchange of some unknown disclosure. Before I had to dwell on such things, Joe snapped back to his senses and cleared his throat.

"Yes, apparently so. Girl's living as an Aristocrat and everything."

My face scrunched around the confusion, the sudden truth that was so hard to accept. *Why hadn't he killed her?*

Conversation halted around our little table, scrawled with graffiti and runes depicting the Old Gods. All around us, the vibrant hub of the Drunken Stag continued, each high-pitched shrill of laughter – mostly from Missy Baloo – ringing a head that suddenly ached. I squeezed my eyes shut, determined to fight through this growing anxiety.

"Come on, let's go to your room." The chair scraped against the stone floor, as Joe stood to his impressive height. "We need to talk in private."

* * *

LOCATED up two flights of stairs, our rented room had a pristine view of the town. The narrow streets, cobbled haphazardly and marbled by the snow, were bustling despite the ungodly hour. Roamers and Traders alike filled the winding streets, bordered by cottages with stone foundations, wooden walls and grass roofs that were almost completely covered with snow. Further to the ground, braziers blazed in the night, attracting a whole company of men, women and children: half homeless, the other half simply stopping for a breath of warmth, before returning to the snowy wilderness.

Drunk's Redoubt was not a big town, but it was in a pristine location for travellers and Merchants alike. At the boundary between the Forest and Glacier Territories, the grand forests of the east were all but drowned by the jagged, rugged mountains of the west. Just over the initial peaks that sleepily lay behind the town, the first of the thousands of glaciers that ruled Glacier Territory sunk lethargically down the mountainside, scraping the dirt below. On a calm day, with no wind and when the town was subject to a rare and short silence, one could detect the haunting creaks of the moving ice, like faint whispers on a fleeting breeze.

"What's so important then?" Campbell's deep voice brought me from my wayward thoughts. Pulling the curtains and shutting out the outside world, I wandered to the fire and set to work removing the contacts: a simple task that always knotted my stomach.

Behind me, Joe sat on the edge of the four-poster bed, directly opposite the fire blaring quite happily. The only source of light in the room, it illuminated the cloth-covered walls and the piles of reindeer furs. If nothing else, we would be warm.

"On my way here, I travelled through Bear's Folly – you know the place, right?"

Yes, I did know the place. A small town – or a large village, depending on one's perspective – Bear's Folly was cute and rugged in equal measure. Wooden huts encircled a central fountain, constantly frozen by the bitter chill, racing down from the mountains. From what I remembered of my visit there, the inhabitants of Bear's Folly were equally icy.

"Whilst I was there, a Messenger relayed news of Mason's conquest – in finding Alira, I mean. Clearly in awe of this new Lady, the Messenger said how taxes will be increased to fund a new celebration."

"Celebration?" I frowned. "What celebration?"

"Damned if I know." Joe chuckled nervously.

"Well, when is this grand celebration supposed to be?"

"No one knows."

"What? How can he plan a celebration and not know when it is?"

"Gods know that. But I'll tell you this – it's got something to do with this woman pretending to be you. This *Pretender*... Mason's waiting for her to *do* something."

"What? What's he waiting for!" I was becoming angry, my voice rising of its own accord. "He's been looking for Alira for one-hundred-and-eighty-three years – to *kill* her because she's the End of Everything – and now that he has her, he does absolutely nothing?"

"Girl, calm down –"

"No, I won't! For years, you've been telling me that if Mason gets me, he's going to look into my eyes and then I'll be dead. Because he thinks I'm *somehow* going to destroy his world and everything in it, and only when *he* kills me will *Alira's* cycle of rebirth finally end! And yet, as soon as he finds this Pretender, he does...nothing?"

Countless possibilities entered my mind, each more horrific than the last. I scrunched my fingers in my hair, pulling against the roots. "Oh Gods, what's he planning for her? Is he going to torture her? Publicly? Is that what this celebration is all about? Is he raising taxes so he can construct some horrific machine in which to tie me to and slowly – "

Campbell's arms wrapped tight around me. Only then, with Campbell's comfort seeping through my tatty jumper, did the tremors take a hold. I remained in his embrace, consciously slowing my panicked breaths, my entire frame shaking with fear.

Eventually, I curled up before the fire, a fur blanket draped over my shoulders. Heat quickly punctured the layers, spreading hot fingers over the inked skin of my back. It was too hot, but I endured. The heat seemed to purify whatever shivers were left in me.

After a while, Campbell took a deep breath. "Regardless of what he's planning or what he's waiting for, the fact still remains that Mason has been duped by a Pretender, and that is the one fact I just can't seem to grasp."

"Well..." Joe sighed, hands in his pockets. "She had a very convincing story: kidnapped since birth, left locked away in a bunker somewhere until she escaped. Masonians found her wandering the wilderness and, rumour has it, she was practically feral. Kicking and screaming to the Old Gods themselves."

"Clearly has your anger then, girl." Campbell smirked and I rolled my eyes.

"Doesn't have my eyes though," I shot back.

"There are rumours of eye-colour procedures in some of the more...*scrupulous* towns." Joe folded him arms, shuffling his weight from one foot to the other, unable to keep still. "She must have a pretty sordid fascination with diamond eyes. Jeez, I can't even imagine what she went through to have them." Joe visibly shivered.

"But it still doesn't explain why she'd pretend to be me in the first place. I mean, she's clearly gone to a lot of effort just to risk Mason killing her."

"What d'you think, Campbell?" Joe said, after some time. "You think Mason's just playing her?"

"No, I don't think so. Mason's a cruel son-of-a-bitch and such things aren't below him, but the fact that he's called off the search for the *true* Alira suggests he believes this Pretender completely. Be too costly a stunt otherwise. He's been waiting over one-hundred-and-eighty years, after all."

"Is that why he's believed her?"

"I'd like to think he's ready for a miracle. Desperation is not the right word, but if I were in his shoes and a beautiful woman with curious eyes suddenly landed on my doorstep, I'd believe her. I mean, why would she lie about such a thing?"

Indeed, until recently it was always thought that Mason wanted to kill Alira. This Pretender took an enormous risk, not just from Mason himself, but from the other residents of the New World. I was not the only one with a gun, after all.

To Mason, this woman *must* be Alira, because what reason would she have to lie about such things?

But yet, the question remained: *Why pretend to be me in the first place?*

"Right," Joe suddenly declared, standing to his great height and stretching his long, scrawny arms above. "As riveting as this conversation is, the dawn is approaching and I still have Missy Baloo to visit."

"Ha, have fun catching chlamydia."

"Oh, you're hilarious." Glowering, he marched over and rubbed his knuckles hard into my scalp.

Campbell stood to his feet: an equally impressive height of over six foot. The two men slapped each other on the shoulders before holding each other at arm's length.

"You off tomorrow morn?" Campbell asked.

"First light. I'm on my way to Glacial Hollow, to the north." Joe made his way to the window, separated the curtains with a single finger, and stared at the bustling ground below. "And what of you two?"

I thought to this new Rebellion, hiding within the mess of villages and pine trees, and was conflicted by such news. At their core, Rebellions in the New World meant hope, they meant fighting for a world free from Slavery. Of course, they also meant death, and most often for the Rebels themselves. My eyes slid to Campbell, and the tightness of those lips surrounded by dense stubble, and I wondered if painful memories swirled around his skull.

Still, perhaps we should find this... *Ashworth?* He might have information about this Pretender, this supposed celebration or why – at the very least – Mason was keeping her alive. The birth of this new Rebellion, at the exact same moment as this Pretender's remarkable appearance, seemed too opportune to be a total coincidence.

"We'll continue to Roam East, into Forest Territory," Campbell replied, before I could say anything.

Campbell clearly thought running after Ashworth was a bad idea, for I was certain he'd considered it.

Joe turned his head, his finger still embedded between the curtains. "Are you sure that's wise? The Woodlands are right next to Fjord Territory – to Mason."

"True, but Woodlands is the largest Territory, by far."

I missed the trees. Albeit mountains and glaciers were beautiful, it was a struggle finding food on a scree slope. At least in the Woodlands, I could climb a tree and wait for prey to saunter by, which was tenfold more likely than on a mountain side.

"Yes, it's a big Territory," Joe said. "Nonetheless, I think you should steer clear of the more southern territories for a while. Get as far away from Maelstrom and the rest of the Fjordlands as you can."

"Where d'you suggest then?"

"North, to the Icelands."

"The Icelands!"

I groaned inwardly and cursed in two different languages. The northern Ice Territory was plagued by a never-ending cold that struck the hearts of every living being who dared reside there. The snows never thawed. The lakes never melted.

The only fools who lived up there were those who could survive on ice fishing, and the occasional battle with a polar bear. The latter could go tits up pretty darn quickly.

The only other source of food was the Slushy Sea, at the very edge of the map. It was said to be home to whales, and fish the size of small houses. But the sea itself was treacherous, littered with shifting ice bergs. In the past, many brave sailors attempted to hunt in the Slushy Sea, only for the seabed to become their tombs. I dread to think how many eager seamen met such a grizzly, wet end.

No, everyone in the Icelands were either brave, foolish or just plain mad.

"I'm not going to the Icelands!" I said. "We've been managing around here just fine, thank you very much."

"No…" Campbell sighed. "Joe's right. If Mason does end up killing this Pretender, you're back to being the most wanted woman in the New World. We need to lay low for a while – and don't you even mention this new Rebellion to me, girl! We are keeping our noses firmly out it!"

Campbell had strong opinions about Rebellions, for he alone survived the last one. According to him, Rebellions only brought death and attention, something we both needed to avoid.

"Fine," I grumbled.

"Good," Joe boasted a toothless smile. "May I suggest heading through Waterman's Quarry? Innkeeper's a mate of mine. Tell him I sent you, and he'll give you room and board for free."

"Thank you, Joe," I said, standing to my feet. We hugged each other, free of the jibes or the snide comments or the little irritations that drove us both mad. Yes, despite everything, Joe was a good man. He was my friend.

"Take care, girl," he said.

Joe Matheson opened the door and disappeared into the corridor, leaving nothing but a wink of a seafoam eye.

4

The road to Waterman's Quarry was long and arduous.

A winding stretch of dirt and gravel, the only hint to the road's edges were the dirtied wheel tracks from carts, slicing through the snow. Hundreds of footprints lay between these tracks, like some unspoken boundaries. If one dared to vary from the path, they'd disappear into the shadows of the forest.

Straddling the border of the Snow Territory, the rugged terrain of the Glasslands – or the Glacier Territory – dwindled in both scale and severity. What once lay towering mountains, that sliced the dirty white clouds, fell into huge plateaus dominated by trees, or rocky outcrops home to caves and trickles of water. Canyons cut their way through these plateaus and formed spectacular waterfalls. They roared their bubbling way down the cliffs and formed seething, calamitous pits at the base.

The Snowlands had the highest precipitation rates in the New World, and allowed evergreen trees to flourish in their thousands. Fir, pine, spruce... All manner of trees, their emerald needles dotted with snow, their trunks frosted with severe cold.

It also led to the Snowlands being dominated by lakes.

All different sizes, some spanning the entirety of the horizon, others no bigger than a millpond. In the winter, the waters froze. For the larger lakes, this perpetual freeze only reached a few metres below the surface. The smaller, shallower lakes froze entirely, their waters resembling a clear glass lens in which to stare aimlessly at the lakebed, and all the unfortunate critters that had met an icy grave.

But it was in the summer – in those two short months the snows melted – where the real beauty of these lakes shone in the overhead sun.

The water boasted their true colours. Blues, opals, greens... Even deep, rusty reds. Each lake housed a different colour that gleamed in the sunlight.

As a Herder, I had spent most my life in the Snowlands. I had seen the lakes begin to thaw, their unique colours pooling on the surface of ice, suddenly becoming so fragile, like thin panes of cracking glass.

For now, the wonders of the Snowlands would remain in mystery. Campbell was marching us on at breakneck speed, determined to reach Waterman's Quarry within the week. Other than the occasional rustle of the trees, the world was silent. No birds, no animals. Just our boots, crunching what was remained of the trodden, dirtied snow.

"It's quiet," I said. I rearranged my rucksack, my hunting rifle positioned upon my shoulder.

"Yes is it," Campbell replied. "Storm's coming, I'd reckon."

"D'you think?"

"Ai, ever heard the expression: *The calm before the storm?*"

"Of course, but I didn't really think that had any... What's the word?"

"Credence?"

"Yeah, that."

Campbell shrugged, his hairy hands grasping the straps around his shoulders. "These things always come from somewhere, and it's true, you'll see. As soon as it's calm and quiet, a storm'll greet you soon after."

"I'll hold you to that."

He chuckled.

The clouds grew thicker by the minute and soon enough, it started to snow. White specks dotted my hair, cooling my scalp.

"Told you." Campbell smirked, casting a squinting glance to the sky.

"Hardly a storm."

"Well just you wait, before long it'll..."

Campbell's words disappeared beneath a frown. He stared forwards, his chapped lips parted and his eyes taking on an experienced sharpness. I followed his gaze and saw nothing but ominous shadow, interspersed with healthy flakes of white. Dread sank, spreading through the tips of eager fingers, stroking the rifle on my back.

"What is it?" I asked.

"There's something up ahead."

Campbell's eyes did not waver. I followed his gaze again and my finger twitched.

"I don't see anything," I said, yet cold air shivered in my bones. "Masonians?"

"No."

"An animal then?"

"I'm not sure..."

Campbell edged forwards. He unsheathed his sword, the blade glistening as the metal scraped against the scabbard.

Close at his heels, my eager fingers found my rifle. The wooden butt pressed into my shoulder, my hunter's eye aiming.

Our footsteps were light and careful; only the briefest crunch of snow foretold our movements towards the strange object. Difficult to distinguish, it resembled two thick poles that did little but sway in the breeze.

Whatever it was, it didn't seem alive.

"Ah shit..." Campbell sheathed his sword and marched quickly towards the object.

Closer still, the snow left little doubt as to the fate of the two men, swinging from makeshift gallows at the side of the road. Hands tied behind their backs, only the black hoods protected their modesty. The men's naked bodies, bruised and bloodied, were already beginning to discolour and swell. I held my breath as I joined Campbell, the sickening odour of rot sticking to my throat.

"Bandits?"

"Mason." Campbell took a large step and ripped a damp piece of paper off the top of the pile, nailed into the right man's ankle. His eyes skimmed the hand-written lines, his expression twisting with each smudged swirl of ink. I managed a peek over his shoulder and saw only the emblem of a large stag, with antlers radiating the entire width of the paper.

"What does it say?"

Campbell cleared his throat, taking a few steps back from the corpses, perhaps trying to escape the stench.

"*The Honourable Lord Mason hereby declares that all collaboration with the Free People, or to withhold information regarding the aforementioned party, is punishable by death.*

"*Behold the consequences if such warnings are ignored.*

"*A substantial reward and a rise in status will be given for any information regarding the Free People, and in particular, the location of Mikael Ashworth.*"

Rebels. The two men butchered, hanged and left to be ridiculed, were rebelling against Mason.

I swallowed hard, forcing my tongue to still whilst Campbell absorbed this information.

Such examples of Mason's cruelty were hardly new to us. In the eleven years I'd been Roaming with Campbell, I'd seen countless swinging bodies. Mostly Slaves, executed for some ridiculous plight their Masters endured, then left to feed the bugs and the birds on some abandoned road in the northern Territories. I'd stare at those bodies, bloating with decay, and say a silent prayer to the Old Gods, to ask Odin himself to come down and spite Mason's cruel, sadistic hide. Hatred bubbled inside my belly, like it normally did when I considered the lives lost to Mason's horrific regime. Normally, Campbell would remain silent and stoic by my side, absorbed in his own prayer, fighting his own hatred.

For me, that afternoon was no different: I whispered my prayers, I relished the familiar ball of heated fire, rising up my gullet.

Yet, for Campbell, this execution order was a little too personal.

For a while, he simply *glared* at the words. Next, his fists clenched hard, the satisfying crunch and scrunch of the paper reflected in a face that twisted into something almost unrecognisable. Campbell's knuckles turned white, as if Mason himself was hiding within the swirling lines of ink.

Finally, when the paper could no longer bow to his wishes, Campbell threw it to the ground and marched ahead. I scurried behind as the paper turned to grey mulch in the slush.

Campbell stopped. I went to his side, about to question the sudden change in pace, when I saw his solemn stare.

"Should we go another way?" I asked; my voice soft, my accent prominent.

Campbell shook his head.

We continued in silence, the road long and bordered by more hanging bodies, swaying in the breeze.

* * *

THAT NIGHT, we camped in the forest. A healthy fire crackled, its warmth radiating in each flicker of orange light. The snow subsided, allowing the forest to erupt with nightly noise: the screech of a white fox, or the hoot of an owl. Small creatures scuttled between the branches, or climbed trees to observe us with fearful curiosity.

I'd shot us a hare for dinner. Not a lot of meat on it, but I'd skinned it, and set it over the fire. The delicate scents of roast meat tickled my nasal hairs, goading my impatient stomach to growl. I only prayed there were no bears or wolves in the vicinity. The killing shot alone was practically a dinner bell.

My loaded rifle sat patiently as I turned the spit, just in case.

Ever since the road, neither of us had said a word. I was dying to; my voice box was twitching.

The Free People. Rebels, by any other name.

A deep sigh escaped my lips. Images of those swinging bodies kept sticking to my eyelids, flashing every time I blinked. If Mason had already started the Rebel eradication, perhaps it was a blessing we didn't go after Ashworth. Yes, maybe Campbell was right, and Roaming the New World, avoiding Rebels and Masonians alike, was the best option after all.

Maybe Ashworth's jaunt was nothing more than a fool's dream. After all, should one be discovered conspiring against Mason, death would be their kindest punishment.

Poor Campbell knew that better than most.

I flicked my eyes to Campbell. He remained ever so still, simply gazing into the fire, lost in his own thoughts.

"Are you thinking about the execution order?" I finally asked. My voice was weak and croaky, doing little to steal Campbell's stare from the burning embers. Clearing my throat, I repeated the question.

"I'm thinking about the Free People's Rebellion," he finally replied.

Twiddling my thumbs, I rocked back and forth on my knees.

"Do you think they'll do it?" I asked.

"Do what?"

"Kill Mason?"

"Mason can't be killed."

I bit my tongue, but it wriggled free. "I'm not sure I believe that. I mean, Mason might not die naturally, but shooting him –"

"Girl, I stuck my sword right through his heart. I thrust in the entire blade, only to watch him pull it from his body, drop it to the floor. All he did was smile..." A sudden exhale of breath, to rid the assault of old memories. "I'm telling you: the bastard can't die."

A short silence.

"Was that in your rebellion?" I asked, carefully.

"It wasn't *my* rebellion."

"No, but you were a general, right? High up in the rebellion-ranks at any rate."

Campbell closed his eyes, either out of agitation or regret. I couldn't tell which. "I fought for what I believed was right."

"You *were* right." My tone was certain and unbreakable, and drew Campbell's sad, glistening eyes to mine. "Your rebellion may have failed, but you took a stand against Mason and – from what I've heard – gave him a right kick in the balls."

I expected Campbell's lips to quirk up into a smile, but they remained stubborn, fixed into a grimace.

"You know nothing about what happened in Gainstorn," he said.

"No, but I know you weakened Mason. Dunno *how*, like – but he retreated back into his Palace and locked himself away for months. In that time, how many Slaves did you free?"

"Not enough."

"Campbell..." I removed the roasted hare from the fire and carved the meat, the knife's blade reflecting Campbell's dejected expression. "You beat yourself up too much about it. The Dagger Rebellion was one of the most successful – "

"*Successful?* How was it *successful* when the majority of its fighters are dead? Johnson, dead. Kemble, dead. Caroline, Alice – " He stopped abruptly, a bubble catching in his throat. He swallowed hard a few times and regained his composure. "Harrison Dagger, the bravest, most decent man I have ever known... I was forced to watch as Mason cut off piece after piece and...a-and made him..." He broke off again and my heart ached.

"Campbell..."

"And what did I get, huh? I got exiled. *A fitting end for a disgraced Aristocrat.* While my brothers and sisters-in-arms were tortured and executed, all I got was a few broken bones and an order to get the hell out of Fjordlands by sundown. *Pfft*, a fitting end indeed. I should have been put in the dirt, not left to wither away, with nothing but the memories of what that monster did to those I loved."

I knelt down beside Campbell as slow trickles of water escaped his eye. "But you have me... A-And if you were put in the dirt, Mason would have got me too."

Campbell's eyes, a shocking mix of red and blue, found mine. And he smiled, just briefly, shining a thousand emotions.

He pulled me into him, wrapping his arms around me with a firm squeeze.

"I will never let anything happen to you, girl."

I closed my eyes, safe in Campbell's embrace, and sighed.

5

Waterman's Quarry was an odd place. An old mining quarry turned into a settlement, the town filled the base of a large crater, dug into the ground in the vain search for precious jewels. Now, the quarry was no longer active, with the only reminder of its past being the old mines honeycombing the steep walls, serving as water storage. Indeed, the entire town had a sophisticated plumbing network that fed the grand fountain in the middle of the square. Water spurted upwards, froze in the cold, and then rained small balls of ice down to the waiting crowds below, congregating to the Quarry in their thousands.

Or at least, that's what they usually did.

When Campbell and I entered the town, with their little thatched huts and gardening patches, the place seemed completely deserted. Even the cows were missing.

Uneasiness grew in the pit of my stomach.

"Err, Campbell, I don't like this..." The town should not have been this empty, this...*ominous*. "Can't we just carry on to the next town?"

"I ain't passing off the opportunity for a free bed with fur covers, not after these past few nights. No, c'mon, let's find the inn and see what's happening."

The inn, being the largest and most elaborately painted building in the town, was not difficult to find. I stared up, hoping to find a hanging sign detailing its name. Two metal loops remained over the door, but the sign had been removed. Such a sight was unwelcome, and did little to settle the growing foreboding.

The door opened with a haunting creak, echoing in the emptiness of the inn.

An unused fireplace made the air damp and heavy. Beams of sunlight shone through the windows, and the cracks in the walls, illuminating the thousands of specks of dust that floated in the stagnant air. The inn itself looked to have been empty a long time and yet, Waterman's Quarry was usually such a vibrant hub. I'd seen that very inn bustling with people, flooded with colour and mead, and both in equal measure. Laughter once cleaned this air, heavy not with dust, but the deafening cacophony of children shrieking with joy, or men and women guffawing with merry indulgence...

All of that had gone. Thrown somewhere unseen, with the last of the town's visitors.

What's happening here?

Campbell headed straight for the counter. A small bell rested on the rutted wooden surface, just itching to be rung. Sure enough, its high-pitched call clanged uncomfortably throughout the room. Half the town probably heard it.

As I inspected the head of a stag above the fireplace, an overweight bald man came stomping down the stairs.

I forced a blinding smile. "Good afternoon, mate. We were told that—"

"No, no – we're closed. Off with you!"

The innkeeper was a beast, with more hair on the back of his neck than the rest of his body combined. A thick sheen of sweat shone on his forehead, shedding slow, greasy drips. *At least his apron's clean*, I thought.

My smile dropped with a loud thud. "Sorry, there seems to be some mistake, we were told we could find a room – "

He bared yellowed teeth. "Are you deaf, girl? I said off with you!"

"We're here on Joe Matheson's recommendation," Campbell said, sauntering over with one hand on his revolver, the other playing with the intricate handle of his sword. "He said you'd be able to provide for us."

Something shifted in the innkeeper. He seemed to exude an impossible mix of dread and anticipation.

"Oh," he said, in a much calmer tone. "Right you are. I have a room for you. All ready and waiting, with no charge. Any friend of Joe Matheson is a friend of mine."

"Pay you to say that, did he?" I said with a teasing smile, as he led us up the creaking stairs.

The innkeeper grew shy, avoiding my gaze as two extra sweat drips ran down his neck.

"Something like that," I heard him mutter.

* * *

"Oh Campbell, I don't like this at all."

Pacing before the fire in our little room, I had my hands upon my hips and glared at Campbell, sprawled out upon the bed, reading a book he found in the top draw.

"Everything's fine," he said. "Now stand still, you're making me nervous."

"How is *everything fine*? This entire town is deserted, Campbell! A-And he obviously doesn't expect us to stay here!"

Campbell finally graced me with a look, however tiresome. "Really. Please explain that one."

"A *single* bed, Campbell – just look!"

Shaking his head, Campbell returned to his book. "You're ridiculous."

"I'm not r...rid-r-r-ridiculous..." I untied my Herdinese tongue. "I'm just cautious, Campbell. This whole situation just doesn't feel...*right*."

Why was nobody in that town? Why, when Waterman's Quarry thrived off passing trade and travellers alike, did the town's merchants slam their doors in our faces and demand we move on to new pastures? I'd no doubt that slimy innkeeper wanted nothing to do with us, and only by our association with Joe did he allow us to remain under that roof. But yet, as I stared at the walls riddled with woodworm, or the frayed sheets upon the bed, why *wouldn't* he want customers in his inn? Odin knew the entire town could do with some refurbishment, so its reluctance to host paying visitors just did not make sense.

Campbell perched on the end of the bed, rhythmically tapping the book against his palm.

"Okay, girl. As soon as the horizon starts to glow, we'll carry on. Just one good night's sleep without the fear of wolves coming to eat us – please, that's all I ask."

Nodding my head, I thought that a fair offer.

* * *

THE WOODEN STAIRS creaked as I descended. Each step was old and warped, the pounding of hundreds of past feet scuffing the mahogany, reducing it to soft splinters. *They need a runner*, I thought.

The emptiness of the inn struck me as I reached the central dining hall, gnawing at my belly, reinforcing the uneasiness that had never quite deserted.

Inns and longhouses were never *empty*. It was a simple fact that just...*was*.

They were hubs for chatter and trade, sex and gossip, food and drink. To see one as neglected as that poor dining hall, with the chairs turned upon faded tables and the once homely hearth reduced to nothing but ashes...

Even the air smelled sad.

"Can I help you, girl?"

I jumped and reached for my hunting rifle.

"Whoa there!" the bald innkeeper said, forcing an uneasy smile. "I mean you no harm... Simply asking a question..."

"Sorry, mate." I presented my empty palms. "Force of habit – you just scared me."

"Ain't no reason to be scared here, girl," he said, quickly.

"Don't doubt it."

Was I lying to myself? I wasn't quite sure.

Coming to rest on one of the bar stools with my chin in my hand, I watched the innkeeper wipe down the clean counter with a dirtied cloth.

"You usually this quiet this time of year?" I asked, watching him methodically move the cloth, back and forth, back and forth.

"Not usually, but been a strange year. A whole manner of strange happenings."

"Such as?"

"Mason finding Alira, for one."

My eyes slid from side to side, watching the wet streak from the cloth glimmer in the late afternoon light.

"You heard about this celebration?" I carefully asked. I watched for any change in the motion of the cloth, but his rhythm remained steady.

"Ai, all the Territories are talking about it. Damn tax increase has almost bled me dry."

"Know what he's celebrating?" The innkeeper and I locked eyes for the briefest of moments, but he quickly shuffled up the counter.

"Nay."

"It's something to do with Alira, apparently. He's waiting for her to do something."

"I wouldn't know about that, girl."

"Hmm..." His entire mannerisms just reeked lies. I didn't trust him, although I didn't trust anybody. Other than Campbell, of course. And Joe, despite his infuriating attitude.

"You're not from around here, are you?" the innkeeper asked, finally gracing me with some eye contact. There was something...*off* about his stained stare. I sat up tall upon the bar stool, should the moment present the need for a hunting rifle, and a bullet to a bald cranium.

"You tell that from my accent?"

"Ai, you're a Herder. Must be good at hunting."

"I've been known to shoot the odd rabbit or two."

"Rabbits..." His gaze wandered to the rafters above, housing nothing but cobwebs and bird nests.

Life sparked within him. He dropped the cloth and smiled at me with hideous, yellowed teeth. "I've got a job for you."

"Err... Okay..." The dubious stare I gave him was either not noticed or ignored.

"Go and shoot me some rabbits for dinner, and I'll give you a free extra night."

"I don't think we're planning to stay –"

"Nonsense! You just go and hunt those rabbits, and we'll come to some sort of arrangement."

A spurt of doubtful laughter rattled against my throat, yet my smile soon sank.

"You're serious, aren't you?" I gestured to the empty room. "You run an inn, for Odin's sake! Since when do your guests shoot their own dinner?"

"Supplies are running a bit low, given the lack of visitors these days..." The innkeeper just smiled widely, patting the counter. "So, off you go. I'll pay you for the excess."

I thought of the stash of gold coins we had, hidden deep inside the lining of Campbell's rucksack. Twenty pieces, at the most. Hardly anything; enough for a box of bullets, maybe two if we could barter. Sighing, I took an annoyed glance across the glistening counter, and conceded that some extra money trounced the sheer oddity of such a request. At the very least, it would get me out of the town. So, I pushed myself from the bar stool and headed for the door.

"Oh, and girl!"

Reluctantly, I stopped, putting all my weight on one leg and sticking out my hip. "Make it three – no four rabbits! That will keep you occupied for a while, right? Don't come back without those four rabbits, you hear me, girl! *Four!* And don't –"

But I had already slammed the door shut.

* * *

WATERMAN'S QUARRY seemed to have woken up a little.

Women in tattered trousers and fur coats raked soil in their gardens, men in cloaks shuffled hay in the stables.

No children.

Must be inside, I swiftly convinced myself.

Other than the resounding echo of a dog's bark, bouncing off the Quarry's high walls, there was silence.

One of the women met my eye. Greasy brown hair, matching eyes, and a face scoured by a hard life, she did little to acknowledge my friendly smile. Instead, she just ploughed aimlessly through the wet dirt.

Feeling ever more like an outsider, I continued on without another glimpse.

The road up the quarry was steep and laborious, with loose stones that could slip at any moment. It was a perilous journey that the ice did little to help.

I wondered how many trucks and vehicles had shaped those roads, or those very walls, from the solid rock beneath. Did they ever find the precious artefacts they were digging for, with a desperation that destroyed an entire landscape?

Away from the sad, stagnant air of Waterman's Quarry, I breathed deep. Cold air expanded inside my lungs, but I welcomed its chill. It was fresh, freeing.

I peered over the cliff to view Waterman's Quarry. Tiny toy houses surrounded a minuscule fountain. They seemed so small, so insignificant compared to the grand wilderness outside their little bubble.

Indeed, *wilderness* was the right world. Trees and snow, rocks and boulders, mountains in the distance, still air and a setting sun that turned the horizon glorious shades of gold and crimson.

Feral, untamed, unconfined by laws or politics. Beauty and adventure and death, all rolled up into a spectacular landscape, left to grow free of harm and exploitation.

All except for Waterman's Quarry: the huge hole carved into an otherwise pristine landscape, then left to grow empty and sad.

It was a travesty. An outrage.

How dare they destroy a pristine landscape in their vain search for riches! Hadn't the Aristocrats gotten enough gold? Enough diamonds? And to leave what remained of such blasphemy as an ugly cesspit of a town such as Waterman's Quarry...

I kicked a rock unfortunate enough to cross my path. It rolled a few miserable metres before disappearing into the undergrowth.

Screw the extra money. We'd manage – we always had done – and so no, I wouldn't shoot those four rabbits. Four innocent little lives that had probably seen their fair share of death and hardship. It was cruel for their short, hard existence to end on the dinner plate of a fat, slimy innkeeper who made my spine shudder.

They deserved a better end.

A tree towered above me, its welcoming branches open. Obliging, I took one foothold, then another, and heaved myself into its woody embrace.

The structure creaked but remained sturdy. I continued on, climbing the entirety of its great height, before my head popped from the tangle of needles and branches.

I sighed out an endearing breath for my home. Trees glowed orange in the sun's dying light. To my left, a mountain chain stretched along the landscape, their snowy slopes glowing a soft red, marbled by shadows and rocky cliffs. And at their base, a lake, only just beginning to thaw in the subtle spring warmth.

To my right, a field of trees, expanding to the horizon as far as the eye could see.

I sighed again, leaning against the tree as it swayed softly from side to side, and watched the last light of a gold sun disappear beneath the world.

* * *

I RETURNED to Waterman's Quarry when the stars were bright, dotting the sky.

Once again, residents shut their doors when they saw me: a warning to keep my distance.

The inn remained equally sad, its withered facade literally dropping off to the muddy ground below. My feet squelched in that same mud as I approached the door.

Licking my lips, preparing for a conversation I could really avoid, I stepped inside the stale air.

Another man sat perched upon a bar stool. I stared, unaccustomed to seeing another soul in such a godforsaken place.

"Dear Gods, girl – why are you back?" The innkeeper's face was unusually pale, his slimy eyes glazed with apprehension... And perhaps a bit of fear. "You shouldn't be back this early! I thought four rabbits would take you longer than... Wait, where are the rabbits? *Four* rabbits, I asked of you! *Four!*"

"Yes, well mate, all the rabbits have run away," I muttered beneath my breath, approaching with caution.

The stranger had his back to me, hunched over the counter, caressing what I assumed to be a tankard filled with mead, or alcohol of some description. He wore a black trench coat that could not hide the revolver pinned to his hip.

I carefully slipped onto a bar stool a fair distance away.

"But you said you'd –"

"Stop whining," I snapped. It was only four rabbits, for Odin's sake. "I promise to shoot you a deer tomorrow."

"You don't understand girl, tomorrow – "

"Bart." The stranger's deep, sonorous voice echoed around the emptiness of the inn. Walls trembled. "We've run out of a cider. Be a good man and grab another barrel. I want to buy this fine lady a drink."

The innkeeper fell silent and subdued, like a suspicious lamb standing outside the slaughterhouse.

"Well?" the stranger said, louder.

"Err, yes, of course..." He plodded off around the corner, muttering all the way.

Once he was firmly out of earshot, I shyly observed the man beside me.

"Thank you," I said. "For getting him off my back, I mean."

"My pleasure." His gaze remained fixed to the wall ahead, his only movement being the rhythmic lifting of the tankard to his lips, as though drinking to a tune.

I tilted my head, admiring the long scar on his cheek, shimmering in the light from the few meagre candle flames. It matched the colour of his cropped, silver hair. The more I stared, the more I realised that his hard face and crooked nose did little to conceal the raw strength, brimming inside veins not worthy of a man of his fifty-or-so years. Indeed, he almost pulsated the aura of a thirty-year-old, with all the drive, ambition, and power such an age promised.

"So," he said after some time, still staring at the wall. "Why didn't you shoot those rabbits? That rifle on your shoulder is a fine piece of kit, so you're no stranger to hunting."

I tittered quietly to myself. "I wasn't going to spend the best part of my evening on a wild rabbit chase through the forest."

"Wise choice. A situation that involves a young, attractive woman, alone in the forest, can never end well this time of night."

I immediately bristled. "I can take care of myself."

"I don't doubt it." There was the briefest smirk upon thin lips, but it quickly disappeared. "Bart the Innkeeper wasn't impressed though. Why do you think that was?"

"Probably missed his dinner," I muttered beneath my breath.

The stranger did not comment, instead gracing me with a full view of his scarred face. Grey eyes shone like two pebbles at the bottom of an icy riverbed.

"You're a Herder?" he said, one hand upon his knee, the other fondling his tankard.

Without a word, I nodded.

"Strange to see your kind in a place like this."

"I was Herder. Now I'm a Roamer."

"Why the change?"

"None of your business."

He smiled, exposing a cracked tooth. "You're smart to be wary. But perhaps a little foolish to be so secretive."

"Why would I tell you my past?"

"Why wouldn't you? Unless you have something to hide."

My heart began to pound hard, methodically against my breastbone.

"Whatever," I said, as a small snake grew and coiled around my gut. "Don't see why I should tell strangers my history."

He inclined his head, a suppressed smirk ticking the corner of his mouth.

"My name is Alden," he said. "There, we are no longer strangers."

The snake would not retreat but grew larger, expanding into strained lungs. Pushing myself from the stool, I stood to my feet.

"It's been nice talking to you, Alden." I turned my back to him.

"You travelling alone? Dangerous for you to be travelling alone."

I debated whether to ignore him; to continue up the creaking stairs, hide in the dusty single room, and lock the door. But there was something about his tone that made my hackles rise. I felt the need to prove myself.

"I'm not travelling alone," I replied, standing tall and strong. "I'm with a companion. I did travel alone though, when I was small. Made it on my own just fine."

"Interesting." Another sip of drink. "And this companion of yours, know where he is?"

The hunting rifle weighed heavy on my shoulder.

"No..." I said, carefully. "Why would you ask?"

"I would just like to know the location of Campbell Anders. He seems to have disappeared from the town and I'd very much like to speak with him." Alden turned in the stool, glints from his revolver catching my eye. "Pure curiosity, you understand."

My jaw clenched hard, my teeth almost cracking beneath the sound of Campbell's name, spoken by another. A stranger knowing his name – *knowing that he was here* – was most definitely not a good sign...

I took a step back and Alden's lips twisted into a triumphant smile.

"Do you know how long we've been looking for him? My, you Roamers are mighty difficult people to find, especially those who have secrets."

Panic grew in my stomach, rising like bile.

"I don't know what –"

"And then we heard that Campbell Anders had arrived in Waterman's Quarry... Oh, a good day indeed." A dull, metallic laugh reverberated around the tankard. "So we came, and sure enough, Bart said how Campbell had arrived and taken a room for the night. Funny thing is, he never mentioned Campbell had company. I would even go as far as to say that Bart the Innkeeper sent you on a wild hunt for rabbits to get you out of the town. After all, if you hadn't walked through this door ten minutes ago, I wouldn't know you exist."

Of course, the single room...

"Where's Bart?" I asked, caressing the dagger on my thigh.

"Oh, don't you worry about him. Needless to say, he won't be leaving that cellar in a hurry. Aiding members of the Free People's Rebellion holds a high price."

"We're not Rebels," I said – quickly, desperately. "I swear to you, we never even knew about the Free People until –"

"It's no matter." Alden tipped the tankard high, finishing the last drips of his mead. His throat convulsed as he swallowed, emphasising shadows on gaunt cheeks. "Campbell Anders is the last surviving member of the Dagger Rebellion. I'm sure he has some interesting information that Mason will find useful for quelling this latest uprising."

Mason.

The hunting rifle flew into my hands, aimed at Alden's temple. "What are you? A Masonian Captain or something?"

Alden stood to his full height, his black trench coat falling. "I am a General."

A sharp laugh escaped my throat. "A *Masonian General,* is it? Well, you've wasted your time with us – we're *innocent!*"

"Said by all traitors. Do you know how many times Campbell proclaimed his innocence before Mason finally squeezed the truth out of him?"

"That fucking bastard can go to Hel."

"Ha, that's been said before." Alden approached with slow steps, his leather boots pounding against the floor. "I've no doubt it will be said again, but Mason will always endure. You, however, will not."

Footsteps echoed against the hollow wood, softening those splinters upon the stairs...

I turned, abruptly met with the sight of half a dozen men, all marching closer. Long royal blue coats, a brown belt, a sword on one hip and a silver revolver on another. Evil eyes shone from beneath fur hats, their leering, smirking stares puncturing my clothes. *Masonians.*

Get out, was the one thought I had, going round and round my skull and unable to escape. *Get out of here, girl!*

More of those pounding footsteps, behind me.

I spun around. One step forward and the tip of the barrel would touch Alden's leather waistcoat. A flash of orange heat scorched my back, the entire inn smouldering.

"No need to make this difficult," he said, his tone soothing against the crackling air. "I can put in a good word for you, ensure my men treat you with respect."

I cursed in my native tongue and spat on the floor.

A change of eye contact, a subtle nod. Arms encircled me. My assailant grabbed the gun, tried to rip it away. I fought against him, the gun tipping up to the ceiling as my finger convulsed against the trigger.

Two shots fired into the rafters. Splinters rained down from above.

The fire grew. Smoke clouded the inn, the immense heat forming beads of sweat that pebbled my brow, then my lungs began to burn...

Get out, get out!

I kicked blindly behind me. The Masonian grunted, his hold of the gun loosening. In his weakened state, I sacrificed my rifle and escaped the prison of his arms.

Alden did not bat an eye as I ran straight past him.

I threw myself outside, coughing.

Heat and smoke hit me like a train, a wall of fire blazed in the night. Men and women screamed their way from their burning huts, only to be cut down by Masonians.

How many Masonians were there? Forty? *Fifty?*

Bodies littered the ground, sinking in the cold mud that thawed in the heat.

Campbell! Where's Campbell? But Alden had already said he was missing, that Waterman's Quarry had been scoured, but there was no sign of him. I clung onto that hope as I frantically searched for an exit, but the steep walls of Waterman's Quarry meant there *was* no way out. I was trapped in a burning cesspit.

The road. I just had to make it to the road!

Two Masonians blocked my path. I grabbed my dagger, my palm sweating.

They laughed to each other as they unsheathed their swords, wolf-whistling and puckering their lips.

One hunting dagger against two swords.

In a moment of madness, I threw the dagger. I missed my target by a good three inches, the blade embedding in the Masonian's shoulder. His pained scream echoed against the night, merging with the sounds of death.

In their stunned stupor, I banked left and ran.

I dodged bodies and fires, both filling the air with the nauseating stench of meat. Vomit threatened in my stomach, adrenaline pushing me forwards – to the road which was so, so close!

Something hard hit me from the side.

I fell into the mud, ears ringing. Smoke hindered the view of the stars, my vision bordered with flames that reached higher and higher and –

Run, girl!

I turned on my belly, trying to find a foothold in the slippery mud.

A boot slammed into my back, pressing me down. I screamed, my hands and fingers sliding aimlessly, my legs kicking but to no avail. The boot descended, curving my spine. I groaned in agony, my lungs compressed against the cold ground.

Fingers entangled my hair, pulling back my head.

"You'll pay for that stunt with the dagger, you bitch!" Someone kicked my legs apart and stood between them. Two others held down my arms, pressing them deep into the mud. I struggled, but their multiple strengths easily overpowered mine.

They quickly retreated. They released my arms, my legs, the crushing weight of the boot upon my back.

Fear festered. I scrambled to my feet. There was a gap between flames, my window of opportunity beckoned!

Firm hands grabbed my upper arms, dragging me back towards the burning inn. I screamed and struggled, trying to kick and jump and bite and *anything* that would weaken his hold of me.

When the blade of a curved knife tickled my throat, I stopped dead. One move, and I'd be wearing a dress of my own blood. I did not even swallow.

"See gentlemen?" Alden's husky voice boomed around us. "*That's* how one subdues a wild animal."

Muffles words and curses from the surrounding men.

"Now," Alden whispered in my ear. "Where's Campbell?"

I don't know! I tried to say it, but one false word and my throat would slice into the blade, pressed firm against my larynx. My only response was a series of fast, shallow breaths.

"Look, General!"

Like a phoenix rising from the ashes, a figure appeared. I strained my eyes, blood roaring past my ears, and saw Campbell's familiar features emerge from the veil of smoke.

"Ah, speak of the devil..." Alden smirked. "We've been waiting for you, Campbell."

Surrounded by Masonians, Campbell unsheathed his sword and held it high. His pale face met mine, our eyes meeting in the briefest moment of pivotal, hopeless understanding.

"Let her go, Alden," he said. Was he afraid?

"Oh, I don't think so. She either comes with us, or her body is left for the crows. Your choice."

No, don't do it, Campbell! I tried to shout again, but the knife simply pressed harder. I squeezed my eyes shut, the rising urge to scream stopped by the sharp pressure of the blade.

Campbell panicked. "Please, she's innocent in all of this!"

"Not for me to decide. I guess time will just have to tell."

Wood crackled and creaked as the filthy, rotting inn of Waterman's Quarry collapsed into a fiery mound. Millions of sparks floated up into the sky, like orange stars on a bed of black smoke.

Alden raised his elbow and flexed his muscles. Bright specks dotted my vision. I held my breath.

"*No!*" Campbell's loud voice echoed through the ruin. The clang of a thrown sword sounded. "*I surrender!*"

6

The dull, repetitive rhythm of the tracks lulled me in and out of consciousness. Stuck there, in a windowless room of a darkened train carriage, Campbell and I sat in silence.

How long had we been travelling?

I could not answer. I did not know.

My eyes were stinging, salty and dry. I had since lost the energy to cry. What was the point? I knew they were taking us to our deaths. I had accepted it.

The events of Waterman's Quarry kept playing inside my head, over and over again. They knew Campbell was going to be there, but *how*?

Joe's face flashed before me, those seafoam eyes shining with immaturity and perhaps... *Betrayal?*

No, impossible! I shook the scandalous thought away, before it could cement itself.

Joe Matheson may have lacked some morals, but at his heart, he was a good, kind man. He'd helped me for years, he'd known Campbell for even longer than that. To suddenly turn on us, his *friends*, made about as much sense as Campbell inviting the Masonians himself.

No, somebody else knew we were there. Perhaps someone had overheard our plan, maybe the entire ambush was happenstance on whispers, rumour, or a fleeting part of a random conversation...

Whatever the reason, Campbell and I were now locked in a damp train carriage, at the mercy of evil people who wanted to see us suffer.

Once again, I was a wanted woman. This time, they didn't even want *me*.

As Alira, I had been running from Mason my whole life, for twenty years. The irony now was that Mason would find me, yet it wasn't even me he was looking for.

Now, trapped in that train carriage and being taken for slaughter, I realised Campbell was the reason our hands were shackled, secured against those freezing metal walls. Campbell, the man who had kept us safe for eleven long years, was now the reason we were going to die.

"So..." The harsh spit of my voice percolated the metal space, bouncing off the walls and causing Campbell's saddened expression to focus on mine. His eyes ran down long tear marks, etched into the dried mud on my cheeks.

"So what?" he whispered.

"They've arrested us for conspiracy. For treason."

"Yes, they have." Campbell rearranged his position, leaning his greying temple against the wall.

I glared at him. "Why, Campbell? Why are they after you, *now*, when the Dagger Rebellion ended over two decades ago?"

Campbell took a deep, laboured breath, his head bowing low. He seemed utterly exhausted. He did not reply.

I wiped my tongue over my teeth, coating my entire mouth with acid. "Is it about the Free People? You said yourself that you knew Ashworth."

A bitter, dejected huff rattled around Campbell's chest. "I know a *name*, girl. Nothing more."

"But then why – "

"I have no idea!" His voice ricocheted off every wall, bouncing hard against my eardrums. "Girl, I've been Roaming for twenty years, and in all that time, Mason has not given me one thread of thought, so why have I suddenly become important to him again? Hell if I know! But I'd be dammed to drag you down in the shit with me. You know, you fucking *know*, that if I had *any* inclination that Mason was after me, I would have got you the hell away!"

As Campbell's eyes glistened with tears, a hard knot formed in my stomach. Though I understood his drive to protect me, I would never leave him, no matter how far he wished to throw me from the lion's snapping jaw.

For a while, I remained listening to the motion of the train. The repetitive *thud-thud, thud-thud,* that had kept me company for – however long it was.

"Campbell?" I asked, tentatively.

"What?" he snapped.

"Will they take us to Mason?"

A pause that was almost as heavy as the guilt.

"Yes," he said.

A sad little noise, halfway between a moan and a scream, escaped me. I squeezed my eyes shut, ignoring the searing pain in my eyeballs.

"Girl, listen to me." Campbell shuffled forwards, the metallic clang of chains following his every movement. The chain was quickly taut, but he was still too far away. "Look, I'm going to get us out of this, okay?"

"But how? They're taking us to Mason a-and –"

"You just leave the technicalities to me. But you need to promise me something, okay?"

Campbell's glacial-blue eyes sparkled with emotion. They were *pleading*.

"Anything," I replied.

"Whatever happens, you must do exactly what I say. You won't like it, and you don't have to, but it will be the *only* thing that's going to save our skins… Girl, did you hear me?"

"Yeah, I-I promise. Campbell, what are you going to say to them?"

I waited for his response.

It never came.

* * *

THE METAL CREAKED and clanged as the compartment door slid open. White light flooded into the small space, stabbing the back of my retinas. I squinted in the painful light, just able to distinguish four Masonians.

They dragged us out by our shackled hands. Campbell first, then me.

Rain splattered against my face, sinking into hair caked with mud. It had been a long time since I'd felt the cool patter of rain upon my skin. I mumbled in my native tongue: a small prayer for our safety.

A swift kick to my shin. I grimaced around the pain, biting my tongue.

I chanced a look at my surroundings. The train had stopped before some great building, constructed from white marble that disappeared into the grey rainclouds. Through a marble arch was a courtyard, housing a statue of a stag, made from solid gold. Its antlers protruded out, its very stance exuding power. It even included the animal's golden testicles.

A fence surrounded us. Twice the height of Campbell, it spread out around the complex, bordered with barbed wire and interspersed with metal towers, sat below huge spotlights.

This luxurious settlement quickly revealed itself as a prison.

I mumbled again in my native tongue, wondering where we were.

"The Masonian Barracks," an accented voice – *my* accent – rose up from the rain. "Speak English. Herdinese is not a welcome language here."

I met the source of the voice. A Masonian, his bright red hair flattened by the rain, and his thick features dotted with smallpox scars.

I scowled at this man – this traitorous *Herder* – who had defiled our shared history, our shared culture by donning that blue Masonian coat. I cursed loudly in our native tongue, willing the Ancestors to come down and spite his treacherous hide.

That caught his attention. Hands scoured my hair, yanking back my skull until I met those two seething green eyes.

"Bold words from someone who struts around in Roamer gear." His attention slid to Campbell. "And with Roamer allies. Where's your Herd, little girl, or did they all die in the snow?"

I spat in his face.

He reared away, wiping saliva from his bent nose, cursing beneath his breath. Grinding his jaw in a hideous grimace, he marched towards me with fists clenched...

And hit General Alden's open palm.

"Captain Tallis," he said, his tone low and sturdy. "There are matters more important than this little tart. Mason is due to arrive any minute. See that his convoy is met."

Ripping his clenched fist back into his own possession, Captain Tallis bowed his head and dutifully obliged, glaring at me as he passed. He was soon out of sight, disappearing through the archway.

Alden turned to us. In this light, I was able to get a full view of his face. A slice here and there, some deeper than others, with the majority of his scarred features being centred by that monster running the entire length of his cheek. The scars melded with his crooked nose and chipped teeth.... The man was hideous.

"Time to talk, little girl," he said, smiling. "Mason will certainly want to chat to you. A girl as pretty as you... Well, he might not even stop to chat."

Spidery fingers dug into my arm, and dragged me towards the Barracks.

Run, girl! The words came fast and true, clawing themselves into my mind until I couldn't dislodge them.

I frantically searched my surroundings, looking for a way out of this raining hellhole. I kicked and struggled and dug my heels in the ground and –

"Wait!" Campbell's voice rose up behind us, frantic and desperate. "Alden, I swear to you, she knows nothing. She's not old enough to be born from the Dagger Rebellion, and too wild to be involved in this one!"

Alden stopped, his grip intensifying. Tingling sensations rushed down my arm and into my fingertips.

The rain intensified, pattering against the tarmac.

Alden turned, so fast I almost stumbled.

"Say that's true, what am I going to do with her, hm? Release her back to the wild like some dog?"

"Nothing of the sort." Campbell licked his pale lips. "Send her to Maelstrom."

Words failed me. I simply stared, mouth open, and my questioning – confounded – eyes wondering what I was hearing.

Behind me, Alden cackled. "Maelstrom? And live life as an Aristocrat? I've seen rats that have more etiquette than this one."

Saliva pooled in my mouth, just ready to spit.

"No," Alden continued, stepping back towards the Barracks. "She'll go to Mason. He'll decide what's to be done with her."

"No, wait!" Campbell rushed forwards. His chains were yanked back, yet still he persisted, pulling against them. "Mikael Ashworth – son of Laura

Isenhauer and Hamish Ashworth. Born on the *Third Day of the Third Month*, two days before Gainstorn."

Alden stopped. He shuffled his weight from one foot to the other, like a wild stallion raring to go. "And you said you were innocent," he said, with a mean sneer.

"I don't know anything about Mikael Ashworth, but I knew his mother. After what happened at Gainstorn, Laura fled, taking a baby Mikael with her."

"Fled to where?"

Campbell laughed softly, shaking his head from one side to the other. "Oh no, send the girl to Maelstrom, and I swear to tell Mason all I know. Send her to Mason or kill her... Well, you can torture me all you want, but I won't budge."

"You said something similar last time, if I recall."

Something flashed in Campbell. Some deep despair that flicked to the surface, before being buried beneath renewed resolution.

"That girl is the only thing I have left," he said, slowly. "Take that away from me, or harm her in *any* way, and I will have nothing left to live for."

There, through the pattering of the rain, I struggled to accept the terms Campbell offered. He couldn't just *throw me away*, not now – not when Mason's knife was tickling his throat. I wanted to be with him! To be by his side as I screamed our mutual pain, to comfort him as Mason, Alden – *whoever* – prized out whatever information they thought Campbell might have!

"I'm giving Mason an easy choice here, Alden," Campbell said, after some time. "Send her to Maelstrom, I'll be cooperative, and you'll have an early night."

"That's all well and good, but I don't think this one's cut out to be – "

"Enslave her." Campbell's words fell on deaf ears. I could do nothing but watch, dumbfounded, numbed with the coldness of his words.

Slavery? That was his plan?

"Campbell, *no!*" I shouted, the reality of his terms forming a noose around my throat. "Campbell, let me stay with you, let me – "

"Enslave her. Let her be sold to an Aristocrat in Maelstrom," Campbell said, loudly, his eyes glazed with red moisture. "Just let her live out the rest of her young life somewhere other than these godforsaken Barracks…"

Captain Tallis appeared.

"Lord Mason's waiting in his office, Sir," he said. His accent sent hot rods of anger prickling down my spine, the sound of his cultural betrayal twitching at my tongue.

"No, Campbell!" I shouted again through the rain. "No, I'll go with you to Mason, he can do anything he wants to me, just let me stay!"

"Girl…" The same plea arose behind eyes the colour of glaciers. "Remember what you promised me."

"I take it back, I –"

"Maya." Unshed tears glimmered. *"Please…"*

Alden flung me to Tallis, who gripped me painfully tight with both hands.

"I need a phone!" Alden yelled.

Sure enough, a Masonian arrived with a large box carried by two arms. Alden opened the box to reveal a phone, on which he quickly spun the dial and placed the handset to his ear. Thus began hushed conversations with the Higher Powers.

I swallowed past the hard lump in my throat, my own tears mingling with the rain as I met Campbell's miserable stare.

"Campbell, you tell him what you know and he'll kill you – you *know* that!" Why was he doing this? Why was he throwing me to the cold shackles of Slavery and condemning himself to death?

Desperation ruled my senses. As my hair was soaked and battered by the falling Fjordland rain, I suddenly remembered who I was. With startling clarity, I realised I could utilise my real name, my label, as the ultimate bargaining tool. Maybe, just *maybe*, I could use my destiny to my advantage, for the first time in my life…

"Please…" I whispered, as my tears merged with the rain. "J-Just let me stay with you, m-maybe I can bargain with Mason, maybe I-I –"

"Girl." Campbell's panicked, stern glare flushed away any *bargain* I could possibly produce. "Don't you *dare* force me to watch you die."

Tears streamed my cheeks as I considered our future, *his* future…

"But he'll kill you," I said, my voice shaking.

"I know he will," he said, reservedly. "But I signed my death warrant to Mason a long time ago. You, on the other hand, did not, and I will die with a smile upon my face knowing that you're somewhere *far* away from him."

"But I'm not going to leave you here to be butchered!"

Beside us, Alden was wrapping up his conversation.

Campbell's mouth tilted up into a small smile, his glass-like eyes shimmering. "The good news, girl, is that you don't have a choice in the matter."

The phone box slammed shut.

"Take him to Mason," Alden ordered. "The girl goes on the next Slave transport to Maelstrom. Congratulations, Campbell. The Big Man concedes to your offer."

Tallis shoved me towards the train compartment.

"*No! Campbell, no!*"

"Bye, girl," he whispered with a shake.

"*Campbell!*" All English left me. I cursed and yelled and roared in my mother tongue, my willpower consumed with pure, blind panic.

Tallis was surprisingly strong. He flung me into the train with little effort. I collapsed onto the floor, scrambled to my feet, and flung my shackled self to the exit just as the door slammed shut.

Campbell's face, streaked with tears and rainwater, flashed behind my eyelids.

I kicked the door until my toes broke. I scratched the metal until my fingernails bled. My shoulders became bruised, my coat scuffed and shredded as I bashed myself against the door again and again and again...

The entire compartment shook and strained, but the door would not budge.

Eventually, hopeless, I fell into the corner. It was no use. So, I did all I could do: I wailed so loud, distant wolves joined me in chorus.

* * *

When they finally came for me, the world had slowed into a viscous motion. I was numb, without feeling.

Yes, my bones and muscles ached, but the pain did not register. Yes, my dry throat begged for water and my stomach growled for food, but I did not care.

Even my eyes, agonisingly painful beneath the lenses, were nothing but small inconveniences compared to Campbell's absence.

Absence, not *fate*. I couldn't think about Campbell's fate because the word *death* kept forming soon after. He wasn't dead. I couldn't accept it. *I wouldn't accept it!*

Somewhere before me, the compartment door creaked open. Two Masonians entered the van. Tallis was amongst them.

"Come, Wild One," he mocked. "Time to do as you're told."

Mindlessly, I obliged, and limped out of the compartment. Tallis held my chain like a leash.

Outside, a black van loomed through the rain.

The van's rear doors opened. It contained two rows of people, one on each wall. Some wept quietly, others silently succumbed to their fate. All were chained.

"Get in," Tallis ordered behind me.

Without a world, I stepped into the van and took a seat. My empty gaze fixed ahead as Tallis secured my chain to a loop on the floor.

Before long, we were on the move.

The road was bumpy and uneven. Shocks rippled up my spine, making me grimace.

Someone coughed ahead of me. This single vocal noise, echoing in the small space, was the only sound for the entire journey.

* * *

WE ARRIVED into Maelstrom just as a loud, chipper voice declared the time.

"It is 8am and the morning sales are about to start! Come on, join us for this week's auction! New merchandise has arrived from all corners of the five Territories and oh – ladies and gentlemen – don't we have some good'uns for you!"

Outside, a great crowd cheered. A whole cacophony of *let's see them,* and *I'm willing to pay double my last offer,* filled the enclosed space.

The harsh scrape of a baton down the side of the van, rattling a head so painful, I was sure blood trickled from my nose.

Doors burst open.

Cheering, light — there was too much of each. I tried to cover my eyes, but the chains forbade it. I was left squinting as a Masonian released our chains from the floor.

The man before me got out first. Greasy hair, and a face marbled with red and blue, he was led from the van without complaint, much to the roaring crowd's joy. I was next, following with similar numb obedience.

I was led up wooden stairs to a stage, in the middle of a crowd. Hundreds of Aristocrats surrounded me. I stared at their strange garments: colourful dresses stitched to remarkable detail, or the fur coats and shawls, or the sea of top hats and long jackets that filled the crowd.

I stared at the unfamiliar, stunning architecture of Maelstrom, with its tall houses and pointed tile roofs; with decorated facades of black and white; with stained glass windows over flower beds, and with emerald green ivy spreading up walls. I stared at the fountains that spurt water that didn't freeze, and the trees and golden statues that littered the market square.

The crowds didn't notice the market stalls, setting up their wares for the day: merchandise of the finest quality. No, all attention was focussed on the new meat, being led in chains to the stage in the centre of the square. Once free people, we were now on show for the whole of Maelstrom to fight over, with gold coins and squeals of excitement.

It was sickening.

The sun was warm against my face. I closed my eyes, absorbing its rays into dirtied skin.

The roar of the crowd increased as the auctioneer hopped up.

"Behold the next generation of Maelstrom's Slaves!"

More cheers, more euphoria.

"Eight slaves are on sale: five men, three women! All of working age and...*delectable assets*." The auctioneer's lecherous insinuation won him a few more cheers.

The auctioneer: soft skin, soft features, soft hands. Never worked a hard, or *honest* day in his life. His only comfort was to sell innocent human beings into Slavery. The one thing in his wretched existence that made him feel powerful, that made him feel more important than the reality of his insignificant life.

Masonians took residence at each corner of the stage, batons in hand, their beady eyes watching for any act of disobedience. I squeezed my eyes and fists even tighter.

"And now, let the buying begin!" A raucous cheer. "The first: a man from the northern Snowlands."

A grumble, the rattle of chains ,and the hurried shuffle of footsteps as the man beside me was pulled forward, on show for the world.

"Oh he's a looker, ladies! Twenty-nine years of age, a hard worker. Good with his hands, *if you know what I mean*." More whistles, catcalls.

The rip of material, the muffle of clothes falling to the floor...

"You see, my friends: a fine specimen! Now do I hear three-hundred? Three-fifty! Four! Four-fifty! Going... Going... And *sold* to Mr Shaw of the Maelstrom Greenhouses!"

A grand applause stifled out the groans of losing Aristocrats.

"And now... Well, who do we have here!" Someone walked before me. My own chains rattled. My arms were yanked forwards, my feet sharply following. Still, my eyes remained closed.

Calm, girl... They'll ridicule and undress you, but you're alive. You'll get through this. Remain calm...

"Oh, ladies and gentlemen – what a prize this one is! Born a Herder, now a Roamer, and fluent in both English and Herdinese, this one has seen some sights! But, I warn you now... Dubbed a *Wild One* by our Masonians, she may be a beauty, but she's not to be taken lightly... I'd recommend her only for the hardiest of Masters!"

Tremors ached in my bruised, battered muscles.

"But," the auctioneer called in his loud, overzealous tone. "Ladies and gentlemen, don't let appearances fool you... She is strong, hardy, and has quite the fight in her... So, do I hear five hundred?"

A cheering roar.

Cold fingers slid down my coat collar, and with one flawless movement, ripped my coat in two. More hands grabbed the sleeves, more tearing of material, and then the frosty morning air bit through my jumper. My shoulders hunched up through the catcalls and leering comments, protecting myself from the hundreds of stares that cut through what remained of my clothing.

"Do I hear six hundred?" the auctioneer called. "Seven? Oh, my dear people – look at this Wild One! I think we can do better than seven hundred!"

Wild One.

Visions of the wilderness, of the snow, the mountains...

More footsteps, the greedy, groping hands of Masonians twitching to touch me. Cheering, catcalls...

Visions of reindeer, my Papa smiling at me with his eyes full of loving mirth...

Campbell.

I cracked.

Infuriated eyes shot open.

The chain jumped into my hand. A quick pirouette and the metal links struck one Masonian, rendering him to the ground with a bloody gash on his face.

Someone came up behind me. I threw my head back, crunching his nose. An elbow to the jaw and he fell to his knees with a hollow thud.

The crowd screamed in protest, Aristocrats fleeing. Men yelled, leading their wives and mistresses from the scene, protecting their loved ones from the Wild One who was systematically cutting down every blue-coated man she saw.

More Masonians, more batons. I waved the chain in the air, looping it with precision. Numbness combined with angry adrenaline: a chemical reaction that kept my motions steady and patient...

A Masonian lunged at me. The chain struck, his shrieks filling the space.

Next came another. I spun, dodging his strikes, and whacked him between his shoulder blades. His spine arched, his face contorting, but he did not fall. Furious eyes glared at me, a jaw grinding hard.

Something hit my legs. I yelped, my balance failing, my concentration broken.

The Masonian before me swung his arm. I stumbled back. Wood collided against my jaw, splitting my lip.

Searing pain. Ears ringing. World spinning.

I doubled over, watching the string of red dribble from my mouth. The chain slipped from my fingers.

The crowd began to cheer.

Legs shaking, I tried in vain to stand to my full height.

The last thing I saw was a swinging baton, and then there was blackness.

7

Water splashed against my face. Cool and refreshing, it soothed the swelling of my head, my lip, my cheek...

I stirred upon the hard ground. I tried to move – to rearrange my tightly folded limbs – but everything ached with a throbbing, repetitive pain that spread burning claws into every muscle, every bone. A small groan escaped the dryness of my throat.

Water. I needed water.

As if the Allfather himself heard my prayers, a cup rested against my swollen lip. Water found my parted mouth, tipping inside. It soon raced down my chin, tickling my collarbones as the water just kept on coming.

"Slower... *Slower*..." The woman's shrill voice echoed. "Don't drown the girl, for God's sake."

The water sloshed in more manageable mouthfuls. I drank greedily and without restraint, feeling it slip and slide all the way down my gullet and wash away the metallic taste of blood.

All too soon, the water disappeared.

I licked my sliced lips, wincing through the sting.

The pain shocked life into my muscles, rousing them from their cold, still state of unconsciousness. Memories of Bolton Square rushed with the first trickles of fear. Lingering in the background, cowering like some terrified puppy, was a single question: *where was I?*

Slowly, cautiously, I forced my scratchy eyes to open. My amber contact lenses burned with the movement, and in one sharp and startling moment, I realised with great, numbing relief that they were somehow still fixed onto my eyeballs.

I blinked through the perpetual sting. Blurs sharpened, forming lines and boundaries.

The room, though not necessarily dark, was dingy, and stank of stale air and damp. Barrels surrounded me, and against the far brick wall was perhaps the largest wine rack I had ever seen. To the other wall, a collection of hessian sacks, labelled with staple household ingredients, mostly flour.

As for the three figures standing before me, the woman was the most prominent. Obviously an Aristocrat, her skinny frame was covered in a lime green dress, her bare arms encased in a shawl. Though it was made from silk, or so the material's sheen eluded, the most luxurious item of her attire had to be the headscarf, held in place by a large emerald. It complimented the woman's eyes, the colour of stone, and were surveying me with a curious mixture of respect and pity.

"Good, you're awake. About time too, it's ghastly down here." Each syllable was expertly enunciated. *Oh yes,* I thought, *you're definitely an Aristocrat.*

Bound and injured, in the company of Aristocrats, only meant one thing. I groaned around the sudden realisation, at the word that kept screaming at the back of my head.

Slavery.

Instinctively, I looked at the two other figures. Both young men, dressed in black trousers and buttoned-up shirts, remained passive and polite, and completely stationary unless otherwise instructed.

That word kept singing at me again – louder, this time.

The soft light was enough to stab my brain. I tried to inspect my injured head, but I was still restrained and could reach no higher than my neck.

"Oh for pity's sake, unshackle her – she's not a dog."

One of the men, albeit hesitantly, removed the metal restraints from my wrists. They fell to the floor with an almighty clatter that rattled my skull.

Thick lines of blue encircled both wrists, speckled with raw flesh. I prodded them carefully, inspecting the damage. I felt my swollen skull, grimacing as the bloodied lump fell victim to my scrutiny.

"There's no lasting damage, or so I've been told." The woman readjusted the shawl around her frame, raising a pointed nose to the surroundings. "God, it really is horrendous down here."

"Who are you?" I croaked.

"Ah! She speaks! Oh, my dear, I was beginning to think they lied about your English fluency. Your accent though…" She visibly shivered with delight. "Ah, but you asked me a question. Well, my dear, my name is Emilia Eynesbury."

She spread out her arms and graced me with an extravagant bow. Each knobbly vertebra protruded from her dress. As she deftly rose to her full height, I couldn't help but wonder how she had maintained such lasting dexterity. Despite her flawless skin, she easily encroached seventy.

"Where am I, Emilia Eynesbury?"

"You are in my home."

"And why am I in your home?"

"Dear God, you ask a lot of questions, don't you?" She rolled her eyes. "Well, I must say, I somewhat admire your curiosity. But first, I would like to know your name."

I remained silent.

Next came the stare of disapproval from the Enunciated Emilia. "Darling, it's the height of bad manners not to introduce yourself, particularly as you're in my home – albeit the wine cellar is hardly the place for formal introductions."

The water sloshed in the bucket. My mouth craved its cold caress, and I wondered quite dreadfully if Emilia Eynesbury might feel the need to remove it should I be difficult. It was a type of torture that was – apparently – not below Aristocratic nature.

"Maya," I replied. "My name is Maya."

Emilia's thin lips smiled in appreciation. "Good, we're getting somewhere. Well, Maya, do you have a last name?"

"In English, it's Wolf-Charmer."

"Wolf-Charmer?" The skin burrowed between eyebrows that were almost non-existent. "Ah, a Herder name, of course. Maya *Wolf-Charmer*... I'm not sure I like that. *Miss Wolf-Charmer*... No, no, that won't do at all. *Doe* – oh, that's much better. Right, Maya, whilst under my service, you will hereby be known as Maya Doe. I hope you find that agreeable."

I used precious energy to scowl.

"Oh, don't look at me like that. I've no need for flouncy Herder names, and Doe seems a good alternative. It's short, punctual and rolls nicely off the tongue."

"But my name's not Doe."

"Nobody's name is *Doe*, my dear girl, that's the point. *Jane Doe, John Doe*... A communal name for those who have none."

Too tired to argue, I let the matter slip. *Fine then, Maya Doe it is.*

"Will you now tell me why I'm in your home?" I asked. *Unchained as well*, although I didn't remind her of this fact, for fear she might rethink and restrain the *Wild One* trapped in her wine cellar.

"Oh yes, the dreaded topic. Well, my dear, may I stress that you are in no fit state for any more violent antics, and Mr Tomlin here has been ordered to use any means necessary to subdue you, such as the need arises."

Something bubbled from my throat and sounded very much like a laugh.

"With all due respect, Emilia Eynesbury, but if I were to attack you, I would have done so already." My face twisted with pain as I tried to move my leg.

"Quite," Emilia said. "Well then, so be it."

Standing up straight, she cleared her throat and said, completely nonchalant, "I bought you."

There it was. The solid, unbreakable fact that I was now a Slave, with what remained of my life exchanged for meagre pieces of gold. I laughed around the audacity of it all, that these Aristocrats – these *people* – expected me to just do what they said, without question.

Campbell's face raced back to me, hitting me with as much force as that Masonian baton, and I wished nothing more than to be at his side – be in a cell, or a grave. Guilt should have ballooned, for I knew I'd just rejected his noble sacrifice, but, bound before Emilia Eynesbury, I just didn't care.

"Well, I'm glad you find this so amusing," Emilia said, holding her nose high at my stretched, grinning lips.

"Why the Hel would you buy *me?*" I asked, forcing my manic laughter aside. "I'm the *Wild One*. You saw me attack those Masonians."

"And I should think so!" Emilia said, puffing up her shoulders. "I am a firm believer that there is a time and a place for stripping a woman bare, but that place being Bolton Square for the whole city to see is certainly not in my books, I'll tell you now.

"But, as you've so rightly pointed out, you are the *Wild One* – this needs to be addressed. After your little stunt, I got you for an exceptional price, and I am perfectly prepared to lose that money should I feel the need to remove you from my household."

"Remove me to where?"

"The gallows, I expect."

The gallows. Oh, how easy would that be... Just to step off the edge of the world and be free from all the pain and misery the rest of my life would entail.

"You should do it," I whispered, my voice hollow and empty. "You should send me to the gallows now, just to get it over with."

"Oh what rot!" Emilia's sharp tone made me jump. "One does not break the nose of one Masonian, and almost cripple another, to simply give up!"

I huffed around such a notion. Slavery was a swamp, steaming with the excrement from a sordid reality. What was the point in living when life was such a cesspool?

Yet, the more I thought about such an end, the more I realised that *yes*, I did want to survive. I wanted to feel the snow crunch beneath my boots, or see a red sunset bleed across snow-tipped trees.

"Indeed," Emilia said, "I do believe you only fight like that when you have a burning desire to live, which – as it happens – is one of the reasons I admire you."

Another laugh, stale and bitter, erupted from my throat.

"If you *admired* me, then you'd let me go!" I glared at Emilia's stony eyes and was met with equal harshness.

"Perhaps you're not as clever as I thought," she said, lifting her nose. "At any rate, it's almost time for tea. Mr Atkinson." She turned to one of her little stooges. "Show Miss Doe to the shower room and get her cleaned up."

And, just like that, she turned on her high heels and clanked her way towards the stairs. "Girl smells like a ruddy rat's arse," she muttered as she left.

* * *

WHEN MR ATKINSON heaved me to my feet, I was unprepared for the shriek that escaped my throat.

Pain, *everywhere*. I had never understood such searing, burning, breath-stealing pain.

I envisioned those Masonians, wielding those batons, and maiming and murdering for their own sick pleasure, and a fog of red covered my eyes. That same red reminded me of that sunset, high above a town called Waterman's Quarry. Perhaps, one day, when I had escaped that shithole, I might venture back to that town, if only to wallow in its charred remains.

"I can manage," I snapped, pushing Mr Atkinson away. By some miracle of the Old Gods, nothing was broken, but I limped shakily on.

"Up the stairs, and then to the left," he said behind me. His tone of voice was soft and understanding. It was a tone designed to calm those in distress, or to comfort. A voice you would gladly hear after a nightmare, or during the inner struggle to cope with a bereavement.

Against everything I expected, his voice was kind.

The stairs took me a while. Every step twisted my face, forced a bubble at the back of my throat. I gripped the handrail for support, hauling my battered body up the thousands, and *thousands* of stairs.

I collapsed to my knees at the top. I fell forwards, catching myself with shaking arms. The cut skin on my wrists stretched with the movement.

"Here, let me help – "

"I said I'm fine." I pushed away his gentle touch. "I don't need help from a fucking Aristocrat."

Mr Atkinson laughed: a sad, hollow laugh. It did not fix joyous vibes throughout the air.

"You think I'm an Aristocrat?" he asked, quietly.

"Sound like one." I grabbed the handle of the door and pulled myself up with an exhausted groan. "...You... You dress like one, too."

The End of Everything

On Mr Atkinson's instructions, I turned left. I didn't have the energy to venture right, to see if there was an exit at the end of the wooden corridor.

Besides everything, I craved a shower. The feel of the hot water soothing my sore muscles, wiping away the dirt and blood of the last few days. I needed to wash away the evidence of what happened, so I could properly feel the memories etched onto my consciousness.

Slowly and carefully, I stumbled through the corridor. Wooden floorboards creaked beneath my unequal steps as doors bordered on either side. One was open, revealing a small room housing two rickety bunk beds, capable of holding four people. I spotted a bucket full of wet, dirty laundry next to the bed, not that dissimilar to the one I drank water from, and quickly carried on with my stomach lurching.

"I'm not an Aristocrat," Mr Atkinson said, still plodding behind me. "I was born in Uma's Grotto, in the Icelands. Captured by the Masonians eight years ago, on the 18th *Day of the Seventh Month*, bought for three-hundred gold coins by Mr Doncaster, then for two-hundred-and-sixty by Ms Eynesbury, four years ago."

Listening to his story, my steps slowed.

"See?" he said, coming to my side, those two brown eyes shining. "You and I aren't that dissimilar after all."

I chanced a look at this man. Only slightly taller than me, he had an air of one that was born in the icy north: broad shoulders, tight muscles, thick skin. That being said, his round face and thick mop of curly brown hair gave him the look of an innocent child. His most defining feature, it was sad to say, were the glorious mess of acne scars, denting what would otherwise be a flawless complexion.

"*Eight years*," I whispered. My mind wandered back to that stage in the middle of Bolton Square, with the crowd cheering over the rips of material. "How have you just been sitting here for *eight* years?"

His brow furrowed. "I don't follow."

"Why haven't you escaped?" I gestured to his smart attire. "There are no chains, no shackles or restraints. Why haven't you run?"

Mr Atkinson's face twisted into a nasty scowl.

"Because I value my life, Maya. I tried to escape once, when I was under Mr Doncaster's service. All that got me was four broken bones, and one-hundred lashings on a whip spiked with metal." He visibly shivered, his eyes resembling spheres of freshly cut glass. "Never again will I endure that."

Without another glance, he carried on walking.

Stumbling behind, I thought of witnessing such a scene. Of this poor man strapped to a wooden pole, blood and flesh pouring off his back as he endured lash after lash after lash...

Would I be able to endure such torture?

"Does Emilia Eynesbury do that?" I asked, quietly.

"Do what?'

"Use lashing as a punishment?"

Mr Atkinson stopped, hands in his pockets, and stared at the floor with his innocence restored.

"No, thank the Gods. She doesn't agree with it. Thinks such things are below Aristocracy." He cast his eyes up to me. "All things considered, she's not a bad person."

I scoffed bitterly beneath my breath, doubting that.

"Trust me," he said. "I've been under the vile hands of men – and women – who want nothing more than to see us suffer. Speak to any of the other Slaves here and they will tell you the exact same: Ms Eynesbury is a blessing. Never was there a better Mistress."

"I refuse to believe anyone who buys a human life is a *good* person."

"Really?" He raised two bushy eyebrows. "She didn't have to buy you, y'know. She could have left you to the Masonians – one was already excited and unbuttoning his trousers, from what I hear."

I swallowed hard, fighting the tremors that ached. Mr Atkinson saw this and his gaze softened.

"After they'd have their fun with you, they would have killed you, and not kindly. Ms Eynesbury saved you from that fate. You owe her your life."

"I owe her nothing!"

"If you believed that, then you wouldn't be crying."

I angrily slapped the tears from my cheeks.

"Maya..." Mr Atkinson said, that gentle tone resurfacing. "Please, I'm not asking you to be happy here, and I would be lying if I said that any of us would choose this life. But... Please, don't do anything stupid."

"Ha, like run away, you mean?"

"If a Slave is seen roaming the streets without their Master, they are instantly taken to the Barracks and never seen again. Do you want that fate?"

"I want to be *free!*" My voice echoed down the corridor, vibrating the wooden walls.

Mr Atkinson remained quiet, his shoulders rising with a large, hopeless sigh.

"We all do, Maya," he eventually said. "But sometimes freedom has too high a price."

* * *

WATER RAN DOWN MY BODY. Warm, clean, seeping into my skin and cleansing me of all the shite I had trudged through.

Mud coalesced in the base of the shower, each dirty particle racing round and round the plughole. I watched the water with curiosity, wondering where it would go. I imagined myself disintegrating in that shower, following the water on its path to freedom, and reforming far away from Maelstrom. Far from Slavery and Ms Emilia Fucking Eynesbury.

I thought of Campbell. Of those glacial-blue eyes shrouded with pain and terror, and the fear of death. Was he still alive? I almost wished he was not. At least then he would be free of the suffering.

Yes, for his own sake, I wished Campbell was dead.

I *knew* he was dead.

The tears came. A roaring torrent, merging with that dirty water. I slumped in the shower, covering my face to drown out the sounds. Mr Atkinson was waiting outside the door and I didn't want him to hear me crumble.

And I was crumbling. Badly. Completely.

Where was my resolve? My fighting spirit? My insatiable urge to run back to those Barracks and save the man who became my second father?

That girl was still in the train carriage, wailing to the moon.

This girl, the one in the shower, was debating how to live her life, and I hated myself for the choice I was making.

You're doing this for Campbell, I thought to myself, over and over. *Be cooper-*

ative, and they won't kill you. Campbell died so you could live, and don't you dare screw this up.

Yes, Campbell died so I could live on. He knew what would await me at the end of that Slaving Line, and yet he did it anyway. He must have known Slavery would be better than whatever was waiting for me in those Barracks.

My fate with Mason.

No, I wouldn't mess this up. I would be good and respectful to my fucking Mistress, and clean her clothes and brush her hair. To do anything other would be an insult to Campbell. An insult to his memory.

But I couldn't just give up. I couldn't just stop wishing for the feel of freedom beneath my toes, because what was the alternative? To be a Slave for the rest of my existence? To do as I was told, to bask in the greatness of Emilia Eynesbury?

Pfft, not bloody likely.

Campbell made a deal to save me – I understood that, entirely. I'd be damned if I were to let his sacrifice go to waste, for me to die beneath a Masonian baton, or to hear my own neck snap beneath the taut, tight rope of a noose. Yet, I couldn't just sit and ponder what my life *could* have been if we'd never set foot in Waterman's Quarry. I couldn't just *carry on* living an unliveable life.

No, I would escape this fate. I refused to remain a Slave for the rest of my days. But I had to be smart, cunning. I had to bide my time, to be *cooperative* simply until my moment of glorious opportunity beckoned. All I needed was time and, thanks to Emilia Eynesbury, I had buckets of the stuff.

But – in one year, or maybe two or three – *when* I managed to escape this nightmare, I expected to survive. That was my promise to Campbell. *That* was the reason he offered me to Slavery.

He wanted me to *survive*.

"I made a promise to you, Campbell," I whispered, clean water dripping from my lip. "And I intend to keep it."

When I finally exited the shower, a pile of pressed clothes was on the floor, next to the sink.

A black pencil skirt and a white blouse. Not too revealing, nor something I would regard as a Slave's uniform.

The End of Everything

When I imagined the Slaves living in Maelstrom, I imagined men and women being led in chains and dressed in rags, continuously whipped.

Reality was far different. We had a communal bathroom at our beck and call. Albeit simple, it included all the niceties – even hot water. There were no chains, no locks on the door, no barriers of any kind.

It all seemed too easy to escape...

I shook the scandalous thought away. If it were *easy* to escape, there would be no more Slaves in Maelstrom. No, whether by fear or action, Slaves did not escape because – for whatever reason – they knew it was impossible. The punishments: dire. That simple mentality gave all Masters and Mistresses throughout Maelstrom undeniable, unbreakable obedience. Clearly, whatever horrors lay indoors were far, far better than what lurked outside in the shadows.

The sooner I understood this, the better.

Tying my wet hair up in a bun, now clean from dirt and returned to its chestnut sheen, I chanced a look in the mirror.

My diamond eyes shone. Free from the contacts, my eyes exploded with light and colour. *Don't hide us away again*, they seemed to scream, *please don't imprison us again.*

But, as I stared sadly at the mess of black and blue upon my pale skin, I realised that if I wanted to survive – to keep my promise to Campbell – I needed to hide who I really was. Gone was the girl with diamond eyes, born of Wulfrick Wolf-Charmer.

At that very moment, Maya Doe was born. A nobody. A girl with an insignificant name and an insignificant appearance. A girl whose amber eyes, although striking, were not strange or dissimilar from any other eye colour.

"Hello, Maya Doe," I said to myself.

With a reluctant breath, I reached for the contacts, lying precariously on the edge of the sink.

* * *

"My, you look like a new woman," Mr Atkinson remarked.

I certainly didn't feel like a new woman, yet forced a thin smile.

The clothes were scratchy and restrictive, not at all what I was used to. Hel herself invented heeled shoes.

Clanking and limping in equal measure, I asked, "Okay, Mr Atkinson, what now?"

"Firstly, call me Orzo. *Mr Atkinson* is getting rather laborious to listen to."

"*Orzo?*" I scrunched up my face. "Is that your birth name?"

"No, but everyone calls me Orzo. Except for Ms Eynesbury, of course."

"But *of course*," I mocked.

Orzo led me through the house: a myriad of elegance and sophistication. As we traversed the corridors with wallpapered walls and large portraits of stiff-looking Aristocrats, countless artefacts proved the wealth of *my owner*. Golden statues of animals and half-naked women; clocks emblazoned with mother-of-pearl; entire vases encrusted with diamonds, sapphires, emeralds – all home to extravagant bouquets of flowers that sent their strong, floral scent radiating in all directions.

Dusting and cleaning all of these relics were Slaves. All men. All in the same black trousers and button-up shirts, all less than forty years of age. And all were looking at me, their eyes portraying a curious mix of pity, desire and gratitude. It was unsettling.

Orzo opened a door and led me inside a room doused in mahogany. A chandelier dropped from the ceiling, strings of glass raining down and catching the orange flicker from a healthy fire, contained in a marble fireplace. The majority of the room, it seemed, was a social gathering point. There was very little in the way of functionality, other than a couple of chairs and sofas, pimped up with cushions and throws. On one of these sofas, stretched out like the Goddess Freya herself, was Emilia Eynesbury.

"Oh, good God," she declared, those stone-coloured eyes looking up and down. "There was actually a girl under all that mud."

I bit my tongue, for insults were itching.

Sitting herself upright, Emilia Eynesbury rearranged her headscarf: blue satin, this time held in place by a large sapphire that matched the colour of her navy day-dress.

"So, I assume you've had time to come to terms with your new establishment?"

Still, I remained silent.

"Oh come now," she snapped. "All this silence is certainly not becoming. I assume you haven't washed away your voice. Give those vocal cords some exercise."

"What exactly would you like me to say?"

"*Ma'am*, for one. Every time you speak to me, you shall refer to me as *Ma'am*."

My knuckles whitened, stretching the scarred skin.

"Anything else, *Ma'am*?" I hissed through gritted teeth.

"Oh, much. But first, I shall give you your duties." Standing to her full height, Emilia Eynesbury wandered around the room, her head held high. Indeed, she looked down her straight nose at absolutely everything, even the décor. "As you are no doubt aware, the majority of my household is male-orientated. For the most part, I find this very agreeable, but it will be nice to have some female company. In the future, I will expect you to help dress me, bathe me and ensure that my personal wellbeing is extraordinarily high. However, until then I will assign you more menial duties. To break you in, for lack of better words."

My tongue twitched with acid, just aching to spit at Emilia Eynesbury's subtly lined complexion.

"And what *menial duties* will you have me perform?" I said, and then, "*Ma'am*".

Emilia Eynesbury simply looked at me, her thin lips rising into a smug, practised smile.

"Oh much." She beckoned me to sit down. "So, shall we go through the list?"

8

Wipe. Mop. Scrub.

That's all I did for the next four weeks. I scrubbed dried food off the floor; I polished away the streaks of rubber from posh shoes, and the fingerprints that marred priceless artefacts...

My hands, cracked and dried from the chemicals, burned as I pressed the cloth deeper into the grooves between the tiles. My fingernails yellowed, the softened nails flaking. Two permanent bruises formed upon my knees as I knelt for hours and hours upon the marble.

My only solace was that my ordeal from Bolton Square had healed. Other than a slight discolour to my cheek, all my injuries had been wiped away.

I was a clean canvas, ready to be painted once more.

Unfortunately for any eager artist, Orzo was on my shoulder, ensuring that I did not step out of line.

"Don't chew with your mouth open," he said, as was his usual dinner conversation starter.

"Oh piss off," was my usual reply.

Orzo smiled at my prickly attitude, his tongue wrestling with a particularly stubborn piece of meat.

Dinner was nothing more than potato and lamb stew. Cooked in a large pot and left to boil since lunch, it was a gloopy mess of meat and vegetables that did little but settle my growling stomach.

Orzo and I were eating with the rest of the Slaves, yet they remained quiet and preferred their own company, with hunched backs and lowered eyes. They chewed their food in silence, the only noise being the screech of a chair, followed by the clank of bowls in the sink. Then they would return to their duties.

As for Orzo and I... Well, we were a talkative duo.

"Y'know, you really should learn some etiquette whilst you're here. Emilia Eynesbury is a good tutor in the matter, she used to run a finishing school y'know."

"Ha!" That was hilarious. "Of course she did. No wonder the old bag has a stick up her arse."

"Oi! You can get hanged for saying something like that."

I rolled my eyes. The lenses were scratchy beneath my eyelids: a constant reminder of my predicament. Save dwelling on sour futures, or the past (for the past was still too raw to remember), I thought of the man sitting beside me.

"Orzo..." My tongue rolled around the name. "...Orzo, Orzo, Orzo... Why the Hel are you called Orzo?"

Orzo grinned, each pitted scar deepening at the gesture.

"It's my nickname. My real name's Otho." Large brown eyes flicked in my direction, a sparkle glimmering in each of them. Heat flushed my cheeks, my own stare quickly dropping to a piece of carrot left at the bottom of the bowl.

"Uh-huh," I mumbled.

The door barged open, and a skinny man with messy curls came bounding into the room, waving a piece of paper.

"Ms Eynesbury's going to the Theatre tonight!" he rejoiced. A dozen eyes flicked up from bowls, all staring at this man with shocked glee.

"Who's she asked for?" one of them said, excitement spilling.

The man quickly scanned the paper, his eyes flicking back and forth.

"Lander..." A bunch of grumbles and an elated gasp rose from the table. "Orzo..."

Perplexed, I frowned at Orzo. He remained unmoving, like a statue, and simply stared to the floor with his eyes wide and his mouth securely snapped shut.

I heard my name.

"Say what?" I startled, eyes wide.

"You're going to the Theatre."

Hating glares cut me from all corners. My muscles tingled, preparing to flee. One sudden sound and these men could quite easily turn homicidal.

I stared at each of them in turn, wondering what to say.

"Unbelievable," one of them meanly hissed. "Do you even know what the Theatre is?"

"Yes, of course I do," I snapped. "What's all of this about?"

Orzo tried to speak, but his words came hoarse and disjointed. He roughly cleared his throat. "Ms Eynesbury partly oversees a number of theatrical productions. Occasionally she attends the opening night, and sometimes she allows a few of us to accompany her. It's a great honour to be chosen."

"A *great honour?*" The butch man opposite almost spat on the floor. "That's an understatement, if I ever heard one."

Shaking his head, Orzo said, "It's a small nicety but it does help."

"Help what?"

"With this life."

"You mean, it keeps us obedient, right?" Scoffing, I jumped to my feet and dumped the remains of my dinner into the sink's dirty water. "The promise of a nice *reward* means we're more likely to do as we're told?"

"Maya — "

"No, if one of you wants to go in my place, be my guest. I'd rather live through another Ragnarök than see my *Mistress's* stupid play."

The man with the paper huffed. "Selfish little girl! Why does she deserve to go? She's only been here four weeks and —"

"*Mr Jameson!*" Those sharply spoken vowels caused a thick silence to suffocate the space.

Ms Eynesbury stood in the doorway. Despite the slightness of her frame, her ominous presence seeped from the seams of her scarlet dress, complete with the obligatory headscarf.

"Ma'am," he said, with no more than a whisper. "My sincerest apologies for – "

"Oh hush! I wish to hear no more of your pathetic jibes of jealousy! This is my decision, and you should all respect that." Her eyes, fuming, snapped to me. "As for you, Miss Doe, you're going to the Theatre whether you like it or not. I expect you to dress smartly and quickly... *Now!*"

* * *

SQUISHED BETWEEN ORZO AND LANDER — a short man with a cropped beard, and eyes that never quite looked in the same direction — we were driven to the entrance of the Theatre.

The early evening sun was still high in the air, illuminating Maelstrom in all its glory. Away from the markets of Bolton Square, Maelstrom continued to excel as a place of luxury and extravagance. All around, the houses became higher, bolder; the cars became more garish, the horses more thoroughly groomed.

Shops beamed at the base of limestone buildings, their facades bordered with scarlet cloth and gold, their pristine windows protecting objects of various colours and wealth.

Further still, and the shops and houses disintegrated into restaurants. Tables shone behind windows, each dining couple or laughing party stuffing themselves with piled plates of food. Flowers in golden vases sat in the middle of these tables, the glasses of wine shining like red and white beacons in the lights from chandeliers.

And there, just ahead, was the Theatre: a glorious building with a domed roof and a spectacular facade of pillars, engravings and statues. Its marble body clashed beautifully against the crimson carpet, rolling like a tongue from the entrance's gaping mouth.

If nothing else could be said about this Theatre trip, I was thankful for the change of scenery. I mumbled something indiscernible, my eyes darting over each intricately carved man and woman, looking down upon us from their obscenely great height.

Peeling ourselves away from the car, the three of us mimicked the statues.

Everything stilled, except for our eyes. They skimmed over every surface, trying in vain to absorb every line, every curve, every piece of utter brilliance.

"Oh, stop gawking," Ms Eynesbury snapped, waving us behind her. Her scarlet dress flowed in waves, rippling over the carpet like she and the Theatre were the same entity.

As I perused the surrounding streets and the mess of roads, scandalous thoughts trickled into my brain. *Escape*, each one kept teasing.

Yet, achingly aware of skulking Masonians, I quickly scurried behind my Mistress. Those thoughts still lingered, rooting themselves inside my bones. Excitement fluttered at the hope of a sudden, fleeting chance at freedom.

The interior of the Theatre was no less impressive: carpeted stairs curved around both walls, illuminated by an enormous chandelier that dripped diamonds. Gold accents glinted in the bright light; bulbous vases embraced bouquets of red roses. A theme of red, white and gold shone from all directions.

Emilia's red dress continued to ripple as she marched onwards. Up the stairs, to the right and then down a service corridor.

We arrived backstage. Costumes and dresses filled the racks to capacity, each bodice straining against the material crushing it from either side. A wall of mirrors overlooked tables filled with cosmetics, all in different coloured bottles, and all reeking of some artificial scent.

Ms Eynesbury opened the first bottle of perfume and gave a subtle sniff. "Here's what you're going to do."

Our chores at the Theatre were no less menial. We were to ensure that all costumes were returned to their proper place, all spilled cosmetics wiped up swiftly and expertly, and – most importantly – we were to be *quiet*. If, and only if, we excelled in all of those endeavours, then were we allowed to watch the production from the viewing hole beneath the stage.

I grumbled bitterly about the injustice of it all. There I was, picking up clothes and helping actresses tie their corsets, or brush their hair, or wipe up spilled white power, when I could be faffing about in Emilia's Residence, doing sod-all in her and Orzo's absence.

I protested this to Orzo whilst Emilia's back was turned, but when I saw his face flushed with unbreakable determination, I considered my position.

For Slaves to work so passionately must involve a reward worthy of such an effort.

Before long, my curiosity was piqued. Why was this reward so revered? Why did Orzo's eyes glisten at the gleeful prospect of this Theatre trip? Perhaps it was time I found out.

So, I worked my little socks off.

I ran from one dressing room to another, dipping in and out of changing rooms, wondering what else I could do to be deemed worthy of Emilia's praise. Of course, I couldn't care less about Emilia, or her pride. I only cared about this curious reward, dangling just ahead of me.

When Ms Eynesbury graced me with a proud smile, I exhaled a sigh of relief.

"Watch the production from under the stage – Lander, you know where to go – and be sure to return at the intermission," Eynesbury said. Sitting before the mirror, she had changed her attire into a spectacular ball gown. Scarlet material, gold accents, and a red feather protruded from the ruby in her headscarf. She was the definition of *extravagant*.

The tip of the feather tickled the ceiling as she stood to her full height. A final grin to each of us in turn, deep wrinkles in her powdered cheeks.

"Now, if you would excuse me, the audience are about to take their seats."

Once Emilia was out of sight, we ran. Lander was at our head, his stumpy legs moving with such ferocity that even Orzo had trouble keeping up.

We arrived at the viewing hole. Small and cramped, it barely fit all three of us, yet we crawled into position and poked our heads through the gap. There, in the underbelly of the stage, we could see *everything*.

The interior of the Theatre was enormous. A circular room with a domed roof portraying a whole manner of painted vistas: mountains, forests, stags and does prancing through the snowy landscapes...

Hanging down from this artistic masterpiece were a collection of chandeliers, smaller than the one in the entrance, but no less splendid. Further down, row upon row of seats separated into three distinct tiers. Taking residence in these seats were Aristocrats.

There must have been hundreds of them.

Men donned their dinner jackets and bowties; women wore elaborate gowns with even more intricate headpieces. It was a colourful mess of luxury and extravagance; a moving kaleidoscope of satin and sparkle that shimmered in the light pouring from the chandeliers.

Closer to the stage, there was a pit filled with smartly dressed people – mostly men – holding up various pieces of equipment. Some were brass, others were wooden, some contained strings and others a mouthpiece to blow in, cheeks swelling. A low drone erupted from a brass instrument, so deep it rumbled in my lungs. Other sounds reverberated up, some high-pitched and squeaky, others low and sudden. There would be sudden pause and then again, the same noises, slightly altered, would float up from the pit.

"What are they?" I whispered to Orzo.

"That's the orchestra."

"What's an orchestra?"

"A group of people who play musical instruments."

"Music?" I grinned stupidly. "We're going to hear *music?*"

When was the last time I had heard *music?* I sang songs and drummed my hands upon the table, and occasionally there would be a bard with a lute in one of the inns, strumming with tales of poetic legend.

But to hear actual *music*... It must have been years.

Above us, box stalls quickly filled up. Private parties, with their private butlers and their made-to-order drinks, were sitting down, observing the ground below with evident superiority.

Actors coalesced at the side of the stage, hidden by large sheets of red chiffon. They wore bulbous dresses, with their faces painted white, and their lips an exaggerated scarlet. White wigs reached over a foot above their heads, and the more I debated such an accessory, the more I wondered how such a piece stayed put. The more immature part of me wanted to casually saunter over and poke and prod until the hairy beast dislodged.

"What are they going to do?" I asked Orzo sideways.

"Opera, I'd reckon."

"What's opera?"

"Wait and see."

A soft smile brightening my face, I leant both elbows on the wooden stage and cast my eyes over the scene. The chandeliers dimmed, their electric bulbs blessing us with the most meagre of light.

The crowd hushed, the once loud rumble of chatter diminishing into whispering breaths. Eyes of hundreds of Aristocrats fixed upon the stage as spotlights glared. I squinted as the beam of light shone directly at us, before concentrating in the centre of the stage and onto Emilia Eynesbury, grinning like a girl a tenth of her age.

"Good evening, ladies and gentlemen!" She spread her arms out beside her, the spotlight catching every gem on a dress that glittered like bloody stars. "A warm welcome to this evening's production of *The Red Rose*."

The patter of applause filled the area.

"And, a very warm welcome to our Lord Mason - "

Mason? He's here?

Everything froze. I forgot to breathe. I *couldn't* breathe.

"...Who we are honoured to have in our audience."

Emilia Eynesbury smiled again, gesturing to Mason with a gracious lift of her arm. More applause, louder this time.

I leaned further out of the hole, my eager – yet terrified – gaze following Emilia's outstretched hand.

But no matter how hard I focussed, faces were nothing but dim pinpricks against the spotlight. I could not see a thing.

Hands grabbed my shoulders and roughly pulled me back inside. Orzo did not say a word. He didn't have to. The warning behind his eyes said it all.

"Mason's *here?*" I hissed through my teeth. The art of breathing returned with a vengeance, my lungs burning with the strain. I gasped in air, the pounding of my heart reverberating into my skull. Blood roared around my veins, blackening my vision with stars.

"Yes, he's here," Orzo quietly replied. Two large hands pressed down on my shoulders, rooting me back to reality. "But he's not here for you, or me, or anyone else. He's here for the show. Relax and breathe steady, you're fine."

"No, Orzo, you don't understand, I-I have to get out –"

"No, you don't, Maya. Running now will put a big red mark over your head. Mason will as good as kill you for ruining the show."

"It's starting..." Lander whispered.

Orzo squeezed my shoulders and through my heaving breaths, I managed to see sense.

Masonians would be everywhere, on the lookout for assassins or Rebels or escaping Slaves. They would easily catch me – it would be foolish to think otherwise. Then, they would take me to Mason. He would be incensed. He would look into my eyes – amber or otherwise – simply for disturbing his entertainment.

Maybe after the show, my scheming little voice thought. *I could escape then, jump into the car of an unsuspecting Aristocrat and –*

Music. It floated through the air, surrounding me, capturing me within its musical arms. *Delicate, exquisite...*

One of the actresses appeared on the stage, the spotlight shimmering against the sequins of her dress. Dancers pranced and spun in the background.

The air shivered with her voice. I was entranced, enraptured by the beauty of such a song, and as the music loudened – became more forceful and powerful – all essence of fear completely diminished. Drowned beneath those musical notes, swirling like water around my head.

More singers came, the loud, rumbling vibration of a baritone quaking in my lungs. Next, the sharp notes of a soprano, shaking the air. Hairs on the back of my neck stood on end, the very air electrified with the music and the voices and the sheer power of their combination.

Soon enough, I was captivated.

* * *

THE STORY WAS at its climax. The music grew louder, dramatic, as the singers wailed their lungs in a final song, and then *silence*.

There was a great musical uproar of sorrow and triumph. A curtain of red fell down upon the stage, covering the scene as applause rose above the music.

"What? No, no — why is it finishing?" I asked Orzo, panicking.

Orzo nudged my shoulder, gesturing to the cleared stage as four men in suits arrived.

"This is the musical interlude," he whispered, as the men set down their chairs. "A string quartet."

I observed the men curiously. All had wooden instruments with strings and a long stick that Orzo would later refer to as a *bow*. They immediately began tuning, odd notes quivering the air, heavy and silent with anticipation.

The men took up their positions with the bow set delicately against the strings. Then, in one fluid motion, arms moved. Music filled the air.

Soft, sublime, enchanting...

How could these pieces of wood and horse's hair create something so profoundly beautiful?

But, no matter how exquisite the music, something was... *Different.*

Difficult to distinguish, there was some faint, underlying tune that never quite made it to the surface. The musicians were talented, of course, and it was not denied that their skill contained musical genius...

But regardless, something was... *Odd.*

"Does it sound alright to you?" I whispered to Orzo. He looked at me like I had two heads.

"Doesn't it to you?"

I shrugged, my eyes fixed upon the instruments, their strings trembling in unison.

"I don't know," I honestly replied. "What instruments are they?"

Orzo leaned close, his warm breath tickling my cheek.

"The big one is the *cello*, the next largest is the *viola*, and then the two smallest are called *violins*."

The hunter within me perked up her ears, listening to each chord, each sound. The world slowed, allowing me to separate each instrument: the bass of the cello, the low tones of the viola, and finally the quick, almost mournful tunes of the two violins.

The violins.

That was it! There was something *off* with the violins. Their tune was...*wrong.* Something scratched in the back of my head; some essence of a memory that was never quite there. It prickled at the surface, like an itch unable to be satisfied.

All too soon, the piece was over. The string quartet rose to their feet and bowed to the loud clattering of hands.

The lights enhanced, showering the entire Theatre with visibility, followed by the drone of chatter as Aristocrats entertained themselves.

Orzo and Lander exited our viewing hole, plodding their way back to the dressing rooms to get more instructions from Ms Eynesbury.

I remained stationary, gazing mindlessly at the violin left on the chair, unable to steal my eyes away...

Orzo grabbed my arm.

As it happens, our duties entailed nothing more than a quick change of dress and a dab of makeup for the actors. Within half an hour, we were back in the hole, excitement brewing in our veins as the lights dimmed, the spotlights reappeared, and music once again encapsulated us all.

* * *

My ears were still buzzing.

Dazed, yet energised — it was a stimulating concoction that I revelled in.

Rocking back and forth on my heels, a small smile stretched my lips as I thought to the finale.

It was beautiful. Tragic, but beautiful.

"Oh, what a splendid success!" Ms Eynesbury declared, marching over with a gigantic grin upon her face. "I could not have asked for a more triumphant opening performance. Oh my days, I shall remember it until I die." She added a dramatic wipe of her forehead. "Lander, is the car outside?"

"Yes, Ma'am. Whenever you're ready."

"Oh, fabulous... Mr Atkinson, have you seen my scarf?"

"I last saw it on the stage, Ma'am."

"Of course! With all the flowers raining down in praise, it must have fallen from my shoulders...

"Miss Doe." I jumped at my adopted name, turning on the spot like a deer in a bullet path. "Be a dear and collect my scarf from the stage. And be quick about it, I'm all but dying for another glass of champagne."

"Err, yes, Ma'am." Smiling as graciously as I could, I nodded my head in obedient servitude, and quickly marched up the service corridor.

Once out of sight, I stopped, removed my heels and ran.

You can do this! I desperately thought. *You can get out through the Theatre!*

This was my moment of opportunity, the chance to leave the stinking shithole of Slavery for the rest of my days! Masonians were at the entrance, but I could run up to the top floor, somehow make it onto the roof. Visions of leaping from one building to another – of traversing Maelstrom without fear of bashing into a Masonian baton – filled my heart with glee.

Oh, how I wanted to be free! How I dreamed of the snow and the wilderness and desire to feel my feet crunch the ice upon a mountainside... I longed to see the sunset reflected in creaking glaciers; to hear the songs of birds at dawn; to throw my limbs into a tree's welcoming embrace and climb to the top of the world!

Now, freedom beckoned, racing my heart and making me understand that one tremendous – *stupendous* – theatrical production did not make me free. Tomorrow, I would rise before the crows squawked, before the sun formed black shadows outside the window of my cell. My cracked hands would bleed and sting, as I drenched cloths in chemicals and scrubbed and *scrubbed* until my fingernails popped off.

No, I would not be subjected to this life.

I was a Roamer, a *Herder*, and I would die a free woman. Not as a Slave hung from the gallows.

The stage was beckoning. I ascended the wooden steps in three enormous leaps...

And stopped dead.

Music.

I shook my head, attempting to shake the memories away, but no – there it was. Tangible, palpable music, pulsating throughout the air.

Slowly, I stepped onto the stage.

What hit me first? The man, most likely.

He was facing away from me, his black dinner jacket convulsing as he moved the bow, ferociously, across the violin's strings. His head rested against the instrument; his hair, blacker than a moonless night, quivered in time to each beat.

The actual music was the second thing that hit, but with tenfold more intensity. The music was vigorous, powerful...

Intoxicating.

The persistent itch that prickled my brain was suddenly extinguished. In its place was enrapture, beguilement... *Gratification.*

The violin pulled me in, each string wrapping around my arms, legs and pulling me further and further towards the precipice of musical ecstasy.

The song was mournful and elated, low and high tunes mixed in with exquisite precision and each note holding such exciting promise that I could think of nothing else. The music encircled my skull, vibrating my very lungs, making me understand just how utterly *magnificent* such a song could be!

It was glorious.

Too soon, it was over. The man lowered his arms; the violin in one hand, the bow in the other. As the echo of music bounced around my skull, I could do nothing but stand and gaze stupidly. The music had winded me, rendered my limbs useless. I was a statue.

The man raised his head, looking to the ceiling. Broad shoulders rose and fell with a large, relieved sigh. Had the sheer magnificence of the music affected him to?

My vision grew hazy, my head fuzzy. I clasped a hand over my temple, my balance failing as everything spun round and round and –

I caught myself before I fell, my bare foot jolting against the wood. It mocked my presence with a very obvious creak.

The man's head twitched.

"It's rude to sneak," he said. His voice was deep and rich, flowing like a glass of full-bodied red wine.

"I-I'm sorry," I stuttered, when I finally remembered how to speak. "I-I didn't know you were – "

He turned to face me. Pale skin clashed beautifully against the black of his hair, his broad jaw sharp against the open collar of his shirt and bowtie. With high cheekbones, a straight nose, and a brooding brow, he was an irrefutably handsome man.

No, not handsome. *Beautiful.*

The most defining feature of this beautiful man's face were undoubtedly his eyes. Large and almost too bright, they sparkled a thousand diamond's worth.

"Mason…" I whispered. A thick coil of dread sank heavily to my gut as I realised the Destroyer of the Old World – the man responsible for *everything* – was suddenly before me. And there, standing before him with as much rigidity as a startled rabbit, was the End of Everything.

And, just like a rabbit staring at a hungry fox, I resembled a block of ice, frozen beneath the power of his presence.

He did not flinch at my sudden understanding, instead responding by a small, almost imperceptible tilt of his head. His eyes dropped to the shoes hanging from my fingers, and then to my bare feet.

"Who is your Master?" he asked, his voice licked with menace.

Fear gripped my throat in a strangling hold. My mouth opened but no sound came.

Mason took a step closer.

"I asked you a question, my dear," he said, dangerously even. "I suggest you answer."

"Emilia..." I managed to gasp, barely audible. "Emilia Eynesbury."

"Hm." Mason placed the violin upon one of the chairs, so delicately it did not make a sound. All too quickly, those deadly eyes flicked up. "And why are you here without your Mistress?"

I stared around, frantically, trying to remember what was asked of me. I had come here for freedom, but that dream was obliterated the moment I found Mason, playing the violin on the stage of an empty Theatre.

Mason moved closer, excruciatingly slowly.

From the corner of my eye, I spotted a red chiffon scarf, almost camouflaged by the red ripple of curtain.

"The scarf..." I said. "S-She sent me here to fetch her scarf."

Mason, now within arm's reach, followed my gaze.

"Ah. I see."

My stare dropped to the floor, directly onto his polished shoes. *Don't look at him*, I desperately thought.

My heart was an animal, clawing its way through my breastbone. Nausea bubbled up my gullet. I squeezed my eyes shut, the amber contacts suddenly so obsolete now the Destroyer of the Old World was breathing upon my forehead.

Two cold fingers rested below my chin, and Mason lifted my head. Against every essence of self-preservation, I saw his eyes. They sparkled gloriously, catching the light from the chandeliers overhead.

I was transfixed. I wanted to stare harder, deeper into those eyes. To absorb every facet of colour, every prism of light that escaped them...

Somewhere in the distance, I heard music.

"Well then," he said. "You better return it to her. People like us don't like to be kept waiting."

His touch left me. As Mason wandered away, the quaking in my knees intensified. I stumbled back towards the wooden stairs, my steps clumsy and uneven.

"Wait," he said.

I stopped, my limbs like lead. "Aren't you forgetting something?"

I peered over my shoulder. Mason held the red scarf between his fingertips.

"Of course…" Head down, I staggered towards him.

He presented the scarf to me. Tentatively, I took it.

"Thank you," I whispered.

Without another word, I ran back to my Mistress.

* * *

THAT NIGHT, I stared at the ceiling.

Alone in a room on a creaking bed, I traced each cobweb, each speck of dust floating throughout the air. I remained silent, listening delicately to the impossible music inside my head.

I had spoken to no one about Mason. That I had met him, that I had seen him play that wondrous – that *delectable* – music. Orzo knew something had happened; he eyed me curiously as I returned to Emilia Eynesbury, the red chiffon scarf in hand, my face pale and shocked. But he had not asked. Perhaps he didn't want to know.

I had met Mason. Mason had *touched* me, and yet I was still alive.

Why was that so hard to comprehend?

When I was little, I always assumed that once Mason saw me, that would be it. One quick stare, a flash of light, and then my body would be left for the maggots. That's it, gone. *Poof.*

The End of Everything destroyed, the world a safe place for Mason to rule over forever.

But there I was. Still alive, still enslaved, still wondering how I survived. It just didn't make any sense.

The song he played kept repeating in my head. Softly in the distance, like a faint rustle of trees on a quiet day. But it was there, hounding me, mocking my naivety.

I had never heard music like that before. Now I couldn't *un-hear* it.

The mystery grew, for the music inside my head wasn't caused by the instrument Mason was playing – a *violin,* or whatever it was called. It was something else, something undeniably beautiful – something powerful and dangerous and just so exhilarating. I wanted to play that music with all the seductive power Mason had…

But I had no idea what instrument it was. I had never heard it before.

It wasn't a woodwind, like the violin. It was something different. Something equally wondrous…

Was this strange music connected to my destiny? Was the simple fact that these glorious, delectable notes swirled around my skull proof that I would – *somehow* – destroy the entire world?

Ha, maybe I should've just asked Mason.

My own attempt at humour sent rushes of cold fear slithering up and down my spine.

Jokes aside, there was clearly an extra layer of complexity to all this.

Maybe Ashworth knew? Maybe, when I eventually got out of there, I would try to find the Rebels, if only to plead for information.

But then Campbell's warning rattled around my skull: that Rebellions brought nothing but death, ruin, and the promise of an impossible dream. Moreover, what would the Free People do if the *real* Alira – the bringer of the apocalypse – suddenly appeared at their doorstep, demanding information about her destiny? I highly doubted my questioning nature would be received well.

Emilia was right: I didn't want to die, by anyone's hand. At the very least, I didn't want to disappoint Campbell.

I glanced at the contact lenses, neatly settled in a small pool of solution, poured from a bottle I found in Emilia's private bathroom. Their amber sheen goaded me, reminding me that I was *fake*. A Pretender.

And lucky.

A deep sense of dread built in my stomach. I closed my eyes, exhaling a slow stream of air through pursed lips.

You're here girl, I kept saying to myself, *you're still here.*

Yes, I was still there, but for how long? How long could I hide who I really was when I was so close to being discovered that night?

Campbell peered at me from the back of my conscious thought. His gentle smile, his sincerity, his caring nature cradled me.

Tears pooled in my eyes, falling like rivers. Each one was mushed and wiped on dirtied bed linen.

No, I should not think like my life was prematurely terminable.

I had persevered that far – *Campbell has made me get this far* – and Asgard and Hel be damned if I was going to let him down this early in the show.

Life was a show after all, and we weren't even at the intermission.

9

Lander came into the kitchen, cradling a piece of paper like it was solid gold, and declared Emilia would be having visitors that night.

Spines were straightened, eyes wide with fearful curiosity. All except me, that is. I just slouched back and slurped my soup.

"Who?" Orzo asked. He resembled a deer caught in headlights: too shocked to move but knowing an impact was inevitable.

Lander fumbled over the paper, his trembling finger tracing each word.

Then, quite suddenly, he relaxed. His hands dropped like sacks of flour; his eyes closed on a heavy, relieved sigh.

"Not him."

The room relaxed. Some resumed conversations, others left altogether as the tension literally dispersed.

"Thank the Gods..." Orzo breathed beside me.

"Mason?" I asked, quietly. "You're talking about him?"

I recalled the Theatre a few weeks prior, those diamond eyes shining bright as music dripped like honey from his fingers...

Orzo took another large sigh and collapsed deeper into his chair.

"Yeah," he finally responded. "He's good friends with Emilia, sometimes he joins her at the dinner parties."

"But not tonight?"

"No, not tonight."

I slouched further into the chair. "Oh thank the Gods..." I mumbled.

"Don't pray to Asgard just yet," Lander grumbled before us, "the Ulster Twins are still coming."

An ice pick shot down Orzo's spine, straightening it immediately.

"Both of them?" he asked, incredulous.

"Yes, as well as..." Lander took a cautionary glimpse at Orzo. "Mr Doncaster."

Orzo deflated. Emotionally, as well as physically, for he cradled his head in his hands and curled over his knees. His back rose and fell with long, anxious breaths.

"Orzo...?" I asked, tentatively. Very carefully, my fingers hovered over his back. Slight hesitation, then they touched delicately against his spine.

Orzo shot up. The wooden chair fell with an almighty clatter. My arm snapped back to my lap as Orzo marched shakily from the room, using the doorframe for support as he rounded the corner, and disappeared.

Perhaps sensing my concern, Lander approached me and picked up the chair.

"Erik Doncaster was Orzo's old Master, before he was sold to Emilia." Lander perched himself on the chair, carefully placing the piece of paper upon the table. He made sure to avoid the spilled soup or breadcrumbs, leaving the paper pristine and highly valued. "Orzo had a rough time under his service."

Echoes of Orzo's history whipped my stomach with quick, ominous blows.

"Do you mean the whip with metal spikes?" I whispered.

Lander took a long sigh, closing his eyes in a pained grimace.

"Look, Maya," he said, tiresome. "Slaves aren't treated well anywhere, but some Masters are tenfold worse than others. Mr Doncaster is one of the bad ones, and the Ulster Twins aren't that great either. Just do us all a favour and please – *please* – be on your best behaviour tonight."

"Ms Eynesbury —"

"These people aren't Ms Eynesbury!" Lander ran an irate hand through his hair. "Just be careful tonight, for God's sake."

He threw himself to his feet and marched angrily out the kitchen.

The End of Everything

* * *

I WAS EXHAUSTED.

Emilia had me polish the hallways, the greeting rooms, the dining rooms, the smoking rooms, the after-dinner rooms – or whatever you'd call them. I spent hours upon my knees, frantically scrubbing the floors, making them shine and squeak with each step. I polished the decorations and statues, dusted the portraits until their golden frames glistened. Even the chandeliers, dripping diamonds, sparkled under my tender care.

By the time the champagne corks popped, a thick sheen of sweat layered my brow. I sat upon my ankles, pushed my palms into my lower back, and stretched towards the ceiling.

"Well, I must say, you've done a splendid job." Emilia smiled as she clanked into the hallway, dressed in a tight blue satin dress with a matching headscarf sporting a magnificent peacock feather. "It seems my tutelage of you is beginning to show."

My shins burned as they stretched, having been cramped and stationary for so long. "I'm simply thankful that Mason is *not* coming tonight, and wanted to show my appreciation. *Ma'am*."

Though my tone was patronising, the words were true. My relief was palpable.

"Oh, his lack of attendance is not for a want of joining. He is simply otherwise engaged, which is a shame, all things considered. I enjoy his company."

"*Excuse me?*" I glared, forgetting my status. "How can you *like* his company? He's a mass murderer!"

"Oh my dear, pipe down!" she snapped, slapping the air with an Aristocratic hand. "Mason is a charming man and holds an incredibly interesting conversation. You should hear the stories he has, the things he's seen. He's over two-hundred years old – he's practically a walking history book! And aside from that, what a glorious opportunity you have, not just to meet Mason, but members of his Social Circle. It's such a shame that experience is wasted upon you – a Herder as well! – so take that frown off your face and start enjoying your position."

Was she serious? I frowned at her, genuinely shocked at her ignorance –

her *arrogance*. That I should *enjoy* being her Slave, that I should *appreciate* meeting the homicidal, *genocidal* madman who killed everyone I'd ever loved in my short and pathetic life. The *monster* who would gladly – eagerly – kill me should he even take one look, one *glimpse* into my real eyes... It was ridiculous, maddening.

Why should I have to put up with this? To put up with *her*?

Each of her words bored as a separate insult, scratching the surface of my skin until I could just take no more of her *bullshit!*

With only a huff, I dropped the polishing cloth. Emilia's face lowered, a rare shadow descending.

"Pick that up," she said, then she grew angrier. "I'm talking to you, Miss Doe! I demand you pick that up at once!"

I spat Herdinese curses. She wouldn't understand them, but who cared! The words felt good rolling off my tongue.

She grabbed my upper arm with the strength of a woman half her age and easily dragged me down the hallway. My heels scraped against the wooden floors, marring its polished surface.

"I have been nothing but patient with you, you ungrateful little girl! I rarely have the need to use punishments, but you really are testing me!"

Orzo appeared, next Lander and then a few others, having been roused from their own duties. They each took one look at me, then at the devil incarnate that was Emilia Eynesbury, and then skulked back into the kitchen, uncaring. All except Orzo, that is. He shook his head, utterly defeated, and closed the kitchen door behind him.

Emilia dragged me before the open basement door and with one swell swoop, she threw me inside. I fell down the first few stairs, regained my balance, and raced up just as the door slammed shut. The click of deadbolts sounded. I was trapped.

I screamed, pounding against the door.

"You will come out when you learn how to be appreciative!" Next, the angry clanks of Emilia's heels as she stomped down the corridor.

In her absence, I wailed.

I cursed and screamed in my native tongue, weeks of hardship and torture and sheer *misery* – not just towards my predicament, but for *Campbell* – balling out of me in droves. My throat screeched, scratching the stone walls of that basement, the desire to be free of that stinking, mouldy place – of *Maelstrom* – so overwhelming that I felt I might collapse on that cold floor and die.

My anger spat at Emilia. That old *bitch,* to declare that I should be appreciative – to *thank* her – for all the experiences I endured, that *she* made me endure. My *owner*. My own personal Mistress...

I jumped down those stone stairs in four long leaps and struck my anger against those unsuspecting flour bags. I punched them with all my might, clouds of white puffing up at each dull, pathetic little thud.

There was a bucket. I kicked it hard and it flew across the room, colliding at speed against the stone wall, shattering. Next, there was a piece of rope, hanging from the ceiling. I pulled it down from the rafters, the wooden boards breaking under my weight, and hurled it through the air.

But no, there was still more to *destroy,* more I had to maim and break to just let my anger out upon *everything!*

There was no time to reach the flour sacks. In my infuriated haste, I turned to the nearest wall and punched it, hard. A dark thud matched the cracking of my knuckles.

Anger left, replaced by a searing pain that spread like treacle up my wrist. A small, surprised wail tickled my larynx. Slowly, I cradled my abused hand to my chest like some hurt animal.

All four knuckles were bloodied, the hand red and starting to swell. I tenderly pressed against the damage, grimacing with each throb. I could not uncurl my fingers.

"*Shit!*" I hissed beneath my breath. *Campbell would be so proud of you, girl.*

I walked blindly back until I hit a wall, then sank down its entire length. I remained sitting on the cold stone, inspecting my broken hand, and tried to resist tears.

Campbell always said I had an anger within me. An insatiable drive of emotion that was unparalleled, unbridled and untamed. *Out of control,* he had once called it, *like a pot of boiling water upon the stove.*

Now, it seemed, Campbell had been right. I was an idiot for it.

What if Emilia decided I simply wasn't worth the effort? She bought me on offer, and I was a gamble, an investment. It wasn't unusual for investments to go sour.

Above me, the first dribble of Aristocratic laughter poured in. Clearly, her party had started. An inward groan, a deep sigh as I remained stuck in that cellar, with nothing but the pain in my hand.

For a good while, nothing changed.

Deadbolts clicked open.

"Ah yes, this must be the basement."

My ears pricked up, hackles rising as new and unfamiliar voices fell down the stairs.

"Ugh, what a charming place…" A woman's shrill voice. Young and powerful, dripping with venom.

"Come out, little Slave… Come out, come out wherever you are…"

"Yes, we've heard so much about you."

The two other voices were both men, both equally unkind.

I shakily rose to my feet, still clutching my injured hand to my bosom.

Three people appeared at the bottom of the steps, all dressed in fine clothing. The woman wore a green dress that shimmered in the dim light. With jet black hair that fell the entire length of her skinny back, she was incredibly slim, with a gaunt face, pale skin, and two emerald eyes that reeked of malice.

The men both wore tuxedos and exuded arrogance. One had a large handlebar moustache. The other had hair the colour of dark chocolate and the same green eyes as the woman, whom he was clearly related to.

Aristocrats, all of them. *Shit.*

A domino of evil grins formed, as they found me at the bottom of the stairs.

"Ah, there you are, little Herder," the woman said, smiling. "Or are you a Roamer?"

The man with the moustache smirked. "Or a Slave."

I remained silent, taking careful steps back until I hit the wall. How did they know about me? How did they know about my heritage? My will to escape Slavery was swiftly replaced with the urge just to escape; to run from that basement and the monsters lurking within. I frantically scanned my surroundings, searching for a gap between their neatly sewed seams, but their wall was impenetrable.

"Oh, why no talking?" The woman tilted her head to one side, judging me. "We want to hear your accent. Emilia informs us how delectable it is."

"Oh please, Verity. You and I both know that you're just here to gauge the competition."

Verity's smile fell like a block of ice. She turned to the man with green eyes and slapped him hard on the shoulder.

"Surely you're past such immaturity, Ivan," she spat with a glower.

Ivan's devilish smile extended to two gaunt cheekbones, then he winked at me. "My sister wanted to meet you. Mason's been talking about Emilia's little Herder Slave for *so* long now, Verity's become somewhat jealous."

Music found my ears, more powerful than before, as unsavoury images floated before my eyes. Of *his* eyes, sparkling like diamonds, upon the stage of an empty Theatre. What had Mason been saying about me? My accent, my heritage, my eyes?

Please, dear Odin, not my eyes...

I swallowed hard, pushing myself further into the wall, hoping to disappear into it.

"S-Surely you have better things to be doing than being d-down here." I stumbled over the words, weakening my position.

"Oh, that accent..." Verity crooned with an evil grin. "I will admit that it is somewhat charming. I think I'll cut out your tongue, so I'll never hear it again."

"Don't you dare touch me!"

"And there we have the anger!" the other man jeered. "Thank goodness Emilia wasn't exaggerating!"

"It's a wonder Mason isn't here," Ivan said. "What with his anger and yours, you two should write a play."

"As if this little whelp can write," Verity said with a vicious sneer.

I had to get out of that basement. I flashed my eyes around the room, looking for an escape. The deadbolts had been opened. That door remained my only way out.

The Aristocrats still mocked me. My anger resurfaced, bubbling like a cauldron of bitterness beneath my skin. I pushed it down, forced my own inner sense to put out that red fire, if only for a moment, so I could escape and make it out of that basement unhurt...

For if anything was certain: *These people are here to hurt me...*

I darted to the stairs. Verity shrieked and stumbled back. The men rushed forwards. Ivan's arms extended but I was too quick – a sharp pivot and the stairs were directly ahead. Light from the hallway shined upon me, seeping through the opened door...

A hand grasped my broken one and squeezed.

Pain consumed my entire right side. I fell to my knees, squealing, trying desperately to loosen the tight grip. Bones crushed and crunched together, beads of sweat dotted my back, my brow, my bosom... The air became thick and heavy, my lungs working hard through the immense pain.

"Does that hurt, my dear? Oh, I do apologise. Here, let me help you..."

He threw an arm around my waist, hoisted me to my feet. The prickly hair of his moustache stroked my ear. "Now isn't that better?"

"Erik, how did you do that?" Ivan asked.

"Take a look," Erik motioned to my bruised hand, swollen and throbbing. "Looks like she broke it."

Verity marched forwards and gripped my hand in a vice-like hold. I yelped, the urge to scream aching at my larynx.

"You really need to watch your anger, little one," she crooned. "Without this, you'd be upstairs by now, running to Emilia and telling her just how mean we've all been to you."

Her grip on my hand intensified.

"*Please*," I choked, the pain reaching unbearable levels. "I-I've done nothing to you!"

"You don't have to *do* anything, darling. We're just here to have a bit of fun."

"Well, Verity is," Ivan mumbled. "I'm just here to see the *Wild One*, to see what all the fuss is about."

My glassy eyes fixed onto Verity's, reeking with sick satisfaction.

"Then what *fun* do you want, *Ma'am*?" I hissed through gritted teeth.

Laughing, Verity threw my hand away like some rotten meat. I audibly gasped, falling further into Erik's hold, my body slumping from the release.

"I enjoy attention." A wide smile slithered across her face. "I'm someone who walks into a room, and all eyes fix upon me. And *only* me."

Her expression soured. Slowly, she came towards me and oh-so-delicately tucked a stray strand of hair behind my ringed ear. Her heavy perfume invaded my nostrils: lavender and thyme.

"Yet, for the last few weeks, all I've heard about is this little Herder-Roamer hybrid, who's been strutting about with Campbell Anders for *however-many-years*, causing absolute chaos wherever she steps."

She fondled each golden ring with a long, red nail.

"Well, I thought this would all blow over after a few days but here we are, *weeks* later, and still all anyone seems to talk about is *you*. The Herder with an attitude problem – can you *imagine?* Well, I'd prefer not to hear your name, your accent, or your voice for the rest of my days. Oh, and please do something about this infernal jewellery."

With a quick yank, a golden ring was ripped from my ear cartilage. It clinked sadly to the floor, bloodied, with bits of flesh hanging off. Through the burning pain, something warm and wet dribbled down my neck, and marred the white lustre of my blouse.

Panic rose, one tense second at a time, as Verity removed a knife from a strap on her thigh. The dress fell back to her ankles in a shower of green satin.

"Come now, darling." She smiled again, touching the knife to my chin. "Let's do something about that accent..."

My jaw clenched, so hard I thought my teeth would crack. The blade of the knife glinted in the light, coming closer and closer and –

"Wait, stop!"

The knife lowered, then quickly raised at the sight of Orzo, flying down the stairs.

"Go back to your Mistress!"

"Please, Miss Ulster," Orzo said, standing as still as his panic would enable. "I have another proposition that may be more amiable."

"Oh really, do tell."

Orzo grew very pale. I saw his kind, innocent eyes lock with the man behind me, still holding me with a grip that was almost suffocating.

Orzo croaked out a hollow name, then cleared his throat. "Mr Doncaster, please take me as tonight's pleasure. Leave the girl alone."

Visions of that morning stabbed behind my retina. Of the sour memories whipping Orzo directly in the face, of the terror that now clung to his very bones.

"Orzo, no!" I shouted, only for the knife to shoot into my mouth. It cut my lip deep and scraped against my teeth. Verity Ulster scrambled for my tongue like her very life depended on it.

"Verity!" Erik pushed her weaponised hand away. "Let's hear what the good man has to offer us."

Clearly bored, he dropped me to the floor. Blood quickly pooled in my mouth. I spat it out, the metallic taste growing nausea.

Erik grinned at Orzo, his eyes large and leering. "Ah, Mr Atkinson. It's been a long time."

Orzo swallowed hard, his eyes squeezing shut as every fibre of his being begged him to walk back up those stairs…

But he didn't. He stayed exactly where he was.

"Sir, I should be grateful if you would use me instead."

Erik clearly liked this idea: the flies of his trousers were straining.

I tried to speak, to beg Orzo to shut up and go back up those stairs, but the blood pooled more forcibly and turned my pleads into strained splutters.

"I graciously accept that offer, my dear boy." Erik smirked. "Yes, it's most certainly been a while."

Orzo tried to smile.

"Well, that's all well and good but what about this… Well, *this*." Verity stabbed a pointed nail at me. "With respect, Erik, how is your fun going to satisfy us all?"

"Come on, Verity," Ivan said, highly amused. "You don't want blood stains on your dress."

She thought about this long and hard, and returned the knife to her thigh.

"Well, quite," she said, before marching off up the stairs.

"Ivan, would you please remove the Herder from the basement." It was not a request from Erik, but a polite demand. Ivan, his mouth twisted into a hard smirk, hoisted me to my feet. I struggled as I passed Orzo, trying to speak some sense into him. Blood trickled in streams from my mouth, and Orzo merely nodded in sad recognition.

He was unbuttoning his shirt when the basement door gently clicked shut.

* * *

IT WAS the middle of the night. Emilia Eynesbury had already retired. The guests had left, including Erik Doncaster.

No sign of Orzo. He was not in the Dormitories, although I had been assured that he was alive. He simply did not want to see anyone.

He certainly did not want to see me.

Guilt is a terrible thing. It consumes you, wrecks you from the inside out. Never before did I feel guilt like it. The knowledge of what Orzo did for *me* – to save *me* – filled me with such shame that I almost wished the Ulster Woman *had* cut out my tongue. At least then my big mouth wouldn't get me – or him – into any more trouble. Without the ability to speak, I would not be able to talk back to Emilia, or get myself locked in a cellar, or build myself such a terrible reputation that three complete strangers felt the need to *teach me a lesson*.

This was my fault. All of it.

This had to stop.

* * *

OF ALL THE people Emilia Eynesbury expected to knock on the door of the ornamental Tea Room that morning, it was not me.

"Oh, come in Miss Doe," she said, simply to be polite. "What can I do for you?"

The stitches and swelling on my lip made talking quite difficult, but I endeavoured to enunciate every word. I spoke slowly, and with absolute resolve.

"Miss Eynesbury, please forgive my intrusion this morning. I am aware that you probably have better things to do than to listen to me... But, but..."

I took a deep breath. My eyes burned at the acidity of each tear.

"I just want to apologise for last night. I know my actions were completely uncalled for, and disrespectful, and I am so, so sorry for – "

A small gasp. My eyes squeezed shut, releasing a torrent of liquid guilt down my face. Emilia Eynesbury, sensing my sincerity, sighed gently.

"I appreciate that, Miss Doe. But I'm not really the one you should apologise to, am I?" She waited until my sad eyes met hers. "Mr Atkinson is in the attic room, recovering. I suggest you pay him a visit."

I nodded in thanks, fighting the anxious urge to bite my lip.

"One more thing, Ma'am?"

"Yes, Miss Doe."

"My anger," I breathed, my stomach tight. "I-I don't know how to control it sometimes. Will you help me?"

For the first time, I saw in Emilia's face something akin to relief. That, and a deep sense of accomplishment.

"I'd be delighted to," she replied.

* * *

Orzo was lying face down on the bed, concealed under a thin white sheet. A glass of water was at his side, along with a few slices of stale bread. Both were untouched.

A single wooden chair lay beside him. Tentatively, I eased myself into its creaky confines.

"Hey Orzo," I whispered. Slowly, those empty eyes flicked to me. I saw them scan my facial injuries, and then to the bandaged hand in my lap. The other held the stems of two bluebells, picked from a vase downstairs.

"What are they?" His voice was so small, so tired...

"They're for you," I replied, gingerly placing them next to his uneaten food. "I asked Emilia, she said it was okay."

"You actually asked her?"

"Yes. I didn't want to get you into even more trouble..." My eyes swelled. Swallowing hard, I forced a smile and tried to keep my calm composure. I was there to be supportive to Orzo, I was there to apologise. Crying would accomplish neither.

My stare fell to Orzo's bare shoulders. White scars crisscrossed his skin, foretelling the torture of years passed. I unwillingly wondered what new marks had resulted from my idiocy.

More tears burned, and I could no longer hide them.

"I'm so sorry, Orzo," I whispered, as tears fell. "I know I'm uncontrollable but you warned me and I didn't listen and now –"

"Hey, hey…" Orzo said softly. He put a warm hand on mine. "It was my choice, remember?"

"To save me, to stop her from…" I licked the raised stitches on my lip.

"Look, who's to say they wouldn't have tried to hurt you even if you had behaved? They're sadistic people, Maya. You can't alter your behaviour to try and predict unpredictable actions."

"That doesn't change the fact that you saved me. And I'm so sorry I had to put you through that, but… *Thank you.*"

Orzo closed his eyes on a deep, relieved sigh.

"Don't mention it," he whispered.

10

SUMMER

The floor was polished to a high shine when the sonorous tone of the doorbell rang across the hallway. Dropping the cloth in the bucket, I stood to my full height, patted down the creases in my skirt, and dutifully answered.

The cool summer breeze and fresh scent did little to alleviate the shock of Mason, standing on the porch of the Eynesbury Residence.

"Good morning."

The sun shone on his hair, turning it inky black. It framed his beautiful features perfectly as the faint notes of strange music were carried by the breeze.

I froze, transfixed by those eyes, their beauty… I hadn't seen Mason since the Theatre, yet images of his eyes kept encroaching into my everyday routines, blinking behind my constant thoughts of freedom. Now, as those same eyes sparkled beneath the bright summer sunlight, they continually mocked my dangerous situation.

A nearby car horn honked.

"Oh, good morning, um…" I gulped hard, trying to find the words. Mason was clearly finding my stuttering amusing. "Um… Do you, I-I mean… Do you want to come in?"

"That would be nice."

I manoeuvred myself to allow Mason inside. With the hands in the pockets of his long grey coat, and his navy shirt opened at the collar, he sauntered into the corridor. Even the wooden floor creaked at his presence.

I pushed the door closed, allowing its loud clink to soothe my frenzied mind. *Keep calm, girl.* Mason did not know who I was, nor was there any reason for him to. My contact lenses were lifelike and secure. Besides, he had already found *Alira* and she was, for whatever reason, still breathing inside his Palace. The fact that she was a Pretender was an inconvenience to him, yes, but one that greatly benefited me.

"I'll grab Emilia Eynesbury." Confidence was feigned as I marched past Mason with my head held high.

"Aren't you going to take my coat?"

My breath stuttered. "Oh, yes… Of course."

I gingerly took the garment, his eyes flicking to the bandage on my hand.

"Did one of my men do that?" he asked.

"Huh? Oh, no." I flexed my hand, sore but healing, and met with Mason's quizzical stare. "I punched a wall. It's fine."

Mason expertly hid a chuckle as I led him to a nearby drawing room.

"I'll go and find her," I said.

He muttered a word of thanks and wandered around the room, admiring the ornate decorations with hands inside his trouser pockets.

As soon as his back was turned, I rushed from the room and quickly met Lander, coming out of the guest bathroom. He carried a bucket of cleaning goods and startled as I pushed Mason's coat to him.

"Take care of this," I whispered.

"Wait, who's coat is it?" He searched for a label inside the collar.

"It's Mason's."

"What?"

"I know, I know – he's in there…" Lander paled as his eyes fixed to the open door. "Just take care of that."

Lander objected but I was already up the stairs. I quickly found Emilia, fingering a book in the library, and she was quick to raise both her eyebrows when I relayed news of the visitor.

"Well I hope you offered him a drink? *No?* No matter, no matter – he hasn't been waiting long. Goodness, Miss Doe, calm yourself!"

Like a swooping eagle, she soon boasted her signature smile to the Destroyer of the Old World.

"Darling, what a pleasant surprise this is! Please sit down." With a quick swoosh of her gold dress, she was inside.

Outside the room, Lander and I skulked a little further down the corridor, easily in earshot.

"Forgive my unannounced intrusion, Emilia. I am aware it is not the politest."

"Oh nonsense, it's always a pleasure to entertain you. I just hope you received the welcome you deserve. I am still training my new Slave."

Anger bubbled, the pot simmering at her words. I took a deep breath and remembered the technique Emilia had taught me, only two weeks ago.

Breathe in for four, count to five, exhale for seven.

In my meditation, familiar notes of music crept upon my ears. Their presence was near constant, and though they were not entirely unwelcome, I resisted falling into their seductive tune. Particularly now, when memories of Mason's violin followed his echoing footsteps on Emilia's wooden floor.

"Ah yes," Mason said. "You are referring to the Herder girl?"

"The very same. She has been a bit of a whirlwind, I must say!"

"I have no doubt. Well I can assure you, although some prompts were needed, she was perfectly pleasant."

"Oh, I am glad." Emilia audibly sighed. "However, I did notice that she neglected to offer you a drink?"

"It's of no concern. I would have declined regardless."

This seemed to calm Emilia, who continued with a softer tone of voice. "May I enquire as to your visit here today? Not that I don't enjoy your company, of course, but I am rather intrigued."

"Well, firstly, I would like to apologise on behalf of some members of my Social Circle. I do not condone the poor treatment of Slaves without their owners' permission, and especially without their knowledge."

"Your apology is greatly appreciated. Though, I shall admit, that it was less to do with your Social Circle, and more the behaviour of Miss Doe."

"The Herder?"

"Yes. She was particularly boisterous that afternoon."

"This is a very fortuitous development, seeing as she is whom I'd like to discuss."

Lander's eyes slid towards me, mirroring my own concern. Butterflies hatched in my stomach, swarming around my intestines, and allowed the first few trickles of nervous nausea to climb up my gullet.

"Oh?" Emilia casually enquired. "How so?"

"I would like to propose a deal."

"I'm intrigued, darling. Do tell."

"Miss Doe has been on my radar for quite some time now. She travelled with Campbell Anders for a great many years, and although it is claimed she knew nothing of the Free People's Rebellion, I cannot discount the possibility that she knows more than she is conceding."

"I hardly think she knows anything of great importance."

"That may be the case, but the cynic in me cannot overlook it." A low chuckle filled the room like a softly breaking wave. "Besides, she sounds like far too much trouble for someone as esteemed as yourself. As such, I would like to take her off your hands."

"Off my hands?"

"For a generous price, you understand. In fact, I am willing to pay a great deal more than her worth. It really is an offer you cannot refuse."

The clanks of Emilia's heeled shoes as she paced the room.

"My goodness," she said, almost in disbelief. "That is an incredibly generous proposition... However, I am afraid that I must refuse. I have made more progress with Miss Doe in these past two weeks than I have in the past two months — it would be a shame to forfeit all of that progress by sending her to a new establishment now."

A long pause weighed heavily on the room.

"Emilia," Mason said, very slowly. "I believe there has been a misunderstanding. You see, you appear to think you have a choice in this matter. I am taking Miss Doe whether it pleases you or not."

The air both crushed and carried me. I was shocked, terrified...

"The only thing we have left to discuss is how much I am willing to pay you. Please note, my generous offer is exponentially decreasing with every second of displeasure you show. I am not above taking Miss Doe out of this house for no more than a penny, do you understand?"

"Yes, of course," Emilia spluttered. "And rest assured that both Miss Doe and I are incredibly fortunate to be in this position. Miss Doe is a lucky girl to be heading to your establishment."

"Good!" Mason's bouncy attitude completely lifted the shadow that had descended. "Please inform Miss Doe that she has two hours to get her affairs in order before transport arrives for her."

"Of course, Lord Mason."

Heavy footsteps approached the hallway. Lander and I darted around the corner just as Mason appeared.

Breathe in... One... Two... Three...

"Your coat, Sir."

I paraded towards him like a mountain lioness: sure, confident. My hands had a will of their own, however, and gripped the coat with brute force.

"Ah, thank you, Miss Doe." Mason smiled, lifting his entire face. For a moment I was stunned, entirely spellbound, at just how handsome he was...

I shocked myself by own disclosure and my stare tumbled to his kneecaps.

"You're welcome, Sir," I whispered. Mason observed me for a few moments, those bright eyes falling to my shoes, then up to my face.

"What is your birth name, Miss Doe?"

My eyes grew wide as my inner voice, loud and petrified, screamed inside my head. *My name? No, you can't know my name – that name will kill me!*

"Maya." An involuntary swallow. "My birth name is Maya."

It wasn't a lie. My Pa did call me Maya when I was born, before Mason's men came and slaughtered him. A flash of rage accompanied the thought, but this was no time for the pot to simmer, and I forced the heat down low.

Oblivious to my turmoil, Mason merely smiled, his eyes catching the light from the chandelier above. They sparked a whirlwind of colour.

"Well then, Maya Doe, I shall see you soon."

With a final flash of a smile, he was gone, leaving nothing but the sick, reeling apprehension for my future, spent deep in the bowels of Mason's Palace. And there, for reasons I could not explain, I heard the faint, almost joyous tones of unknown music, bouncing around my skull.

* * *

I WAITED in the Drawing Room.

Orzo stood by the doorway, admiring my solid composure with a sad smile on his face. Lander gazed out the window, eagerly looking out for the transport that would take me to my new home.

Emilia was less than pleased about the arrangement, but her hands were tied, and so she elected to take a rather diplomatic approach.

"Remember to do exactly as you're told, Miss Doe," she said, for the fourth time that hour. "Mason is not a patient man and I daresay you'd push him over the edge in no time at all. And for God's sake, remember your breathing exercises."

Exhale... One... Two... Three...

Contact lenses scratched behind each eyelid, as if they knew. They knew I was being sold to Mason and they wanted my diamond eyes to shine bright in his presence.

The room filled with an ominous silence. The clock above the fireplace laboriously ticked away as the sun lowered, filling the room with a soft golden glow.

I remembered the last sunset I witnessed as a free woman, atop that tree, far above the cesspit of Waterman's Quarry. That seemed so long ago now. I wondered if there was anything left of that town, save piles of smouldering black ash.

"They're here," Lander declared, standing to his full height.

Life suddenly returned into Emilia, who shot out of the room like the very floor might buckle beneath her.

"Ah, good evening to you!"

Mumbled voices in the hallway. My name was called.

Cement poured into my legs, rendering them stiff and heavy. Orzo gently uncrossed his arms and moved towards me.

"You'll be fine, Maya," he said. "Remember, this is a promotion, not a punishment."

I huffed beneath my breath. The only way this would be a *promotion* was if I was a simple girl called Maya Doe, with minor anger issues and natural amber-coloured eyes.

But I was none of those things. I was a lie. I was a fraud, and I was being bought by the very man who wanted me dead.

That evening, I was collected by a Masonian thoroughbred: stocky, broad-shouldered and with short, muscular legs. Given my history with Masonians, I was shocked when he offered a large, almost *friendly* smile.

"Evening," he said, his platinum hair glinting in the dying sunlight.

I hugged Orzo, then Lander, and expressed my sincerest goodbye to my *former* Mistress. She expressed some words of good luck, and a slight expression of concern, but most of her attention fell upon the large casket of money that had just been delivered. Indeed, Mason had paid a lot for me. The notion of *why* was concerning.

Fighting back unsettled tears, I stared at my fumbling hands rather than meet the faces of those I'd left behind. Orzo's reaction hit the hardest, for he seemed genuinely concerned about my new venture. In the end, I found his worrisome stare too distressing.

I remained staring into my lap when the car grumbled to a start.

When I finally looked up, Maelstrom bathed in golden light. Tall houses cast long shadows over cobbled streets, the summer flowers still blooming against the black and white facades. Despite the late evening sky, Aristocrats walked arm-in-arm with their spouses, or coagulated in sociable groups.

It amazed me to see such dignified people, enjoying their daily lives, when the entire city clawed for blood. How many innocent people would be sold the next morning? How many of these seemingly *refined* Aristocrats had cheered and gawked at each new, scared offering? What made it worse was the sense of decency, of civility, these people possessed, the evident superiority they spewed on anyone who did not fit into their little bubble.

The hypocrisy was sickening.

"Very quiet back there, love," the Masonian driver called back.

"I'm not your *love*," I replied, simply too scared and too tired to make my words sound as bitter as I meant them. Nevertheless, it caused a toothy smile.

"Just an expression, I don't mean anything by it." A pair of aqua-coloured eyes kept flicking to me in the rear-view mirror. "What's your name?"

Still no reply.

"Well, my name is Jayson. Jayson Montgomery, and it is such a pleasure to meet you, Miss *Whatever-your-name-is*. Been in Ms Eynesbury's care long, have you? She's a lovely woman, if a little eccentric. Still, it's a wonder that – "

"Oh, will you shut up," I snapped, glaring at his reflection.

"Ha, ha! Got your attention though, ain't I?"

I rolled my eyes. "Congratulations," I dryly muttered.

I stared vacantly out the window. We were approaching the outskirts of the city, as the buildings were replaced by trees.

"I don't know why you're so upset. It's a real privilege to be serving in the Palace."

Breathe in... One... Two... Three...

"Perhaps I just want to be free," I said.

"Free? No one is ever free. The outside world is brutal. Starvation, molestation, murder... The list goes on. At least in Maelstrom, there's order."

"There's also Mason."

"Yeah, that's true. By Odin, they don't make bastards like him anymore."

I startled, hastily looking for impossible eavesdroppers.

"Are you sure you're allowed to talk about him like that?" I asked, frowning.

"Like what, the truth? Don't see why not. Mason refers to himself in far worse language."

"Really?" It was somewhat refreshing to hear that Mason did not have any preconceived ideas about his *civility*.

"He's brutal though, make no mistake. You'd better watch out for him when you're in the Palace."

"Yeah, many people seem to be telling me that." A long sigh through pursed lips as the buildings of Maelstrom disappeared entirely.

"Nah, you'll be fine," Jayson said. "If you're ever worried about anything, just come to me. I may be a Masonian but I'm not half bad, considering. Who knows, might be able to put in a good word for you."

"Thanks," I said, finally meeting his sincere stare.

*　*　*　**

IT HAD BEEN an hour since I'd left Emilia Eynesbury. The sun had set, the moon had risen.

The trees grew thicker, more crowded. The car was enveloped in a sea of green needles and pinecones, the air thick with an earthy, heady scent. I breathed deeper, surrounding it around my lungs. This was the closest I had come to the wilderness, and by Odin did my muscles ache for it.

The car, though vintage and fancy, was expressly designed to transport Slaves. The handles were missing and the usual contraption to open the window had been removed. The interior of the car itself was spacious and clean, created to goad Slaves into a false sense of security. To allow them to have one last glimpse at freedom, to be close enough to touch it with outstretched hands before serving a new Master.

"Heads up, we're almost at the Palace."

It pricked my senses, like a startled rabbit. The golden gates to Mason's Palace loomed ahead.

Two golden stags stood to attention on either side of the gate, their large antlers radiating in both directions. The gates themselves were enormous, the gold glinting in the beaming headlights. The car stopped directly before the gates, and for a small moment I imagined what it would feel like to escape that car, to disappear into those trees.

The gates opened in one, fluid motion. Gears shifted and we grumbled onwards, into the estate, perused by the golden eyes of each stag.

First, we passed areas of cultivation. Vegetable patches, young and recently raked, spread up and down an entire acre. Next, huge greenhouses with their elaborate structures looming high, and each glass panel, though seamless, frosted with condensation. Great orchards followed, the trees arranged in neat lines: apples, pears, plums... Cherry trees burst with blossom, the petals blowing in the gentle wind, like specks of pink snow.

Continuing on, the estate widened in both scale and grandeur. Grounds were exceptionally manicured, expertly arranged. Deer roamed freely across acres of green fields, bordered by forest. We meandered through trees, by lakes, abreast to marble fountains and gold glinted statues... The road was bordered with small spotlights, illuminating the flower beds, the ornamental gardens, the streams that trickled in slow and steady motions...

There, in the distance, Mason's enormous Palace loomed.

With walls of polished granite, embellished with chunks of shimmering quartz, large columns bordered a grand entrance, supported by two curving staircases. They met at the base of the Palace and morphed into a large fountain, propelling water into the air like streams of pure silver. Balconies extended from tall windows, their curtains closed, but muted light hinted of chandeliers behind.

A scurry of footmen rushed to the car and opened the door wide. Gravel crunched beneath my heeled shoes, and I craned my neck to see the top of the building. Yes, certainly impressive.

"Good luck," Jayson called from the car. "I'll see you around, Miss...?"

"Doe... Err... Maya, I mean... Maya Doe."

"Well, see you soon, Maya."

Another grumble, and the car crunched its way over the gravel driveway. Deer eyes lit up like small beacons as headlights shone through the trees, and then the very trees themselves seemed to envelop the car.

All too suddenly, I was alone.

"Miss Doe," someone called from the entrance, atop those granite stairs. "This way please. Don't keep us waiting, it's late and we have a lot of work to do."

I gazed longingly around the emptiness of the Palace grounds, at the cool blades of trimmed grass. Everything seemed so calm, so open for the taking... My legs twitched.

"Don't..." A voice arose behind me, subdued and quiet. A footman stood by the fountain, his entire body stiff and rigid. "Snipers are on the roof and Masonians patrol the grounds with dogs. You'll never make it."

A hard swallow, those manicured ground looking a little less bright.

"Thanks," I mumbled, then took crunching steps towards the Palace.

The man called again, clearly irate. Incredibly tall, he easily appeared as I climbed those granite steps.

"Good evening, Miss Doe," he said. "My name is Bentley. I am the Butler here."

"Bentley," I repeated, unable to hide a smirk. "Bentley the Butler?"

"Yes, and remove that attitude, I have no need for it." His stare could cut ice. "Now, follow me."

The interior of the Palace was no less splendid. Inside two mammoth doors lay a small corridor, lined with jade columns, bordered with clean white marble. Ornaments were everywhere, lining the walls, filling the gaps between the columns. Cluttered excellence.

Further still, and my mouth dropped, for we had arrived into a huge, gigantic space. A staircase weaved around the circular circumference, stretching to the first floor, and then to the second, and then to the third. It was the hub of the Palace, connecting every floor, every room, every nook and cranny that enormous place held.

At the top of the stairs lay a domed stained-glass window that completely covered the ceiling. This colourful mound of glass lent to the name of this space: *The Dome Room*.

In the centre of this Dome Room was a golden table, supporting a vase: a huge thing, encrusted with precious jewels, containing a spectacular bouquet of flowers. They stretched high — far too high to be real — but their glorious colours clashed beautifully with the veined white of the marble. My eyes followed higher, reaching to the very peak of the saffron-coloured petals, and merged into the bottom drip of a goliath diamond chandelier.

Almost the diameter of the room, the chandelier must have been made of hundreds – no, *thousands* of diamonds. Were they real, glass? I couldn't tell, but each one caught the light and sparkled just as vehemently as Mason's eyes. It was glorious.

Never in a million Ragnaröks did I believe that such a luxurious abode existed. But there I was, ogling a chandelier the same size as my childhood home.

"Come, Miss Doe," Bentley urged, quickening his pace. I hurried behind him with echoing clanks. He led me down a small wooden service corridor, then down a staircase. Grandeur instantly ceased. Corridors became cold and damp, and more than a little musty. We were Downstairs, where numerous Palace kitchens interspersed with sleeping Slaves.

Bentley quickly led me to a small office. A singular lightbulb hung from the ceiling, overlooking a wooden desk that was, to say the least, disorganised.

Menus littered its wooden surface, along with guest lists, cleaning rotas, pens, pencils, even a spoon and a polishing cloth. The walls were no less bare, for each contained a wooden corkboard. These, too, brimmed with paperwork.

Without pause, Bentley the Butler sat behind the desk, directly opposite me. He fumbled with his mess of clutter, allowing me to study his features.

An incredibly tall, lanky man, Bentley's brown hair was slicked back against his skull. Only just greying at the temples, his gaunt face lined with more than what it should have at his age. I guessed he was somewhere in his fifties, though he appeared far older.

I rocked onto my heels, my hands behind my back, my tongue wrestling with the last remaining stitches on my lip.

"So, you've come to us from the Eynesbury Residence, but you've only been in service for two months. Well, I hope you're a quick learner, Miss Doe."

"I do my best, Bentley Butler."

His stare cut my smile.

"Word has reached me of your attitude and I implore you to drop it. I don't have to remind you that you are in Lord Mason's Palace, and proper manners are imperative. I will not protect you should you make an arse out of yourself, is that clear?"

"Yessir."

"Good, now let's see." More muffles of paperwork and then a tentative knock on the door. In walked a young woman who was strikingly beautiful.

"You asked to see me, Sir?" Her glorious blue eyes set like sapphires against smooth porcelain skin, framed with vibrant red hair. Tall, slim and only a few years older than me, she was absolutely stunning.

"Maya Doe, please meet Miss Anya Whittaker."

Anya boasted a blinding white smile, shaking my hand with a confidence that was not reciprocated.

"Pleasure," she said. "Please let me know if you have any questions, or if there's anything I can do for you."

"Can you get me out of here?" I joked. Bentley rolled up a used menu and bonked me on the head with it.

"Ah, I'm afraid we'd both be shot if I did." She smiled awkwardly. "Not that there *is* a way out. Place is tighter than a virgin's arse."

"Miss Whittaker, please..." Bentley grimaced.

* * *

Bentley soon left me within Anya's seasoned clutches. Leading me down the service corridor, we eventually came to the Slave Dormitories. Two adjacent corridors, one for each gender.

Anya and I shared a room halfway down. Each room contained a bunk bed and a small metal wood burner, as well as a sink and a toilet. Only a shower curtain hid our modesty whilst we shat.

Communal showers were situated at the end of the corridor. I proclaimed my absolute disgust of this, far from wishing strangers of either gender to gawk at my bruised body. Anya merely shrugged, stating that I'd get used to it after a while, and at the end of the day, it was safer for all Slaves to shower together.

"Masonians aren't above coming into the shower rooms," she said from the top bunk, later that evening. "Remember there's safety in numbers."

I curled up on the bottom bunk, the scratchy woollen blanket just covering my head, concealing my real eyes from my new roommate. I hid the lenses under the bed, soaking them in a new batch of solution I'd swiped from Emilia's bathroom before I left.

"Is it dangerous here?" I asked, tentatively.

Anya seemed to take a long time before answering.

"No more than anywhere else," she eventually replied.

Our silence was so heavy, so threatening.

"Is Mason around?" I asked. The thought of him residing somewhere above was...disturbing.

"Mostly, yes. He's around for breakfasts and dinners, not so much during the daytime."

"What's he like?"

Anya sighed. "Just stay on his good side, do what he says, and don't – for God's sake – talk back to him."

There was a tone to her voice that screamed more questions.

"What happens if you talk back to him?"

"Nothing good," was all she replied.

Soon Anya fell into a deep sleep. I was wide awake, watching the remaining minutes of my existence tick aimlessly on. It was unfair, barbaric. I should have been outside in the snow, not left to die in a mouldy room, forced to shower with other Slaves so we could be safe in our nakedness.

But what was the alternative? To dash through the Palace grounds, only to be taken out by a sniper? Or, should I be captured or discovered, stand before Mason with diamond eyes fluttering?

A heavy sigh inflated my chest. I wasn't abandoning my dreams of freedom. I simply had to store them somewhere, to tuck them away in a little box which I could open every time things grew a little too overwhelming. Escape was still possible – I genuinely believed that. I had to.

As I watched the slacks above me move with Anya's dreams, faint tones of that strange music trickled into my ears. I rubbed my eyes hard, relishing their freedom, and tried to ignore the impossible music. It did not work.

The music followed me into my dreams.

11

Dawn birds sang to the rising sun. Downstairs was alive with activity. Footsteps reverberated across hollow wood, into the very walls.

I chose to wash in the sink, not having the confidence to bare all in front of two dozen strangers. How many Slaves were in the Palace? The walls could hide a few dozen more without my knowledge.

Uniforms for this establishment consisted of a plain white blouse and a black pencil skirt. The only peculiar addition were the scarlet red heels, which were tall and annoyingly loud upon the wood.

"These are new," Anya said, as she struggled to fasten them. "The Mistress wants us to wear them. God knows why, I mean, it's not as if we don't walk a lot." She scoffed sarcastically beneath her breath.

This was the first time anyone had referred to the *Mistress*. It was almost an admission of her existence, as though she had suddenly become real and not a figment of my imagination.

I wanted to storm up to the Pretender's bedroom and shake priceless information out of her. *Why* was she here, *why* was she still alive? A complete stranger knew more about *me*, *my* destiny than I did, and to say this was frustrating would be an immense understatement. No doubt I'd claw her fake eyes out the moment I saw her lying face.

"Will I be serving Alira?" I asked, gauging Anya's reaction from the corner of my eye.

"Not really. I might ask you to do something, like prepare food or the like, but you won't serve her directly. No offence, but I don't think she's best pleased that Mason's bought you here."

Pfft, I thought, *the feeling is mutual.*

"Why not?" I asked. Indeed, I'd never met this woman, and I'd sure as Hel never given her a reason to hate me, so why did she already despise my presence?

"Oh, I wouldn't worry." Anya giggled, though it seemed a little forced. "Give it some time. You learn to be resilient."

"What do you mean?"

"Doesn't matter," she mumbled. "Anyway, let me introduce you."

Anya led me to a little kitchen tucked away at the end of the corridor.

"Here is our base of operations," she said.

Admittedly, the kitchen was charming. Wooden counters lined each wall, covered with a granite worktop cluttered with kitchen items. Of particular interest were the selection of teas, neatly displayed between the kettle and the gas stove: easily thirty varieties, and each one had an unfamiliar name. There was a small window on the far side of the room, above the sink, and a large wooden table with five chairs. Just out of sight, as I would later realise, sat a little pantry, full of staples and delicacies alike. A chef's wonderland.

Crowded into this little kitchen, huddled around the table that lay beneath bulbs of garlic and strings of herbs, hanging from the ceiling, were three women.

Two stared at me, one was engrossed in her morning porridge. The latter was bulbously pregnant.

"The new girl, Maya, is it?" one of them asked. She was a striking woman with hooded almond eyes and silky black hair. A rare beauty.

"Er, yes," I replied. "How do you know my name?"

There was a subdued giggle around the room.

"The Mistress told us. She was moaning about you quite a bit yesterday."

"Ah yes, the *Mistress*..." I raised my eyebrows, crossing my arms across a thin waist. "I've heard she isn't too pleased that I'm here."

"She'll get over it. Besides, Mason's happy and that's the main thing." The girl with the almond eyes rushed forwards and dutifully shook my hand – it was a very *Maelstrom* greeting that took me by surprise.

"My name is Luna, she's Tia." She pointed to a blond girl with tanned skin and blue eyes reeking of suspicion. "The whale over there is Hallie."

The pregnant girl gave a sarcastic *ha-ha* and continued eating her porridge. Her head was bowed so low, the tip of her brown hair tickled the rim of the bowl.

I stood awkwardly at the door as they regaled their duties for the day: serve meals, serve drinks, and clean up after Aristocrats. In basic terms, their job was to keep the *Masters* happy, whatever that entailed.

Apparently, the Powers That Be were not yet comfortable with me serving food to them. Instead, most of my duties fell Downstairs: chopping vegetables, washing dishes and laundry, polishing silverware… How *wonderful*.

On the face of it, my chores seemed mundane. But, as those first two weeks wore on, exhaustion quickly grew.

Great callouses formed on my heels and soles, my toes wrecked with blisters. Cuts and abrasions easily formed, healed and reformed anew, scraped by the shoe's rigid frame. Yet I hobbled on with my piles of dirty laundry, or stood for hours before soapy dishwater. My nails, already flaking and soft, were on the verge of popping off completely. Dried blood oozed from the grooves around the nail bed, like some perverted picture frames.

Clearly, Mason bought me because he wanted another Slave, yet why *me*? Apparently, the Bolton Square Slave Auctions occurred multiple times a week, so he had ample opportunity to buy another woman – or even another Herder, should he have just liked my accent.

But no, he dragged me – *Campbell's little Wild One* – away from Emilia's clutches, leaving crates of gold in my shadow, simply for me to…*clean*? I hadn't seen him since Emilia's hallway, so he clearly didn't want information about Campbell *(thank the Gods),* so what other reason was there?

Maybe he wanted to own a last little piece of Campbell. Such a sordid thing would hardly be surprising for a man who killed two billion people, enslaved countless more, and had killed everyone I'd ever loved in that cold and wretched world. My eyes burned with angry moisture at such hard truths.

The End of Everything

At our prescribed mealtimes, I would join the other maids in the little kitchen, beneath the bulbs of garlic and strings of rosemary. Most of the time, it would be in silence, our muscles aching, the air heavy with exhaustion. Occasionally, however, someone would attempt to start a conversation. It could go either way: ending with stony silence, or a gossipy chat that had our ears sharpened and our tongues dripping for more. That afternoon, it was the latter.

"Mason's having a dinner party at the end of the week, have you heard?" Tia said, as she lifted a forkful of mashed potatoes.

"About bloody time," Anya said. She gave me a quick sidelong glimpse. "He hasn't hosted one for a while and normally that's a sign he's in a bad mood."

I wondered what constituted a bad mood for Mason. I'd only ever met him twice, and both times were reasonably civil. The chance encounter in the Theatre may have been the most dicey, and dangerous, but even on that occasion, Mason wasn't necessarily in a *bad* mood.

Was Verity Ulster in a *bad* mood? Was that why she tried to cut out my tongue?

"What happens at these dinner parties?" I tentatively asked.

"The usual. Go up, make sure everyone's well-fed and drunk. Same as normal, just with twenty more people."

Hallie grumbled and slouched low in the chair, almost sliding beneath the table. "I hope he's going to let me have a chair this time, all that standing around will kill my back again."

"When are you due?" I asked, though it was a silly question. Any longer and the baby would have popped out of her belly button.

"Not long now, another month at the most." She stared sadly at her bump, her hand running up and down its impressive curvature.

Hallie's baby was a curious little being, and it confounded me. Surely a sadistic man like Mason would have Hallie thrown out of service, or – worse still – removed Hallie's unborn baby entirely. Clearly Hallie was allowed to keep it, but what would happen after the birth? Hallie's time would be rather stretched, and Mason did not sound like the type of man who'd prioritise a baby's needs over his own.

A curious thought popped into my head.

"Who's the father?" I asked, loudly.

Hallie's narrowing eyes shot to me. "None of your damn business."

Her abrupt and rather prickly response cemented the – seemingly obvious – fact that Mason was the father. Why else would a very convex Hallie be in that kitchen? It made so much sense.

"I'm sure he'll get you a chair," I said, managing a friendly smile.

Hallie did not return my gesture and her stare fell back to her bowl of mashed potato.

"It might be worth having a practise session with us one night this week," Anya said, completely nonchalant, as I sank further and further into the chair. "It'll make the big night a little easier if we can go through a few things first. Y'know, make it all a bit more comfortable for you."

For a moment, I listened to her kind words and felt the sure, unmistakable crunch of anxiety inside my stomach. Then, I became difficult.

"I'm not serving at Mason's dinner party," I said, absolute.

All four of them just stared at me.

"Don't be ridiculous," Tia snapped. "Of course you are."

"No, I'm not."

"Look," Anya said, irritated, turning in her chair to face me. "I know you haven't been in service that long, but this is a big deal. Mason doesn't just hold dinner parties for the sake of a few drinks, he does it to show off, to remind his deplorable Aristocratic pals where the status quo is. For you to hide away down here, simply for the sake of being difficult, will most certainly irk him."

"You really think Mason is going to want a Herder freak like me serving drinks at his dinner party? Not likely, that's why they have me hidden down here, so they don't have to see me or hear me. Ha, Gods forbid they like my accent so much they try to cut my tongue out." I motioned to the marks on my lip, raised and discoloured but otherwise completely healed.

"You're only down here because they want to gauge how you're going to react," Luna said. She was in direct sunlight, her ebony hair falling like waves of oil down her back. "It's standard practise to see how you're going to behave before they release you to the *civilised* folk. Hell, once this dinner party is up, you're going to be let loose Upstairs with us."

"All the more reason to stay down here then," I muttered with a defiant cross of my arms.

Anya clicked her tongue at me, rolling her eyes.

"You're Mason's new pet," Tia said. "He's going to want to show you off."

"Why would he want to *show me off?*" I was an abomination. A savage. An orphaned little girl who had spent her entire life crawling through mud and excrement, and eating animals raw. Why in Hel's name would anyone admit such a creature was working in their kitchens, serving them food?

As if she read my mind, Tia scanned my features.

"You're gorgeous Maya," she said, quickly and not in the least bit friendly. "Mason evidently knows this – hell, everyone knows it."

My jaw dropped, exposing a tongue that itched to form a snarky reply, yet was unable to do so.

"Obviously he wants to show you off, Maya" Anya said, after some time. "Mason doesn't own beautiful women to keep them hidden away."

* * *

LESS THAN FORTY-EIGHT hours to go until the dinner party, and my resolution remained solid, unbreakable, and all too reckless. I'd stay low, stay hidden, and stay *far* away from all Aristocrats. The more sensible part of me begged myself to reconsider, to grovel before Anya, so she'd take me beneath her obedient wing. My Herder side, however, had a very different tone. She was angry, bitter, just so goddamn indignant. Why should I serve my enslavers? Why should I give those pompous Aristocrats the pleasure?

Perhaps they would lock me Downstairs forever, away from their Aristocratic eyes.

Hope would be a fine thing.

Hope. Such a little word. It flicked in and out of conscious thought, when I least expected it. That morning, it fluttered across my skull whilst elbow deep in dishwater, cleaning the breakfast dishes from Upstairs.

Ahead of me, the open window allowed the warm summer breeze to gently caress my face. My hair was down; a great cascade of chestnut waved down my back, and as each strand of hair was tickled by the breeze, I wondered if this summer heat had melted the lakes in the Snowlands.

I wondered if the grass had punched its resilient way through the shallow snow, or if the birds were singing in their nests. Perhaps bears roamed carefree through the emerald green valleys, or dipped inside the colourful lakes for a midday refresh. In my mind, the Brüster Mountains still owned their snow-capped peaks, immortal as they punctured the sky. They were dominant guards over the wondrous summer Snowlands, watching with grandeur as yellow flowers tilted their small heads to the sun.

At that exact point, hope fluttered. It was the hope that I would see such sights again, that I might one day crunch the Snowlands beneath my boot.

Perhaps, one day, when the time was right.

Three short knocks brought my attention down with a thump. I startled around and was met with a smiling Anya, hanging sheepishly around the door.

"Sorry, I didn't mean to startle you." She made her way into the room, stepping into the sun with hair resembling red flames.

I shrugged and turned back to the window. The hope had been scared away, startled by her presence. So, my attention fell upon the manicured grounds, and then to the driveway. Three Aristocratic cars parked on the gravel, polished by male Slaves who sweated in the strong sun.

Anya hopped skittishly to my side, leaning her skinny frame against the counter. She observed my hands in the dishwater and asked what I was doing, which seemed a little redundant. I replied truthfully, if not a little sarcastically, then wondered why she acted like I was some raging wildcat about to pounce.

"The Mistress has a job for you," she said, and my heart sank. "Only, it's a bit of an odd request. I'm sorry to have to give it to you but she asked for your name specifically."

Oh Gods, what was this woman having me do now? I grabbed the nearest towel and tried in vain not to strangle the darn thing.

"What is it?"

"She's asked you to retrieve a book for her."

"A book?" I raised my eyebrows. "Why is she asking me to do that?"

Anya fumbled with her hands, wondering how to proceed. "Please don't be offended, but can you read?"

"Yes," I replied, absolute. That was mostly true, I *could* read, though not very well and my spelling and grammar were atrocious to say the least.

Still, my confession calmed Anya, who visibly relaxed and smiled away her obvious awkwardness.

"Oh, good! That's going to make this book thing a *whole* lot easier!"

Realisation popped like an annoying lightbulb.

"Oh," I said with a large sigh. "She thought I couldn't read, right? She wanted me to fetch a book because she thought I'd struggle with it."

Gods, what had I ever done to this woman? But then, maybe I was just the excuse. Maybe she really resented Mason for owning another *beautiful* lady. Couldn't say I blamed her – not because I was apparently beautiful, but because *I* resented him owning yet another human life. It was sickening.

Before me, Anya awkwardly shifted from one foot to another.

"But you *can* read," she quickly said, as if to save any further insult. "So this should be easy for you!"

"What's the book?"

"*Articles that Define the Normal Autocracy in Civilisations....* Or something along those lines. You'll get it I'm sure! I mean, how many books can there be, right?"

* * *

CLEARLY, in all of her years at the Palace, Anya had never seen the Reading Room.

Bookcases lines every available wall, each one cramped with literature. All different sizes and colours – some with leather linings, others simply held together with string. This was perhaps the most ornate, complete, *beautiful* room in the entire Palace.

I wandered around the circumference and scanned each book. Some were fiction, some were factual, some were simply memoirs of a time long since passed. My red heels clanked loudly against the wood as I slowly made my way around, fascinated with the history, the unlimited *imagination* that lay scratching at my fingertips.

The chandelier dripped blood-red rubies and fit perfectly within the warm mahogany of the room. A fireplace, bordered with mottled marble, lay unused and somewhat dejected before a velvet loveseat that had clearly seen better days. At the far end of the room, a large window overlooked the grounds on this glorious summer's day, with a wide cushioned ledge for even the most seasoned book lover to curl up upon, and watch the world tick by.

But, by far the most magnificent thing in that room was the utter *beast* of an object sitting in the corner. It was hard to describe: a bulky thing with a flat top and a smooth, curving ledge. Below this ledge was a stool, cushioned with red velvet. The base of the object was empty for all except three golden pedals. As I moved closer, the intricate golden detail on the object's flawless, dark wood left little doubt: this was one of the most beautiful objects I had ever seen.

Delicately, a finger stroked its surface. Silky smooth. Sparks raced up my fingers, as though it was electrified, and travelled up into my hand, my arm, my chest.

I was a moth being dragged to the light. In the back corners of my mind, a little light flashed on and off, warning me to keep my distance. I didn't understand the music, I had no comprehension of what it was, what it was doing to me… I should have been terrified by this music, all too ready to run far away from it, but yet… I couldn't.

I was entranced by it, helplessly pulled further into its musical light, just like that doomed moth.

Slowly, I lifted the cover – the *keylid*. Huddled inside were a series of black and white… *Buttons?* No, *keys*. Made out of ebony and ivory, they reflected the light.

My fingers moved across them, caressed them. Intrigued, I placed a delicate, careful touch upon one. It was cool beneath my fingertip. With a held breath, I pressed down.

Music erupted. A singular note, sudden and delicate. A shiver raced. The hairs on my arms, my neck, pulled against my skin.

Another key pressed. I closed my eyes, feeling the notes caress my head, effortlessly wiping musical bliss inside my skull.

Somehow, this instrument, whatever it was, was the source of the impossible music inside my head. For months it taunted me, but now I knew. I'd heard its inner structure quiver with delight, and I wanted *more*, to be closer to that music, to be surrounded, consumed by it…

By their own admission, my fingers wanted to caress the keys, to press them down with feral ferocity. They splayed themselves out and a chord filled the room. A shaky exhale, my eyes closed tight as I focussed on each beat, each quiver.

My other hand touched the keys, and I just wanted to press them...

"Can I help you?"

I startled, both hands snapping back to my side. Stumbling back, my focus turned to the door. An involuntary gulp as Mason's blazing eyes stared back at me.

"Erm... I was just looking for a book... Sir."

Mason took careful steps into the room, his stare fixed and intense. The uniform he wore, reminiscent of a Masonian one insofar that it comprised of the long blue coat and black boots, exuded superiority from between the neatly sewn seams. My eyes sank to his black weapons belt, containing a silver revolver on one side, and a long, sheathed sword on the other that glinted silver, gold and sapphires.

He had switched from civilised Aristocrat to the Destroyer of the Old World, simply by changing his clothes.

"You don't appear to be looking for a book, Miss Doe," he said, his voice licked with menace. He stood on the other side of the instrument.

"I was, but –"

Mason slammed the keylid.

Agonised musical notes shivered the air. I stumbled back.

Mason expressed a sharp, toothless smile that was the exact opposite of happy, and placed a possessive hand upon the instrument's smooth surface.

"But I, erm..." I suppressed the urge to tremble. "I was looking for the book, but I got distracted."

My guilty eyes fell upon the instrument. It stared longingly back. My fingers twitched.

Mason followed my gaze and ran his hand across its surface.

"One can easily get distracted in here," he whispered to himself.

Snapping out of his reverie, Mason stood up straight and glared. "Why, may I ask, are you looking for a book? It almost sounds like your Downstairs duties are not keeping you sufficiently occupied."

"What? No, no, nothing like that..." My stomach tightened as those dangerous eyes bored into me. "Alira, I mean, the *Mistress* asked me to bring her one."

This seemed to calm Mason. His posture relaxed, his eyes dimmed.

"Did she now? How curious."

I remained quiet, my fingers frantically fumbling. My heart was like a wild animal, my reflexes brimming, my muscles readying for a fight or flight.

"What book?" Mason asked.

"*Articles Defining Normal Civilised Aristocracy.*"

Mason seemed to show a genuine smile. "Do you mean: *The Articles Defining Normalisation of Autocracy in New Civilisations?*"

"Er, yeah. That one."

"And the Mistress has asked to read it? How curious."

My throat was suddenly dry and in desperate need of something stronger than water. But still, I couldn't help but wonder... "Why is it curious?"

"Because it's frightfully boring," he said with a smirk. "I daresay she has simply chosen the book to challenge you, and not given any thought as to the contents."

A sarcastic *pfft* escaped me, which I quickly hid with a cough. Mason clearly saw my attitude but did little to comment, instead asking, "Are you literate?"

"Yes." I sighed, unable to hide a tiresome tone. "Why does everyone keep asking me that?"

Clearly amused by my frustration, Mason chuckled to himself and wandered to a bookcase on the far wall. Stroking a long finger against the leather book bindings, he seemed to be looking for something.

"The Herder Culture, though fascinating in its own right, is not known for its literacy expertise. You communicate with your voices, not with letters."

He pulled a book from its mahogany home, flicked briefly through the pages, and then presented it to me. "Here, read this."

Tentatively, I took the book. It was heavy, with a green leather binding and letters that were unnecessarily small. For a moment, I hesitated, wondering why he wanted me to read the book in the first place, and perhaps a little scared as to the consequences if I did. Yet, the ramifications for *not* doing as he asked seemed a little more worrisome. My future inside Mason's walls did not bode well if I refused to comply with his ever-so-simple requests.

Using my finger as a guide, I spoke the words as best I could, using my intellect to aid my frequent guesswork. My words were slow, my eyes straining for some time before I eventually closed the book with a dejected sigh.

"I might be a little rusty," I said.

A slow smirk formed on Mason's lips. "I've heard worse. I daresay the Mistress underestimated you."

I forced an awkward smile, dropping my gaze to the book, and noticed the title, in silver letters: *Moonsilver*.

Confused, I frowned. "This isn't the one she's asked for."

"No, it's not. This is for you."

"For me?"

"Think of it as a way to brush up your literacy skills."

Stunned, I could do nothing but gawk at the book Mason had given me. Then my senses slammed back and I gasped out a surprised, "Thank you."

"There is one condition," he said, his eyes darkening. A shadow descended over his features, instantly reminding me that his eyes, though beautiful, could kill with a single look. "A little bird has informed me that you're refusing to serve Upstairs at my dinner party tomorrow night. I trust you are aware just how inappropriate that would be. I daresay it would cause me great embarrassment."

"I don't want to embarrass you, Sir –"

"No," he cut in. "You really don't."

"But – "

"Are you going to argue with me, Miss Doe?"

"No, I'm not…" I shifted my weight from tall heel to another, my stomach contracting. "It's just, no offence, but surely you'd be more comfortable with me out of the way? Besides my obvious lack of *esteem*, I've never served at a dinner party before and what if I fu – I mean, screw it up?"

Mason showed a wide smile, lifting the shadow, and only intensifying the shimmer of those diamond eyes.

"You're a smart woman," he said. "I'm sure you'll manage."

Knowing deep in my pounding heart that there was no way out of this, I agreed.

"Good," Mason said, evidently pleased. "In that case, enjoy the book."

He wandered back to the grand instrument.

"I won't keep you from your other duties," he said.

It was a polite invitation for me to leave, but I was halfway to the door when I remembered, "Oh, what about the Mistress's book?"

"Ignore that. I'll inform her that you can, in fact, read to a certain level. I've no doubt her interest in the book will diminish shortly after."

I nodded, made it three more steps, and then stopped. A niggling thought wormed its way into my brain, filling me with such paradox that I remained numb to all movement.

"Anything else, Miss Doe?" Mason called behind me.

I turned, licking my lips. "May I…"

I hesitated. Did I really want to know this?

"May I ask you a question, Sir?"

Mason thought for a moment, scanning my mannerisms, my blatant pull of the status quo.

"If you must," he replied.

I hugged the book tight into my chest, like my very soul was nestled between the pages. "Campbell," I whispered. "Is… Is he dead?"

Mason did not move. He remained staring at me, his jaw tightly clenched, his body filled with heated rigidity.

"Yes," he eventually replied.

Of course he was. I knew this, I had done for a while now. But yet, as that singular word of confirmation passed Mason's lips, it hit me with full, unfiltered force. Suddenly I was back in that train carriage, wailing my despair to the distant howl of wolves.

I swallowed the painful lump in my throat, fighting those wails, pushing them down into the rising ball of hate. Mason's confirmation merely enforced that he, The Destroyer of the Old World, was responsible for it all. I wanted to scream, to release this pressurised ball before it popped in Mason's face.

Breathe in… One… Two… Three…

Somehow remaining silent, I traversed the last few shaking steps to the door.

"One last thing, Miss Doe."

With a clenched jaw, I turned to see Mason with his diamond eyes blazing.

"Don't you ever touch this piano again," he said.

12

It was the night of the dinner party.

From within the confines of my Downstairs bedroom, I observed the tight black dress with disgusted curiosity.

"Why again are we being made to wear this?" I asked, grimacing. It showed too much of me for comfort.

Anya, already dressed to impress, put two warm hands on my shoulders. "Don't worry about it. I'll be right there with you, okay? You're not alone in this."

Something in my chest warmed at the sight of Anya's kind smile, and as she helped me squeeze into the black dress, I wondered how someone as pure and as generous as she had managed to survive at all. Nine years, she'd been at that Palace. *Nine years.*

"There, you look lovely." Anya smiled, zipping me up. "Hair could do with a trim though, when was the last time you had it cut?"

I fondled the dried ends, pondering that exact question.

Anya was surprisingly blasé when I told her of my meeting with Mason in the Reading Room. She had almost expected it.

"We're his possessions," she had said. "He likes to interact with us every now and then. Aside from anything else, it keeps us on our toes."

What she could not understand, however, was why he had given me the book. Apparently, it was much unlike his personality to offer any sort of niceties to Slaves *in my position* (whatever that meant). She suggested I keep such an occurrence to myself, save *worrying* the other maids (again, whatever that meant).

Nevertheless, I agreed with her. *Moonsilver* remained safely tucked under my bed, next to the stolen bottle of solution.

Every time I replayed the events of that Reading Room, the *piano* in my head sang back.

The notes were quiet at first, floating listlessly in my skull. Like falling feathers, they allowed their presence to be known without overpowering my senses.

But now, the music became more urgent, more demanding. They were seeking attention, bouncing around my skull, determined to make their presence known.

The urge to go back to that piano, to hear those exquisite notes, was almost suffocating. I wanted to dissolve into the music, to fall headfirst into its chasm and be carried by each chord, each note...

I thought of Mason's touch upon its smooth contours, his possessiveness of it, insofar that he banned my touch after only three powerful caresses. I recalled that night at the Theatre and wondered whether Mason felt the same draw, the same possession over his violin too. Was it as strong as it was for the piano? Stronger even? Perish the thought.

* * *

THE CLOCK NEARED 8PM. The guests would arrive any minute. I was absolutely shitting myself.

Standing in the Dome Room with a tray of champagne flutes, I debated whether I could feign sickness and be excused Downstairs. Then I'd chastised myself for such a thought. Mason's warning to me in the Reading Room was remarkably clear: serve the guests, or pay the consequences. I certainly did not want to embarrass him.

The dress was tight against my slim curves. Low at the front, it allowed the roundness of my breasts to be observed in anxious detail. My cleavage was not something I had the desire to parade. No doubt I'd receive lewd stares from Aristocrats.

Would the Ulster Twins be coming that evening? Likely, considering they were part of Mason's Social Circle. What about Erik Doncaster?

My blood boiled with sick memories. I recalled the terror behind Orzo's eyes, the way he reluctantly undid each button as the basement door snapped shut...

I cast my eyes to Anya, standing beside me and looking like a Goddess, then to Tia, and then over the hall to Luna and the pregnant Hallie. What would happen to them if I screwed up here tonight? Would Mason make them pay for my insubordination? I had already done that to Orzo. Never again.

An outside breeze carried voices up the jade corridor. Aristocrats soon poured in.

Before long, the Dome Room was full of them, dressed in luxurious extravagance with expensive jewellery and designer spouses. Dresses of exceptional quality stroked the marble floor, a whole manner of precious gemstones glinting with every subtle movement. Men strutted around in tuxedos, laughing with gleaming white teeth, their hair and beards exceptionally manicured.

Somewhere in the mass of people, I bumped into Emilia Eynesbury.

"Ah, good evening Miss Doe." She beamed, her grey eyes observing me up and down, her magnificent peacock feathers bouncing from her headscarf. "You look a much better sight than when I last saw you. Clearly this establishment agrees with you."

"I wouldn't go that far," I nervously muttered. "How are Orzo and Lander?"

"Oh, fine, just fine. Mr Atkinson asks about you a lot."

"He does?"

"Oh yes." A small smirk worked its way through Emilia's thin lips. "I believe he holds a candle for you."

"What does that mean?"

Emilia tittered to herself, sipping her champagne, and engaged in loud conversation with the Aristocrat next to her.

Confused, I shook my head at that enigma of a woman and continued my rounds.

If one thing about me was memorable, it was my accent, and as such I made a point to remain silent. Instead, I dutifully smiled at Aristocrats, determined to keep my vocal cords still.

It was all going rather well.

"Oh, look, the rats have returned from the sewer." Verity Ulster's sneer cut through the flesh of my tongue, just aching to retort. I inhaled deep, my attitude safely hidden, and merely smiled in greeting.

"I must say," she said, blocking my only exit with a jutted hip bone, drenched in a silver gown. "I've never seen you looking quite so... *Delectable*. I hope these Masonians are treating you as well as your cleavage is."

Oh, and there it was. The childish, unnecessary remark about my appearance. I swallowed the curses aching at my throat, and did my best to smile.

"No words?" she crooned, thin eyebrows raised. "Come now, darling. Let me hear you."

I smiled tightly. "Excuse me, Ma'am."

She grinned a blinding smile and pinched my elbow between two long fingernails. "That accent is still charming. Just wait, I'll cut it out of you soon enough."

"With the greatest of respect, *Ma'am*, this is Mason's Palace. To go around cutting the tongues out of his Slaves is quite disrespectful."

Her pale face developed a sinister shadow, and clashed gloriously with her scarlet lipstick. "Oh, trust me. Mason and I are *very* good friends. I'm sure I can convince him otherwise."

A shadow in the corner of my eye foretold the arrival of her brother, Ivan. He observed me briefly, before gently grasping his sister's bare arm. "Surely you have better things to be doing, dear?"

Verity considered this for a while, blessed me with a ferocious green glare, then stomped her way through the crowd. Ivan remained, leering.

"What, you want to cut my tongue out too?" I said, dryly.

Ivan's lips curled into a smirk. "I don't know, I might have use of that tongue."

Stunned, I remained motionless as he swiftly took a flute of champagne and joined his sister in the crowd.

"Allfather save me..." *How do these people live with themselves?*

"Hey, are you alright?" Anya asked, materialising from the waves of fine material. "I saw you talking to the Ulster Twins."

"Yeah, fine."

"Don't take it personally. Ivan's all talk. Whatever he says, he has the highest respect for Mason, and wouldn't dare touch any of his Slaves without his expressed permission."

"And what of Verity? She's the one who really seems to have it in for me."

Anya frowned, her bright blue eyes focussed on the bubbles in the champagne. "Yeah, she's something alright," she muttered. "Stay out of her way for now, the novelty of you will wear off after a while."

"Ha, yeah. I hope my tongue remains attached until then."

"Hey, as long as Mason doesn't fuck you, you'll be fine." My eyes widened in horror. "Oh c'mon, that's the only reason she hates you. You're her new competition."

This was all getting too much. I took a big breath, straining against the dress's tight fabric.

"Relax," Anya said, softly. "You're easy pickings if they can see you're scared."

"I'm not scared."

"Yeah, tell that to your face."

I tried to glare but it just materialised as a feeble little look from the corner of my eye.

Anya quickly scanned the room. "Come on," she said.

She led me to the edge of the Dome Room, to a group of men sipping their champagne. "Excuse me, Doctor Grant?"

One of the men turned. He had one of those faces that was impossible to age, although the greying temples suggested post-fifties. Nevertheless, he smiled like a man more than half his age when his sharp eyes found Anya.

"Good evening," he said.

"Arnold, allow me to introduce Maya Doe." She gestured towards me. "She's the one I told you about."

The man smiled again and held out his hand for me to shake. Still shocked at this strange Aristocratic display, it took me a moment to react.

"Maya, this is Doctor Grant."

"Er, hi," I said.

"My pleasure," the Doctor said, kindly. "I'm the General Practitioner for the Palace. Bentley has my pager should you need anything, and Anya knows how to contact me."

This man – an *Aristocrat,* of all people – was genuinely concerned about the welfare of Slaves. The notion was intriguing, to say the least. Although, as I observed the way he stared at Anya, or the way his eyes sparkled when she laughed, I soon realised the exact reason why he was so willing to please her.

There was the briefest of conversations before Bentley demanded Anya and I return to our duties.

So, there I was, parading around with the champagne flutes and trying in vain to avoid tipsy Aristocrats. An hour must have passed before the deafening chatter became subdued and distracted.

Numerous eyes were fixed on something. Joining the communal stares, I saw Mason walking down the spiral stairs. Dressed in a tuxedo, images of that night in the Theatre raced to me. I thought of the song, the violin, the way he moved the bow across the strings with such delight, such *passion*. How could a musical instrument invoke such a reaction from him? From us both?

The piano inside my head loudened, ever so slightly.

Beside Mason, linking his arm with all the prestige of a boastful peacock, was a woman.

All in white, she was a beautiful creature with long blond hair and an elegance that radiated through every pore. As she descended, she presented a beaming smile to all around her, her teeth glinting as bright as her extravagant diamond necklace.

I observed this woman closely, then inwardly sneered at our blatant dissimilarity. She was far taller and skinnier, with bones clearly protruding from skin that was artificially tanned, and a face portraying a type of beauty that was nothing but superficial. I wondered, rather unkindly, what she looked like beneath the layers of expensive grime on her cheeks.

On their way to the Dining Room, our eyes locked for the briefest – and longest – of moments. I stared at those opal-like eyes, engrossed in the iridescent twinkle they produced.

But, although beautiful, they did not sparkle on a moonless night. They could not fluoresce in the dark or catch the golden light of the fire. They did not stare at a lonely piano with such ferocity, the music encroached around them.

No, you are definitely not me.

* * *

THE DINNER PARTY was in full swing.

Standing with Anya at the edge of the Dining Room, I could not help but be impressed. A long wooden table was in the middle of the room, set with gold placements and candelabras. It was affluent and sumptuous: a grand support on which Aristocrats could devour their first of five courses.

Mason was at one end of the table, with the Pretender to his left and Ivan Ulster to his right. A delightful little smirk curled my lips as I spotted Verity Ulster sitting on the far end, as far away from Mason as possible. Those green eyes flicked up to him continually throughout her meal.

The Dining Room itself was huge, with wooden walls and floors, and a large fireplace that radiated delicious warmth during the cool summer evening. Large windows sported spectacular views of the grounds, the forest, and the snow-capped mountains in the distance, just visible in the dying light.

Finally, as was the case for all rooms in the Palace, a spectacular chandelier overlooked the table, hanging from an ornately painting ceiling. It allowed Anya and I to monitor the entire table and swiftly refill any glass that was a little too depleted.

"Thank you, Miss Doe," Mason said, as I refilled his glass with red wine. "I'm pleased you acknowledged our little chat yesterday by gracing us with your presence this evening."

A nervous lick of my lips, being sure to catch the singular drip of red wine hanging from the neck of the bottle.

"Wouldn't miss it, Sir," I quietly replied.

Opal eyes burned my skin as I continued to fill glasses.

"You talked to her?" The Pretender's voice was high and delicate, like a crystal vase.

"Yes. Miss Doe originally refused to serve us tonight. I felt obliged to remind her of her position."

Ivan Ulster eyed me as I poured the red wine into his glass. It was a lecherous, uncomfortable stare that invoked shivers up and down my spine. Those shivers did not disperse as I continually perused the table.

"Oh, you *must* hear her accent," Emilia remarked as I passed her.

After the entrée dishes had been cleared, I noticed Hallie on the other side of the room. Head bowed, she swayed from side to side, her bulbous belly barely camouflaged by her black dress. Against everything I had assumed, Mason did not provide Hallie a chair to rest on. Hours had passed and my feet and legs were already aching with the strain. In her pregnant state, it must have been torture for Hallie. Her ankles had swelled considerably throughout the evening, spilling around the straps of her heeled shoes.

A chair was needed, desperately. I tried to ask Anya, but she immediately *shushed* me. I grumbled beneath my breath, searching around the room, wondering what to do.

Luna and Tia suddenly appeared with the dessert course. Tia presented a dish before Mason, then Ivan.

I clicked my tongue at her, grasping her attention for mere moments before she glared harshly and marched from the room. Luna was gone before I could summon her. Bentley was preoccupied in the kitchens.

Hallie's swaying intensified. Was she going to faint?

"Anya, she needs a chair," I hissed out the corner of my mouth. Anya, who had also been observing Hallie, sent me an agreed glimpse, followed by a defeated shrug. It was her way of saying there was nothing we could do.

Why won't anyone help her?

Tia returned with more dessert dishes. I tried to grab her attention, to at least fling her irritated eyes over to an increasingly unstable Hallie. When she actively ignored me, I openly glowered at her bouncy golden locks.

A cough brought my attention to the table.

"Miss Doe, is anything amiss?"

The Pretender glared at me, those opal eyes so full of... *Hatred.* It took me by surprise.

Why did all these strangers hate me?

The table fell silent beneath the combined stares of twenty-one Aristocrats. Mason's eyes were the brightest of all, and I suddenly recalled his warnings about humiliation.

"Erm…" I licked my dry lips, debating how to respond. But as I noticed Hallie, her eyes closed and her sways becoming more prominent, I puffed up my shoulders and took the biggest gamble of the night.

"Ma'am, please may I get Hallie a chair?"

Anya bristled. Hushed whispers oscillated down the table.

No reply, so I said, "It's been hours and she looks like she's going to faint."

The Pretender turned on her chair to see Hallie, staring at me with exhausted horror.

"Oh?" The Pretender's expression soured. "Do tell me, Slave, why should I allow Miss Osborne a chair? It's hardly my concern."

Mason observed me intently. Our eyes met for the briefest of moments before I fixed my attention to the Pretender, acting all high and mighty with a goddamn smile on her face.

"Forgive me, Ma'am, but I'm just thinking of the wellbeing of the dinner party."

A low drone of doubtful laughter percolated. The Pretender practically cackled.

"For *our* benefit? Please, do explain."

I took another glimpse to Hallie. She was pale… So incredibly pale.

"If I may be so crude, fainting could result in a miscarriage and it would be shame if you were all disturbed from an enjoyable dessert. Think of the fluids."

The Pretender's pale pink lips formed an ugly grimace.

"I'd rather not, if it's all the same to you." Then she straightened her spine and snapped, "Miss Whittaker, bring a chair in."

Anya wasted no time in bringing a chair, and Hallie outwardly groaned as she eased herself down. Colour flushed her cheeks.

As the dining table settled into their dessert course, I chanced a final look at Mason. He held the glass of red wine to his lips, trying to hide his smirk.

Once the guests had finished, they settled in the Green Room: a smoking room, so named for the expansive collection of jade ornaments. A few wooden tables and a black marble fireplace remained the only other pops of colour in a room choked with smoke.

I followed Anya with bottles of whiskey when a tight hand dragged me to a nearby corridor.

I squealed, ready to use the bottles as batons.

"What the *hell* were you doing?" Bentley hissed through gritted teeth. Dots of sweat lined his forehead. "Tia told me what happened. What possessed you to *dare* speak out of line like that?"

"Hallie was in trouble!" I said, no less emotional. "A few more minutes and she would have collapsed – how could I just stand there and do nothing? Besides, it worked, didn't it?"

Bentley could not think of a proper retort.

"Clean the table," he snapped. "Don't set foot in that Green Room otherwise the Aristocrats will be wearing you as a bloody corset by the end of the night."

It was unclear if he was exaggerating.

* * *

THE GUESTS HAD STARTED to filter out. Some stayed the night, such as Emilia Eynesbury and the Ulster Twins. Others, such as Doncaster, had their chauffeurs wait in the Slaves Dormitories, waiting aimlessly until they were called to transport their drunken Masters. Indeed, most of the Aristocrats were drunk. This was a shock, as I'd always assumed Aristocrats enjoyed alcohol in a quantity that was befitting their civilised status. Evidently not, for I'd already heard one sorry sod vomiting the remains of the party in one of the bathrooms.

I wondered how drunk the Pretender was.

Wiping the wine and food stains off the table, I contemplated exactly what she was to Mason. Clearly, he wasn't going to kill her, at least not yet, and although that fact was baffling enough in its own right, why was she still alive?

With a despondent sigh, I thought of Campbell. He told me, in no ambiguous terms, that Mason would be the literal death of me. That he would kill me to prevent the End of Everything.

Clearly Campbell was wrong.

Oh Campbell, you poor bastard.

Tears threatened to emerge. I quickly wiped them away with the cloth.

As the last of the Aristocrats left or retired, the grand clock over the fireplace chimed 3am. Only two hours of sleep before the morning chores.

I wandered to the window, and easily spotted the distant mountains, shining in the moonlight. What mountains were they? I had no idea, but they were no less impressive, no less beautiful. I wondered what was on the other side...

No, girl, my inner mind chastised. *Stop thinking about such things.*

What was the use of dreaming about free lands when I was stuck there, cleaning up vomit from overindulged Aristocrats? The fact that these people cared more for their dessert than a poor girl's miscarriage only reinforced that I served monsters. Those monsters would happily kill me without a moment's thought, and they would certainly enjoy it.

The clock chimed one last time, and I debated whether to catch those two hours of sleep. My limbs ached, my bruised and battered feet screaming for some reprieve. But as the pearly light of dawn tickled the horizon, I admitted there was simply no point. My body would demand more than those two measly hours, and I could not risk a grumpy disposition during breakfast.

Apparently, I was required to serve Upstairs now.

Pfft. Clearly, they thought I was sufficiently *broken in.*

No, I would stay awake and fight the urge to collapse. Whilst the rest of the Palace slept, I could even have a shower. The thought was more exciting than it should have been.

The first thing I did was to remove my red heels. The delicious stretch of my foot on flat ground... Such agonised pleasure, and I outwardly groaned.

Limping onwards, I silently traversed the Dome Room.

Then I heard something from one of the adjoining rooms. So subtle at first, I wondered if I'd heard anything at all, but... No, there it was again.

I held my breath, listening. There were voices, for sure, but they didn't seem to be having a conversation. No words could be distinguished.

Shoes in hand, I tiptoed towards the sound. It was coming from a room that was hardly extravagant, just containing a few sofas and a lonely ornament cabinet. But the door was closed and concealed those curious sounds.

Tentatively, I pressed my ear against the wood.

The intense moans of a couple wrought with ecstasy assaulted my eardrums. I recoiled, my cheeks burning.

Their moans swiftly grew loud and laboured... And then nothing.

Muffled movements from inside. Footsteps.

Blood rushed. I darted into a nearby open room, hugging my shoes close. Cautiously, I peeked around the corner.

The door clicked open and Mason's footsteps echoed around the empty Dome Room. Throwing his dinner jacket over his shoulder, he made his way up the marble staircase and out of sight.

A few moments later, the loud clinks of red heels as Tia appeared. She was smoothing down her dress, her hair tangled and matted. Soon enough, she too had disappeared, the sound of her shoes diminishing beneath silence.

Did anyone else know that Tia was sleeping with the Destroyer of the Old World? But then again, how could they not? There were thirty-*ish* Slaves in that establishment and gossip was a ripe apple, passed from one Slave to another.

Hallie's bulging belly flashed across my retina, and I wondered quite horribly if Mason was gradually working his way through his stock of beautiful Slaves. The thought was quite nauseating, but one I could not shift.

The first strained flutters of panic. I rushed Downstairs with the hopes of finding Anya. If anyone should know what went on behind closed doors, surely it was her?

But Anya's bed was as cold as mine, unused and unloved.

Where was she?

A rather unpleasant sight of Anya and Mason infringed upon my mind. I pushed it away just as quickly, determined not to dwell on my own sordid assumptions.

Moonsilver's green binding winked at me, still hidden beneath my bed. Is that why Mason gave me the book? To gain his trust, to coerce *me* on to that sofa?

The mere thought was horrific.

Sighing, I flicked through the pages. Unknown words mocked my gaping holes in the English language. I thought to the Pretender's petty reading request, or Mason's amused little smirk as I demonstrated my lacklustre reading skills. Such Aristocratic ridicule was just so goddamn predictable. Perhaps it wouldn't hurt to brush up my literacy skills. At least then they'd have one less thing to mock me with.

Yet, visions of Tia walking out of that room, her hair matted and her dress creased, kept encroaching. I was afraid that reading that book, that by succumbing to Mason's reading request, suddenly meant I was free game. That I was sport, jumping from one room to another while Mason skulked the darkened corridors, a wineglass poised in his hand and a salacious grin upon his lips.

No, it had to remain a secret. No one could know, not even Anya, because even she had suggested I keep it hidden, to fling it under the bed and forget about it. Was that why? Did she envisage my feet squeezing into Tia's shoes?

Yet, I was stubborn and determined. There had to be a way.

A sweet little lightbulb popped.

Smiling, I tiptoed my way to the showers, saw they were empty and then speedily showered. Once clean and dressed, I grabbed the blanket from the bed and silently ran back Upstairs.

By some gigantic stroke of luck, the Reading Room was not as dark as I anticipated. Moonlight poured in through the window, illuminating that cushioned windowsill. It beckoned me closer.

I obliged completely, wrapping the blanket around my shoulders. Slaves' nightclothes, consisting of grey t-shirts and cotton trousers, were comfortable but not warm, so I enveloped myself within the blanket and thanked Odin it was summer.

The piano loomed in my peripheral vision, almost daring me to touch it. For a few moments, I simply stared, casting my lying eyes across its smooth surface. The music inside my head egged me on, begging me to caress each key, to shiver at each note...

But yet, as I sat on that windowsill, I resisted. Mason's warning still rattled inside my head, flicking around each persistent note. The piano grew more frustrated, almost *desperate*. I pushed down the impossible music, so I could focus on the matter at hand.

The book smelled of old paper and damp as I peeled the pages apart. I studied the small text, grimacing at each word. Half made sense, half didn't.

As I aimlessly flicked through all five-hundred pages, I realised that I didn't have to *understand* the words, I simply had to say them. My tongue needed to practise them, caress them, to work with my eyes so that when any Aristocrat fancied a taunt, I could recite something as intricate as that spidery text with little more than a squint.

I listened suspiciously to my surroundings. Silence sang back.

I whispered a few words to the room. They reverberated softly around the space, but did not cause anything to stir.

Smiling, I continued to whisper the book. Some words were harder than others, knotting my tongue. Still, I persisted, saying them again and again until their clarity was clear.

I continued to read until the dawn birds chirped their morning song, at which point I closed the book over my hand, and watched the sunrise bleed across the horizon.

13

There was a murmur of activity well before the clock chimed 5am. Groaning, I took one last, longing look at the sunrise, and then tiptoed my way Downstairs.

Anya was still not there.

My forehead lined with concern. Unwillingly, I considered all possibilities for Anya's disappearance and more disturbing scenes flashed back in unison. What if she was in trouble? Should I wake Bentley? Where *was* Bentley?

My panic grew, squeezing my lungs tight. Then Anya reappeared. Her hair was large, her eyes tired, and she still wore the black dress. The panic fell to my blistered feet, making room for the frustrated glare I was sure to spit as she walked in.

"Where the Hel have you been?" I snapped.

"What's it to you?" Her tone was tepid.

"Sorry." I sighed, wiping away that glare. "I was just afraid something bad had happened to you."

Anya's entire posture shifted, lightened. Smiling, she hugged me tight within those skinny arms, her seemingly carefree attitude wiping away the sludge of concern in my stomach.

"I'm fine," she said, confidently, before heading to the shower.

BREAKFAST in the Palace was a rather casual affair. There was a breakfast buffet set up at the side of the room, full to the brim with edible delights: bacon, eggs, smoked meats and fish, cheeses, fruit and breads and honeys and jams... My gurgling stomach kept leering at it.

Standing around the edges of the Dining Room, we remained motionless with freshly brewed coffee, tea, juice and an artisan pastry tray, and waited for the Aristocrats to rouse.

Aside from ogling the buffet, I noticed a chair had already been set up for Hallie.

"Thank you for last night," she said. "I don't know what would have happened if you hadn't spoken up like that."

I shrugged, for I was unaccustomed to thanks and it made me uncomfortable.

Finally, the first Aristocrat awoke.

"Good morning, ladies," Mason said, marching into the room with a pile of letters beneath his arm. We chimed a reply, then set to work with pouring breakfast necessities.

Mason remained quiet as he casually opened letter after letter, periodically sipping on his morning coffee. He looked so... *Normal.*

When I was a child, I expected Mason to be a terrifying beast of a man, constantly covered in blood. Little did I know, but he was also an Aristocrat, acting with as much esteem and civility as such a title promised.

But then, I'd seen his cruelty first-hand. His Masonians butchered my Tribe, he killed Campbell. Sometimes, monsters didn't look like monsters.

I tilted my head, scrutinising the bulging muscles beneath his white shirt, and wondered, quite horrifically, if Tia had a choice in their night-time exploits.

But as I watched Tia refill his glass with juice, I saw how relaxed she was. Indeed, how...*awed* she was of him. No, that was not a woman serving her rapist. That was a woman serving her lover.

As the morning wore on, more Aristocrats joined the table. All of them had a hangover of some severity, and it was rather amusing.

"Coffee, Sir?" I enjoyed watching Ivan Ulster convulse as the smell of caffeine hit his nauseated state.

"Fuck off," he grumbled beneath his breath. I wandered back to Anya's side, unable to hide a smirk.

All in all, breakfast seemed to go by rather smoothly.

"Excuse me, Sir." Captain Tallis was suddenly standing at the entrance of that Dining Room, his ginger hair and scarred skin flashing memories of Campbell's sacrifice, of my enslavement. That traitorous Herdinese accent spilled my senses with a broiling rage.

Visions of Campbell being led away in chains, the desperation in his voice – *his eyes* – as the last trickles of hope washed away in the grey Fjordland rain...

Breathe in... One... Two... Three...

An audible exhale. Anya's bright blue eyes slid towards me.

"Maya, what is it?" she whispered.

Anger twisted my stomach, infecting each strand of muscle. Soft nails punctured my palms and I tried dreadfully, *desperately*, to regain some control.

"What is it, Captain?" Mason called down the table.

"The Trader is here. He claims to have some vital new information about the Free People's Rebellion."

That fucking Rebellion was the reason I was enslaved.

Exhale... One... Two... Three...

I clenched the coffee pot hard. Sharp heat did little to stave the growing cloud of red.

"What a surprise." The ruffle of paperwork as Mason flicked through his letters. "Very well, send him in."

Tallis called somewhere unseen, reappearing with a man whose familiar voice contained so much immaturity, my eyes popped wide open.

"Mmm, something smells good." Joe Matheson produced a wide smile, rubbing his hands together like some excited little schoolboy. "Don't suppose there's any spare going for a hungry Trader, eh?'

The coffee pot slipped from my fingers. It crashed to the floor, spilling the hot liquid.

Joe met my confounded, *anguished* gaze, and his smile plummeted.

"Shit…" he breathed.

Tallis groaned, cursed loudly in Herdinese, and marched forward.

"Keep calm everyone, I'll deal with this." The metallic *swoosh* of his sword being unsheathed.

"No, wait!" Joe shouted, holding both hands in hopeless pleading. "Don't hurt her! Let me explain…"

His words fell silent, crushed beneath the realisation that kept hitting me again and again, like some thunderous waterfall.

I was unable to move, unable to speak, utterly unable to pull my eyes away. Joe became a blur, a disjointed truth, and although I knew he was pleading with Captain Tallis, I was unable to accept that he was there, in that Dining Room, selling information to our mutual enemy.

He was once the Trader I called *friend*. Not anymore. Now, he was the traitor who sold Campbell's name to Mason.

Everything shook. Tremendous, horrifying shakes as my eyes filled with tears of acid. I was numb, dead of everything except that pure, uncontrollable *hatred*…

Anya cradled my head, forcing our eyes to meet. "Maya, look at me!"

I could not move, my eyes staring blankly ahead, to the blurred image of Joe holding Tallis back with two outstretched arms. Tears streamed down my face as my thumping heart physically ached.

"Maya, please honey, you have to look at me…"

Somewhere in the sea of seething red, my eyes slid to Anya.

"That's it," she whispered. "Come back to us…"

Sensation slammed like a speeding train. I surrendered to my panic attack and fell to the floor with a great thud.

"Please, Captain Tallis!" Joe shouted, somewhere ahead of me. "Look at her, she's no danger!"

"No danger? Do you have *any* idea what this little bitch is capable of?"

"Just give me five minutes, *five* minutes to explain myself to her. I can calm her down!"

"Best of luck with that," Ivan said, with an evident smirk. "She looks like she wants to rip your throat out."

And I did. Gripping Anya's supporting arms, I threw my seething glare to

Joe. His colour dropped to his new, expensive shoes.

Exhaustion rose, and as the simple strain of my emotions took their toll, my body surrendered to the defeat. My breaths slowed; the tremors lessened. The fight or flight reflexes had been subdued, thrown to the back of the room until the next pot of anger was placed upon the stove.

"Mr Matheson." The chair screeched as Mason stood to his feet. "Your presence has caused quite the stir. I am rather annoyed."

Joe licked his dry lips. "Please, Sir, I take full responsibility for her outburst."

Mason huffed as he marched across the floor. Gripping my upper arm with a crushing hand, he hoisted me to my feet and dragged me across the room.

"Matheson, with me – *now!*" If his booming voice wasn't enough, the intensity of that glower had Joe Matheson scuttling in no time at all. Tallis lingered close behind, his sword now sheathed, but a hand hovering dangerously close.

Mason found the nearest open room and threw me onto a patterned rug.

"Get up," he spat. I obliged, not because I was afraid of Mason's temper, but because I was simply too tired to argue with it.

I perched onto the nearest seat: a plush armchair that would have been comfortable any other day.

Joe scurried inside and Mason slammed the door so hard the chandelier hummed.

"Well, what a marvellous display!" he snarled; first to Joe, then to me. "Tell me, Miss Doe, do you remember our little chat about humiliation, hm?"

"Lord Mason, please understand," Joe said, his voice trembling as those defensive palms reappeared. "This is my fault, entirely."

"Oh, I do not doubt that at all." Mason glared. "But I don't really care about accountability, Mr Matheson. I care about manners, about civility, and you barging into my home, unannounced and with a great Herdinese insult floating above your head has not put me in the best mood!"

"Sir..." My voice was small, my accent so loud and prominent. Their attention flocked to it, like bees to honey. "Please, whatever you do to me – to *us* – please, just let him explain... I *need* him to explain..."

Mason thought long and hard about this. I could feel his judgment weigh down upon me, then flick to Joe Matheson, who was visibly sweating.

"Alright, Miss Doe," he said. On first impressions, he seemed calm, but then he roughly grabbed Joe by his collar and beat hot breath against his forehead. "Let's hope you have a good excuse, Mr Matheson."

Mason threw him to the floor, then settled against the wall, watching us.

Joe crawled closer and put two clammy hands upon my knees, trying to catch my eye.

"Maya? Maya, look at me..."

Simply because I was too exhausted to care, I did.

"I'm sorry," he said, wearily. "You have to believe me, I am so, so sorry."

"Why?" My throat was dry, my voice hoarse.

Joe sighed, his eyes – once bright and full of mirth – now appeared so dull and lifeless they matched the colour of the green-grey clouds outside.

"I was a mule for the Mulch Gang," he said. "I tried to smuggle goods into the Fjordlands, but I was caught by Masonians. The only way I could save my skin was by telling them I knew where to find Campbell Anders."

"But we were innocent," I said, my voice rising. "We didn't know anything about the Rebellion!'

"Campbell has always been a wanted man, ever since Gainstorn he's been –"

"But he was punished for that!" I switched my angering stare to Mason. "You already punished him for that!"

The hostility behind Mason's eyes forced my attention to Joe.

"You have to believe me, it was the only way." His throat convulsed with a laboured swallow, and I knew he was holding back sobs. "When I met you, that night at Drunks' Redoubt, I told you to go to Waterman's Quarry. I knew the Masonians would be waiting for you there."

Joe cradled my head within his hands and forced a small, despairing smile. "But I didn't tell them about you. Yes, I sold Campbell's name, but you are innocent of all that happened at Gainstorn... Girl, you weren't part of the deal.

"So I told the innkeeper to get you the hell out, before the Masonians arrived." His voice broke, tears spilling. "You're not supposed to be here, girl – *why are you here?*"

I was there because I was stubborn. I didn't shoot those four rabbits, like I was supposed to. I watched my last sunset as a free woman and returned to Waterman's Quarry hours earlier than I should have. Then I met Alden. Then I started to fight.

"I returned early," I said, almost dazed. "I was captured. Campbell made a deal with Mason to have me enslaved in return for all he knew about Mikael Ashworth. Now he's dead and I'm here and it's all your fault..."

Joe squeezed his eyes closed, a singular tear falling.

"Please..." he said. "Please try to understand why I did what I did."

Reaching my tether, I angrily shook his hands off.

"Do you have any idea what you've done to me, Joe? The danger you've put me in?" Could Joe Matheson see the fear behind my contact lenses? Maybe.

"Get away from me." I grimaced at the sight of him.

"Maya, *please*..."

I examined the features I once found handsome, and felt nothing but disgust. "You have important information to relay, Mr Matheson," I bitterly spat out. "You shouldn't keep the Master waiting."

Swallowing the rest of his tears, Joe stood shakily to his feet. Mason opened the door in a silent order. A sulking Joe obliged, plodding to the door with each foot weighted by past choices.

"I'm not done with you, Mr Matheson," Mason snarled as he passed. "Wait for me in my Office."

"Sir," Joe whispered, nodding.

The door slammed shut. Then, I was left alone with Mason. His temper was palpable, spreading through his skin like pure, humid heat.

With a shaky breath, I wiped my cheeks clean and stood to my feet. Just too tired to feel the hate that still lingered, I refused to spend another second in Mason's presence.

"I need to get back to work," I said.

Only then did Mason push himself from the wall, skulking closer.

"Anger is a funny thing," he said, those eyes fluorescing. "It's powerful, maddening. I understand that, Miss Doe. I understand that entirely."

Mason gripped my arm.

"But mark my words, should you ever exhibit such lack of control again –

at Matheson, me, or even a fucking pigeon – I might feel the need to teach you a thing or two about *real* anger. Do you understand me, Miss Doe?"

"Yessir," I breathed, unable to look at him.

"Wonderful."

And then, finally, he released me.

* * *

CLEANING my mess proved to be an arduous task. It continued well after the breakfast buffet had been cleared.

Nevertheless, I was dutiful and precise. The floor was polished to a high shine when the lunch cart lazily rolled into the Dining Room.

For the rest of the day, I was silent and dignified. Dinner was hard, but I forced my head high as I poured Mason's wine, kept my gaze glued ahead as those diamond eyes kept flicking in my direction.

Only when the lights went out, when Anya was sleeping soundly, did I finally crumble. For hours, I silently cried.

Joe Matheson. That wretched, traitorous *bastard!*

I wanted to tell Campbell. I wanted to scream our betrayal to the stars above, to howl the name of the man responsible for *everything.*

For the next week, I remained in a numb haze. Devoid of feeling.

I imagined the Snowlands that were once my home, and turned my skin into the same icy wilderness. An exterior of pure numbness, not easily thawed.

By doing that – by cutting myself off from all emotion – I was able to cope. If I opened up to feeling, if I scratched away that top layer of ice, then the realisation of my enslavement – the *truth* of why I was in it – would destroy me completely.

My only company was the music inside my head. It bounced softly against my brain, caressing the pain that Joe's truth had inflicted. I ached to play the piano, to rid myself of that pain and to be solely, unconditionally absorbed in each of those musical notes.

But that was not possible. Mason himself had banned me from ever touching it again. I did not want to test him.

Escape loomed, louder and more forceful than ever. The urge to race across those dewy grounds, to clamber up those tallest trees, was so powerful, so consuming. I needed to inhale the frosty air, for those wispy snowflakes to tickle my nasal hairs... Gods, if anything, I just needed to be outside...

But, I couldn't. I was still stuck there, trapped within the walls of the Palace, waiting – seemingly endlessly – for the moment when I *could* run, when I could justify a dance with death and race towards those mountains. The moment itself remained elusive, and I'd be damned if I broke my promise to Campbell in a fleeting drive of reckless emotion.

So, in an effort to occupy myself, I remained in that small kitchen, doing as I was told, washing dishes and cutting vegetables.

That was my life.

If I ever saw Joe Matheson again, I would kill him.

14

It was a peaceful night. The Palace was still.

The moon disappeared behind thick clouds that brought torrents of rain, smothering the world in shadow. Rain slammed against the window, thousands of tiny patters dulling the music inside my head. Anya snored softly above me, oblivious to the outside world.

I could not sleep. My eyes were wide open. Just staring ahead, listening to the rainstorm outside.

So preoccupied with my empty thoughts, I barely heard it.

A whimper. Heavy breaths floating in the air.

I perched onto my elbows, listening intently. It sounded like a pained gasp, echoing down the corridor.

I crept out of bed. It creaked ominously, but Anya remained unstirred. After fitting my contact lenses, I cautiously opened the door and peeked my altered gaze in both directions.

Empty.

Must be my imagination, I thought.

Anguished cries bounced down the corridor. I recognised them immediately.

"Hallie..." I whispered.

I ran down the corridor, passing one, then two doors before I reached the room she shared with Tia. I knocked frantically on the door as the cries grew louder.

"Hallie, open the door!" The only response was more laboured gasps. "Tia, are you in there, open the door!"

Still nothing. Another pained breath followed by a small, almost imperceptible, *"Help me!"*

I bashed my shoulder against the wooden door. It buckled but did not break. Again, I bashed it, ignoring the pain that zapped up my arm, that shattered my icy exterior.

The door buckled just as another contraction hit her. Hallie groaned and grimaced, her face bright red and her hair licked with sweat. She was lying with her legs splayed on a pile of blankets, soaked with amniotic fluid and blood.

I swore loudly in my native tongue and dropped to my knees before her.

"Hallie, how far apart are they?"

"I-I dunno..." she breathed. "But... B-But something's not right..."

Not caring for decency or even goddamned permission, I lifted her night dress and took a look for myself just as a horrified Anya burst through the door.

Luna appeared then, the kitchen staff tagging along behind. All of them gasped, some of them ran away, and the remainder just stood stoic in the corner of the room.

"Luna, we need towels and water," I declared. "Anya, get that Doctor."

"Why, what is it? What's wrong?" Hallie's desperation was evident. I squeezed her sweaty hand.

"The baby's in the wrong position," I said, calmly. "But don't worry, I'm going to help you through this."

I chanced a concerned look at Anya. She understood the warning behind my eyes and leapt from the room like a pronghorn.

"Right," I said. "I need you to resist the urge to push, okay?"

She nodded her head, beads of sweat trickling down her temple.

Luna rushed in with towels under one arm and a bucket of water in the other, then ushered out the bystanders. The bruised door closed with an almighty slam and the room grew stuffy and hot, almost suffocating.

Time was not on our side. Gently, I placed both hands upon Hallie's round belly and tried to rearrange the baby inside of her. Luna's eyes bulged as she saw the baby shift and turn beneath the skin.

"Don't push, Hallie!" I ordered as she arched her back, screaming.

A little more... Just a little more...

The baby was shifted, Hallie's body more than ready.

"Hallie, *push!*"

She squeezed her eyes shut and pushed her little heart out. The baby's head was crowning.

"I can see it! Come on, Hallie, push!"

Through all the sweat and the tears, a small baby's cries filled the room. Hallie collapsed, panting, as I cradled the new life she had created: a tiny being, no bigger than a loaf of bread.

Something warm exploded within my chest: a deep, powerful sense of longing that I couldn't quite explain.

The music inside my head loudened, ever so slightly.

Smiling, I said a small welcome in my native tongue and placed him delicately on his mother. Hallie gasped out a laugh, her eyes welling with pure joy. A small smile of my own as I contemplated his uncanny resemblance to Ivan Ulster.

"Huh, who would have thunk," I whispered.

* * *

ONCE CHECKED BY DOCTOR GRANT, Hallie and her baby were left to rest and recover.

Unable to sleep, the rest of us had congregated in the little kitchen. Sitting around the table, Anya, Luna and I quietly sipped our tea. Tia had also reappeared, and was forced to join us, seeing as her room was now somewhat occupied.

"He's just so beautiful," Anya remarked. Luna and I hummed in agreement.

"He is," I said, with an incredulous shake of my head. That prompted a few raised eyebrows. "I just didn't realise Ivan Ulster was the father until his kid popped out looking like a mirror image."

"Who did you think the father was?"

"Mason."

That granted me a few surprised chuckles.

"Why on earth did you think that?" Tia asked with a cynical smirk.

I shrugged. "Well, y'know... Seeing as he shags an awful lot of people around here, I just automatically assumed."

Tia frowned at me, her blue eyes full of suspicion, before she shook herself out of her stupor. "Yeah, Mason's a lecherous dog."

I almost choked on my tea.

"Well he is." She shrugged two bony shoulders. "Ain't no denying it."

"You can see why I thought Hallie's baby was his then," I said, wiping split tea from my chin.

"I suppose. Bit of a null point though, seeing as Mason can't have children."

"What? Why?"

"It's not exactly a subject one brings up with him, Maya." Tia rolled her eyes.

Deflated, I slouched in the chair as deep grooves formed on my forehead. Then again, Mason's infertility was probably a good thing. If what Tia said about his promiscuity was true, the New World would have been overrun with his progeny.

Still, it would be wonderful to have a baby Downstairs, keeping us company while we prepped vegetables, cooing as he tried to catch the lonely bubbles floating up from the sink.

Maybe that was why Mason allowed Hallie to keep her son. To remind us that, despite everything, the world needed a little coo every now and then.

Or maybe Mason just wanted another Slave. A free one, this time.

"Maya," Luna said, smiling, as the first light of dawn glimmered outside. "Sorry, but I have to ask: how did you know what to do back there?"

"Oh." I giggled, delicately placing the cup on the table. "I helped my Pa deliver reindeer calves when I was little, and how different are people, really?"

Sitting round that little wooden table, we all laughed out loud as the dawn birds began to sing.

* * *

The End of Everything

As one might have expected, Hallie was out of action for a few days following childbirth. Mealtimes were strange without her presence.

I was envious of her, spending all of her time Downstairs with her son. I'd been craving a cuddle with him.

Unfortunately, on that particular morning, the closest thing I had to Hallie's baby was the presence of his papa, sitting a little further down the table from Mason.

Ivan Ulster had been staying at the Palace for a few days now. Apparently, it was due to some important new information regarding the Free People. Whether such information was sold by Joe Matheson was unknown, but the most shocking aspect of his visit was that his own son had been born less than a week ago, and he hadn't even seen him. What made it worse was his complete lack of interest: he hadn't even bothered to ask about the baby's health.

All Aristocrats were arseholes, but that seemed a new low, even for them.

A sharp nudge brought my attention back to that dining table, and that Mason had run out of coffee. Sighing, I clanked my way forwards with the full pot at the ready.

"And what of our contacts in the Snow Territory?" Mason asked, his deep voice reverberating around the room.

"There are mixed reports," Ivan replied, spreading a thin layer of butter on his toast. "The word is that Ursa's Leap is where the majority of the meetings are held."

Ursa's Leap. An interesting little town. The remains of some gigantic bear were discovered at the base of enormous overlooking cliffs.

Mason hummed to himself. "What are these reports based on?"

"Increased sightings of known Rebels."

My attention piqued. *Rebels near Ursa's Leap, huh?* I'd have to pay that quaint little town a visit when I eventually escaped that luxurious dungeon.

"Including Ashworth?" Mason asked.

"No, there's no sign of him." Ivan reached for a small plate of red jam. "Though I hear the local people have been aiding him."

One could practically see Mason's ears perk up. As did my own.

Local people? Were they talking about Herders? This was fortunate, for Herders were less likely to kill one of their own, should Ashworth decide the

End of Everything was just an extra hindrance to their cause. Couldn't say I blamed him either. What use was liberating the New World when I'd somehow destroy everything anyway?

I sighed my silent frustration to the Dining Room.

"Is that so?" Mason took a delicate sip of hot coffee. "How interesting."

A small knock at the door.

"Ah, come in Miss Osbourne," Mason said, smiling.

Tentatively, if not a little shyly, she made her way with both hands clasped before her. She gave a polite nod to Ivan, simply out of courtesy, then fixed her attention to Mason.

"So," he said, returning the cup to the saucer with a delicate little *chink*. "Congratulations on the birth of your son, Miss Osbourne."

"Thank you, Sir." She easily beamed, her entire face lifting despite the puffiness around her eyes.

"I trust you are fully recovered?"

"From childbirth? Yessir, I'm feeling much better."

"Excellent!" Mason produced a calculating smile. A sudden chill descended upon the room, shooting icicles down my spine. I chanced a sideways glance to Anya, then to Luna and Tia opposite, and met our mutual, shared concern. All apart from Hallie, that is, whose innocent glee shadowed her outwardly senses.

"In that case, Miss Osbourne," Mason said. "The time has come to discuss the future."

"Sir?" The chill worked its scheming, sadistic way into Hallie's bones, chipping at her smile one lingering second at a time.

"If you are capable of returning to your duties, then I see no reason why your son should stay in this establishment."

The smile vanished, replaced with startling panic. She bounced from one foot to the other, unable to stay still for long.

"But... Sir, I'm... I'm confused." A swift, panicked smile. "You'd... You promised me I'd be able to keep him, here at the Palace..."

"Oh, Hallie." Mason smiled. "I lied."

A tear came then. Small and singular, it flowed slowly down Hallie's pale cheek. We all felt the punch in Hallie's gut. All of us had been completely sucked in by Mason's false promise, his cruel jibe at *hope*. That we might see

Hallie's baby grow into the beautiful child he would become. Mason enjoyed ripping that hope away from us, along with Hallie's baby.

"Please, Sir," Hallie said, trembling. "I-I'm more than capable of looking after him and – "

"It really isn't open for discussion." Slowly, he took another sip of coffee. "In fact, the question you should be asking yourself is where I intend to send your son, once he is removed from your tender care."

Hallie's panic grew, her eyes wide and fearful.

"No, not there... Please Sir, I am *begging* you, I'm – "

"The Orphanage is a fine institution, Miss Osbourne. After all, the children are fully cared for until they're sold. That's certainly more than I can say for other establishments in Maelstrom."

Slavery. This pure, innocent, beautiful baby boy was being sold into instant Slavery. I could see the fear swell inside Hallie, imagining all the different scenarios her son's future could entail. It pained me to see more parts of her die, as each new thought became more horrific than the last.

"Please Sir... Anything but that..." She squeezed her eyes shut, desperate to shut herself from that room, that conversation, that *future*... A sharp inhale, the cries close to bursting. She turned to Ivan.

"Ivan, *please!*"

Ivan simply bowed his head, stirring milk into his tea.

Tears broke the barriers of Hallie's eyes and streamed down her face. She gasped short, high breaths before slapping those tears away, standing tall with some newfound resolve.

"Then send me too," she said, her head held high. "If you're sending him away, then please send me with him."

Mason just chuckled to himself, shaking his head from side to side.

"Oh, why would I do that? You've proven yourself to be a valuable asset over these past few years, and obedience like yours is difficult to come by."

A dark shadow descended over Mason's features, that handsome smile dissolving. "Besides, why would I deny Ivan the pleasure of you? Who knows, maybe in a few years we'll be having this conversation again. Another son maybe? Or a daughter perhaps? Maybe Ivan should just learn to put a fucking sock on it."

Ivan closed his eyes, defeated, his jaw clenched shut.

"Regardless," Mason continued, his tone lightening, "I have organised transport to take your son to the Orphanage tomorrow morn. I expect to see you in this Dining Room that evening, is that clear?"

Trembling, Hallie supported herself against the back of Ivan's chair. It creaked under her weight, causing Ivan's head to twitch, ever so slightly.

"Off you go, Miss Osbourne," Mason crooned, the ceramic cup suspended in his hand. "You wouldn't want to neglect your son now, would you?"

Hallie inhaled all the air her lungs could manage. Holding herself upright, she forced a stagnant smile to Mason and excused herself from the room. The doors clanked closed, then her despair echoed across the marble.

I bowed my head, fighting back tears. Beside me, Anya was visibly shaking.

"Sir," Tia said, carefully, her voice nearly breaking. Obviously irked, Mason lowered the newspaper he had just started reading and openly glared at her. "With the greatest respect, the four of us are more than capable to both jointly care for the baby, *and* pick up any lost work from Hallie."

A brief pause, then Mason summoned her closer with a smooth curl of his finger.

"Tia," he said. "If you ever speak of Miss Osbourne's son again, I will *break* you – do you understand?"

Tia could do nothing but nod glumly as she returned to her station.

Everyone remained silent as Mason spent the rest of his breakfast devouring the morning news.

* * *

ANYA SLAMMED her bony shoulder to the door of Hallie's bedroom. The bruised wood swung open, revealing an empty room with nothing but a pool of vomit steaming on the floor.

"They're not here..." Anya whimpered, slapping a solitary tear from her face.

I threw my trembling fingers through my hair. Gods, how could I even understand what she was going through? How could I dare look at Hallie and say everything would be alright? Because it wasn't alright. It was far from it.

"Over here," Luna said quietly, dejectedly. She was standing at the entrance to the kitchen, her hair blown back by a cool breeze.

Cautiously, we came to her side.

Hallie held her son against her shoulder, bouncing him up and down, softly humming in his tiny ear. She alternated stares between her son's button nose and the outside world, blowing in through the window. A small herd of deer resisted the weather, grazing quite peacefully on the grounds ahead. Smiling, she pointed to them.

"Look at them... Can you see the deer, hmm?"

"Hallie?" Luna asked, braving a few steps forward.

Hallie briefly met our gazes, allowing a short glimpse of her red, swollen eyes before turning her attention to the free animals outside. Touching her head against her son's, she resumed her humming.

I wanted to run to her – to comfort her. But the more I thought about it, considered what I would say, the more I understood that I... Well, I just didn't know what to do. So, I remained motionless, like a statue, all my inner courage faltering beneath the shadow of those grey clouds.

"Hallie," Anya said, crying. "Please, just... Say something..."

Hallie gave her son a huge, audible kiss. She graced us with a maddening smile. "Aaron, that's a good name, right?"

She turned to her son, drooling quite contentedly upon her shoulder.

"That will be your name: Aaron Osbourne."

15

Mason was truly a monster.

To know the torment, the devastation he was inflicting on poor Hallie... To understand that he was so readily subjecting an innocent life – a *baby* – to a whirlwind of suffering... And he didn't even care.

It was almost too much to stomach.

It was sickening, watching that *bastard* of a man eat his dinner so calmly, with such lack of emotion. To empty his wineglass with each carefree sip, every selfish swallow.

No guilt. No remorse. Just a pure, carnal desire to watch everyone suffer.

At least Ivan was having difficulty stomaching his dinner that night.

Later still, when the Palace was either asleep or entwined with passion, I crept to my little windowsill in the Reading Room. The blanket wrapped around my shoulders, trying in vain to disperse the chill. Despite my best efforts, I could see Hallie's desolate expression; the innocent glee that morphed into something quite unrecognisable. I recalled how happy we were when I brought little Aaron into this world, and then chastised myself on a memory that had now become so tainted.

I squeezed my eyes shut, ignoring the burn from the contacts. Then I whispered words from the book gifted by the man I despised.

The End of Everything

* * *

SHOUTS.

Gunshots.

I startled awake. *Moonsilver* fell from my lap, clattered to the wood.

Thin strips of light bordered the door to the Reading Room: a frame that concealed the thunder of countless feet. Angered shouts from Masonians, terrified shrieks from men, women...

I jumped to my bare feet. The blanket slipped from my shoulders. With shallow breaths, I frantically searched the room. *Hide, girl,* I desperately thought. *Hide!*

The door to the Reading Room burst open. Tallis marched inside, his face twisted with murderous intent.

"*Tallis, wait!*" My Herdinese beg merely infuriated him more. He spat something indiscernible, wrapped his spidery fingers in my hair, and dragged me shrieking from the room.

Dazzling light bounced off every bit of marble, each gem, hitting my retina with painful stabs. I wrestled with Tallis's grip, my scalp almost peeling with the pressure. My feet slipped and slid on the polished floor and he hurled me into an adjoining room.

I landed with a slam.

Two hands grasped my shoulders and hoisted me upright. Blood rushed to my head, rendering my vision black and dizzy.

"Maya, come on!" Anya shouted, pulling me to the side of the room.

As my vision cleared, other Slaves lined up against the walls. Masonians were in the centre, surrounding the luxurious upholstery with their swords unsheathed.

"What's going on?" I asked.

Clutching my arm with both hands, Anya's breaths quickened. "It's Hallie, she's gone!"

"*What?* And the baby?"

"She's taken him too. She caused a diversion in the other side of the Palace a-and made a run for it!"

My eyes darted around the room. I saw Bentley, the footmen, and most of the kitchen staff. A shaking Luna was directly opposite, her head bowed, her eyes squeezed tightly shut. The cleaning staff were just being filed in, the last in a long line of terrified, hysterical people who had been roused from their slumber because of a mother's desperate gamble to save her child.

A loud buzz of fearful chatter, until Mason's thunderous footsteps echoed around the space. He arrived gripping Tia by her wrist, her long limbs on show and her modesty only concealed by a short silk nightdress.

Shirtless, armed, and excessively angry, Mason threw a squealing Tia into the room like she was some useless piece of cloth. She hit the floor with a loud thud, only to be hoisted up by Tallis and thrown next to Anya and me.

"It's late, so I'll get right to the point." Mason spat the words with such ferocity the very air trembled. "One of you knows where Hallie Osbourne is. I suggest you step up and save us all from a *very* long night!"

A silver revolver was in his hand, gripped tight. Scars shone brightly on his knuckles as he paced around the room, his abdominal muscles taut, his chest pulsing with each angered breath...

"What about you?" He pointed the gun to one of the kitchen Slaves, a woman in her thirties who broke down in tears. "No? Fine then, how about you?"

The gun moved on, scanning every one of us.

He made it to the footmen. One of them avoided his gaze.

"What about you, Mr Fuller?" Mason glared. "Do you know where Hallie Osbourne is?"

Guy Fuller mumbled a weak, inaudible reply.

Mason lifted the gun and shot him between the eyes.

"Wrong answer!" he barked.

The lifeless body of Guy Fuller slid down the wooden wall, leaving a trail of blood and grey brain matter.

His patience dangling by a fiery tread, Mason stormed to the centre of the room.

"We are going to be here for a *very* long time unless someone starts talking!"

As if Odin himself cowered beneath Mason's wrath, two Masonians appeared at the doorway. In the middle of them, motionless and reserved, was Hallie.

"*No!*" I squeaked, rushing forwards. Tia sharply pulled me back.

"Ah..." Mason said. The anger seeped out of him in three long exhales. "Hallie, we were just talking about you."

She shook herself free from Masonian hands, prepared to meet Mason with her head held high. Tucking the revolver in the waistband of his slacks, Mason approached her.

"Where's your son?" he asked, dangerously even.

"Mr Ulster found her, Sir," a Masonian replied. "He found her navigating a ditch and brought her to us. Mr Ulster is currently on route to the Orphanage with the child."

A small, irked smile tickled its way through Mason's lips, surrounded by nightly stubble.

"Be thankful Ivan is a better man that I am, Hallie," he said.

Hallie did not respond. She glared at Mason, her hate evident.

"Ah, no words? No pleading for your life?" Mason moved ever closer, his voice turning soft and delectable. "Come now, Hallie, let's not disappoint your son by simply giving up."

"I'm not giving up, Mason," she said, emotionless. "But I'm not begging you. Why should I? You don't deserve my begs."

Mason smiled; a horrible, evil smile that wiped all remaining colour from Hallie's dirtied face.

"Shame," he mumbled. Two hands rested on Hallie's shoulders and gently slipped off her stolen coat. It fell in a heap around her filthy feet. "I must say, I almost admire you for running. Out of all my maids, you're the one who has surprised me the most."

Mason's hands rose up, slinking their way up her shoulders, her neck. Hallie's ragged pants intensified as he squeezed her head between both hands. He tilted her face to meet his, and as she took her final breath, I remembered the one rule drilled into young'uns from our first breath...

Don't look Mason in the eye.

Hallie screamed as Mason stared into those hazel eyes. They remained locked, unable to pull their eyes away even as the blood trickled down her face, or as her screams – so ragged and grating – became nothing but dull echoes in the chandelier beads.

Hallie's life slipped away, and he *smiled*...

When she was lifeless and silent, Mason released her. She dropped to the floor with a hollow slam.

"Let Hallie Osbourne's insubordination be a reminder to you!" he shouted, circling the room with his diamond eyes bright and bloodshot. "You try to escape, you will *die*. You disobey me, you will *die*. Is anything about this arrangement decidedly unclear?"

There was a mixture of words and shaking heads.

"Good!" he barked. He ordered his men to return us Downstairs, and left the room.

We stepped over Hallie's corpse on our way out. Her bloodied eyes were still open, gazing into the abyss.

The bodies of Hallie Osbourne and Guy Fuller remained there until morning; a reminder to us all.

16

AUTUMN

The trees were changing. A chill extended its spidery fingers down the mountains, turning the once bright emerald leaves into little red and gold beacons of colour.

In the grounds, stags rutted with calamitous intensity. Their spectacular antlers pierced the frosty air, their warm breaths forming clouds of mist with each low grunt. The sharp clatter of ivory: two stags battling for dominance in the dim morning light.

I admired the sights before me, craved the feel of frost upon my skin, and wondered when the world would return to its wintry hibernation.

In the little kitchen, I dried the dishes Anya washed, and wondered what the world was doing in its other, epic Territories.

Had the Snowlands' lakes frozen, like lenses of clear glass? Had the blizzards returned in the northern Icelands, wrapping the trees with blankets of snow? I reminisced to the smell of pine needles in the Woodlands, the echoing creaks of glaciers as they fell lethargically down the Glasslands' mountains.

It was amazing, how the world could alter in such short a space of time. Even in the two months since Hallie's murder, the Fjordlands' seasons had shifted with vigorous intensity. It was almost as if the very air wanted to hibernate, to return to an icy slumber.

It was a feeling I knew rather well.

The Palace had returned to relative normalcy – or the closest approximation. The other Slaves seemed to bounce back rather well, all things considered. Such sights were hardly new to them. How many unjust deaths had Bentley witnessed, in his thirty years at the Palace? Too many, probably. Far too many.

Yet, such sights shocked me. Hallie was their friend, after all, yet they acted as if she'd just been moved to another establishment. They were subdued and quiet, sometimes offering the odd memory of Hallie, but otherwise forgetting she ever existed at all. Eventually, their behaviour became less of a shock, and simply became part of the daily routine.

From my station in the Dining Room, serving wine and coffee, I saw the scattering of visitors over those two months. Some were Aristocrats, others were contacts from other Territories. More often than not, it was Emilia Eynesbury.

The Pretender occasionally appeared for meals, but such a sight was rare. Usually, it was only when Mason was in an exceptionally good mood. They laughed and giggled, and generally conversed, but it was hardly what one might call riveting conversation.

A noticeable absence was Ivan Ulster.

This was curious, considering his high social standing. I daresay he was classed as Mason's *friend*, if Mason even had such things, and so his absence was a continual mystery. I wondered if Hallie was the catalyst for his sudden antisocial behaviour. After all, he had gifted her to Mason on a silver platter, and condemned his own son to Slavery. Surely, that must have tarnished the view of his own self-worth?

Maybe he was deep in meditation, reflecting on the terrible things he had done.

I imagined a future Aaron Osbourne, having grown into a strong and handsome young man, discovering the fate his mother endured, the acidic salt his father rubbed upon them both. He would seek revenge, storm into the Ulster Residence and shoot that meditating son-of-a-bitch directly between the eyes.

I believe they call such things *poetic justice*.

Alas, such things were too good to be true. Ivan Ulster was, according to Mason, simply away *on business*... Whatever that meant.

That afternoon, one frosty afternoon with the clouds low in the sky, we had plates to wash and more plates to polish. Mason was hosting a dinner party in a few days' time – the first for a while – and our lack of numbers made preparation difficult.

The Pretender's limitless requests also mocked our short numbers.

So, I aimlessly dried the plates handed to me by Anya, while Luna and Tia chopped vegetables. A simple life, indeed.

At least the idle chatter of the room dulled my inner, *impossible* piano. As the weeks progressed, so had the music. It was so persistent, impatient. Always there, fluttering inside my skull like a buzzing bee. Humming helped, for I would synchronise my voice with the music's beat, and that seemed to calm its insistence. That afternoon was no different, and my voice delicately traversed the space as we continued to chat.

All was rather tranquil until there was a resounding knock on the door.

Expecting Bentley or one of the kitchen staff, we were all unprepared when Mason walked in. He was in full uniform, including a full belt of weapons that my dread noticed instantly.

Tia and Luna stood to their feet, the chairs screeching behind them. Anya and I grabbed towels with such force our knuckles turned white.

"Afternoon," he said, scanning us all.

Anya mumbled a vague reply before asking, "What can we do for you, Sir?"

"Nothing at the moment, Miss Whittaker. I'd like to have a quiet word with Miss Doe."

A large bubble caught in my throat, rendering me silent and still.

Witnessing my ballooning agitation, he formed an annoying little smirk.

"Well then," he said. "Follow me."

* * *

CLIMBING those marble stairs in the Dome Room, it suddenly dawned on me that I had never seen the Palace's upper levels. Only then, trailing Mason through the labyrinth of marble and wooden corridors, did I truly understand just how *enormous* that place was. Doors were everywhere, equally spaced down the tributaries of corridors. What did those rooms hold? Beds? Baths? Bookcases?

The sway of Mason's blue coat came to a stop, directly before a large wooden door, intricately decorated with golden fibres.

Mason swiftly unlocked the door, and entered with me in tow.

"Take a seat."

He gestured to a leather chair that sat before a huge, mahogany desk. Easily encompassing a third of the room, the desk was certainly a beast. It was also entirely covered in paperwork; a complete, disorganised mess. For a man as particular as Mason, this surprised me.

Mason took residence between the arms of a goliath leather chair, on the other side of the desk. He took a moment to declutter some of the desk space, grouping various bits of paper together and looking surprised when the odd lost fountain pen reappeared. During this time, I cast my eyes across his office.

Incredibly large, bookcases lined most of the back walls. One of these bookcases housed a small mirrored hole, housing a few bottles of whiskey and some decorative glass tumblers. Behind me was a large window that overlooked the driveway below, bordered with thick curtains the same colour as a fancy claret I'd served the previous evening.

There, just at the side of the window, was a violin. Smooth, shiny and exquisitely made, the violin was poised atop a golden stand. It was obviously loved, revered.

No sheet music.

Mason suddenly sprung to his feet and poured a tumbler of whiskey from the little drinks' nook. Expecting him to enjoy the glass, I was stunned as he presented it to me.

Hesitantly, I took it. The rich smell of the liquor punctured my nostrils. I simply stared at the amber liquid, unsure of what to do.

"Drink it," Mason said. "I need you to be calm, but your mannerisms strongly suggest otherwise."

"Sir?"

"Quite frankly, Miss Doe, you look like you're about to shit yourself," Mason said, lowering himself to the chair. "So drink, settle your nerves."

What the Hel, I thought, and downed the contents in one large mouthful. I coughed as the alcohol burned my throat, unaccustomed to such things after months of sobriety. I sighed at the growing warmth in my belly, yet was unable to relax in his company.

"Thank you," I said. Fear and hate coalesced, fighting with each other, neither side willing to declare victory. So, I remained impartial to both emotions, and simply met Mason with my spine straight.

"Pleasure." Mason watched as I delicately placed the tumbler on his desk. "I feel obliged to inform you that you are in no trouble. I simply want to ask you a favour."

"A favour?"

"You see, a young Herder has come into my possession whom I believe holds critical information about the Free People, specifically Mikael Ashworth. The only obstacle is her dire lack of English. *Your* English, however, is exceptional." Mason graced me with a small, almost imperceptible smile. "Now, seeing as my Herdinese is a little rusty, I should be very grateful if you would translate for me."

"Oh," I said, a little startled. Of all the things I expected when I entered that office, this was not one of them. "Sir, forgive me, but why isn't Tallis translating?"

"Because, strangely enough, the young girl isn't particularly enthused with speaking to the man who butchered her family." Mason's sardonic look chilled the warmth in my stomach.

"Ah, yes, I see." I licked the haunt of whiskey from my scarred lips. Again, it would not bode well to ignore his simple requests. "Yeah, sure I'll translate."

"Excellent." Mason smiled, before fighting through the mound of paperwork to reveal an ornate telephone. "They'll be here shortly."

"They're ready now?" He was clearly prepared.

"They are downstairs as we speak," he said.

"Oh, okay... Out of interest, what if I declined?"

Phone in hand, there was a flash of amusement. "Saying *no* to me really isn't in your best interests though, is it Maya?"

"No," I conceded with a sigh. "It's not."

There was a brief phone conversation. In Mason's lack of interest, my eyes returned to that *beautiful* violin. I remembered the night I met Mason, all alone in a Theatre filled with nothing but the electric, delectable music. How could Mason have produced something so pure from such a small, delicate instrument? Somewhere in my head, the piano notes grew in intensity, willing me further into the violin's wooden shell...

"Admiring my possession?"

I startled, turning to see scrutinising diamond eyes.

"Sorry," I mumbled.

"Don't be." Mason smirked. "It's an exquisite instrument."

"It is," I said, honestly. "But, if I may, it's also... *Baffling.*"

"Baffling? Do explain."

"Well..." I licked my lips again. "When I saw first you in the Theatre, when I was still Ms Eynesbury's, you were playing the violin..."

"Yes...?" Mason hummed before me.

"But... It wasn't just that you were playing the violin... It was something *more* than that. Almost as if the music was controlling you, that you *were* the music...?" I shook my head incredulously. "I can't explain it."

Mason huffed out a sigh, standing to his impressive height and strolling around the desk, both hands inside his pockets.

"Tell me Maya, why are you so interested in that night? It was months ago, surely such things would be forgotten by now."

Both hands fumbled nervously in my lap. "The violin just jogged my memory."

"Ah, I see." For a moment I wondered, quite excitedly, if he would play the violin for me. To find it somewhere in that cold, sadistic heart of his and indulge me in just one moment of complete, musical bliss... Just so I could hear the music, just one more time...

Mason's hands rested on both my shoulders, gracing them with a delicate little squeeze. Everything tensed.

"Curiosity is a dangerous thing, Maya," he said. Two thumbs ran down the ridge of my shoulder blades, pressing firm.

"It was an honest question," I breathed.

"And I am reciprocating with an honest answer." His hot breath burned my ear as he leant in close, heating those seven gold rings. "My music is no concern of yours. I strongly suggest you push it from your mind."

My heartbeat pounded, pressed up at the base of my throat. But yet, despite my reservations, I remained conflicted. I was torn between my fear of Mason, and my utter longing to *understand* him. To understand the music. To understand *me*.

"Yessir," I eventually replied.

Mason removed a stray piece of chestnut hair and pushed it behind my ear.

"Good girl," he said. A sharp flick of those golden rings, then he stood to his full height. "You seem to be missing one."

"What?"

"The dent in your ear."

"Oh..." I fiddled with the damaged ear cartilage as Mason returned to his chair. "There used to be another one, but Verity Ulster pulled it out."

"Why?"

"She just felt like it. She originally wanted to cut my tongue out, so I'd say I got the better end of the deal."

Mason laughed softly to himself. "I daresay you might be right. Regarding your ear jewellery, I'm intrigued to see that there are seven, formally eight rings. I'm correct in deducing that's how many people you've killed?"

"In self-defence, yes."

Mason arched an eyebrow, almost admired. "It's rather refreshing to see someone who can take care of herself."

"I only did what was necessary."

"I do not doubt it," he said, and his smile grew. "Nevertheless, I should start watching over my shoulder in case you stalk me with a kitchen knife."

"What would be the point of that?" I said, with a spiteful curl of my lip. "You can't die. Campbell himself said he stabbed you right through the heart and yet, here we are."

Mason laughed softly, the sound reverberating around the room. "That he did," he said. His attention dropped to his pile of paperwork, either searching for something or looking inside his own depraved soul.

"How much did Campbell tell you?" he asked.

"About what?"

"Gainstorn. What did he divulge about that night?" As much as I tried to hide it, Mason saw my hesitation. He placed both elbows on the mounds of paper, leaning forwards. "Simply for my own curiosity, you understand."

Rearranging myself on the seat, I pulled my rumpled skirt down, and took a deep breath.

"He was always incredibly vague about Gainstorn. He never told me what happened, but I know that it weakened you."

I chanced a look at Mason. Although analysing my every motion with rigorous intensity, he remained calm. "He told me that, when you locked yourself away for all those months, it gave him the opportunity to free a bunch of Slaves."

"All of that came at a price, of course. I trust you know that when I eventually found Campbell, I did not make life pleasant for him."

"Or Harrison Dagger, for that matter," I bitterly scoffed.

A broad, callous smile worked its way across Mason's face, from one defined cheekbone to the next.

"I enjoyed cutting out his tongue. Perhaps I'll allow Miss Ulster the same pleasure with you."

My jaw quickly clamped shut, my hands squeezed tight. Mason revelled in my fear and leant back in the chair, smiling. "But after this interrogation, hey?"

The bastard winked at me just as there was a knock on the door.

On Mason's orders, in walked a particularly bedraggled Tallis. Mud caked his hair, and a deep gash dwarfed his selection of smallpox scars.

"Had a rough night, Captain?" Mason mocked.

Tallis remained silent and gestured to the girl he trailed behind him, on a rope leash that encompassed both her wrists.

At eleven or twelve years of age, she was a pretty little thing with long golden locks and eyes resembling pots of honey. Muddy rags drenched her frame, scratches and cuts decorating full cheeks that would have otherwise been so innocent. Against everything I tried to stop it, pity prickled at my features.

This girl, whoever she was, shared my history, my sorrow. Much like mine, her Tribe had been butchered by Masonians. Was it for sport this time? Or information? Which option made her story better?

"Maya, get two chairs from the adjoining room."

I obeyed, reappearing with two wooden chairs: one for Tallis, the other for the little girl. She perched upon the edge, her eyes empty and cold. I tried to see inside of those eyes, to glimpse the life that must have been in there, but she remained still and stoic, a statue of flesh and bone. I doubted she even knew where she was.

"What have you found out so far, Captain?" Mason asked.

"Nothing yet, I'm afraid," Tallis replied, wiping the mud from his face with the sleeve of his blue coat. "She's a stubborn little bitch."

"Then maybe you shouldn't have killed her family," I muttered.

"Miss Doe..." Mason's stern glare had me apologising to Tallis through gritted teeth. "That's better. Well, shall we begin?"

"Sir, forgive me, but what is *he* doing here?" I was in no mood to have my accent or my people's name be coated in the same stinking mud that soaked Tallis.

Tallis scowled at me in response, grinding his teeth.

"Tallis is here strictly to observe, to ensure that nothing of what she says gets *lost in translation*, if you catch my meaning."

I did catch Mason's meaning. Admittedly, I was a little insulted by it. I bit back my retort and turned to the small creature who sat next to me.

For a small moment, I wanted to apologise to her. To make her understand that, despite my current interrogation, I was *on her side*. Yet, as blankness remained behind those honeyed eyes, I admitted that was a conversation for another time.

First, I said hello. Then I asked her name.

No reply, but her eyes flicked briefly in my direction once she heard our mutual language.

When she still did not respond, I told her my name. *Maya Wolf-Charmer*.

That seemed to spark her attention. She asked me if I was a Slave here. I nodded, then tilted my head to Mason and innocently stated that he wanted to ask her a few questions. For the first time, those honeyed eyes sped to Mason, took one glimpse into those diamond eyes, and then squeezed tightly shut.

"*I want to go home*," was all she kept saying.

"Oh this is ridiculous!" Tallis snapped, berating me with an icy glare. "Leave her with me, I could get answers out of her within five minutes."

"What you'd get is a bunch of lies befitting the active imagination of a ten-year-old!" I shouted back. Tallis sunk back into his chair, a little startled.

Mason, of course, was loving my fiery display. His smile even grew as I snapped, "Just give me time! T'is no use threatening her when she's this young a-and scared… A-And – oh for the sake of Asgard!"

I turned my back to Mason and tenderly touched her shoulder. She winced under the pressure but did not shake it off.

I asked her name. It took her a few tries but she ultimately breathed it out: *Heidi Ice-Dancer.*

A beautiful name. A soft, beguiling, gorgeous name that her muddied face and sorrowful expression did little to emphasise.

A tender smile formed upon my lips. Only then did I notice the obvious discomfort from her wrists.

"Take these off her," I said. Mason's eyes widened at my bossy display but agreed with a growing smirk. Heidi Ice-Dancer rubbed her sore, discoloured skin. She leaned a little further in my direction, perhaps trying to fall into our mutual language.

I asked her again if she would be willing to cooperate with Mason, simply to answer his questions as best she could, not to fret if she couldn't. I saw Tallis bristle out the corner of my eye, but strenuously ignored him.

Finally, she agreed.

Mason leant forward with a smile that lied warmth. "Ask her what she knows about the Rebellion."

Heidi knew quite a lot about the Rebellion. Her Tribe had traded goods with many Free People, Mikael Ashworth included. Mostly food, clothing and primitive weapons: bows and arrows, and the like. I wondered sadly if all that trading was the reason her Tribe was murderous sport for Masonians.

The name Mikael Ashworth was understandable, even in Herdinese, and Mason's ears grew.

"Where is Mikael Ashworth now?"

Heidi did not know. Apparently, the last time she saw him was on the border of the Glasslands.

Visions of glaciers, the desire to feel the cold wind on my cheeks, the subtle creek of ice slumping down mountains…

"Yes, Maya, you were saying?" Mason prompted, eyes and ears brimming.

I cleared my throat. "Heidi remembers him mentioning a little town just inside the Snowlands. She thinks it's *Bear's Folly*."

"She *thinks*?" Mason scowled. "I need more than mere opinions from her, Maya."

I shuffled uncomfortably in my seat.

"It's difficult to interpret. She's certain it's Bear's Folly but there were other towns as well. Ashworth seemed to give conflicting orders each time he spoke."

"She's right, Sir," Tallis cut in. "It almost sounds like Ashworth was lying purposefully, to leave very little trace on his whereabouts should one of the Tribe be interrogated."

Mason absorbed this information slowly and carefully, his hands vertical against his lips.

"Ask her..." he began, then faded out as he restructured his inner thoughts. "Ask her if she ever saw an Aristocrat."

"Sir?"

"Get on with it, Maya."

Stunned, I shook away my confusion and asked Mason's careful question. Heidi thought hard, racking her memories for several moments, then shook her head.

"*Dammit!*" Mason hissed into a clenched fist. Another short moment of contemplation before he said, "Ask her if she ever met Ashworth in person."

Heidi had only ever eavesdropped on Ashworth's conversations, and each one gave conflicting information.

"That wasn't Ashworth," Mason said, growing increasingly vexed. "That was a decoy, several decoys by the sounds of it, and each one tasked with giving false locations."

Heidi could see her words had irritated him. She sent a worrisome glance to me, which I tried to dispel with a nervous smile.

"One last question, Maya, if you'd be so kind." I turned to await his order like the dutiful Slave I had become. "Ask her if she's ever heard of a woman called Svenja Svellec. It might help to relay this woman has golden teeth."

That seemed awfully specific.

But I did as I was told, and asked Heidi what seemed to concern Mason most of all.

To my utmost horror, Heidi refused to answer.

I asked the question again, hoping she had blanked out the first attempt. But no, she remained absolute. Her only response: "*I can't tell you that.*"

Stunned, I faced Mason with my eyes wide.

"She says – "

"Oh, I know what she said," he said, glaring. "That, I did understand."

Heidi could see the blood begin to boil, the swirling cauldron of diamonds begin to intensify. She pleaded with me, trying to make me understand that some ingrained Tribal law forbade her to ever discuss it.

The Herder Culture was a superstitious one. Bloody mammoths could be falling from the sky, and her beliefs still wouldn't let her budge.

Her position swiftly grew dicey. Tallis bristled upon his seat, his fingers twitching for the knife, and I had absolutely no doubt that he'd torture Heidi to readily spill information. No, I had to break her before he did, before her blood trickled.

In an attempt to persuade her, I calmly explained that no magic or hex would ever befall her if she told us.

I could see her eyes fill with hope. Colour rushed back to those young, delicate features. I was winning her over!

All until Tallis opened his big Herdinese mouth and warned her, in rather graphic detail, what bits he would chop off if she didn't start talking.

As Heidi burst out in hysterical tears, the swarm of furious bees hatched from somewhere unseen. Outraged, I jumped to my feet, slammed both hands on the desk, and berated Mason with a cutting glare.

"Mason, *get him the Hel out of here!*" I pointed a sharp finger to Tallis, moving his jaw like he was chewing on a piece of bone. "I had her eating out of my *fucking* hand, and then he goes and ruins it!"

Tallis jumped to his feet.

"Like Hel you did!" he yelled, beads of spittle flying from his mouth. "You're wasting time!"

"I *had* her!"

"The *only* thing you had was a false promise of safety that was *clearly* getting us nowhere!'

"And what did you do, huh? Just casually inform her what bits you were going to chop off? That's a brilliant trust tactic if ever I heard one!"

"You want me to *lie* to her, is that it?" Tallis threw his arms out to the side. "Go on then, tell her everything is going to be fine, *lie* to her like Campbell Anders lied to you!"

"Don't you dare bring Campbell into this..." I said, my finger outstretched, my voice even and low.

Tallis knew he'd got me where it hurt. He smiled, exposing his yellowed, crooked teeth.

"Don't forget whose side you're on, Maya. At the end of the day, you'll always be Campbell Anders's little Wild One."

Wild One. It had been a long time since I'd heard that particular nickname.

I continued to yell at him in Herdinese. Tallis responded in kind, and we continued to furiously berate each other in a language Mason had no hope of understanding. Sitting and observing us with a callous mix of annoyance and pity, it was this unwilling ignorance that made him yell, *"Enough!"*

Tallis and I stopped dead. I bowed my head in obedient servitude, my hands clasped tight before me.

"Both of you, *sit down.*"

Silently, we obeyed.

Poor Heidi, caught in the midst of our screaming match, had reverted to her old catatonic self. She curled herself into a ball, her small limbs barely fitting upon the chair as she gently rocked back and forth.

"Now," Mason began, eyes closed and rubbing an aching temple with two fingers. "It is quite obvious that neither of you are going to get anything else from that girl. And Tallis, don't even think about harming her. Her mental state is factitious, to say the least, and I'm certain any physical or emotional pain would render her absolutely useless to me."

Tallis nodded; annoyed maybe, but in agreement nonetheless.

"Nevertheless," Mason continued, "I need that information. Do either of you have any suggestions of how to get it?"

In the same amount of time it took for rain to start falling from the sky, I had an idea.

"Enslave her," I said.

Mason just looked at me.

"You've got to be kidding me," Tallis said, sneering.

"Think about it... I can try and keep working on her, try to get out the information you need." I chanced a look to Mason, who was listening with intrigue. "Besides, we're one Slave short since... *Y'know*. We could use an extra pair of hands."

Mason considered this for some time, weighing up his options, flicking his stare from me, to Heidi, and then back again to me.

"Alright," he finally mumbled, chewing on his tongue.

"You agree?"

"Yes, I agree. She will become part of his establishment. Maya, she is your responsibility. Be sure to get her cleaned up and trained, and should she tell you *anything* that you deem is important, you inform me immediately. Are we clear?"

"Yessir."

"Good, now all of you, get out. I've had my fill of Herders for today." Without another look, he produced a sheet of clean paper and began scribbling something down with a golden fountain pen.

Tallis gave a small courteous nod, glared knives at me, and then left the room.

I brought Heidi out of her stupor and ushered her limping body to the door. Mason called my name.

Curious, I turned to see his leering gaze.

"I think I'll allow you to keep your tongue," he said, smirking. "After all, I rather like it when it's angry."

Stunned, I quickly left the room with my jaw clenched shut.

* * *

Needless to say, the girls were not happy when I declared little Heidi would join our ranks.

"Well that's just brilliant," Tia muttered, pacing around the room with both hands upon her hips. "As if we didn't have enough to worry about!"

Anya and Luna were both in equally foul moods, their stares judgemental and their arms fastened tight across their bosoms.

"Oh shush," I said, wiping the mud from Heidi's cheeks with a damp cloth. "You know as well as I do that she's safer here, with *us*, than in most places in Maelstrom."

"How can you say that? She's refusing to relay vital information about the Rebellion! Do you realise how dangerous this is for her?"

I met Heidi's large, seemingly innocent eyes, and allowed a small smile to work its way across scarred lips.

"I think this one can take care of herself just fine," I said.

Before me, Tia paused her infernal pacing and glared with large dimples on her forehead. "What the hell is that supposed to mean?"

I made sure to give each of them a knowing smirk, and then helped Heidi down from the counter.

"Come on now, girl, let's hear you."

Heidi took some persuasion, her brown eyes assessing us. Then, to the complete shock of the room, she gave a cheeky shrug.

"Hi," she said, quietly.

Tia, in particular, did not appreciate Heidi's innocent little wave. Her brow furrowed even further, her spine curving as she relentlessly hit us with barely suppressed fits of anger.

"Are you telling me she can speak *English?*" A burst of hysterical laughter, bitter and stagnant. "Oh, you have *got* to be kidding me!"

"Little bit," Heidi said, pinching the air. "I understand, I don't speak good. English words hard."

I smiled at her accent, so thick and heavy and just so goddamned nostalgic that I wanted to throw it back to the wilderness where it belonged. Guilt rose, for she deserved to be outside in the snow, not left to rot here with the rest of us. But then, better for her to rot here than elsewhere in Maelstrom. At least here, I could wipe away the splotches of decay from her face.

Still, Heidi's English fluency – though limited – also acted in my advantage. Heidi was obviously a little bundle of information on the Rebellion, and might help put the pieces together, not least about this mysterious golden-toothed lady.

Of course, there was another reason to have little Heidi within our ranks. A reason no one would ever expect... I smiled quite triumphantly at the thought.

"How did you know she can speak English?" Anya asked me.

"It was when Mason ordered Tallis not to harm her. Relief hit her like a bloody train. Ain't no denying she understood everything that was said."

Seeing that little girl's smile, the way those large eyes looked up to me with such gratitude, made my heart swell. I patted her on her shoulder before meeting the heavy fog of tension, quickly suffocating.

"Maya," Anya said, deathly quiet. "Are you trying to tell us that you've *lied* to Mason?"

Lying was such a strong term for what I'd done. It was such an exaggeration of events and it didn't sit well with me. After all, the word *lying* implied I did something wrong in saving this little girl's life.

"I didn't lie – Hel, you know I *can't* lie. Mason just didn't ask the right questions and so I didn't feel the need to tell."

"We're all going down for this, do you understand?" Tia's voice was low and frantic, her chipped nails stabbing the air before her. "Because *when* Mason finds out about this, he is going to kill every single one of us!"

"Tia," I said, calmly. "He's not going to find out."

"How can you be sure?"

"Heidi can't really speak English, she just *understands* it. That changes everything."

"Really? How?"

"Look," I said, leaning against the countertop. "Heidi isn't going to be talking to anyone, so no one will have a clue that she can understand them. So, they're not going to worry about what they say in front of her. What we have here, ladies, is a *spy*."

The word weighed heavily on the room, cut only by Tia's bitter chuckle.

"A spy? Oh please, why the hell would we need a spy?"

My personal reasons for wanting a spy were none of their damn business. My connection with the music, or Mason's connection with his, currently lay at the top of the espionage checklist. Flying in a close second was why the Pretender was still alive, even if she elected to hide away in her bedroom most of the time. Then, hanging healthily at the bottom, was *how* I'd destroy the world. Obviously, the apocalypse wasn't going to happen with a mere sneeze, but if I knew *how* I was supposedly going to end the world, maybe there was some hope to change my destiny?

But my inner pondering was something the inhabitants of that kitchen did not need to know. Nevertheless, Tia's blatant disregard for Heidi's potential was sure to pull the fuse on my temper.

"Dunno, Tia," I spat. "Maybe you'd just like to know when Mason wants his little whore back."

Tia took three steps and slapped me hard on the cheek. Strings of chestnut whipped my face, stings skipping across skin.

"That was uncalled for," Tia said, her voice shaking, tears festering. "You don't know *anything*."

She was right. I had no clue at all what Mason did to her, what he was *still* doing to her on a regular basis. My body shivered at the thought.

Guilt ballooned. An apology quickly formed but Tia flew out the kitchen and slammed the door.

"Leave her," Luna said, her eyes fixed to the floor.

"She tells Mason?" Heidi asked with mild horror.

"No, honey, she's not going to tell him," Anya replied. "She just needs some time alone."

An awkward silence hung in the room. I caught Anya's eye and tried to gauge how she felt about a situation that had quickly escalated out of control.

She simply stared at me, unreadable.

* * *

THE NEXT TIME I saw Tia, it was in the Dining Room.

She was still and stoic, standing next to Luna, staring blindly ahead. I tried to catch her eye, to send apologetic stares hurtling towards her, but she actively ignored me.

Standing next to Anya with a bottle of wine, I chastised myself on my own stupidity.

Fighting amongst ourselves never accomplishes anything, Campbell always used to say.

Gods, I missed him.

When Mason arrived for his evening meal, he cast an acknowledging stare across us all, and fixed upon me a little too long. He stood directly before me, took a gentle hold of my chin, and manoeuvred my face for his scrutiny.

"Have you been slapped, Miss Doe?"

I sucked the scar on my lower lip, staring at the open collar of his white shirt. I did not reply.

"I hope it wasn't dear little Heidi," Mason said, dangerously. "Perhaps she needs a lesson in manners before she's tamed."

"No!" Tia gasped from across the room. "It was me, I did it."

Mason's increased the pressure on my chin. "And why, may I ask, did you slap her, Miss Kingsley?"

"I insul – " I began, but Mason squeezed my chin hard between his fingertips.

"I didn't ask you," he growled.

"Miss Doe commented on something that really isn't her business," Tia said quickly. "I lost my temper."

"Oh yes, and what was the comment?"

"It relates to our deal, Sir," Tia quietly replied.

"Hm," he purred. "Interesting."

He released me. I stumbled forwards, catching myself at the last minute. Ice sank heavy in my veins as Mason pushed that singular strand of chestnut behind my ear.

Without another word, he sat down to enjoy his meal.

Tia glared shards of glass, only intensified by Mason's stony silence. I wished for another Aristocrat or an informer or *something* to cut through the quiet.

It was a relief when Mason enquired about Heidi, and her elusive information. I stated that she polished up like a new penny. Of course, I also relayed that – so far – her information ran dry.

Heidi had immediately closed down after I brought up the subject of Svenja Svellec. Clearly her agitation with that topic was not forced, it was genuine stubbornness. One could even say, undeniable fear.

"That information is imperative, Maya," Mason said, slicing a serrated knife through prime rib. "I trust you are aware how important it is that the girl talks quickly."

"I do, Sir," I said. "Leave it to me."

***

THAT NIGHT, Heidi was asleep in the room Hallie and Tia once shared. Tia was now sharing a bunk with Luna, for memories of Hallie still stuck to those wooden walls. That room, with the floor still stained with childbirth, was a horrid reminder of Hallie's demise. I can't say I blamed Tia for not wanting to sleep in there again.

In the room I shared with Anya, we listened to the crackle of the wood burner and chatted about the little girl I had so casually flung into everyone's care. The questions about Heidi fuelled more about my own life, my own past. Whether I'd belonged to a Tribe, or ever sold goods to Rebels.

Next, she asked me where I'd travelled, what I'd seen. Memories flooded my eyes with tears, but I did not push them away. I let those memories rise and consume me, the last lingering images of my Pa being the most painful to reminisce.

Eventually, left in silence, I watched the burning embers of the fire, following each golden spark.

"You shouldn't have said that to Tia," Anya said, after some time. "That was unfair of you."

I sighed despondently. "I know. I regret saying it. Will she forgive me?"

"Probably. She's an understanding creature once she's had time to stew things over."

A breath of relief. The last thing we needed was cracks forming in our steady foundations, lest we all wanted to crumble.

"What's the deal with her and Mason?" I asked, unable to stop myself.

"The *deal*?"

"Yeah, I mean... Tia's not... He's not forcing her, is he?"

Above me, the wooden slacks creaked with a long sigh. "No."

"Oh, good."

"It's hardly *good*, Maya," Anya snapped.

"No, I know but... I mean, at least he's not... *Y'know*."

A terrible silence appeared out of nowhere. I shuffled my legs against the cool bed sheets, the frost still biting at the walls.

"She was raped," Anya said, subdued. "It was almost two years ago now. She was cleaning ornaments in the Green Room when it happened."

"Who was it?" I asked, my voice delicate.

"Dunno, some Masonian." The bunk creaked with another sigh. "In the following months, it almost destroyed her. Every day, a little bit more was chipped away – you could see it plain as day, every time you looked at her. That's when Mason offered her the deal."

"The deal? You mean, to sleep with him?

"The deal to *protect* her. So long as she's with him, no other man – Masonian or otherwise – is able to touch her."

She laughed bitterly beneath her breath. "It's the only deal he's actually kept."

I recalled the way Tia looked at Mason with such...*fascination.*

"Does she love him?"

"No, she doesn't. But she respects him. Think of them what you will, but at the end of the day, I truly believe Mason saved her life by offering that deal."

"I'd hardly go that far."

"You didn't see her before, Maya," Anya whispered. "Remember that before you say anything else."

17

Mason took a delicate sip of his morning coffee. "Miss Doe, I trust you are aware that Joe Matheson shall be attending the dinner party tonight."

His sudden and all too *infuriating* remark jolted my hand. The coffee sloshed out a little too quickly, spilling down the side of the ceramic cup and causing Anya to rush to my aid with a napkin.

"Be careful, you idiot girl," the Pretender piped up. She had decided to join Mason for breakfast that morning, and ensured her disdain for us was evident.

"Apologies…" I mumbled, my forehead lined and my weight shuffling from one red heel to another. "With the greatest of respect, Mason but – "

"*Sir*," Mason snarled, snatching the milk jug from a little way up the table. "And I implore you to think before you sour my good mood."

Biting my tongue, I nodded and made my way slowly back to my station.

Joe Matheson.

Why the fuck was Joe Matheson coming to Mason's dinner party? I happened to voice that question, in politer terms, to Mason when conversation ran dry. As usual, I was answered with a glare and an equally stony silence, so I compelled myself to drop the subject. I remained motionless, gazing at a point in mid-air and idly licking the scar on my lip.

A rumbling drone of thunder brought my attention back to that Dining Room. Raindrops speckled the windows, foretelling the arrival of a storm outside. The mountains in the distance had substantially more snow, and I wondered what the Palace would look like bathed in icy white.

"I doubt it will be too long now, my dear," I heard Mason mutter, gradually coming out of my reverie. "There is no point stressing about such things. It is beyond our control."

The Pretender closed her heavily lined eyes, fighting the nervous biting of her lip.

"But it's been *months*."

"It can take years," Mason said, gently. "Such timelines are not unheard of."

"*Years?*" The Pretender audibly gasped, bringing two bright red nails to her pink lips. "But that can't be the case – how can you possibly wait that long?"

Mason grinned. It was almost empathetic.

"I've already been waiting an awfully long time. I'm sure I can wait a little longer if I have to, Alira."

Alira.

The very whisper of that name – from *him* – caused every hair on my body to stand on end. I squeezed my eyes shut through the burn of the contacts, and willed my wild heart to slow to its usual, repetitive rhythm.

"Yes, I suppose," she eventually said.

As they engaged in more laborious conversation, I wondered what exactly they were discussing. What was she waiting to *do*?

More importantly, what was Mason waiting for?

I thought back to rumours of a grand celebration and wondered, quite absentmindedly, what such a thing would entail. Would there be fireworks? An orchestra? Dancing?

My, I hadn't danced in an awfully long time.

Campbell and I used to dance. We'd find a longhouse with a drunken bard, slam our fists on the table and then spin, arm in arm until one of us collapsed. I'd sing at the top of my lungs while a grimacing Campbell covered his ears, and we'd drink tankards of mead until our heads spun. I could practically smell the smoke burning in the central hearths, the wooden longhouses full of idle chatter and drunken revelry. They were the definition of freedom.

I cast a longing gaze to the mountains in the distance, only just visible through the dull grey of rain, and expelled a shaky stream of air through pursed lips.

Some days were easier than others. This was not one of those days.

* * *

HEIDI'S ENSLAVEMENT hit her like a tonne of bricks.

Once the shock of those first few days lessened, other emotions rose up, consuming her with a cauldron of feeling she just didn't know what to do with.

She cried a lot. It was the only thing she could do. The memories of what happened to her Tribe – *her family* – had finally caught up in one ginormous leap. Most nights, her softened weeps filled the small corridor, seeping from the edges of her bedroom door. In the day, she became silent and dejected, doing what I'd ask simply because she just didn't know what else to do.

Guilt consumed me, but I knew I'd done the right thing. What would have happened if she was sold at Bolton Square, left to the mercy of a man like Erik Doncaster? Ironically, despite Mason's presence in the Palace, Heidi was safer with me than she was anywhere else. Yes, I'd done the right thing.

On the night of the dinner party, she remained in the little kitchen, polishing silverware. I had asked if she was alright, but on the third one-word answer, I had given up trying. Heidi would eventually come to terms with her situation – we all did.

The rest of us were in the process of preparing for the party. I had the extra job of preparing for Joe Matheson.

I was thankful for Mason's warning. Should I have bumped into him, completely unprepared, I would have clawed his eyes out.

For now, I forced all of my anger into the wayward strands of my hair, trying to calm the feisty locks, forcing them into the scruffy bun on the back of my head.

I was mumbling Herdinese *Curses of the Old Gods* when Anya paraded in the room with two dresses over her arms.

"These are for us," she declared, neatly lying a garment per bed.

"What about the ones we wore last time?" I asked.

"They like us to have *variety*." Anya rolled her eyes.

I held my towel secure and inspected the dresses. Made out of a fine black material, they looked marginally looser and far more comfortable than the skin-tight monstrosities we were forced to wear last time. They also covered our cleavages, which I found to be a great relief.

Of course, as Anya held it to the flicking lightbulb, it was completely backless with just two measly strings of pearls securing the two sides.

"Bloody brilliant," I bitterly remarked.

Too enraged for decency, I threw the towel around my ankles and stomped my way into the dress. I was forcing my arms through the sleeves when Anya muttered, "Oh shit."

I paused, half my breast still exposed.

"What?"

Anya manoeuvred my body so she could see my back, and the large black tattoo inked there.

"What the hell is *this*?"

"It's Jörmungandr. Y'know, the World Serpent?"

"Yes, Maya, I know who the big-ass snake is. I'm asking why the hell I've never seen it before."

"Because I usually get undressed at three-in-the-morning when I take a goddamned shower." I shook off her hands and quickly secured my modesty. "What's the big deal?"

Cheeks flushed, Anya looked horrified as she threw fingers through her hair.

"Maya, you can't go out parading that thing!"

"That *thing* is my culture, Anya!"

"No, no – I didn't mean it like that, I – "

An impatient knock on the door halted Anya and revealed Bentley.

"Only ten minutes to – oh," he said.

I flipped them both the finger and continued to get ready.

"Maya, you don't understand – the Aristocrats will give you absolute *murder* if they see that!" Anya's hands sought sanctuary in her hair as she turned to Bentley. "Sir, what are we going to do?"

As Bentley's thin face formed a tight frown, I remembered the lewd stares and cruel remarks about my cleavage. My face grew pale.

My tattoo was bold and obvious and just screamed *Herder*. What would the Aristocrats say about *that*?

"Wear the other dress," Bentley snapped.

"But she'll be different to the rest – "

"She has no choice, Miss Whittaker. Let's just hope, what we're all wearing isn't high on an Aristocrat's agenda tonight."

* * *

So, there I was, back in the tight dress showing too much cleavage, and now with the added concern that I was a noticeable, obvious addition. Standing in that Dome Room with the flutes of champagne, I awaited my fate with a thin sheen of sweat upon my brow.

Please, dear Odin, might I avoid the Ulster Woman. This'd be the time she'd finally cut my damn tongue out.

I took a last longing glimpse to the door of the Reading Room, wishing I could hide away from the entire evening, and found sweet solace in thoughts of the piano.

A bracing chill whipped through the Dome Room. Aristocrats poured in, and as I made my champagne rounds, I found myself looking for Joe so I could stab a broken flute in his eye.

I shook the grotesque image from my mind.

"Your dress is so obvious," Tia mumbled, coming up behind me. This was the first time we'd spoken since the slap and I was rather surprised to see her genuine concern.

"Did Anya tell you?"

"*Pfft*, of course she did. She asked me to tell Mason."

"You're kidding me..." My heart sank to the black veins streaking the marble. "And did you?"

"I had to, Maya. He would have asked about it anyway."

"That's not the point," I snapped, and because Joe Matheson had got me all jittery, "And why does everyone feel the need to tell Mason *everything*? Surely it's not against the rules to keep some things to ourselves?"

Tia simply rolled her eyes, exasperated.

"We all have secrets, only *that's* not a secret. It's a blatant invitation to ask why you're wearing something different to the rest of us."

I audibly groaned, reluctantly seeing her point. The bubbles in the champagne looked so enticing. Perhaps I could sneak a glass?

Shrugging a guilty shoulder, Tia just said, "Keep a low profile."

She wandered off through the crowd of lush material, the flawless skin of her back being the last to disappear.

Shaking away the growing uneasiness, I took a step back and bumped into a shoulder.

It had to be Joe Matheson. Who else would it be?

"Maya..." He had to drag my name from his mouth, not wanting to acknowledge its existence. "Erm, how are you?"

I scrutinised the man I thought I knew so well. The same handsome features were there, of course they were. But there was something decidedly lacking: a huge part of his immature personality that had been wiped clean entirely. It aged him tremendously, those seafoam eyes looking so tired and troubled, it barely looked like Joe Matheson at all.

"Fine, Sir," I brusquely replied, before a short, sharp smile. "Excuse me."

Joe gently gripped my arm. "Please, Maya, just tell me you're – "

"Get your hand off me."

His hand snapped cleanly away, as though burned. "Just let me know if you need any help," he mumbled, quietly.

"What are you doing here, Joe?"

He licked his lips, devoid of all colour. "I've been accepted into Mason's Social Circle."

"Well, congratulations. Clearly selling Campbell's name worked well for you."

"That's unfair, Maya," he said, his gaunt cheeks reddening. "You have no idea the situ– "

Joe's pain dissolved, that lying mouth twisting into a charismatic smile.

"Good evening, Lord Mason."

The words were barely out before a hand took a champagne flute from my silver tray.

"The same to you." Mason took a large mouthful, his diamond eyes scanning from neat head to toe. "I must say, Aristocracy suits you, Mr Matheson."

"It is somewhat different than what I'm used to, yes." He tittered to himself, and I was overcome with the urge to stick my fingers in his eyes.

I exhaled a long stream of anger, regained my posture, and was about to make a swift exit. Mason put his hand on the covered skin of my back, rooting me in place. Warmth spread from his splayed fingers into my inked skin.

"I trust Miss Doe is treating you well?"

The warning was not easily missed. Joe's smile dropped for exactly two seconds, and then reappeared brighter than ever.

"Oh yes, she's actually been quite delightful."

I smiled sweetly and hoped both men were unaware of the rage that was so, *so* close to boiling over.

Mason increased the pressure between my shoulder blades, ever so slightly.

"I am immensely glad to hear it," he said, his tone lightening. "It's always so refreshing when people get along, don't you agree, Miss Doe?"

I nodded in startled agreement.

A flash of scarlet foretold the arrival of the Pretender. This was obviously the first time Joe had met her, for he scrutinised every bit of her body with such intensity that Mason's hand dropped from me, and curled around *her* back in a blatant display of possession.

"Alira, may I introduce Mr Joe Matheson," Mason said, gesturing to a blushing Joe. "He sold me the whereabouts of Campbell Anders."

"Ah, yes – I've heard a lot about you," the Pretender replied, flashing a smile so bright it clashed with her ruby jewels. Her opal eyes shimmered a multitude of colours from the chandelier above, fixing Joe's gaze upon them.

"My," he said, genuinely startled. "I've heard descriptions of your eyes before, Ma'am, but they truly are beautiful."

"Oh, why thank you." She smiled, colour imposing on cheeks that were already painted.

Wishing, with all my bodily strength, to be elsewhere, I politely excused myself and continued my champagne rounds. Large beads of anxious sweat trickled between my breasts.

"Keep it together, Maya," Anya mumbled as she passed.

Against everything I did to try and avoid her, the Ulster Woman spotted me just as we were heading into the Dining Room. She scrutinised my appearance, yet soon took her rightful seat at the table. I continued on, relief hitting my head and turning it light and bubbly, just like the champagne I was forced to serve.

Joe Matheson was seated opposite Verity Ulster, with whom he was now in deep conversation. His character had returned to its normalcy, exuding a type of charisma and charm that could potentially woo any woman. I wondered quite sickly if such charms would work on the Green Witch.

"Lord Mason, I wonder if I could ask a favour of one of your Maids?" a young man called from the middle of the table, his mousy hair slicked back and his features resembling both male and female qualities. "Only, I've happened to come across a Herder delicacy which I am rather intrigued about."

A Herder delicacy? There was no such thing.

Mason saw nothing unsuitable with the request and agreed with a smooth wave of his hand.

"Oh Little Herder-girl, come this way please," the Aristocrat crooned.

Ignoring Anya's pitying stares, I clanked my way over to this Androgynous Man, who proceeded to remove a silver tin from his pocket. The man beside him covered his mouth, stifling immature laughter.

"May I ask what this is, Sir?" I asked, taking the cool tin.

He made a pitiful attempt at a Herder name that literally had no meaning.

"Go on then, Slave," he said, when I just frowned at the tin. "We're so very intrigued about what it is."

Cautiously, I opened the tin, revealing a piece of raw fish.

I pondered the meaning behind this *delicacy*. After all, I was hardly a stranger to eating raw fish in my twenty or so years.

That is, until the smell hit me.

My eyes and mouth clamped shut, determined not to react to the disgusting, vile, utterly *foul* stench picking at my nostrils.

"Jeez, what is that?" someone asked.

"Fermented fish." He giggled loudly.

"Well eat it already. Fucking stinks."

For a moment, I imagined turning the stinking tin of acidic, rotten fish to its owner and stuffing it down his throat. What would be an appropriate Aristocratic adjective for such a thing? *Enlightening,* perhaps?

Feeling the amused stares of most Aristocrats at that table, Mason included, I picked the delicacy from the tin. Almost translucent, it was pale pink in colour and lined with grey veins. The vile odour intensified, and some Aristocrats gagged into their napkins.

I opened my mouth, then closed it as I lost my nerve. My stomach begged to heave, eyes watering with the stench. I stuck my nose over my shoulder for a last long breath, and quickly dropped the fish in my mouth.

It was warm and slimy against my tongue. I immediately began chewing, closing off my senses. I gagged with the taste – *and oh Gods, the smell* – and fought the powerful urge to spit it all over that table. I quickly swallowed once, then twice for good measure.

I formed slow, careful breaths as nausea threatened. With every inch of control, I willed my stomach to settle and returned the small tin with a sweet smile on my face.

"Not bad, not bad at all," the Androgynous Man said, then he turned to his friend. "Darling, I believe you owe me fifty gold coins."

He praised himself over his winnings as I slowly – carefully – made my way back to Anya. I retched a little, merely wiped my face, and turned my composed form back to the table with both hands behind my back.

An Aristocrat ordered a top up of wine. I went to her aid, bottle in hand.

"There's a bucket in the prep room," Bentley whispered as he passed, on route to Mason with the first course of oysters and lemon.

I quickly filled the wineglass and slipped through the adjoining door to the prep room. It was a half-way point between the kitchens and the Dining Room, where all food was stored and counted before being served.

A rogue kitchen Slave held a beckoning bucket. Without a second thought, I stuck my fingers down my throat and easily vomited, twice. The kind lady covered the bucket with a damp towel, smiled tightly, then rushed back Downstairs.

The open bottle of red wine was still in my hand. The taste of rotting fish lingering on my tongue, I spat in the bottle and returned to the Dining Room to refill glasses.

* * *

THE EVENING PROGRESSED with a sickening haze. My stomach was sensitive and disagreed with the delicious scents of food. It growled and grumbled, spurring a few suspicious stares. Except from Joe Matheson, that is, who actively avoided me.

Once the dessert course was finished, the plates cleared, I served the sweet wine when the shrill laugh of Verity Ulster rattled my sore head.

"Little Herder," she said, her crooning voice echoing around golden candelabras. "Do tell us why you are dressed differently to the other Slaves? We are *very* curious."

"It's simply a...wardrobe malfunction, Ma'am."

"Oh dear, you're going to have to do much better than that... Mason, darling, why are your Slaves dressed inconsistently this evening?"

Mason delicately wiped his mouth and replaced the napkin on his lap.

"It seems Miss Doe has a Herdinese tattoo that was deemed inappropriate. It's a small inconvenience, Verity, nothing more."

A small, relieved smile tickled my lips, which Verity was quick to notice. Her smile grew nasty.

"Oh, but I would very much like to see this artwork! Particularly if it is as inappropriate as you say. Why, let's all have a giggle, shall we?"

"I happen to agree with Verity," the Pretender added, her eyes shimmering with a vicious mirth. "After all, Herdinese artwork is said to be riveting."

"Oh, I am fond of Herder Culture. Why, I even own the tattooed skins of Herders at home. It would be wonderful to see it on a live specimen for a change."

My stomach lurched, though I could not tell from what.

"Oh, Verity!" Emilia's enunciated syllables echoed across the space. "This is no time to undress a woman! We are at dinner, for goodness sake!"

"But we have eaten our fill this evening, and there's only so much wine a lady can yet consume. Even you, Emilia, can admit that it would be ample entertainment before the port is opened."

"Oh, please Mason..." The Pretender grinned, grasping his arm like an excited child. "Do indulge us."

Mason seemed to contemplate this for a few agonising moments, before a swift nod.

"Oh fabulous! I am such a fan of art!"

"Mr Matheson, would you do the honours? As a former *companion* of Miss Doe, I've no doubt you've seen all her artwork before." The Pretender gave a salacious little giggle.

To my utmost horror, Joe agreed to the request, coming to stand at the end of the table, directly opposite Mason.

I remained still, unable to move, to *think*... Everything became a bubble, the time ticking on and yet stopping entirely.

Verity snatched the bottle of dessert wine and placed it defiantly on the table.

"Off you go then, Slave. Don't keep us waiting."

I found Bentley and endeavoured to find some unspoken words of advice. He simply gave a small, sad incline of his lip, his eyes silently begging.

My legs moved of their own accord to stand before Joe. I was shivering wildly, the urge to run from that room almost irrepressible.

Joe placed his hands upon my shoulders. He offered a small, reassuring smile that did the exact opposite of what it was meant to convey.

I gripped the lapels of his black dinner jacket, squeezing my eyes shut. He slowly began lowering the zip, but their stares cut through me, burning my skin one blistering inch at a time. I took a hasty step back, struggling away from Joe's hold.

He tightened his arms around me, pulling me back to him. I met his eye and behind their seafoam colouring, I saw his pleads, his *desperation*.

Do as they say, his eyes begged.

I closed my eyes again, imagining the feel of freedom, the crunch of snow beneath my foot. I clung to that image as Joe slowly lowered the zip.

Tendrils of black ink peeked from inside the dress, and as Joe moved the zip further down, a sea of gasps erupted from the table.

The zip came to rest just above my buttocks. Joe gently parted the two halves of the dress, allowing my back to shine in all its inked glory.

Jörmungandr slithered his way up and down my spine, looping himself several times before he grasped his own tail between his teeth. The markings were bold and traditional, reminiscent of the Old Gods that all Herders worshipped. I personally found my tattoo beautiful. It was meaningful and stemmed from a time where I found strange comfort in the knowledge that a second Ragnarök could not occur, so long as the Jörmungandr on my back kept tight hold of his tail.

Clearly, the Aristocrats in that Dining Room held a rather different opinion.

"Oh my dear Lord, who in the world would get something like that engraved on their skin?" Verity's disgust was palpable, as were those of the other members of the table.

"I hope she realises that dragons are meant to have wings."

"What else do you expect – all Herders are as thick as deer shit."

"It's not a dragon, darling, it's a snake."

"That's even worse!"

"Oh, how utterly terrible."

"Well, what a blessed waste of time!" Verity said. "I was expecting artwork, not some drab attempt at such. I do apologise, that was a completely wasteful five minutes."

The screech of chairs as Aristocrats stood to their satiated feet.

Bentley rushed forwards to clean the table, giving me a knowing nod on his way.

A quick slap of Joe's hands, for the anger was steadily rising and I needed to get out of that Dining Room. I tried to zip up the dress, but my hands were trembling. The zip kept catching on the fabric.

"Here, let me," Joe said, calmly. Too shaken to argue, I meekly stood as Joe finished dressing me, wiping the tears from my cheeks before anyone could notice. Joe gave a miserable nod and made his way out of the room with his fellow Aristocrats.

"Anything else, Sir?" Bentley's voice echoed across the emptying room.

Mason was still present, sitting in his chair.

"No..." he said, his head bowed and his attention...*strained?* His fist was clenched tight on the table as he concentrated. Very hard.

A few more seconds and he seemed to zap from his reverie, removing the napkin from his lap and standing to his full height.

He walked towards me as I was finishing my attire, both hands in the pockets of his dinner trousers.

"Take the rest of the evening off, Miss Doe," he said as he passed. "You've had a rough night."

* * *

BOOKS TREMBLED as I stormed into the Reading Room, slamming the door so hard even the piano strings yelped. The music in my head had all but been disintegrated beneath a furious rage that was trying to burst its way out.

I removed my heels and threw them to the floor, one by one. One of the heels dented the wood but I was too enraged to care.

I paced around the room, my bare feet slapping against the cold floor.

How dare they. How *dare* they!

Was I embarrassed? Disgusted?

Blistering *fury* rose fast up my gullet.

I squealed a small and pitiful wail, then bit my hand hard to stave the worst of my angered screams. The pain seemed to help.

Small red teeth marks pierced my palm, and as I licked away the blood, I wondered what I had done to deserve this fate.

My back slipped down those hundreds of books, Jörmungandr himself not able to hold me up. Two long legs stretched before me, the cold soothing my burning skin.

Exhale... One... Two... Three...

A pressed hand upon my heart. It beat wildly into my hand.

I leant my head back against the bookcase and willed my heartbeat to slow. Listening to the sounds of those laughing, cackling Aristocrats, it was almost a relief when the music found me.

It was so delicate, soothing the anger in my belly, willing my heartbeat to slow to its normal, tranquil state. It caressed the inside of my skull, wiping away the rawness of what I had endured.

The music was comforting me.

My eyes found the piano. The piano stared back. Leering, *begging* me to come and feel it's warm, soothing embrace.

For almost an hour, I simply stared, unable to do anything else.

In the end, with the Aristocrats otherwise engaged and my hands tingling, I took a few careful steps.

The draw from the piano intensified, pulling me closer and closer until I was directly before it.

Mason's warning echoed in my ears: *Don't ever touch this piano again.*

But how would he know?

If I touched a delicate little finger to those smooth ivory keys, then no one would be any the wiser.

I smiled at the piano. It would be our little secret.

Tenderly, I lifted the keylid.

The music intensified, egging me on. It was as excited as I was.

The soft pad of my finger stroked the white surface, revelling in its smooth coolness. Oh-so-delicately, I pressed down.

A singular note erupted through the air. Gorgeous, *exquisite*...

I exhaled a slow, shaky breath, the music filling my very core, finally satisfying that torturous *itch* I never knew I possessed...

Very carefully, my finger moved to the next key.

Another note filled the air, fluttering in the empty space. It was just so peaceful...

Loud footsteps erupted in the Dome Room, Aristocrats laughing and giggling to each other.

I lost my nerve. Visions of Mason teased that I could not be discovered.

I gently lowered the keylid, protecting keys that were screaming for my touch. I fought the urge incessantly, begging my inner mind to understand my precious position, arguing with hands that wanted to run their way up and down that beautiful instrument...

I pulled myself back, cutting myself from the piano's warm embrace, and felt sharp stabs of agony in my head.

I ignored them, collecting my abused heels from the floor. The piano called me, *begged* me. Trembling fingers grasped the doorknob and turned.

Music came screeching and shrieking and *suffocating!* I grasped my head, feeling each note scratch inside my skull, pounding my brain.

I fell to the floor, shaking, my jaw clenched. The piano still screamed, demanding I get back over there and finish the song I was *destined* to play.

Gone was the sweet, sensible guise of the music. Now came a torrent of anger, of desire. The music wanted me, digging its claws into my flesh, pulling me closer and closer...

My ears buzzed, blood trickled from my nose, my eyes squeezed tightly shut through the skull-splitting *pain!*

I chanced a dizzy look at the piano. It glared back, and within that *impossible* look, I saw Mason's ferocity, his wickedness...

Tears streamed down my face as I stumbled shakily from the room. I made it Downstairs. Anya was elsewhere, her bed empty and cold.

The music was deafening. I stuck my fingers down my ears, trying to burst my eardrums, trying to release the painful pressure inside my head. It was no use. The music continued to hound me, to maim and yell at me for my stubbornness.

I apologised again and again, willing the music to understand *why* I had to leave, *why* I could not finish the song!

Finally, after an age, the music relaxed.

Audibly gasping, I lay on my back and listened to the music's stern tone.

Play the song, Alira, it seemed to say.

I promised I would. Oh Odin Allfather, I promised...

* * *

IT WAS THE NEXT MORNING. The music, the *pain,* had not abated.

Tenderly, I pressed a palm against my eye, trying to diminish the pickaxe that stuck there. My dry eyes stung and itched, and I realised I'd slept in my contacts. I audibly chastised myself, and quickly cleaned and reinserted them just before Anya burst in, still in the previous night's dress.

She took one look at me, dropped to her knees, and cradled my head like a mother inspecting her sick child.

Despite everything, I was required to serve at breakfast that morning.

Questions would be asked for any notable absence, and I couldn't risk any musical discovery. No, I simply had to persevere.

But still, the music was there, tingling in my head, mocking the dull throb of agony that brought a fresh wave of nausea with every peak and trough.

So, there I was: all cleaned up, swaying back and forth and resisting the urge to vomit in the coffee pot.

As usual, Mason was first down to breakfast. He spotted my grey complexion and took a gentle hold of my chin, to scrutinise my health. A slow tilt of my face, into the young day's light. It was too bright, too harsh. I squeezed my eyes shut, and snapped my chin back into my own possession.

A low hum in Mason's throat, but he did not comment further.

The newspaper was ready and waiting as he sat for breakfast. Slowly and carefully, I made my way to his side and poured his coffee. The scent was rich and pungent, and did little for my lingering nausea.

"Do not throw up on me, Miss Doe," Mason glared.

Aristocrats trickled in over the next hour, the most interesting addition being the Pretender. Dressed in high-waisted white trousers and a matching crop top, her toned midriff was on show and her hair falling like ribbons of pure gold. Her lips were painted a bright scarlet red, and although her face was still plastered with cosmetics, she looked stunning.

The Pretender openly grimaced at my presence but relaxed once assured I was safe to serve food.

A few more Aristocrats marched in, including the Androgynous Man and his gambling friend. They were slapping each other on the back, evidently pleased with their night of mischievous antics.

My stomach dry-heaved at the memories of that rotten, raw, *disgusting* thing they made me eat.

I turned my back to the table and clasped a hand upon my mouth.

"Still with us, Miss Doe?" Mason asked, observing me from the corner of his eye.

"Yessir," I replied, swallowing hard. With Mason's permission, Anya left her post and brought me a glass of water. It was cold and fresh, sliding down my throat like pure ambrosia.

"Err, Little Herder-girl, we require coffee here, darling."

I shoved the glass of water to Anya, holding my breath through the stench of caffeine. Both men decided it would be a good morning to mock my appearance.

Mason blared down the table, "Behold the result of your actions, gentlemen."

Both men stilled, icicles forced down their spines.

"If you insist on feeding my Slaves rotten food for your own immature amusement, be sure it is safe to consume." He shook the newspaper out wide. "I'd be much obliged if you did not make my Slaves ill."

A brief exchange of quizzical looks, but they sincerely apologised nonetheless.

I meekly returned to my station.

Tia stepped forward to fill the Pretender's morning glass of orange juice, but she swiftly covered the glass. She persisted to glare at Tia in such a way it almost *dared* her to come closer. A little stunned, Tia stepped back to her station.

"You were with *her* again last night, weren't you?"

Mason lowered the newspaper, very slowly. "What?"

"You heard me," she hissed beneath her breath. "That whore of a Slave you cavort with."

"Whom I cavort with, and when I do so, is none of your damn business." Mason hunched his shoulders, waiting to pounce.

But the Pretender remained strong and swallowed her hurt. "Mason, I am *Alira*."

"You are my *guest*," he snapped. "Do not presume your position here is unconditional, my dear. You have a job to do, and I will not be satisfied with you until it is completed."

The Pretender looked him up and down with an ugly grimace. "Of course, and then you'll be able to throw me away whenever you feel like it, won't you?"

"Oh don't be so melodramatic." Mason shook out the newspaper wide. "When the time is right, you will conceive my child and we shall revisit your social standing."

Conceive his child.

Child.

The entire world slowed into a dull, repetitive motion. The rain outside, the crackling of the fire, the groans of hungover Aristocrats... All of that disintegrated beneath the weight of that one, horrific sentence...

Once Alira conceives his child. Once I conceive his child...

Like petrol thrown on a dwindling flame, the world was kick-started with dizzying motion. I was flying, moving at one-thousand miles per hour as every single conversation I'd had with Campbell raced back. As every single *nightmare* dissolved beneath a new terror, even more wretched, sickening and frightening than the last.

The throbbing in my head intensified. Nausea bubbled.

The light was too bright. The room was too noisy. The truth was too fucking *atrocious!*

Vomit rose.

I ran from the room. The bathroom was too far – I would never make it in time.

I rushed inside a small sitting room and vomited in an ornamental vase. Large retches wrecked my body, the horror of that Dining Room expelled in a series of gut-wrenching heaves.

Anya was suddenly behind me, holding my hair through the worst.

When my throat burned and my body had nothing more to give, I collapsed beside the vase. It was a pretty thing: white ceramic, with blue and lilac illustrations of birds and reeds.

Anya knelt beside me, wiping away the tears that had been squeezed out.

"Is that any better?" she delicately asked.

I could not reply. I simply sat there, unable to move or think or do *anything* but replay the contents of that terrible conversation.

Somewhere in the distance, more footsteps arose.

"With the greatest respect," Anya spat, "but Maya's clearly not in the mood to be talking to you, *Sir.*"

Joe Matheson's small, feeble voice drifted through the air. Did he know? All that time he knew Campbell – he knew *me* – did he know the real reason Mason wanted to find me?

"Anya, do you mind?" I pointed weakly to the vase, filled with my vomit. "I'm sorry to ask, but I'll make it up to you."

She just graced me with a concerned look. "Are you sure you want to be left here with *him?*"

"Yes, I'll be okay."

Nodding, she placed a tender kiss upon my forehead. Such a sweet gesture. Then she lifted the vase with two hands, and exited.

Joe shut the door behind her, leaving us alone in a dimly lit room.

Deceit spread between us, soaking everything: from the collection of purple loveseats, to the bearskin rug, and then finally to the dull diamond chandelier.

Moving shadows of rain streaked a pale face illuminated by the dull silver sky.

"Did you know?" I asked, after some time.

Joe took a long time to reply.

"Yes."

Tears came, burning my treacherous eyeballs and escaping in slow, thick streams. I thought of Campbell: his glacial-blue eyes, the black stubble upon his chin, the way he smiled and hugged me and said how everything was going to be alright…

"Did Campbell know?"

Joe rested on both knees. His hand lifted, perhaps debating whether to place a soothing touch upon my shoulder. He decided against it.

"Yes, he did."

And there, just like that, the man I respected above all others became the greatest liar I ever knew.

"Why didn't you tell me?"

"How could we?" Joe's saddened face twisted into something quite pitying. "You were just a child. How could we possibly tell you something like that?"

"That's no excuse, I should have been told."

"I know that now. I'm sorry."

"What am I?"

Joe dropped his gaze to the marble floor, licking life into lips that just wanted to be still and silent.

"You're his mate – it's the only way I can describe it. You're the only one biologically capable of producing a child for him."

"Why?" The small word weighed heavily on the room. "Why does he want a child so much that I exist in the first place? Why has he been so determined to find me, to find all the others who were born before me?"

"I don't know..." he said, his face wrought with pity. "All I know is that by giving birth to Mason's child, it's...the end."

The End of Everything.

"That can't be possible. How can having a child destroy everything?"

"I don't know, girl, I – "

"No, no – this doesn't make any sense," I said, as my entire existence unravelled to reveal its dirty, frayed seams. "Why would Mason *want* to have a child if it means everyone – *everything* – is destroyed?"

"I swear to you, I don't know. Campbell only said how imperative it was that Mason does not find you."

And that was why they lied to me. Why they told me, for all those years, that Mason wanted to kill me.

Heck, all the New World knew that Alira was the End of Everything. It only made sense that somewhere down the line of whispers, the truth had twisted and deformed into something far from reality. It was those incorrect rumours that fuelled the lies Campbell fed me, one spoonful at a time.

Was the truth any better than those lies?

No. It was not.

"Listen to me, girl," Joe said, his hands upon my shoulders. "You need to stay focussed. I know it's a lot to absorb but you have to keep your head in the game. Your true purpose doesn't change the fact that *Mason cannot find you.*"

"I'm scared, Joe," I whispered, as more tears ran down my cheek. "I'm so, so scared..."

"Oh, sweetheart..." He wiped the tears from my cheeks with the rough pad of his thumb. "But you're also *strong* – so much stronger than I am, than anyone else here. You can *do* this."

The urge to be comforted, to be *protected,* stabbed its way through my chest. In one quick movement, I threw my arms around Joe Matheson's neck and squeezed him tightly, burying my face in his woollen jumper.

Joe was stunned. His arms were filled with concrete as he just did not know how to react.

But then, as my body shivered with suppressed cries, those arms softened and curled into a warming embrace. He sighed into my neck, holding me close until my tears had run dry.

* * *

Hours passed.

Lying in bed, the world spinning around me, I had a bucket at my side and continually threw up my fear.

My fear of being Alira. My fear of being Mason's.

The piano was taunting me. It stabbed painful notes inside my skull, laughing at my torment. *You're going to have Mason's baby*, it seemed to cruelly sing.

My skin crawled at the mere idea, the slightest notion… Regardless of what Campbell said, or how it was supposedly going to end the world, I found the concept of my destiny physically repulsive.

The Pretender made it even worse. She *knew* Alira's destiny, and yet there she was, drinking tea with him, berating him for screwing other women when the reality of *their* relationship was far, *far* worse.

Is that what Mason was waiting for? Were they trying to conceive?

In the dark recesses of my mind – in the little back corners were only the foulest thoughts materialised – popped a frightening, unwilling visualisation of what would happen if Mason ever found me. Visions of what he would want, the logistics of how he would do it, rose up like bile. I vomited more of the noxious mix as music cackled.

But, of course, what about the music? It was clearly connected to this in some perverted way, but *how*? The Pretender didn't hear it – she couldn't have! Only the *true* Alira heard the music.

So, did she lie about it? Did she use the music to deceive him? No, surely not. Mason was an intelligent man and would be able to see through any musical lies. He would know if she was truly hearing the music.

My heart froze in my chest: *He will know if she is hearing the music.*

For the first time, I thanked the Old Gods for that rotting fish. I thanked Hel herself for forcing it down my throat.

That so-called *delicacy* was a splendid excuse for my musical illness.

I contemplated my position. Food poisoning would normally last a few days, a week at the most. If my symptoms lasted any longer, suspicions would be raised.

Even if Mason himself contemplated what caused my plight, the last thing I needed was Doctor Grant examining me, for fear he'd shine a light in my eyes. Now, more than ever, it was imperative that my contact lenses remained a secret. Those two little pieces of amber glass were the only things protecting me from rape.

I threw my hands to my face, hoping to hide myself away from the world. How did it come to this? How did the uncontrollable Wild One become the feeble little girl throwing up musical torment?

I needed to understand what was happening to me. I needed *answers.*

Through the throbbing, I stumbled to the wash basin. The water was refreshing as I washed my mouth out, then greedily guzzled three handfuls.

I waited for the nausea to subside, then ventured out into the corridor. It was dark and still. Slaves were busy in their own duties. This was fortunate. I needed solitude.

Outside, rain plummeted. Large droplets slammed the stained glass as I traversed that grand marble staircase.

At the bottom of an empty corridor, Mason's Office loomed. The door, framed with thin strips of light, screamed the monster that resided there.

I threw my sight away, unable to stomach it.

Portraits of mean Aristocrats berated me as I stumbled on, using their golden frames to support myself. I gently peeked into open rooms and held my ears to others, but my target remained elusive.

Thunder trembled. I finally saw it.

The door was rather understated, being wooden with only a few delicate threads of gold. But the voice that softly sounded from inside left little doubt of its resident.

For a moment, I just stood motionless, hearing Mason's song – *my* song – be hummed by a stranger. By someone who had no comprehension of the beauty, the power, the *gratification* such wonderful music promised. It was a travesty.

The sickness came first, then the anger.

How dare she. How dare she tamper *my* song with her lies!

The music willed me on, caressing my head for the first time in hours. I marched forwards and slammed a tightly clenched fist against the shimmer of gold...

The humming stopped. Movement from inside. The sharp clicks of a turning key.

The door opened to reveal a smiling Pretender. The smile dropped when she saw me, replaced with a disdainful frown.

"What do you want, Slave?"

My bloodless lips curled.

"What do I want? I'll tell you what I want." I took slow, forceful steps into the room. "I want you to listen to me very carefully because I am done with this fucking bullshit."

I slammed the door closed. "You are going to answer every single question I have, and you are going to answer them quickly, and truthfully."

"Oh, am I?" She folded her arms across her tight bosom.

"Yes. You are."

"How dare you." She formed a disgusted sneer. "Mason will have your head for this."

A maddening laugh escaped my sore, ragged throat. I turned my back to her.

"Oh, I don't think so..." I faced her with an amber lens placed delicately on my finger, and one diamond eye sparkling. "As it happens, cutting off my head is the last thing he will do."

18

The Pretender's chambers were not necessarily large, but they were extravagant. A four-poster bed lay against the wall, covered with golden cushions and decorative blankets. Aside from a fireplace adorned with jewels and marble, it contained a series of wardrobes, a small desk, and a dressing table, almost completely covered with cosmetics. A door lay on the far wall, which I presumed led to a private bathroom, and just before the desk lay two large windows that overlooked the manicured gardens.

The distant mountains were no longer visible, smothered with the same grey cloud that descended over the Pretender's pretty little face.

"Alira..." she breathed.

I smiled curtly, replacing the contact lens with a smooth lift of my finger.

"Now," I said, watching with small accomplishment as she supported her trembling body against the bed frame. "Calling Mason would not bode well for you, would it?"

"H-How?"

"Doesn't matter. The only thing you need to understand is that we cannot survive without each other. I'm sure you've gathered by now that I don't want to be Mason's...*mate* – or whatever the Hel I am. At the same time, you need to keep Mason occupied, because once he finds out you're not who you say you are..."

The consequences were best left unspoken.

"So *please*..." I said through the first trickles of fear. "Please help me..."

Just as the Pretender eased herself to the bed, exhaustion filled my limbs. I collapsed onto the small stool before her dressing table, caressing my sore head. I suddenly felt a lot older than my twenty years.

As the rain slowly washed away the shock, the Pretender's mouth closed into defiant resolution.

"What can I do to help?" she said.

I released the breath I didn't know I was holding. The pressure of my fingers felt good as I scraped them through greasy hair.

"Tell me everything," I said.

The Pretender simply looked at me. "I'm going to need a bit more than that, love."

"I was always told that Mason wanted to kill me, and only by way of your conversation this morning do I realise he wants me for something...*different*."

Could she hear the shaking in my voice? It was hard to tell.

"Everything," I whispered, "I need to know *everything*. What I am, what he is, how I'm the End of Everything... Please, I *have* to know..."

Residual shock deformed into a grotesque sneer.

"You've got to be kidding me... Do you mean to tell me that you know *nothing* about who you are? *What* you are?" She jumped to her feet, pacing around the room like her very skin was on fire. "This is just *perfect!*"

"Keep your voice down!"

She eventually did and fell against the soft mattress.

"Look," I began, trying to find some common ground. "You have to understand that I am by no means pleased about this either."

"Maybe so, but the last time I checked, your life wasn't on the line."

"My *life* has been on the line since the moment I was born!" I threw my hair back and pointed to those seven golden rings. "You do realise how I got these, right?"

"This isn't the wilderness, Ali -"

"Don't call me that," I snapped. "That's not my name."

"Oh, I'm sorry, has the fact that your eyes are diamonds suddenly eluded you?"

I collapsed into a heap on the floor, my head throbbing. "Just tell me what I need to know."

The Pretender thought about this, her tongue fighting with her wisdom teeth. Eventually she agreed to my request with an annoyed nod.

"Thank you..." I massaged both temples as the first question came easily. "What am I?"

"You're the only one who can have his child," she emotionlessly replied.

"Why does he want a child? I mean, he's hardly fatherly material."

"He believes the birth of a child will grant him ultimate control over the world."

"But..." I frowned. "Doesn't he have that already? He's already immortal and no weapons can kill him."

The Pretender shrugged two bony shoulders.

"Well, that's what he told me. He's been wanting a child since Ragnarök, but out of all the *Aliras* that have been born since then, you're the only one who's made it to adulthood."

Over one-hundred-and-eighty years. That was an awfully long time to crave ultimate power. My body shivered at the thought of what he would do to get that power, and I swallowed the threatening nausea.

But still, the sheer longevity of his search meant he was open to all other deceptions, the Pretender being the most prevalent.

"How do you trick him?" I asked. "I mean, aside from your eyes... No offence but they're very different to Mason's and they mustn't have been the only things to win him over."

Those opal eyes flicked to me with thinly veiled contempt.

"I know things," she said. "I know things that only a true Alira would know, and I've been able to play those things rather well."

"Like what?"

"Well, the anger, for one."

"What?" I never even considered my anger to be related to Mason, or my inner destiny. But then I recalled the stories of Mason's insatiable anger, or the pure, bursting rage the night he killed Hallie. It was an anger I knew all too well.

"Your anger is a consequence of your species. You can't control it, one could argue you're not meant to. I played my anger off rather well during the first month here."

"But why would you do that? Why on earth would you surrender to him knowing what he is? What *you* would be to him?"

"For all of this!" She threw her arms above her in some grand display. "I wanted a palace, and gold and jewels. I wanted people to gasp with awe when I walked into a room, and Slaves to do everything for me without complaint... I want to be appreciated, revered, *wanted*."

Those arms fell slowly to her side, like spoons dropped in honey. "And I have that. For now, at least."

"But Mason's still going to find out about you. What happens when ten years have gone by and you've still not produced a child? Don't you think that's going to make him a bit suspicious?"

"I still have time to worry about that. Apparently, it can take years before I'm ready for the Connection."

"What's the Connection?"

The look she gave me was filled with resounding pity. "Oh, honey," she said, "you really have no idea, do you?"

"I wouldn't be here if I did."

"No, I suppose you wouldn't." She flicked a wave of golden hair across her shoulder. "At any rate, the Connection needs to be made before you're able to conceive. Your brain won't let you be intimate with him until it's been formed, and so he's obliged to form it. It's like some ingrained, basal instinct you both have."

"What exactly is the Connection?"

"He looks into your eyes."

All air shot out of me in a series of painful coughs. My throat, already burned from the vomit, stung and shredded with each lungful of air.

"But that will kill me!" I managed through the splutters.

"No, it won't," she said calmly. Too calmly. *How was she being so calm about this?*

"That's why I have diamond eyes too," I solemnly realised.

"Well they're not just for looking pretty, are they?" The Pretender rolled her eyes.

Nausea threatened once more, more powerful than before, and had me scrambling to the bathroom. I threw my head in the toilet and heaved those three handfuls of water back before they had time to be absorbed.

Lingering at the door with her hands clasped before her, the Pretender looked glumly on.

"You need to see a doctor," she said. "I wouldn't be surprised if those Aristocrats poisoned that fermented filth they gave you."

"It's not the fish," I squeaked from inside the toilet, a long drip of spittle hanging from my lip. "It's the... It's the music."

I wiped myself clean, then lifted my flushed face to see the Pretender's whiten completely. The makeup she wore was so evident, like orange blobs on an otherwise ghostly complexion.

"You're hearing the music?" she said, barely audible.

Without another look, she threw her hands through her hair and marched back into the bedroom. I quickly staggered after her, collapsing against the bed's golden sheets.

"What do you know about the music?" I asked desperately, feverishly, as the music thudded its way around my skull.

The Pretender didn't stop pacing. She pulled and tugged on her golden hair, her midriff inflating as she took great gasping breaths.

I endeavoured to help her through her panic attack, enforcing the same calming technique that Emilia had taught me all those weeks ago.

It worked: her breathing slowed, her face returned some colour. Once she took a delicate seat upon her stool, her long limbs stretched out before her, I calmly repeated my question.

"It means you've Come of Age," she quietly replied. "That's the one thing I'm playing dangerously close. He thinks I haven't reached it yet – he claims it could take years for me to – and before that happens the Connection cannot be formed."

"What does it mean?" I asked, breathlessly. "Why do I *Come of Age?*"

"It shows you're ready. That you're biologically fit enough to survive his stare, to produce a child for him. His stare *will* kill you if he tries to form the Connection before you're ready. So, the music acts as a little signal that your time has come, that you've passed puberty unscathed..." She formed a bitter *pfft* between pursed lips. "I should hear a bloody trombone after all I've been through."

Realisation hit with the clash of outside lightning.

I had *Come of Age* the night I saw Mason play a beautiful song on a violin, all alone in an empty Theatre. I had *Come of Age* the moment strange and serene notes from a peculiar instrument found my head, remaining there ever since.

Listening to her words, it was now so brutally clear: if Mason ever found out who I was, he would form this...*Connection*. Then, there would be nothing but my anguished screams as I tried to push him off.

I dry-heaved into my lap, my stomach having nothing more to give.

"You tried to play the piano, didn't you?" she asked, delicately. "What happened? Did someone disturb you before you finished the song?"

I shook my throbbing head. "I lost my nerve. I heard the Aristocrats, so I ran away from it."

"You can't run away from the music, Alira. It's one purpose is to unite you with Mason, and it will persecute you if you try to fight it."

"How can I stop it?" I breathed, my hand caressing my pulsating temple.

The Pretender looked down to her white trousers, listening to the pounding rain outside.

"Mason's visiting a contact in Maelstrom tomorrow afternoon. Persevere until he leaves, and then meet me in the Reading Room."

* * *

I WAS SLUMPED on the kitchen table.

A bottle of pills stared at me. They were from Doctor Grant: a gift to save me from the pounding headache he was convinced was due to dehydration.

Since then, I had been carefully sipping water. I must have consumed litres of it, but the throbbing did not abate. I had taken the painkillers, letting them slide down my burned gullet. They didn't help.

The music still taunted me, mocked me.

What would happen if I swallowed all of those pills, grinding them between my teeth? Would the pain stop in the afterlife, or would the music follow me there too?

I knocked the bottle off the table. Shards of glass skimmed everywhere, crunching beneath my shoes as I wandered on trembling legs to the window.

Finally, Mason was leaving. I watched the convoy drive away through the rain, bound for Maelstrom and the cruelty that lay within. I grew impatient and bounced from one foot to the other, counting the seconds until the convoy disappeared from my view.

Then I rushed to the Reading Room. The Pretender was already waiting for me.

"How are you feeling?" she asked.

My pallid complexion screamed my current health, so I ignored her question. "How do I stop it?"

She gestured to the piano stool.

The cushion was cool and soft against my buttocks, caressing the gentle curves. Slowly, I lifted the keylid. Music screamed.

Try to avoid your destiny, we dare you.

Carefully, even a little hesitantly, my fingers rested against those cold keys. Tingles of electricity rippled up my hands, through my arms, striking my very core. Every hair stood on end, and I took a precious moment to truly revel in the sensations.

Standing beside me with her arms crossed and tight, the Pretender watched in wonder.

Both hands pushed the keys.

The tune was delicate at first, filling the air with serene, calming notes.

But as the song commenced, it intensified. My fingers pressed harder, faster. Hands skipped over the keys, the intensity burning my muscles.

My heart was pounding in time with the music, willing me on as I absorbed every facet of that gorgeous, beautiful song. The insatiable urge to get closer to that piano, to *feel* the music inside my very bones as each breath became pained and ragged…

But I could not stop. The music had me, embedding its claws into the very fabric of my being, clinging deep.

Hands danced across the keys; vibrations stroked my skin. The end I had been waiting months – no *years* – for, was drawing closer and closer, willing my fingers faster and faster as the music consumed everything!

Something fluttered inside my head: a cold numbness that stung my eyes.

Finally, when my body had nothing else to give, the notes began to slow.

My finger pressed down upon that final key, the last bite of musical ecstasy lingering in the air.

Silence.

Finally, I could hear silence...

I held my breath, then released a shaky exhale. Warmth flushed through my cheeks, my chestnut hair – always matted and dry – was restored with such glossy vigour that it shone with a ruby hue as I twirled it around my finger. Even my fingernails, which had endured months of torment, returned to their pristine strength.

The music had rejuvenated me. Limbs trembled, yet I felt invigorated, empowered. Every synapse brimmed with newfound power the likes of which I had never experienced. It was intoxicating.

I laughed in spite of myself, picking at my thickened fingernails.

Only then did I glimpse up and see the Pretender. A singular tear trickled down her cheek.

"I-I'm sorry..." I said, because I didn't know what else to say.

Scarlet lipstick had been chewed away, revealing the dullness of those lips as she formed a desolate smile.

"He must never hear you play. He'll know instantly."

I nodded in bleak understanding. A last longing gaze to my piano.

With as much tenderness as a lover's last embrace, I closed the keylid.

* * *

WE WERE BACK in the Pretender's chambers.

She stood by the window, her limbs drenched in a ruby dressing gown as she studied the outside world.

I remained on the bed, revelling in the smoothness of my hair, my hands, my skin...

How could the music do that? How was such a miracle even possible? I caught my reflection in the mirror and even my amber eyes glowed, foretelling the intensity of diamonds beneath.

"Your music is different to his," she mumbled, transfixed by the grey outside. "The backbone of the song is unchanged, but yours is still different."

I remained quiet, simply listening.

"It's like you and Mason are playing two halves of the same song. Only by connecting these two halves will the song be undeniably perfect. Two completely different instruments, fitting together with such harmony, complementing each other so effortlessly."

A quick wipe of her cheek and we returned to ominous silence.

I thought to Mason and his violin, all those months ago. I'd only heard him play the end of the song – or his version of it, at least – but I could still feel the musical draw, the melodic beauty such a display promised.

Had Mason played it for the Pretender? I quickly squashed the surprise bite of envy. But then I thought to *my* song, the side of me that was still hidden from Mason, and relaxed in the knowledge that it was still irrefutably mine.

The piano had just started to resurface, though it caused no angst. The notes were calm and dignified, just echoing in the background like some record player left chiming in another room.

"Does he know my music is a piano?" I eventually asked.

"Yes – he told me he heard piano notes, only once and many, many years ago. Ever since then, he's known your instrument would be a piano. I already knew, of course."

"How did *you* know?" This question had been loitering in the background for a while now, though squandered by the other, more pressing questions that took most of my attention. But now it screamed at me, mocking my own ignorance. How did she know all these things?

At this, the Pretender sighed, tightening the sash of her dressing gown. It clamped around her middle, emphasising her bony structure.

"I met a woman," she replied, still gazing into the empty, outside air. "A strange, curious woman who told me everything about you. She told me what you are to Mason, your Coming of Age and the Connection. Though by no means everything, she told me just enough about you to allow me to *be* you." She forced a wretched smile and tapped the side of her eye. "After I got these done, that is."

"But why would she tell you anything at all?"

"I believe she wanted me to come here. She wanted me to fool Mason, to pretend to be you, though I don't entirely know why. Who knows, maybe she wanted me to distract him, to keep him off your toes for a while."

"Who was she?" I asked, carefully.

Her chest rose and fell on a heavy sigh.

"I don't remember her name, it was many years ago now. But she was a strange woman. I remember thinking at the time how fragile she looked, how small and feeble she appeared to be. But at the same time, she had this strange power that exuded from her very veins. She almost didn't seem human. It was all very odd."

A strange thought popped into my head that threatened more questions than it answered.

"Were her eyes made of diamond?"

"No," she replied. "But she did have golden teeth. That I remember distinctly."

* * *

For the first time in weeks, sunlight fought into the Fjordlands. Gentle rays burst through gaps in the grey clouds, bathing the Palace in a soft autumnal light. It formed streaks of gold on the gardens, catching the trees' changing colours until they glowed like beacons. I was admiring them from the window of my little kitchen when Heidi eventually arrived.

I was glad. I had been waiting for her.

Heidi forced a smile when she saw me. It was a strange smile, conflicted. She seemed genuinely pleased that I was better, yet her predicament did not agree with *smiles*.

Pale skin, bloodshot eyes and dry cheeks, yet it was Heidi's glassy – *hopeless* – expression that filled with me emphatic pity. I crushed her into my warm embrace. She hugged me back even tighter, burying her face into my shoulder.

It was a lovely moment. A pure moment.

But time was of the essence. The sun was close to the horizon and Mason would be back soon.

Tendrils of guilt surfaced. I wanted to stay in that embrace, to feel Heidi's warmth.

I pushed her away and asked her about the woman with the golden teeth. About Svenja Svellec.

Heidi startled, her honeyed eyes now glossed with betrayal.

I kept a tight grip upon her small shoulders, forcing our eyes to meet, allowing her to see my pleas.

I begged her for answers, enforcing that no hex or curse would be her downfall. All she had to do was tell me about this strange golden-toothed lady.

She ripped herself away, rushing to the door. I trapped her with two extended arms. Once more, I begged her and swore upon Asgard – upon the Old Gods themselves – that I would not dare breathe a word to Mason.

Eventually, she conceded.

Svenja Svellec was a curious being, both everywhere and nowhere. Heidi recalled having dinner with her around the Tribal fire, only for the Free People to claim she was in a whole different Territory at the time.

I questioned this, but Heidi was adamant: this woman seemed to be in two places at once. It was maddening.

But when she was around that burning fire... Oh, what stories she used to tell! Oh, by Freya, they were beautiful. She told tales of strange Gods and Goddesses, their temples open for all to discover; of lands filled with jungles and strange, fanciful animals that couldn't *possibly* exist; of coastal towns and white sand beaches; of coral reefs in clear turquoise waters... She told of buildings so tall they punctured the clouds, and great machines that carried entire villages across mountains. Her stories were wondrous.

Heidi sighed out her sadness. I squeezed her shoulder, as a gentle push to continue.

Svenja Svellec, in all of her beguilement, seemed the keeper of all New World knowledge. Even the damning events of Gainstorn were due to Svenja's innate knowledge of Mason's then unknown fragility.

I asked her if she knew what happened at Gainstorn, or why Mason was so weakened as a result. She simply shrugged, unknowing.

At any rate, Heidi surmised that Svenja Svellec was a godsend to the Free People, and was systematically feeding them information at every opportunity.

Although, it was more complicated than that.

Upon further probing, Heidi concurred that this was the view of the Tribe and was, perhaps, not representative of Svenja's true agenda. In fact, she seemed more of a living rumour, methodically popping up at opportune moments, and then disappearing for months at a time. Heidi personally thought she acted to impede the Rebellion more often than she aided it.

Nevertheless, the Tribe found it imperative that she remain a secret. Moreover, Svenja was adamant that Mason would kill her at first opportunity. She never said why.

I asked if she knew where Svenja Svellec was.

Heidi gave a guilty shrug of her shoulder. Apparently, this strange and curious woman was somewhere in the Icelands, although Heidi had no idea how she knew this. No Tribesman or Rebel had told her this, nor did Svenja ever say so directly. It was simply a feeling she had, an indiscernible hunch that her fellow Tribesmen forbade her to ever utter again.

It was a curious tale. I wondered what to make of it all.

The hum of car engines foretold the arrival of Mason and his convoy. Boots crunched against the gravel as half a dozen Masonians entered the Palace.

I thanked Heidi for her honesty. She nodded, tears just beginning to peek behind her eyelashes. My cold heart expanded for this lovely child, and I crushed her into me with such compassion that Heidi was initially stunned to react. But eventually she did, and those two small arms came curling around my waist, holding me tight.

I do believe I made a friend.

19

I feigned illness when Anya came to check on me, wiping cornflour across my lips and cheeks. By all accounts, it worked. I was excused from serving in the Dining Hall that evening.

This was an immense relief. Still coming to terms with my destiny, and the music, I was not prepared to deal with Mason. Hoping a peaceful night's sleep might help prepare me for inevitable conversations with him, I curled up into a tight ball and listened to the raucous antics from Upstairs.

Masonians. Drunken Masonians.

Sleep would elude me until the Palace settled down.

Once silence descended – as the dull thumping of boots subsided – I was wide awake. Either from the music's aftermath, or my own inner turmoil, I was alert and energised.

Sleep was just a word, and not something I felt any desire to be a part of. Grumbling, I grabbed my contact lenses, and my weathered copy of *Moonsilver,* and crept to the Reading Room.

It was cold that night. Tendrils of frost climbed across the window. Each blade of grass, or orange leaf, was encased in a thin layer of ice that shimmered and sparkled in the moonlight. The pine trees were glowing silver, the air crisp and clear. I curled up upon that windowsill, the blanket tightly wrapped around my shoulders, and simply gazed at the beauty of the outside world.

The piano was at my back, the keylid still down to protect the white and black ecstasy that lay hidden beneath. But the music was content with me, and I with it. For now, at least, both our needs had been satisfied.

A shiver prickled its way through my skin. I turned to the window, watching my warmth thaw the frosted glass.

Exhaling a contented sigh, I quietly began to read.

My reading skills had improved tremendously, although a few words still gave me an issue. I practised them again and again until I could taste their complicated sounds.

Harmoniously, was the word proving to be a particular challenge that evening.

Somewhere, glass chinked against marble.

I stopped, my breath held, and listened intently. Like a startled rabbit, I remained perfectly still.

Nothing.

Shrugging, I cast it to my imagination and continued the insufferable word.

The door clinked open.

I jumped to my feet, hugging the book close. Expecting to see Mason, I forced my rational mind to be calm and collected, and simply explain that I hadn't touched the piano and I didn't hear the music and I was all so perfectly innocent...

As a million thoughts whirled around my head, a billion answers stuck to my tongue, it was a shock when Mason did not enter.

"Yikes, it's chilly in here."

I narrowed my eyes at the stranger. In the dim light of the room, only the colour of his hair could be distinguished: platinum blond, falling haphazardly across his forehead. I recognised his colouring, and those broad shoulders, yet the thought vanished just as quickly.

"Can I help you?" I asked, as innocently as I could muster.

The stranger met my squinting features, and his grin grew wide. Slowly, he wandered towards me, both hands in the pockets of his chequered pyjamas.

"Ah, Maya, I thought it was you in here."

I froze, my blood curdling. "I'm sorry, do I know you?"

"Ouch, that hurts," he said with a chuckle. His voice was rather shrill and did little to emphasise his thirty or so years. "I drove you here, remember?"

"Oh." I took another look at this man, scrutinising those thick features and suddenly recalled this Masonian thoroughbred. "Ah yes, I remember now. Jayson, right?"

"Jayson Montgomery, at your service." He blessed me with an exaggerated bow.

"What're you doing here?"

"Meh." He shrugged, those hands swiftly returning to his pockets as he cast those aqua eyes around the room. "I was snooping around the Palace and I heard someone in here. Just wanted to check it out."

"Well, it's only me. I'm not doing anything bad, so you can probably go back to your post now."

"Oh, it's my night off," he said, smiling. "All the Masonians that went to Maelstrom this afternoon were allowed to stay for the night, and of course, dinner."

"Yes, I heard the party."

Jayson inched closer to the piano, and I had a sudden and vast urge to protect it – at all costs. Blanket still around my shoulders, I went beside my instrument and placed a hand atop its smooth surface.

"Oh," Jayson realised. "Of course, you were Downstairs tonight. Food poisoning, I heard."

"I'm better now."

"Certainly look it." The smile he formed was either lewd or caring, it was difficult to tell. "At any rate, I assume I'll see you much more in the coming months."

My fingers curled against the piano, trying to root myself to it.

"Oh, why?" I nervously asked.

"I expect to be getting a promotion soon. I've been a driver for almost two years now, so it'll be nice to do something else for a change."

"You mean start killing people?" I asked, bitterly.

Jayson frowned at my feisty display and crossed two large arms. "Maybe. But it sure as hell beats sitting in a car."

"We clearly have a difference in opinion." I scowled at him, then gathered my book and headed for the door. "Goodnight, Mr Montgomery," I said, curtly, passing him by.

Jayson nipped *Moonsilver* from under my arm.

"Oh, what's this?" He roughly flicked through the pages.

The blanket dropped from my shoulders. I scrambled after him, pleading and hissing. Panic festered.

Literacy aside, *Moonsilver* was my one true escape in that wretched place. A valid excuse to sit up on that windowsill and aimlessly, breathlessly watch the horizon bleed. I *needed* that book!

Jayson opened the book wide. The spine creaked and cracked under the pressure, dirtying the green leather with his sweaty hands and jumping over loveseats to avoid my outstretched arms.

"Oh, so what's it about then? Ah yes, Chapter One... *In a distant valley –* "

"Give it back to me, Jayson – "

"*... There was a young boy who spent his entire life –* "

"Jayson, I'm warning you – "

"*... Believing he was alone in the world, his only companion being the wolf by his side.* Ah that's a lovely opening. Really drags the reader in."

Jayson stopped just by the fireplace, presenting me the closed book with a smug smile on his face. I snatched it back and tucked it back under my protective arm.

"Are you sure Slaves are allowed to read the books in here anyway?"

"Actually, it was a *gift*."

I stomped my way to the crumbled blanket, and threw it around my shoulders like a cape.

"Oh really?" he asked, pale eyebrows raised. "Who gave it to you."

"Mason did, actually."

All amusement dropped from Jayson's face. "You're kidding... Why would he give that to you?"

"Why do you care?"

"I want to make sure he's not going to take advantage of you."

"Oh, what in Hel's name are you talking about?"

"Maya," he said, and licked his dry lips. "Mason doesn't just give shit to people out of the goodness of his heart. And particularly not to Slaves…. Er, no offence."

My heart sank to the blanket around my feet. He was right, of course. Over the past few months, I had often considered the real reason why Mason gave me that book. None of the answers were pleasant.

Shaking away unpleasant mental pictures, I clicked my tongue. "Well, thanks for your concern."

Without another glimpse, I headed to the door.

"See you at breakfast, Maya."

Before I left, I chanced a final look at him. Silently, I observed Jayson perch himself on the cushioned windowsill.

A circle of condensation had formed upon the glass – a consequence of my body heat. I looked on, first confused and then concerned, as Jayson Montgomery ran his hand through the cloudy patch.

Trickles of water sped down the fogged glass, like waterfalls of black ink.

Jayson just stared at them, unmoving.

That last image of Jayson lingered in my mind. Even hours later, as I tapped my fingers in time to the music, I lay upon the scratchy bedsheets and considered those peculiar events.

There was no reason to be perturbed by Jayson's strange mannerisms in the Reading Room. Technically speaking, they were all completely innocent.

So why did I feel so disturbed? Why, above everything else in that wretched place, did the sight of Jayson staring, *leering* over those few trickles of condensation pick caution at my skin?

I pulled the blanket tight against my chin, still hugging *Moonsilver*, and endeavoured to fall into my dreams.

***

I SERVED BREAKFAST THAT MORNING. I was prepared.

Reminiscing of those snowy mountains, or the icicles dripping from caves, I had reformed my icy exterior. Immune to all feeling.

Was I scared of seeing Mason? Of course I was.

But like Hel was I going to show it.

As it happens, all my preparation went to waste. Mason had declined to show up for breakfast that morning. In his place were half a dozen rowdy Masonians, whose only purpose in life was to make us uncomfortable.

Another notable absence was Tia. Although, one only had to take a solid guess where she was, or *who* she was with.

My very skin shivered, repulsion spreading like a fever.

All that remained were Anya, Luna and me. We remained tense throughout those two long breakfast hours, dreading the inevitable moment a Masonian would make a salacious comment or – worse still – smack us hard in inappropriate areas. Our tight pencil skirts only made us ample prey for those despicable human beings, and I inwardly cursed them all.

Poor Anya felt the brute force of these unwelcome actions, gorgeous as she was. Her contempt was difficult to miss.

Jayson Montgomery was at the end of the table, his aqua eyes occasionally flicking to me but ultimately behaving himself rather well. Out of all the Masonians who had bits of bacon hanging from their mouths, Jayson was the most dignified.

He seemed nice, after all, and he did offer to help me when I first arrived.

But yet, he was a *Masonian*. Such a title did not attract decent men.

A Masonian called for coffee. Their blue coats were open, allowing full views of their open collared shirts and trousers. Their weapons were stored in a row just by the door, each silver glint catching my wanting eye. Could I steal one of them? Sneak a gun or a sword, and make a run for it? I forcibly squashed the thought away, before it had time to materialise.

"Well, you're a pretty Slave," one of them muttered, his nose crooked and his greasy brown hair slicked back into a bun. I tried desperately to ignore him as I filled his coffee. It sloshed in the ceramic cup, thick puffs of steam rising.

A hot hand caressed my left buttock.

I startled away, blood rushing to a hand that was so, *so* ready to crack a tooth. My cheeks heated, my heart beating with the same angered tempo as the music.

I sadly stared at the gleaming weapons by the door, pushing aside the desire to put a bullet in six brains, and concentrated on the distant thunder.

When they eventually left, the table was in a sorry state. Grease smeared the polished wood, covered by spots of coffee and tea. The milk jug had been knocked over completely, white puddles clashing against the dark wood. Oats and chunks of almonds scattered the table, blobs of porridge were setting like cement, the fatty grease from bacon shone like cloudy little jewels...

Animals, the lot of them.

I cursed beneath my breath, the grease smearing like some dirty polish. The clink and clank of what sounded like hundreds of plates as Luna stacked them at the other end of the table. On her hands and knees, Anya wiped up the punctured remains of a runny yolk, the egg thrown there simply *because it was fun.*

Fucking animals.

Understandably, all of us were silent. In this quiescence, Jayson Montgomery's shrill voice echoed across the room.

"Oh gosh, made quite a mess, didn't we?" he said, perusing the scene.

We acknowledged his presence with a brief stare but ultimately ignored him. Sucking at his lower lip, Jayson put both hands in his pockets and just skulked in the doorway.

"So... Is there anything I can do to help?"

Exasperated, I threw the cloth on the table and just looked at him. "S'cuze me?"

"Can I help? Hardly seems fair for you to have to clean up our mess."

Shaking my head, I continued to wipe the greasy table.

"No thank you, Sir," I replied, curtly.

"Call me Jayson. I'm sure as hell not a *Sir*."

"*Fine*. Goodbye, Jayson."

"Goodbye, Maya. I'll see you soon."

"Yeah, whatever. See you soon," I mumbled, rolling my eyes.

Heavy footsteps sounded as Jayson Montgomery left with the rest of them, crunching gravel on the outside driveway. Thanks to the Old Gods, for those messy bastards were finally leaving.

"What the hell are you doing, Maya?"

I look up to see Anya's scowl. "I don't follow," I said, sincerely.

"*Oh call me Jayson! See you soon, Maya!*" She angrily rolled her eyes, her tongue clicking. "Maya, he's a Masonian, not your friend."

"I know that and he's not. I barely know him."

Anya threw a warm hand on mine, halting the movements of the brown cloth.

"Remember what happened to Tia," she said quietly. "*Never* lower your guard around any Masonian, no matter how friendly they appear to be."

As Anya disappeared beneath the table, I recalled those slow drips of black water, trickling down the glass.

"Did Tia ever say who it was?"

"No. But she did say it was a Masonian Captain."

Tallis. The thought popped like a bolt of lightning.

"Was it a Herder?" I asked, bitterly.

"She never said. As I'm sure you can imagine, she doesn't like to talk about it. Please don't bring it up."

"Don't worry, I won't."

I didn't have to bring it up. My mind was already settled.

Captain Tallis raped Tia in the Green Room.

How could it be anyone else? He was ruthless and strong, vicious and wicked. If anyone had the means to do something so atrocious, it would be him. I squeezed the cloth hard, exposing the white of my knuckles and each of the small scars that resided there.

The injustice of it all! How was someone, as profoundly wicked as he, be allowed to run free, to pillage and plunder to his heart's content?

All while poor Tia was forced to sleep with Mason to secure her own protection, her own *dignity*.

It was so cruel, so unfair.

As I scrubbed the cloth hard into the wood, I thought back to Jayson Montgomery. At least, in all of this madness, Jayson Montgomery was innocent. After all, he was a driver, not a Captain.

All disturbing stares aside, maybe he *was* just trying to be nice?

I highly doubted this. But still, I made a mental note to give a friendlier tone the next time I saw him.

Just in case.

* * *

Before too long, Anya was called to aid the Pretender with some superficial part of her appearance. Luna was required to clean up after the Masonians, for they had taken the liquor to their bedrooms and made a nauseating mess. As Heidi was still doing laundry, I found myself alone in my little kitchen.

I enjoyed the solitude – the peace of my own company, the tranquillity of being truly alone. Elbow deep in soapy dishwater, I fought with dishes beneath the suds and gazed at the growing storm.

Clouds formed quickly, drowning the sunlight. The distant snow-covered mountains were already fading, smothered by the immense rain cloud approaching from the north. The rutting stags, their wide antlers jutting, took heed of the rumbling thunder and ran with haste to the forest.

Then the sky fell.

Sheets of rain berated the Palace, slamming against the window. I looked on, amazed, and tried to remember if I had witnessed such rain in other Territories.

But no, only the Fjordlands.

Although beautiful, they were definitely the kitchen sink of the New World. Being completely surrounded by the mountains to the North and East, and then the Endless Sea to the South and West, full clouds were squeezed over the Fjordlands. After all, the incessant rain produced the waterfalls the Fjordlands were ultimately so famous for.

Standing with my hands in the sink, I stared out of that little window. During my time at the Palace, I had seen millions of raindrops, countless grey skies... I missed the sunlight, the frosty blue sky, the virgin white of freshly packed snow...

A longing sigh as a car rolled just outside the window. I watched curiously as the shiny black thing, doused with golden accents, switched off its engines and the doors opened to reveal Mr Erik Doncaster.

Poor Orzo.

I angrily slapped the dish cloth, splashing everywhere.

Erik Doncaster took one look into the thunderous downpour, massaged his bushy moustache and then removed his white jacket to protect himself from the weather.

"Yeah that's right, you old pussy," I grumbled to the window. "We wouldn't want your moustache to frizz now, would we?"

"You're evidently feeling better."

I spun on two red heels, dish cloth still in hand, and was met with a smirking Mason leaning against the door frame.

"Oh, forgive me, Sir," I said, turning my back to him. "I didn't realise you were there."

I squeezed my eyes shut, heart hammering. *Keep it together, girl*, I desperately thought.

"You should not have to apologise for your inner thoughts," Mason said, wandering into the room. "I didn't exactly announce my presence."

I took careful note of his footsteps. My sinking heart was heavy on my bladder as Mason lent against the counter beside me, the long blade of his sword scraping against the cupboards.

"What can I do for you, Sir?" I asked, avoiding his scrutinising gaze. I grabbed a towel from the nearby counter and gripped it in a strangling hold.

Did Mason notice my anxiety? It was difficult to tell. Either way, he remained calm and collected, and graced me with a subtle tilt of his head.

"My, two days of sleep have done wonders to you," he said.

I tried to hide the nervous smile from my lips. Instead, I strangled the towel close to my chest, looking anywhere but him.

"Must've needed it," I chuckled beneath my breath.

"Indeed." His lips curved into a smile that was almost...*admiring?*

The towel was becoming a hindrance in my anxious state, so I threw it to the back of the counter. It remained in a miserable little heap as the sheets of rain battered the window.

"I assume you are fit to return to your duties?"

"Yessir. I'm due to serve dinner again this evening."

Mason reached forward and tenderly wiped a ball of soapy foam from my hair. I suddenly, anxiously inhaled. *Please, Gods, don't let him hear the music...*

"Good," he said, lowering his arm. "I look forward to it."

Gracing me with one last smile, Mason pushed himself from the counter and wandered back to the door.

"Oh, Sir..." I said, turning to face him. Mason stopped, diamond eyes sparkling with intrigue. "I've spoken to Heidi. I have the information about Svenja Svellec."

Mason's attention piqued. "And what did she say?"

Deep breaths, girl, I reminded myself. I'd practised this exact conversation with Heidi earlier that day. I knew what information we had mutually decided to divulge, for I'd memorised every word.

"Heidi said a woman called Svenja Svellec used to tell stories around their Tribe's fire. Strange stories, about jungles and paradise beaches and stuff like that." I shrugged a guilty shoulder. "Then she just disappeared."

Mason's confusion was evident.

"That's it?"

I dared not answer verbally, for Mason would detect my lies and I'd be in deep shit. All I did was nod. Thankfully, this was enough.

Mason wiped the annoyance from his face, his broad chest heaving with a defeated sigh. "Well, that's disappointing."

"I'm sorry I couldn't be of more help."

"Why was she forbidden from relaying that? It's hardly sensitive information."

I shrugged again, casting a guilty gaze to the corner of the room. "Herder's are overly superstitious. Hearing stories about impossible lands can be an insult to the Ancestors, or even to the Old Gods themselves. You insult them long enough and your Herd starts dying."

"Yes, superstition is a powerful thing." He disappeared into his own thoughts for a few moments, scanning some imaginary point in mid-air.

A lonesome roll of thunder echoed in the space between us. With it came some ingrained curiosity that I was unable to shake.

"Sir," I chanced, edging closer. "If I may, did such things exist? Jungles, strange Gods and Goddesses? In the Old World, I mean."

Mason seemed genuinely perplexed by my question. "Why do you ask?"

"It's just so different to this..." I weakly gestured to the outside world. "Heidi spoke of the jungles and those exotic islands with such... *fascination*... Surely such things can only be stories?"

"Are you worried those stories will insult the Old Gods?" Mason sarcastically smiled.

"Of course not," I replied, exasperated. "It's just that such things seem... *ludicrous*." I threw my arms into the soapy water, finding a dish and scrubbing hard. "That Svenja woman clearly has an overactive imagination."

Mason's small chuckle tickled the hairs on the back of my neck.

"Do you long to see those jungles? Those exotic paradise islands?" he asked, wandering to my side.

I paused my hectic cleaning and considered all avenues of his question. The immense rain had relaxed its assault, and as my gaze fought through the grey mist, I found the sharp peaks of those snow-encrusted mountains. The usual longing erupted inside my chest, like a dull ache that could not be sated by any music.

"No," I sincerely replied. "Mountains are better."

Beside me, Mason's bright eyes flicked down. He seemed to be contemplating something.

I cleared my throat and said, "Forgive me, Sir. I shouldn't keep you."

"Nonsense. It's been a most enlightening conversation." He wandered back to the door. "See you tonight, Maya."

I listened to the pounding of his boots as they echoed up the corridor. Finally, after an age, they were indistinguishable from the rattle and clatter of metal pots.

Slumping over the sink, I released the time bomb of tension that was so close to popping in Mason's face.

I exhaled a long, extended breath, then – with newfound resolution – stood up straight and faced the window. Those mountains yelled at me, begging me to return to their snowy embrace.

Svenja Svellec's stories could go to Hel.

20

Mornings grew frosty.
As winter beckoned on the horizon, trickles of cold permeated the air. Thunderous storms became less frequent. The dwindling rain turned to sleet, then stopped altogether. In their stead arose the first icicles of winter's impending breath.

Fallen leaves were encrusted in white, each vein protruding from their bodily structures. The trees themselves were preparing for a long winter's nap. Gold and ruby showers of leaves sunk to the frosty ground below, mixing with the last decaying fruits.

As the rutting season ended, dominant stags strutted across the crispy grass, their harem of does trotting dutifully behind. Large clouds of mist erupted from their nostrils, floating into the frosty air as they turned their faces to the sun's gentle light.

I watched them in awe, a small smile on my face. My hands washed those breakfast dishes, and I inhaled the sweet aromas of bubbling jam from the stove.

It had been a few weeks since Mason and I had discussed the strange stories that Svenja Svellec told. I had informed Heidi of what we had discussed, and then sent her Upstairs most mornings on the pretence of *dusting the ornaments*. Of course, she was there to keep her ears open and relay any more news regarding the curious woman with golden teeth.

The first morning I had done so, Heidi was equipped with a short note to Mason, detailing what innocent task I required of her. Heidi reappeared numerous hours later, having done her chores, with no information but still in the possession of my handwritten note, complete with Mason's red squiggles that corrected all my spelling and grammatical mistakes.

I was so infuriated, I drowned the letter in the dishwater. Then I burst out laughing.

Nevertheless, Heidi was a good little spy. I only hoped she could bear as much fruit as the Palace grounds.

The kitchen staff had utilised all they could from the autumnal fruit, but still they had excess. This excess – comprising everything from berries to apples, root vegetables to cabbages – had found their way to us.

"Well what do they expect us to do with it?" Luna had remarked.

Turns out, we could do a lot with it: chutneys, jams, pickles…

Our little kitchen had smelt glorious ever since.

"This is really damn good," Anya mumbled, finger deep in a jar of warm, fresh blackberry jam.

"Leave some for the rest of us," I smiled at her blue-tinted lips.

"Ha, don't worry, we've got plenty." She bobbed her head towards the neatly stacked rows of jams and chutneys that were invading the countertop.

While Anya indulged herself, I washed dishes and Luna dried. We remained in a calm state of tranquillity, listening to the bubbling of the jam and the soft humming from my throat.

The music was becoming louder each day. Little by little, it was harder to ignore.

I often debated playing the piano, to satiate the music as I had done before. Yet, the music both transfixed and terrified me. I did not want to indulge myself in those black and white keys, only for Mason to hear who I really was.

So, I persisted with the music inside my head, humming it softly to the air when Mason was not in earshot. I daresay the others enjoyed it too. After all, regardless of my own destiny, the song was beautiful.

Small footsteps echoed down the wooden corridor, followed by the clanks of red heels. Heidi rushed into the kitchen with Tia close behind. Both were breathless.

"I have news!" Heidi exclaimed, a huge smile upon her face.

Yes, *yes!* This was the moment I had been waiting for, to utilise that wonderful child and overhear the deepest, darkest secrets of Mason's inner circle. Excited, I abandoned the kitchen sink and hastily dried my hands on my skirt.

I asked Heidi what she had found out, if it was something to do with Svenja Svellec.

Heidi shook her head yet responded with such excitement that I wondered if I'd heard correctly.

"Mason's going on a trip?"

"A trip!" Anya almost burst at the seams. "Did he say where? For how long? How many Territor – "

"Calm down, Anya," Luna said, "let her finish."

I translated Anya's questions. "He's going to stay at a place called Frost Manor?"

"Oh, that's the Snow Territory!"

"Anya!"

"I'm sorry, I'm sorry… Okay, yes I'm calm… Is he going anywhere else?"

"He's stopping off at another town but didn't go into detail. He'll be away for about two weeks."

"*Two weeks!*" Anya threw her head back and grinned to the ceiling. Luna's radiating smile passing to Tia, who appeared to be holding back tears of joy.

"What's this trip?" I asked.

"During the colder months, Mason travels the Territories, usually to check up on his contacts and just generally make his presence known."

"Yes, I know that." Campbell always used to bribe innkeepers to divulge any and all information they knew about Mason's annual Tour. "But why are you all so excited about it."

"Because he takes us with him!" Anya beamed, her teeth stained purple.

Somewhere, deep inside the dusty recesses of my cold heart, sprung a warmth that very much felt like excitement.

"We're all going to the Snow Territory?" My cheeks ached with the scandalous grin that lifted its skirt to everyone in that kitchen.

"Well, two of us are…"

The grin threw down her skirt and retreated to her icy bunker.

"So not all of us go," I stated, glumly.

"But still, two of us are getting out of this Palace, seeing new sights!" Anya said, her purple mouth still twisted into a hopeful smile. "That's enough to get a little bit excited for, right?"

I strongly disagreed.

"Who's going?" Luna asked Heidi, who just shrugged.

"It'll be Tia, for obvious reasons," Anya said. I shot my envious eyes over to Tia, who was stifling tears of pure happiness. "…And then usually it was Hallie, seeing as Ivan accompanied him on all his jaunts."

"So… That would mean…" I shifted my weight from one foot to the other. "I mean, there's a free spot, right?"

"Don't stomp on Hallie's grave just yet," Luna snapped, before her face softened. "…But, yes. There's a spot open."

"Huh." Slowly, I wandered over to the bubbling pot of jam and stirred. Rich aromas of caramelised blackberries wafted up in return.

I didn't like this. The whole thing reeked of that Theatre trip when I was Emilia's. Take the Slaves on a nice excursion and they'll be more inclined to be obedient. It was a sick use of power.

But then, I remembered the Theatre production. The first time I heard an orchestra, the voices of the baritones and the soprano as they wailed their lungs to the audience…

It was enchanting.

Yes, the memories might have become tainted by my Coming of Age, but the feelings I felt during the show – the happiness, the excitement, the bewitchment… Those feelings would stay with me till the end.

But, for argument's sake, what if I *didn't* make it on this trip? Mason would be gone from the Palace, so would a good proportion of his Masonian stooges.

Perhaps, should this open spot on the trip just…slip from my fingers, I'd finally find my moment of glorious opportunity…

To escape that wretched place, once and for all.

* * *

THE NEXT FEW days were a blur.

Downstairs became a hub of chatter, the very air brimming with the perpetual buzz of gossip and intrigue. Excitement worked its way across everyone, spurring newfound purpose and propelling them to complete their duties with energised motivation.

I was the only exception.

While the other maids rushed around the kitchen, scrubbing those dishes until they were sparkling, or cutting those thousands of vegetables, I simply remained by the stove, idly stirring the pans of bubbling jam.

Nevertheless, I was in direct competition with the other maids, and they all wanted to please Mason. Mason, the bastard, observed their efforts with an annoying little smirk, and simply graced my disinterest with a confused frown. I elected to show a little more enthusiasm as I made and stored those seventy jars of condiments, just to avoid raising suspicion.

Some days later, Bentley arrived in our little kitchen with a piece of folded paper. We were eating lunch: a delicate creation of smoked salmon and poached eggs, leftovers from breakfast. Outside, the sun had only just peeked above the horizon, illuminating Anya Whittaker's red hair with crimson light.

I watched that hair shimmer as Anya carefully took the folded note. Anya felt the weight of all four stares as she slowly freed the paper from its waxed seal.

It opened with a subtle little crunch. Anya quickly scanned the paper and burst into tears. She covered her face, trying to stifle her sobs.

Luna snatched the folded paper, her eyes quickly moving across the text.

"Anya's been chosen," she said, as Anya lowered her hands to reveal pure joy.

Was Luna happy for Anya? It was difficult to say, for her eyes quickly iced over.

"Congratulations Maya," she glared.

Tension rose, like a flood.

Tia jumped to her feet, her chair clattering to the floor. She marched to the sink, gripping both sides of the basin with a crushing force.

"What has happened?" Heidi tentatively asked.

"Maya has stolen Tia's spot on the trip." Luna glared with a detesting shadow.

"No, no..." I nervously laughed. No, *no!* This wasn't supposed to happen! I had remained impartial to their electric excitement, completely unresponsive to the idea of this *reward*. So why was my name on that list?

Hopes of my impending escape disappeared. Blown away, like the red autumnal leaves.

Tears tickled my eyes. In a desperate effort to push aside their hating glares, I said, "Anya's coming too, remember. Sh-She could have replaced Tia."

"Oh no..." Tia's voice matched the frost outside. "It's definitely you."

Tia turned, her eyes smouldering with unshed tears. "Well done, Maya. You're his new favourite."

Their stares were piercing, *murderous*. Unable to take any more, I hastily removed my heeled shoes and ran.

I had to get away. I had to find my solitude, where I could forget all that I was – what I was *meant* to be – and find an innocent reason why I had taken Tia's place on that list.

Because Luna was right: Mason didn't want Tia. He wanted *me*.

That was why my name was on his list.

I was in the Dome Room. A corridor lay directly ahead of me. I rushed down it, not caring where it went, and burst my panicking body through the door at the end. Then, I found myself on the floor, both kneecaps cushioned by a white bearskin rug.

Hands upon my thighs, I stared up to the chandelier as horrible thoughts raced around my skull. They matched the tempo of the music, now so taunting. It knew I had grabbed Mason's attention and it laughed loudly inside my head.

Mason does not who you are, I desperately reminded myself.

I threw my hands through my waves of chestnut, regrew my backbone, and stood to my full height.

Only then did I chance a look around the room.

In fact, the more I scrutinised where I was, the more I realised that – aesthetically speaking – it was an almost an exact replica of the Reading Room. The same mahogany walls, the familiar marble fireplace. In the place of books, there were glass cabinets, filled with guns: rifles, shotguns, revolvers, even muskets. There was another rack directly below the window that did, admittedly, boast four antique swords, but they were the only blades in the room.

The rest of the space was filled with two things: paintings and stuffed animal heads. A steady collection of deceased creatures hung from the walls, ranging from elk to pronghorn, buffalo to wolf. The star of the room was undeniably an immense moose's head, its antlers radiating out and creating skeletal shadows against the wooden walls. I wished the regal animal was slaughtered for food, and not simple sport.

Below my feet was that monstrous bearskin rug. The poor bear's head was still attached, obsidian glass eyes forever open, and its huge mouth forced open to boast sharp, stained teeth.

My attention moved to two paintings, encased in golden frames, hanging just above the cabinets. Both portrayed the same mountain range, only one at sunset, and the other bathed in silver moonlight.

I stared at those paintings. Although the mountains were large, the focus of both scenes were the waterfalls, just visible through the scattering of pine trees. Both pictures portrayed the immense lustre of snow.

I wanted to wander into those paintings, to be readily seduced by them. All too easily, my mind threatened freedom. Only, this time, I did not fight the memories.

There was a time, long ago, where I had walked between the trunks of evergreen trees. The pines towered high, their emerald needles shining beneath a sky dancing with green and blue light. It flowed as an undulating wave and tinged the snow with a beautiful wintry glow.

My hunting rifle weighed heavy on my shoulder, the snow crunched beneath my boots. A bitter wind howled between the trees, blowing my hair across my shoulders, whipping my face as my milky breath dispersed throughout the air.

The wind propelled me forwards, towards the boundary of the forest. Mountains climbed above, their peaks smothered in snow that touched those ethereal lights. A waterfall cascaded down the rocky side, originating from a glacial stream far above, roaring down into the calamitous pool at the base.

I crouched down, the tip of my coat touching the snow and examined small tracks dotting ahead. The doe must have been close.

I gathered my rifle, found an overhanging rock ledge. Then, I waited.

The aurora continued to fill the sky with colour, the glittering stars only just visible behind the moving light.

Movement ahead. I took my aim.

Out of the evergreen mess walked three black bears. The mother was at the head: a large beast with a tan muzzle and silky black fur speckled with snow. Behind her, and trotting along quite blissfully, were two cubs. They were playing, cheekily nudging one another with their paws, bearing their small teeth.

I lowered the rifle and simply watched. They wandered, quite blissfully, through the deep snow, eventually disappearing into the mass of pines. All around me was wintry beauty: the forest stretching ahead, bordered with nothing but snow, mountains and heavenly lights.

I stayed there for a long time, just gazing. The only company I had was the roaring of that waterfall, and the call of a gliding owl, silhouetted by the sky...

"Amazing, aren't they?"

My mind was wrenched back to that Palace, and that bearskin rug, the moose's antlers, and the whole host of guns dotted around me.

I stumbled back, for Mason leant against the doorframe.

"Admiring my handiwork, are you?" He pushed himself upright and took a few steps into the room, turning to see the mounted elk's head.

"No matter how many Masonians tell me otherwise, I just cannot see you having the patience to be a prolific hunter. But, nevertheless, here I find you. Tell me Miss Doe, what business do you have in the Gun Room?"

"I-I'm sorry?"

"What are you doing here?" His voice was slow and stern.

My eyes searched frantically, trying to remember. "Erm... I got...er...lost back in the Dome Room and eventually found...this."

Mason's lips curved into a smile. "If you're going to lie to me, Maya, I suggest you lie well."

Defeated, I rubbed my aching temples. "We got the list today."

"Ah, the list," Mason said, wandering around the perimeter of the room.

"The list of all Slaves who will be joining me to the Snow Territory. So does your business here suggest that you are unhappy with the result?"

"Yes – I mean, no, I mean..." I closed my eyes, sighing. "Tia is angry with me."

"I do not doubt that she is," he said with a smirk. "But what Tia has yet to realise is that she does not take priority. *I* choose who is to accompany me when I travel."

"But why me?" Nails clawed at the glass cabinet, subconsciously reaching for those guns. "Why did you choose me over her?"

Mason came to a stop, those eyes catching the light from the low sun, fluorescing with the same golden glow.

"Because you intrigue me, Miss Doe."

The tip of my nervous tongue found the small scar on my lip. Pushing down my anxious heart, I said, "I don't understand. I'm a Herder, I'm *nothing*. Why should I intrigue you?"

"Do I need a reason?"

"It would make me feel safer."

"Safe? Oh, but the New World is not a safe place, and I would not want to give you a false sense of security." Mason grinned widely, granting me with an unsettling wink before wandering to the glass cabinet filled with swords.

"At any rate," he continued, tracing his finger across the glass, "in an effort to put your mind at ease, let me assure you that you have nothing to fear. In fact, I daresay your position is advantageous."

"Forgive me, but how is it a good thing?"

"Because I notice you," he said, silhouetted against the window. "Do you think I've not seen the way you look at the mountains? The longing scratching beneath your skin as you stare to the outside world? It's a draw I understand too well. The Fjordlands are beautiful, yes, but they hardly compare to the sheer majesty of the more northerly Territories, do you not agree?"

Visions of that waterfall, and the dancing lights in the sky...

"Yes," I whispered.

Mason slowly closed the distance between us.

"I chose you, Maya, because you are a strong, resilient woman. I've heard how difficult you were when you were first enslaved, how that insatiable fire kept igniting within you. I have only ever seen glimpses of that fire, though I must say it is *spectacular*."

He smiled widely, proudly, and gently touched his finger beneath my chin. "If that fire was ever present in my other Slaves, it burnt out long ago. I would like to keep your inner fire burning bright for a little longer yet, and I do believe a taste of freedom – to satiate that desire to step into the outside world – would keep it alive. Unless, of course, you would prefer that I take Tia instead?"

"*No!*" I gasped, breathlessly, gripping his open coat. The thought of seeing those mountains physically ached. Should that hope be ripped away, it would not only douse my fire with cold water, but remove the fuel indefinitely. I do believe Mason was right: if my fire was extinguished, I would remain a shell of the woman I once was. It was a fate I did not deserve, nor have any inclination to discover.

"No," I continued, a little calmer. "I would very much like to go to the Snow Territory."

"I thought so." Mason's smile inched wider, the tip of his thumb rubbing the soft flesh of my chin. Those two eyes gleamed like yellow topaz, drawing my gaze towards them. They sparkled brilliantly, each subtle flick from side to side allowing them to capture different angles of the afternoon light, each prism within the iris lighting a whirlwind of colour.

The piano in my head grew louder, matching the fast tempo of my heart. I wanted nothing more than to stare into those eyes, to see what secrets lay beneath.

Just one look, my inner music seemed to taunt, *we promise it won't hurt...*

But the music was lying. It was always lying to me.

I released Mason's coat, my hands dropping like cold pebbles. "Thank you," I whispered.

"My pleasure." He smiled and gently pinched my chin. The skin tingled as he removed his warmth. "I look forward to the trip."

The anxious coil of dread rose up, rendering all speech useless. In the end, all I could do was nod.

Seemingly satisfied, Mason replaced his twitching hands in the safety of his pockets.

"Pay no attention to Tia," Mason said on his way out. "She'll soon get over herself."

And then, just like that, I was alone.

Stunned, I cast my lying eyes around the room, trying to decipher the meaning behind that conversation.

But I could not do it. My brain was locked off to all except the music, now so loud and jeering, and just so goddamn infuriating that I threw my hands in my hair and tried to physically pull the notes from my skull.

I ran to the window, leaning over the cabinet of antique swords, and pushed it open.

Frosty air whipped into the room, throwing those long chestnut strands behind my shoulders. There, as a sigh of wind brushed my cheeks, I reconsidered my plan to avoid Mason's trip. Newfound hope, a fluttering of delighted anticipation, rushed inside my chest. Not at escaping, but at breathing that fresh mountain air, of seeing the untamed land rise into a sky studded with stars.

I closed my eyes, my cheeks flushing with the wind's icy breath, and concentrated on the growing bulb of excitement. Snow-capped mountains loomed in the distance, now so close and so tangible that one long reach with my fingers and I'd be able to run a flaked nail through the snow.

Musical notes dispersed beneath the wind's tender touch, and the excited warmth grew. It spread, slowly at first, through my chest, and then my belly, and then trickled down all my limbs until I was consumed. The thrill of those mountains grew with the smile that stretched my lips, and I laughed, the exhilaration of stepping in those snow-encrusted lands, of inhaling that diamond dusted air, filled me with such inexplicable glee that I could think of nothing else.

I remained in that room for a long time, letting the sun's rays warm my skin as the mountains edged closer.

21

Tia and Luna remained icy. Their mannerisms were cool to Anya, and glacial to me. I resented them for it.

Tia's anger, I could at least understand. Luna, however, was infatuated with such a dark sense of jealousy that it clouded her once open and bright heart with a horrid green tinge. It did not become her.

Mason could evidently tell their disdain and did all in his power to intensify it.

"Miss Whittaker, I trust you have adequate footwear for the Snow Territory? Miss Doe, are you in possession of a warm coat?"

We were succinct in our replies, aware of the growing resentment from the opposite side of that Dining Room. Despite this, Mason would only continue to ask more ridiculous questions. More than once, I was forced to dig deep, to suppress the ball of frustration that wanted to rise up and smack him in his smirking face.

Tia's mood continued to sour as Mason's interest in her faded. She spent most nights Downstairs, for it was blatantly obvious Mason was not utilising Tia's beautiful body as often as he used to.

I did my best not to dwell on the reasoning behind Mason's actions.

Nevertheless, his sudden lack of virility had hit Tia hard. I heard her crying some nights, followed by Luna's soft words of comfort.

The night before we were leaving for the Snowlands, their room was eerily silent.

"Will they be ok?" I asked, once the Downstairs corridors became hushed.

"They'll get over it," Anya replied, quiet at first but quickly loudening. "I mean, they're being ridiculous – we didn't have a choice in this!"

A sharp, angry thump on the wall.

"Oh, piss off!" Anya shouted through the panels.

The next morning, the Palace was abuzz with activity. Anya and I gingerly made our way to the back of lining Slaves, surrounded by the jealous stares of every other Slave in that Palace.

All except Heidi, that is. She remained on the outskirts, her small mouth curled into a proud smile, her honeyed eyes wishing us good fortune. I smiled at her in return. We'd see her soon. In a couple of weeks, to be exact.

Two weeks. Oh what a thought! The bubble of warm excitement spread throughout my chest, forcing a smile to stain my lips. I sucked on them, trying to dispel my evident glee, but with little result.

I spotted Tia staring at me, peeking her head from the Dining Room. I easily ignored her.

Pounding footsteps sounded as Mason descended the stairs, a large pile of papers under one arm, and the Pretender linked to another. Both were dressed smartly; Mason in a long black coat and red scarf, the Pretender doused in an unnatural mix of white furs.

The Pretender's pale skin camouflaged with her coat, but not the dark circles beneath eyes that had not slept in many, many days. I tried to catch those opaline eyes, to inch a guess at their concern, but she made substantial effort to ignore me. She stormed past all Slaves like she had a blizzard up her blouse.

"Good morning, ladies," Mason remarked to us both.

Frosty morning air flew into the Dome Room, piercing my bones. It was still dark at that hour, for the moon remained high and mighty, illuminating the selection of vintage cars on the gravel driveway.

A horde of Masonians barged into the Palace, their swords unsheathed, and quickly ushered us out. The Slaves leaving the Palace were abuzz with excitement; those left remained silent.

Anya and I were shuffled into a car that looked rather familiar.

"Good morning!" Jayson Montgomery's chirpy tune erupted from the driver's seat.

"Oh no, what are you doing here?"

"Ha, nice to see you too, Anya."

The doors slammed shut, and I took a small, sad moment to recall the lack of door handles. Still, I remembered the warmth in my chest and did my best to remain positive.

"I thought you were being promoted?" I asked, as those aqua eyes flicked to me in the rear-view mirror.

"Almost. I'm being promoted as soon as this trip is done. Can't bloody wait."

"Huh, don't wish for it to be over too soon," Anya muttered, beside me.

The cars grumbled to a start, the gravel crunching beneath tires as we slowly edged along. The Palace grew smaller, its light gradually forming tiny pinpricks against the black. Around us, the eyes of stags and does fluoresced in the beaming headlights, before they pranced off into the trees. Before long, the gates of the Palace grounds loomed ahead, those golden stags standing watch as the convoy passed.

Soon, we were enveloped by trees. Woody trunks held such shadowy secrets. I cast my lying eyes into each crevice, each space the forest promised.

For an hour, the scenery remained unchanged.

When the convoy stopped, I stared at the steaming train before us. Of course, we'd never make it north in those cars – the journey alone would take two weeks.

As we waited to embark the train, we stood beneath an early morning sky speckled with stars.

Escape. The thought slammed into me, almost crippling. The desire to hurl those limbs into the forest came fast, and my toes tingled, begging me to *run*.

And perhaps I could... Perhaps, despite everything I had considered over those last few weeks, my name on that list was not one of misfortune, but one of *opportunity*. I had been so focussed on escaping the *Palace*, of Mason leaving the *Palace,* that I had completely neglected that my presence on that trip meant that I was already outside the Palace's walls.

Technically speaking, I was already halfway to freedom.

Excitement bubbled, more powerful than anything I'd ever felt before. Through my pounding heartbeat, my eyes darted between those trees, seeing the shadows in which I'd eagerly dive headfirst...

But then a cold, spidery hand gripped the nape of my neck, and in one quick motion, moved to my throat and squeezed.

"Hello, sweetheart..." The cold, sneering spit of General Alden found my ringed ear. "It's been a while since I've seen you."

I cursed at him, loudly, in a language he could not possibly understand yet still found deplorable. His grip tightened until I was cowering.

"Now, regardless of Mason's own reasons for bringing you on this little escapade, I feel the need to remind you of obedience. Should you even *think* about trying to escape, I will cut you limb from limb."

"Like you'd ever be able to catch –"

"Maya, shut up!" Anya shouted, as colour dropped from her face.

Before me, Alden smiled. "I caught you before, little Wild One. Don't you ever forget that."

With a hefty shove, he pushed me to the frosty ground. I scrambled upright, my fists clenched...

Anya took a tight grip of my shoulders. "Don't!"

Slowly, I uncurled my fist.

Alden's smile merely grew and he marched back to his group of Masonians. Tallis was there too, glaring.

"He's the one who captured you, isn't he?" Anya's voice brought a fresh ache across my eyes. With a heavy sigh, I nodded.

* * *

ON THE OUTSIDE, the steam train was a large, metallic beast. A polluting blemish that coughed up smoke into the pristine air.

On the inside, it was luxurious excellence.

There were numerous carriages: kitchens, lounges, bed chambers... All contained a mix of warm mahogany and rich gold, the seats doused in a fine crimson velvet, and the tables polished to such an elaborate degree that one could see their own reflection on the tabletop. Ornaments were neatly scattered about, all secured by some means or another.

Upon each side of the train lay a row of large windows, polished to perfection. I was distracted by these windows as we served breakfast.

Mason and the Pretender sat on one end of the table, opposite Erik Doncaster and General Alden. A tray of pastries lay in the middle of them, surrounded by toast racks, jams, and marmalades, all adding to the faint aroma of butter and coffee that permeated the air. A large window was directly beside them, the outside world whizzing by as the train rocked gently back and forth.

The world was still dim, the tracks bordered with trees. For now, at least, the bright light of the carriage and the dusty dawn made my view of the outside world limited. But still, I kept hope, ensuring all coffee cups were full as I clanked my way up and down the carriage.

"... And we will reach Eagle's Overlook by tomorrow evening," Alden said.

Eagle's Overlook, a spectacular town at the edge of a large, circular caldera. Campbell and I used to visit there frequently. *My poor, lying Campbell.*

Erik Doncaster returned his coffee cup to the saucer with a delightful little *clink*. "Will Ivan be joining us?"

"No, he is still away on business."

"Where is he, exactly?"

"Oh, I can't tell you that I'm afraid." Mason smiled and popped a small piece of pastry in his mouth.

Visions of Aaron Osbourne threatened: his button nose, his inky blue eyes. He'd be four months old.

"Oi!"

I startled, then saw Erik glaring at me with his coffee cup in hand.

"Oh, 'scuze me, Sir." I poured the steaming coffee and continued my rounds.

I served coffee to Tallis and was sure to glare knives at him – an act to which he easily reciprocated. I thought of Tia, as Mason's infatuation diminished each day, and realised quite abruptly that Mason's protection would no longer apply if he moved on to new pastures. Her anger towards me, the Herder Slave who she believed was stealing Mason's attention, suddenly became clear.

Tallis was the cause of all Tia's pain. I despised him.

Rapist pig, I inwardly spat.

Moving on, I filled Jayson Montgomery's cup.

"Thank you, Maya," he said, with a kind smile. I returned the gesture, a little awkwardly, and quickly scurried to Anya's side.

Breakfast continued quite blissfully. The outside world brightened with every second, with rosy hues of light breaking through the trees. All around us, the snow's luminous skin punctured the dark undergrowth.

As the world zoomed by, I stood before the table of murderers, liars and Destroyers and obediently poured more coffee.

Suddenly, the trees dispersed into a visa of rolling hills. A grand expanse of bare, untouched snow, only punctured by the emerald green of fir and pine. The rolling vista eventually fell to the base of enormous cliffs. Row upon row, they merged into the horizon, into a pale pink sky that only the last few glimmers of stars were able to puncture.

Large mountains were to the left of us, waterfalls roaring down steep slopes, disappearing into the tangle of trees. An early morning sun peeked over those mountains, bathing the world in a glorious tinted light. It was ever more wondrous, ever more *spectacular*...

My amber eyes caressed the Woodlands, absorbing each rock and tree, each tint of rose light, each delicate shimmer from the few remaining stars fighting for freedom in the growing morning sunlight.

Before me, a whole host of clicking tongues and frustrated stares blissfully passed me by.

"Would you like me to kick her?" Alden grumbled to the Pretender, who was still waiting for her coffee.

Mason smiled. "No, give her a minute."

The Pretender huffed beneath her breath and granted me a swift kick to the shin.

That brought me back with a pained thump. I bit my tongue then grudgingly filled her cup.

The air was crisp, and as the pink hue dissolved into the bright blue of daylight, the draw of the Woodlands only grew. The rolling hills eventually grew taller, more rugged, and by the early evening the reddening sun hid behind towering mountains that bordered the train on either side. I watched the shadows form and grow, encapsulating the pockets of trees and boulders as the light continued to fade.

Once dinner was served, the sun had disappeared entirely. The light erupting from the carriage hid my view to the outside world, until only my reflection stared back.

Sighing, I completed my duties with that strong itch persisting.

As the evening turned into night, the Slaves retired. Inside our carriage, bunks lined the wooden walls, overlooked by a singular bulb hanging from the ceiling. The carriage itself was cold and damp, and we shivered wildly as we changed into our night clothes. I threw on my tatty slacks and black tank top quicker than a swooping eagle, and wrapped the scratchy blanket around my shoulders.

There were six Slaves in total. Anya, Bentley and I shared the small carriage space with three footmen.

Our bunks creaked as we crawled into their cool confines, the mattresses thin and uncomfortable. But the majority of us settled into a restful sleep in no time at all, the gentle rocking of the train lulling us into our dreams.

All except for me, that is.

Those lasting views of the outside world stuck with me, pulling me away from my dreams as soon as they threatened. In the end, I stared blindly at the ceiling. Anya was below me, snoring quietly. Heavy breaths of four other people filled the small windowless space. It was suffocating.

Eventually, I could take no more. The first glitters of frost permeated the wooden floor, so I pulled the blanket from the bed and wrapped it tightly around my shoulders, then gathered *Moonsilver* from my bag. Hugging it close, I crept out of the carriage.

The train was quiet and deserted. Free of artificial light, the outside world shone beneath a full moon. Snow surrounded us, its untouched lustre foretelling the empty tranquillity of the wilderness.

We were steaming quite happily through the centre of a large mountain range. Huge mounds of rock bordered us on either side, puncturing a sky glittering with thousands of stars. Moonlight caressed the landscape in smooth silver, the mountains casting deep, dark shadows.

It was beautiful. I ached to watch those mountains, to escape into their magnificence, for a little longer yet.

Tiptoeing my way through the starkness of the train, I cautiously entered the dining carriage.

The door clicked shut. As I turned to the beckoning seats, two diamond eyes stared back.

"Oh!" I startled. "I-I'm sorry, I didn't know you were here."

"Nonsense, Maya," Mason replied. Those glowing eyes returned to the outside view. "Please, join me."

My back pressed hard against the door, my arms wrapped tightly around the book. But as the seconds ticked on, the draw of the outside world was simply too much.

Tentatively, I approached him.

Mason was sitting next to the window, his long legs bent and sprawled across the seats, encased in loose lounge trousers. It was unusual to see the casual grey t-shirt that hugged his broad shoulders, or his bare elbow as he supported his chin with a single knuckle. A steaming cup of peppermint tea sat patiently on the table, sending its minty fresh scent wafting to the air.

He was the definition of casual and looked very unlike the man I'd grown to both hate and fear in equal measure. Music fluttered into my head, trickled down into my belly, and slowly eroded the remaining anxiety that still lingered there. Soon, I started to realise that I was almost *relaxed* in his presence. It was an unsettling notion that I tried to ignore.

Curling my legs beneath me, I pulled the blanket tighter around my shoulders, then carefully placed *Moonsilver* upon the table, drawing Mason's eyes to it. He delicately touched the worn leather binding.

"Goodness Maya, how many times have you read this book?" He flicked through the creased, dogeared pages.

"Erm...this is my fourth time, I think."

"My, you must really enjoy it."

"The first few times were simply to improve my English and reading skills. I didn't really understand a lot of the words back then."

"And now?"

"Now, I'm properly reading it. The story is good, and there are only a few words I'm stuck on."

Mason opened the book wide and pushed it across the table.

"Show me," he said.

Without objection, I spoke the first few sentences. The words came easily, my tongue understanding each letter and relishing their taste, their meaning. There were few stumbles or pauses, and I daresay I was expecting the proud smile on Mason's lips as I closed the book in my lap.

"Not bad at all," he said. "So, you came to this carriage to read?"

"And look out the window." I sighed, my warm breath fogging up the glass. "There are no windows where we sleep, and I didn't want to miss anything."

"I can understand that," Mason said, following my gaze. He seemed genuinely entranced by the outside world, his expression calm and filled with such contentment, he barely looked like Mason at all. I watched him with wonder, picking out each handsome detail. He was just so...*enraptured*.

"Forgive me," I said, "but I never expected you to be so...transfixed by the scenery."

"Why not? You are."

"Because I was taken from it. The mountains are my home, and I've not seen them in months."

"But I created those mountains. Everything you see stemmed from my imagination. Every mountain, every waterfall, every cave and crevice – each one was plucked from my conscious thought, carefully and purposefully placed to create something astoundingly beautiful. I put a lot of effort into creating this world, Maya. Occasionally an artist likes to admire his work."

Artist. That was a good description, for there was no doubt the pristine landscape, dramatic in its construction yet exquisite in its perseverance, was created with perfection in mind. It was reminiscent of a flourishing artist's brush, painting layers upon layers upon the landscape until the desired result was achieved.

I thought of my destiny, and Mason's apparent wish to sire the End of Everything, then stared at *this* man, who viewed the scenery with such pride. Why would a man who crafted this world, who shaped it with his bare hands, want to destroy it all? The whole purpose of my destiny just didn't make sense.

"My Pa always likened the world to a canvas," I muttered to the mountains outside.

"What happened to your Tribe, Maya?" he suddenly asked, studying me intently.

I sighed, dropping my gaze, the music wiped away the anger I knew I should have felt. "Masonians. They came out nowhere, killed everything, then burned it to the ground."

"How old were you?"

"A little younger than Heidi."

"Ah..." Mason realised, "that's why you care for her so much."

"I know what she's going through. I know how scared she is, how alone. Especially when you don't have a clue what everyone is saying." I chuckled bitterly beneath my breath.

Mason's face softened into something between pity and admiration. "How did you survive?"

"That's a good question." I sighed, holding the blanket tight. "A lot of those months are a blur to me. It's like I dreamt it, recalling odd bits and pieces but the majority being lost somewhere in my subconscious. Until I found Campbell that is." I smiled to myself. "He caught me trying to pickpocket him."

Mason's jaw clenched. The muscles convulsed beneath the stubble on his jawline.

"You hold Campbell in high regards," he said.

"He was a good man."

Mason suppressed a huff of bitter laughter, a shadow falling. "You clearly don't know about Gainstorn."

"What happened?"

"Something I do not wish to discuss."

Nodding, I mumbled a brief apology. We returned our attentions to the window.

The Snowlands were almost upon us, the towering mountains only growing in height and teasing our imminent crossing. As I stared, I thought about Gainstorn, about the fleeting pieces of information that were never quite in reach. The truth of Gainstorn was a hare, darting between the trees as soon as I found my aim. It was infuriating.

"Why Ragnarök?" Mason suddenly asked. He had returned to the carefree attitude his comfy attire eluded to.

"Hm?"

"I'm curious as to why you have the symbol of Ragnarök tattooed on your back."

"It's not Ragnarök. It's Jörmungandr, the World Serpent."

"But if my knowledge of Herder Culture is correct, isn't he the harbinger of Ragnarök?"

"The what?"

"Harbinger... It means, he *brings* Ragnarök."

"Ah, right." I pulled the blanket tighter around my shoulders. "Well, technically yes, but that's only when he stops biting his tail. The Jörmungandr on my back always has his tail secure, so Ragnarök can never occur."

Mason smiled patronisingly. "It already has, Maya."

"I know. But it still represents order, a sense of calm. I related to that a lot after my Pa died. It felt like everything was spiralling out of control and I needed a grounding point. Jörmungandr seemed to fit that rather well."

"Did it work?" Mason seemed sceptical.

"Yes." I bobbed my head from side to side. "Sometimes. My teenage years were pretty rough, you know how it is."

"Oh my pubescent years were a long time ago now." Mason laughed softly to himself and returned his gaze to the window.

Maybe it was because of the casual way he was dressed, or the peaceful rocking of the train from side to side. Maybe it was the tuneful notes of a piano, caressing my head so tenderly, I almost forgot they were even there at all.

"Mason..." I said, waiting for his diamond stare to find me. "If I may, how old are you?"

Deep furrows formed in his forehead, so I elaborated, "Ragnarök occurred over one-hundred-and-eighty-years ago, but you still must be older than that?"

Mason smiled, casting his attention back to the window as he played with the ceramic handle of his teacup.

"When you don't age, keeping count of all those years seems rather redundant. There hardly seems any point."

I waited, afraid of pushing something he was hesitant to respond.

"I'm two-hundred-and-sixty-five years of age. Give or take a little."

That was an incredibly long time. All that knowledge, all that wisdom he must have collected over those two-and-a-half centuries. Emilia Eynesbury mentioned all the exhilarating conversations she had with Mason, and even I admitted how captivating they could be.

Everything he must have witnessed, everything he must have seen…

"Do I surprise you?" he asked.

"It amazes me. I can't imagine being alive for that many years."

"They have a tendency to roll together."

The train was leaving the mountain pass, running down the steep slopes as moonlight flooded the distant valley.

I leant my forehead against the window, allowing the warmth of my breath to cloud the glass, and disappeared into the scenery. Everything was so calm, so peaceful. Dreams threatened, my eyes rolling with the gentle rocking of the train.

A nick in the track caused the train to jolt. I startled awake, my eyes darting around the space.

Mason had gone. The ceramic teacup had been emptied and lay ignored on the table, next to my book.

I stirred, stretching across the seats like some wildcat rousing from an intense slumber. The moon was still high in the sky, illuminating the Snowlands in all of their glory. Frozen lakes shimmered like flat pearls, surrounded by mountains cemented with snow and small pockets of greenery.

The aurora had awakened from its long summer nap, undulating the sky with pale pink, green and blue hues. It danced above the Snowlands, the only burst of gentle colour against the white and grey.

The aurora was a sacred thing to all Herders. It was said to be a doorway to our loved ones, long since passed. A window to the souls of the departed, where they could look down upon the mortal realm and fill us all with a sense of hope. Of belonging.

"Hello, Pa," I whispered to the aurora, my native language caressing my tongue.

* * *

THE SUN WAS high in the sky when the train creaked and squeaked to a halt.

Healthy flakes of snow wandered down, dousing an already white world. Our feet sank deep as we exited the train, surrounded by towering trees.

"Bloody hell, it's *freezing!*" Anya pulled the coat tight around her shoulders, stamping her feet in the snow. Despite the borrowed coat and boots, our legs were still bare and endured most of the bitter wind.

I remained silent and inhaled deep, freezing breaths. Each lungful cooled my blood, snow tickled my nose and throat. I revelled in the sensations, scrutinising each, swearing to never take advantage of them ever again...

Dogs barked somewhere in the distance.

Three black beasts came trotting over, secured by Masonian leashes. Dogs, I originally thought. Yet, the more I scrutinised their pointed ears and long muzzles, the more I realised that they were less *dog*, more *wolf*.

Anya's warm hand grasped mine as we were led down a path, straddling the train tracks.

This sudden display of affection confused me. I endeavoured to catch her eye but she remained staring ahead, her jaw clenched hard and her face devoid of all colour. Her hand remained tightly bound to mine, unrelenting.

We walked a little further, eventually arriving in a clearing of trees that contained more vintage cars. The Pretender, shivering wildly, was in that warm car's embrace in no time at all.

Activity ahead, the bags being packed and secured. Mason was lost in his own conversation with Alden and Erik Doncaster.

In everyone's apparent disinterest, the trees looked so tall, so inviting. Somewhere ahead, the distant trickle of a stream had resisted the cool chill and was flowing to freedom. I wanted to jump into that stream, to be carried by the boisterous current to new pastures and forget my life in Slavery.

I took another deep breath, my feet twitching in those boots. My legs were bare but I was surprisingly warm. The coat was thick and it was sufficiently early in the day that I could utilise hours of daylight to find some food and shelter.

Yes, *yes* – I could *do* this!

I could escape! I could run though those trees and disappear from the hard, cold eyes of Alden forever! He would never catch me, he would never get the chance!

Anya's grip intensified.

"Don't," she said, in barely a whisper.

Frantic footsteps sounded.

A footman had seen his opportunity. He ran manically to the trees and soon disappeared behind the veil of snow.

Masonians did not pursue him.

I cast my worrisome eyes around the scene, but no one moved. Not one Masonian took any notice of that lone footman. *Why weren't they moving?*

The dogs were removed from their leash. They remained still, but their hackles shot up like fireworks as they sniffed the air. Subdued growls filled their throats.

Mason took one look at the trees, then at the dogs, and whistled.

The dogs took off. They zig-zagged through the trees, beads of snow and mud erupting behind them, merging into the falling snow.

We listened as the pounding of paws dissolved beneath the wind. Anguished screams burst through the trees. Abhorrent noise filled the space: growling, barking, the ripping of material, those haunting *screams*... Anya covered her ears. I remained motionless, unmoving, as the screams grew ever more intense, and then silence.

I thought of the peaceful, relaxed conversation I had with Mason mere hours previously, and my stomach rolled.

As my sadistic music cackled, all dreams of freedom dissolved beneath the snow.

* * *

It was evening when we arrived at Eagle's Overlook.

A heavy cloud still hung low in the sky, yet it had stopped snowing. Despite the still air, temperatures continued to plummet.

Anya was almost on her knees. I wrapped my arms around her, hugging her close to diminish her shivers.

Eagle's Overlook, as its name suggested, was built on a precarious rock ace, halfway up a lonely mountain called Eagle's Eye, so named for its position in an old caldera, though the volcano that created it had long since died. The caldera itself was shaped by the winds and the glaciers, forming a deep basin surrounded by mountains, with the whole geological structure resembling an eagle's head.

The northern side of the basin was rounded, depicting the crown of the eagle. A large mountain at the eastern side of the caldera had spawned a glacier, carving its way down into the main basin, forming a curved valley that was said to depict the eagle's beak. The western side was bordered with a mountain range, and the southernmost part of the caldera had been eaten away by many glaciers, forming a winding network of small valleys and glacial streams that were meant to represent the feathers of the eagle's neck. Eagle's Eye itself was a lonely mountain, separated from its rocky brothers by an old glacier, and was left standing tall in the exact spot where the eye of the eagle was meant to be.

Eagle's Overlook was one of Campbell's favourite towns: it was quaint and isolated, and had one Hel of a spectacular view. As one of the wealthier towns in the Snow Territory, it had many markets and inns, and was filled with a multitude of Merchants and Traders. Any piece of equipment, no matter how rare, was almost guaranteed in Eagle's Overlook, if you could afford the extravagant prices.

At the head of the crowd, Mason's flowing coat was easy to spot. It was late in the day, yet the residents of Eagle's Overlook were all waiting for his arrival. I imagined they were already briefed on adequate behaviour, for Masonians were perusing the scene with their beady eyes sharp, their revolvers poised. Indeed, I doubted the residents had much choice but to clap their hands at Mason's arrival.

The town was exactly how I remembered: a market square, surrounded by small huts and a central well that acted as a congregation point. The two largest buildings were the Silver Moon Inn and the Town Hall, which was decorated with a large and foreboding clock face that chimed loudly on every hour.

A rather large man, dressed in white robes and with tuffs of grey hair on a balding head, came forwards with his arms outstretched.

"Ah, my Lord Mason!" he rejoiced, bowing in a dramatic manner. "It is my sincerest pleasure to welcome you to our beautiful home. I hope that you and your party will be inexcusably happy here."

"Thank you, Governor Cready," Mason replied. "Take my Slaves and Masonians to their accommodation and we will join you for dinner. We have much to discuss before our early departure tomorrow morn."

"Ah of course. I ordered the innkeeper to set up three rooms for your Slaves. You have brought six, yes?"

"Five," Mason responded, smirking. "My sixth made a good meal for my dogs this morning."

And with that, they followed the Governor up the frosted steps to the Town Hall.

The foyer to Silver Moon Inn was warm and cosy, with an enormous hearth that housed an even bigger fire. Above the fire, a stuffed head of a polar bear perused us all, and above that was a stuffed eagle, its wings extended in perpetual pride. Candles were supported by a large bracket made entirely of elk's antlers, and bearskins rugs were everywhere. Other than the innkeeper called Harald, who was a lovely old man with one brown eye and one blue, the only permanent resident was Margot, a fat little tabby cat who snoozed by the fire.

I had visited Eagle's Overlook on many occasions. On all of those occasions, I had spoken at length to Harald. We had known each other for many years, and both eyes widened when he saw me.

I smiled sadly, before being ushered on by the yapping pile of Masonians.

Irony is a funny thing. Before, Campbell always rented the cheapest room available. Now, having been forced into eternal Slavery, I was required to sleep in that same room. No bigger than a box and only housing two beds, a wood burner and a chamber pot.

There was a horrible, salacious smile from the Masonian behind us.

"Sleep well, ladies," he said, and then slammed the door closed.

"Hmm, like rats in a cage..." Anya remarked. I agreed, removing my coat and boots and collapsing into the bed. It creaked ominously but held my weight.

Anya and I idly chatted away for the best part of an hour until we received a knock on the door. A Masonian dropped our bags to our feet before exiting the room, slamming the door shut behind him. Less than a minute later there was another delivery of two wooden bowels of gruel: our dinner.

After this final visit, the door was locked, as were the other rooms down the corridor.

Later that night, nestled in our creaky beds, Anya and I just chatted.

"How many times have you been here?" Anya asked, her arms tucked beneath her pillow.

"Dunno, must be hundreds."

"Wow," Anya said, giggling.

"Well, as a Roamer you need a lot of supplies, and some stuff's difficult to come by at some of the smaller towns. Every now and then, you need to hit a big one, and Eagle's Overlook is the biggest in the Territory."

And it was beautiful. Oh, so beautiful.

"What was it like being a Roamer?" Anya asked, pushing her face further into her pillow.

"It had its ups and downs, but it was my life, my freedom." A wave of pining sadness which I hastily pushed aside. "What about you?"

"What about me?"

"What did you do before…this?"

Anya sighed and turned to face the ceiling, ignoring the rafters riddled with cobwebs.

"Oh, I was a waitress at a local inn, down in the southern part of Fjord Territory. Not far from Apple Grove, if you know the place?"

I did not know the place, but nodded regardless.

"Well, my mother died in childbirth, and my father was a drunk who used to get frisky with all the women in the village, so I went to work for the innkeeper at the only inn I knew."

"How did you get here?"

Anya remained silent for a moment, lost in her own memories.

"My boss," she replied, quietly. "He couldn't pay the tax for his inn, so he gave me up instead. I was fourteen."

"Gods Anya, I'm sorry."

"Don't be. It's not your fault, any more than it is mine."

"Did Mason buy you at Bolton Square?" I asked.

"No, he bought me from another establishment in Maelstrom."

"Which one?"

Anya seemed to wait a long time before answering. "Someplace different to this," was all she replied.

A hard swallow, and I left us to the silence. We remained listening to the bitter wind, whipping down the chimney and rousing the dying sparks in the wood burner.

"Are you sleeping with Mason?" Anya suddenly asked.

I startled, fighting the pang of anger, and fear, and confusion.

"No," I eventually replied.

"He wants you to."

I swallowed hard. "I know."

"Are you?"

"No, I'm not." I sighed, wiping my exasperation away with two sweaty palms. "He's a monster, Anya. I would never give myself to him."

An ominous silence weighed heavily on the room.

"Anya?"

"Yes?"

"Have you and Mason ever... *Y'know*?"

"No..." She chuckled a little. "Wouldn't do well to spoil the assets."

"What does that mean?"

Anya turned to me, her bright blue eyes so large and vibrant. "Don't you know? Mason orders me to sleep with his guests."

My eyes widened in horror. "What? But, why?"

Anya huffed bitterly. "Usually it's to entice information, or to persuade them to do something Mason wants. Sometimes it's simply as a reward for their good behaviour."

Another hard swallow. All of Anya's nightly absences suddenly made sense.

"Oh, honey don't look at me like that. I'm fine, honestly."

"But it's not fair, it's — "

"Trust me, it's much better than the last establishment I was at." She threw her arm behind her head. "Besides, some of them are rather attractive.

At any rate, this is a holiday for me. I can't wait to shag someone on *my* terms, rather than Mason's."

I sucked the scar on my lip. In an effort to stave the awkward silence, I asked, "What do you think of Alira?"

"How d'you mean?"

"Well, she's been...*subdued* lately, hasn't she? Just think of this trip – she's had a face like a smacked arse the whole time."

Anya bobbed her neat eyebrows, staring to the ceiling. "Don't blame her, to be honest. She's Mason's mate, and yet he's grown bored of her already. When she first came to the Palace, he was all over her — checking on her welfare, chatting to her for *hours* about her past, their future...*everything*. She was in her element when he was like that. Now she's just grovelling at his feet for any scrap of attention."

I considered this for a while, hugging the covers close to my chin. The Pretender's position was growing precarious, as what my own.

"Did you know what she was? To Mason, I mean. Everyone always thought he was going to kill Alira as soon as he found her. Y'know, because she's the End of Everything and all that."

"You truly believe that?"

"I don't know what to believe anymore."

It was true. My view of fact and fiction had become so clouded that I had no idea what was real or imagination. The boundaries had become blurred and there I was, walking the line between the two and dipping my toe in each.

"Well, at any rate, I also thought he wanted to kill Alira and got a bloody great big shock when she appeared at the Palace and he just let her walk in." Anya shuffled in the bed. "God Maya, you should have seen how he was before."

"What do you mean?"

"The pure...*obsession* he had with finding her. It genuinely scared me sometimes, the desperation he felt."

I imagined the sight: Mason pouring over maps of the New World, interrogating innocent townsfolk, bribing local innkeepers...

"Anya," I hummed. "D'you know why Alira's the End of Everything?"

"No idea, I'm afraid," she replied, then she met my frowning stare. "All I know is that there's a reason why Alira exists, and it's sure as hell not to play *happy families*."

I pulled the blanket towards my chin, fighting anxiety in my belly. It settled in my stomach, cold and hard, like a ball of wet concrete.

"Anya, have you ever heard of someone called Svenja Svellec?"

I held my breath as Anya contemplated the strange and peculiar question.

"No..." she replied, "not Svenja. But Mason has mentioned Sebastian."

"Who?"

"Sebastian Svellec."

"Does he have golden teeth?"

"Oh, I never saw him. I only ever heard Mason saying the name and mostly to Ivan Ulster. Why, is it important?"

"I genuinely have no idea." A laugh burst its way from my lungs and ricocheted around the small room. All these names, all these mysteries. They made my head hurt.

"I'm going to get some shut eye," Anya said, suppressing a yawn. "Night, Maya."

I mumbled the same in Herdinese, quietly removed my contacts, and left us to slumber.

* * *

BY THE NEXT MORNING, the snowstorm had passed, gracing us with a glorious bright blue sky and rays of unaltered sunshine. As we waited for the Aristocrats in the central courtyard, I tilted my head to that sun, absorbing each precious ray.

Jayson Montgomery was around, idly trying to make conversation that I easily ignored. Anya replied with vicious one-word answers, her disdain of all Masonians clearly showing. Eventually he just gave up and skulked away to his fellow compatriots.

The Pretender's frantic breaths hit my ringed ear.

"Anya!" she shouted, her voice audibly shaking. She appeared, still doused in the white fur coat and hat. Kneeling on the floor, flustered and panicking, she had one of the smaller trunks open on the snow-smothered ground. Anya ran to her aid.

"Ma'am, what's the matter?"

"My pearls," she spluttered, those long locks of gold shielding her face. "My pearls are not here – *where are my pearls!*"

Anya crouched down, placing a tender hand on her arm. "I don't remember seeing them on the list Ma'am –"

"No, *no!*" Her voice was trembling. "Y-You don't understand, I-I *have* to find my pearls!"

The Pretender lifted her head and gazed at us through bloodshot, glass-like eyes. It was then we saw it: though she had tried to conceal it with makeup, the dirty grey mark of a bruise encircled her right eye.

I gently touched her shoulder. She startled, but did not pull away.

"We'll find your pearls," I whispered as we locked eyes. "I promise, we'll sort this out."

Mason approached, deep in conversation with the Governor, Mr Cready. The Pretender immediately composed herself, stood to her feet, and left Anya and I to repack the spilled contents of her trunk.

22

A blizzard raged when we arrived at Frost Manor. Ironic, really. The convoy passed between large metal gates, bordered by two eagles with outstretched wings as they tried, unsuccessfully, to be welcoming. Visibility was compromised, the grounds smothered by the blizzard. I wondered if, should the blizzard cease, we could see mountains?

Frost Manor was a remarkable structure of grey rock, with seven towers that loomed above and were only just visible from the veil of snow. A large wooden door – complete with several brass rings – was positioned in the centre of the Manor and led to a protruding balcony. Lined up upon this balcony, even in the blizzard, was the household of Frost Manor.

Mason was quick to disembark once the convoy stopped. Healthy flakes of snow stuck to his clothes as he rushed up the stairs and hastily shook the hand of one of the men. Inaudible words of greeting and they disappeared into the Manor, with us in tow.

As a Slave, I had seen the exuberance of Emilia's Residence, and the sheer magnificence of Mason's Palace. So, as the entrance of Frost Manor loomed before me, I assumed this establishment would be comparable to other Aristocratic homes. What greeted me instead, however, was a mess of dark, indistinguishable wood that created shadows the flickering firelight could not reach. A heavy aroma of damp weighed heavily upon the air, which was chilled and unwelcoming. Very little was in the way of ornaments or pops of luxury, except for the fireplaces bordered with gold. Fires burned happily and healthily, as though recently lit, and the stench of soot easily permeated from a chimney that required a good clean.

All in all, Frost Manor was rather disappointing.

The golden firelight was the only form of illumination. Electric lights stretched down from the ceiling, surrounded with colourful glass designs, but none of them were on. Of course, the blizzard was still raging, and I assumed there had been a power cut.

Mason and the rest of the Aristocrats were swiftly ushered into one of the adjoining rooms. A peek over my shoulder and I saw a grand dining table, full to the brim with food: pork, roast beef, potatoes, and a whole host of vegetables. My stomach growled, loud and impatient. I inhaled the delicious scents of that dining hall and swallowed their teasing tastes.

A man blundered towards our group of Slaves, huddling in the entryway. Dressed in a crimson dressing gown, he had an impressive black beard that reached his navel, and sharp brown eyes covered with crooked wire glasses.

"Shoes off, now!" he barked.

Exhaustion showed through his immensely wide gait, yet Bentley the Butler still puffed up his shoulders and shook the hand of the bearded man.

"Good evening Markas," he said. "I'm sorry our arrival is so late."

"You are *too* late, Bentley," Markas snapped, fondling his beard with fingers covered in warts. "Do you have any idea of the trauma you've put my Master through?"

"Again, my apologies." Bentley bowed his head a second time. "But we all have a busy day tomorrow, and are eager to get some rest."

"Right you are." Markas shot his finger up to the damp air. "Follow me!"

As it happens, electricity was still operational, for the bulbs hanging in the servant quarters cast a dim light across bare concrete walls. We were below ground, for the howling wind had disappeared, replaced with the hollow echo of footsteps from above. The room Anya and I shared was even smaller than the inn at Eagle's Overlook, housing two narrow beds that resembled coffins. Apart from the beds, the room was bare of everything other than two coat hangers, and an electric heater that was evidently not used often. The room, though warm, held a sickly aroma of burnt dust.

The lack of chamber pots also meant the toilet next door was our only source of relief. As a result, no doors were locked.

This created an idea. A marvellous, miraculous idea.

Lying on the bed, I listened to the pounding footsteps from above. There were fewer now, as Aristocrats retired for the evening. Soon, silence filled our concrete room. This created an opportunity. A wonderful, exciting opportunity...

I had survived in blizzards before. Provided I had a coat and boots, which I did, I needed to only make it a mile or two before digging a den in the snow. So long as I kept myself warm, I would survive long enough to make a fire, and I could start hunting once the blizzard had ceased.

Yes, once I made it outside, I was a free woman.

The real question was how I would escape the Manor. No doubt the doors were locked, but there were so many windows, brittle and easily broken, just waiting to be smashed with a mouldy chair.

Masonians probably patrolled outside, their eyes piercing the masses of white, yet the blizzard acted in my advantage. My sprinting body would be hard to spot, particularly if I made it to the trees. If I could *climb* the trees, those vicious dogs would not catch me.

Yes, yes – this could seriously work!

I turned to Anya. She faced the wall, away from me, sleeping soundly. I debated whether to wake her that moment and divulge my elaborate plot. But no, better to scout the Manor, then return for Anya when the plan had been formulated.

Slowly and silently, I peeled away the covers. The concrete floor, glittering with frost, was cold beneath feet so I grabbed the leather boots from under my bed – simply for comfort. Walking on tiptoes, I gently turned the handle to the door, and pushed it open. A sliver of light entered the room, illuminating my face. Holding my breath, I peeked around the door.

The corridor was empty.

My excited heart pounded. The draw of the Snowlands was so strong, clawing its way into my very bones, begging me to return...

But what if I was discovered wandering the Manor? What if some lonely

Masonian patrolled the wooden, damp halls? I gathered *Moonsilver* from under my bed covers, just in case. Mason knew I liked to read, after all.

Holding it close, I navigated the corridor, taking small, slow steps. Upstairs beckoned.

In the emptiness of the corridors, my boots were so loud against those cold, wooden floors. But yet, despite the inherent unease spewing in that Manor, my mind was focussed. I needed to find a room where I could break a window with relative ease, where I could run to the safety of the forest before the dogs could catch me. The first few rooms were useless. The rest were occupied. I would have to try another night.

Dejected, I headed back to the main hallway.

A group of Masonians entered. Four of them, slapping each other's back and laughing. All dressed in their uniforms, but their weapons were notable absences. Even so, they grew cocky.

"Oh, darling, what are you doing up at this late hour?"

The men spread out, blocking my way. One of them catcalled, another made some obscene gesture with his hands.

"S'cuze me," I said, hugging the book close. "I'm on my way Downstairs."

"Oh, can we watch?"

"Yeah, I'd like to go downstairs too." They spat jeering laughs to each other.

They moved around me, circling me, surrounding me.

"Y'know Slave, I'm wondering what you're doing with your boots on."

"It's cold," I spat back.

"We should warm up then, shouldn't we?" He winked at me.

Trickles of fear beaded my tattooed back. The Masonians came closer.

"Back off!" I shouted, desperately searching for a way out, a way through the circle. "I-I'm warning you..."

They whistled to each other again.

A hot hand gripped my shoulder. The book fell to the floor. Another hand grabbed me, spidery fingers sinking deep into muscle. I spun, my fist clenched. I hit an open palm, then more hands grabbed.

I kicked and shouted, threw blind punches that always missed their mark. As one entity, they lifted me from the floor and carried me into an unused room. I screamed then, as loud and as piercing as I could, but someone punched my belly and all air was knocked out.

The lights of the unused room flicked on, dousing the room in an artificial light and emphasising the sickly green of the loveseat I was dumped on.

My wild kicks intensified. My boot collided with something with a crack.

He shrieked, stumbling back, covering his face with two hands. "The *bitch* broke my nose!"

My inner fire reignited, warping the fear, replacing it with a fury I had tried for so, *so* long to control. It matched the seething tempo of the piano notes in my head.

My limbs tingled, my fists squeezed, and every fibre I possessed kicked and *kicked* against those hot, grasping hands.

The loveseat was buckling. I flew my body from side to side, sweat dripping from my brow as I hurled my entire self from one side, then to the other.

The loveseat tumbled, Masonian hands ripped away.

In their stupor, I scrambled to my feet. A Masonian tried to grab me but I was too quick, I was at the door!

I opened the door and ran straight into a hard chest.

Diamond eyes bored into me. I shrieked, throwing myself back into the room. I hit a wooden wall with a loud thud, then sank to my knees, trembling.

The Masonians instantly stood to attention. Bowing their heads with their hands clasped behind their backs, they were quiet and submissive as Mason prowled into the room with General Alden and Captain Tallis in tow.

All three took a careful look around the room. At the battered loveseat, then to me, and finally to the bloody nose of the Masonian I'd kicked.

"Care to explain yourselves, gentlemen?" Mason glowered.

"Sir," the one with the bloody nose said. "We found this little Herder slut trying to escape. We confronted her and then she *attacked* me. You have to understand, she was crazy! We were trying to restrain her, for her own safety you understand."

Liars, they were all *liars*.

"Really? Then tell me, why did she have this?" Mason held up *Moonsilver*, its green skin battered and marked by a muddy footprint. "Do you not think, gentlemen, that she was just trying to find a place to read?"

The Masonians cast a worried look to each other, about to conjure up some dramatic story when Mason yelled, "*Enough!*"

They fell back into their hole, silent.

"We are *guests* here! Does that fact completely bypass your idiotic brains?"

"Sir, we – "

"*Shut up!*" Mason's eyes fluoresced widely. "Do you have any idea of the scale of the insult you have made to Barnabas Price?"

They remained silent.

"No, of course you don't. *Imbeciles.*

"Alden, Tallis," Mason snapped behind him. "Get these four pieces of deer shit out of my sight."

All Masonians were charged from the room, the door slamming behind them.

Mason and I were left alone. Heat radiated from beneath his shirt, his shoulders rising and falling at an alarming rate. I remained on the floor, still trembling, unable to move.

Something wet ran against my lip, so I wiped it away and discovered the blood on my fingers. I had bitten myself in the struggle and had not even noticed.

"Thank you," I whispered, eventually.

Mason made some vague noise at the back of his throat.

Shakily, I stood to my feet, supporting myself against the wall. "I should get back Downstairs."

"Why are you wearing your boots, Maya?" His low voice echoed across the small space. I stopped, my heart beating hard against my throat.

"Sir?"

"You heard me." He turned, berating me with a cutting glare. I backed away until I hit the wall but he quickly closed the space. "Going somewhere, were we?"

"No, I-I wasn't, I-I was just –"

"Don't you dare lie to me, Maya."

Scared and troubled, I could do nothing but suppress great, gasping breaths as Mason looked down upon me. "I'm listening."

"T-The cold was floor..." I shook my head frantically. "I mean the floor

_"

"Yes, I get it."

I bowed my head, unable to meet the ferocity behind those eyes. Mason simply placed a cold finger beneath my chin and lifted my face to meet his.

"I suppose, a smart woman such as yourself would not venture into a blizzard like this." He stroked his thumb against my lower lip, smearing the blood. "Such things would be suicide, wouldn't you agree?"

I could do nothing but nod.

His hand moved to my neck, my pulse pounding into his flesh as he gripped it tight.

"I am in a bad fucking mood tonight, so I want you to listen very carefully. If you ever, and I mean *ever*, sneak out of your Downstairs chambers again..." He increased the pressure against my larynx. "Even if it *is* just to read a book, if I ever see you sneaking around again, after hours, where you do not belong... I will not be lenient with you. Do I make myself clear?"

"Yes," I croaked.

With a firm push to the wall, he released me. I was about to say something, to apologise, to make him realise that I would never *ever* do anything to displease him, for he must never stare into my eyes!

Before I got the chance, Mason shoved the book into my belly.

"Go to bed, Maya," he spat.

Nodding, I hugged the book to my chest and ran with pounding footsteps back Downstairs.

23

Anya suspected something had happened. The bloody stains upon my pillow, combined with my shaken demeanour, left little doubt of my midnight trauma. I simply told her not to worry and that I had bitten my lip in my sleep.

We eventually found ourselves in that dining hall, standing opposite a large buffet full of breakfast delicacies. There were pastries and breads, jams and marmalades, eggs and bacon... A whole host of mouth-watering smells permeated the air.

The dining hall contained four large windows that overlooked the grounds of Frost Manor. Tatty curtains bordered these windows, dyed a rich red, and provided the only pops of colour in a room doused with wood, other than the tapestry behind us. It was an old thing, depicting a hunting scene with a white fox and a series of large black wolves. It was all rather macabre, and it was a relief to have my back to it for most of the morning.

The blizzard had ceased, encasing the world with a fresh blanket of snow. Mountains bathed in a crimson light from the rising sun.

Memories of my freedom, and my eagerness to escape the previous evening, rose to the surface of my mind. I shook them away just as Mason entered.

"Good morning," he said, carrying a large pile of papers beneath his arm.

I gauged him closely. He seemed calmer that morning. There were no bags beneath his eyes, and the exhaustion of our two-day journey seemed to have been wiped away.

This was good news.

Tentatively, I filled up his coffee cup.

"And how are you this morning, Miss Doe?"

"Fine, thank you, Sir."

"Good. I trust you remember all that we discussed last night?" His stare could carve ice.

"Yessir."

"Excellent!" He shuffled the papers on the table before him. "Off you go now, Miss Doe."

Not needing to be told twice, I scurried to Anya's side and shook away her questioning stare, exasperated with the lot of them.

Mason spread butter on his morning toast as a man came into the room. He was a curious creature: rather short and incredibly skinny, his messy shoulder-length hair was coloured a dark chocolate and did little to alleviate the gauntness of his cheeks, nor the dark circles around bloodshot eyes. Ribs stuck out of a pale chest, just visible from the navy confluence of his dressing gown.

"Ah, Barnabas." Mason smiled, standing to his full height and shook the hand of the strange little man before him. "It is good to see you, my friend."

"And you, Lord Mason!" Barnabas's voice was surprisingly low and steady. "I trust your journey was pleasant?"

"Exceptionally."

Thus began tedious conversation between two old friends.

My mind closed off to the boring chat, for it mostly consisted of the usual Rebellion talk that I'd heard numerous times before. Such talk was interspersed with a whole host of names that meant nothing to me.

Besides, I only needed to remember one name: *Mikael Ashworth*. No doubt that name was already on everyone's chapped lips.

A sharp nudge from Anya brought my attention to Barnabas's empty coffee cup. I clanked my way over and hastily began pouring, as dark brown eyes scanned me up and down.

"I don't believe I've seen *you* before, sweetheart?"

"Miss Doe joined us in the *Fourth Month*," Mason said from the opposite end of the table. "She was a close associate of the late Campbell Anders."

The late Campbell Anders. It was still a hard reminder.

"Ah," Barnabas crooned. "She must be a whirlwind of information on the Rebellion."

"Excuse me," I said, more than a little prickly. "But we were innocent of ever being involved with that fu –"

"Language, Miss Doe," Mason glared. I bit my tongue, hard, and returned to Anya.

"Ooh, she's fiery..." Barnabas smirked, his bloodshot eyes leering. "A Herder as well, my you are a rare find."

"She's a bloody nuisance," Mason muttered.

Against everything I tried to stop it, a small smile tickled my lips.

"And what of Lady Alira?" Barnabas asked. "I have yet to meet that lovely woman."

Mason's shoulders rose on a large, irritated sigh. "She is not a *Lady*, Barnabas. She still has much to do before I grant her that particular title."

A singular, angry piano note stabbed behind my eyes. I shook my head, stifling the pain.

"Is she being difficult?" Barnabas asked, stirring the milk in his coffee.

"Oh, no." Mason chuckled to himself. "Quite the opposite in fact."

"Then what's the problem?"

Mason remained quiet, fingering the handle on his coffee cup. Deep grooves formed in his forehead.

"I'm losing my patience with her, Barnabas. Though she has yet to Come of Age, she is under the illusion that she is my equal, and this has annoyed me."

"Ah, I see." Barnabas sipped his coffee. "But what else does she expect? Before she Comes of Age, she's still an adolescent."

Mason's eyebrows bobbed in annoyed agreement. "Exactly, and regardless of how much it frustrates her, I refuse to touch her whilst she's still a minor."

Hmm, I thought, *perhaps he has a sliver of decency after all.*

"How long until she Comes of Age then?"

"Impossible to say. It could be years."

Barnabas exhaled a mucus laugh and joked, "How are you able to cope?"

"I have others at my disposal."

I faced the window, doing my best to ignore his leering stare.

* * *

THE REST of the week went by in a delirious haze. All we did was clean and serve meals.

I barely saw the Pretender, which suited us both in equal measure. She only ever asked for Anya's presence and made sure to avoid me at all costs.

Or, she might have been avoiding Mason.

Whether by accident or design, I always seemed to be in Mason's presence. I served him his meals, refilled his coffee and wine, answered his mundane questions... Such questions ranged from the locations of towns, to where Campbell and I would visit during the winter months, to what I had for breakfast that morning. It's not that I minded answering his questions, it was simply the fact he asked them at all. They were so random, so unnecessary.

As the days sped on, the initial awkwardness of our conversations calmed into something I merely expected. I daresay it had become somewhat normal.

I was contemplating this whilst wandering in the outside grounds of Frost Manor. We had a spare hour before the dinner party that evening, and many of the Slaves were enjoying the fresh air. All except Anya, that is, who entertained a rather attractive young man in our shared bedroom. She was enjoying her holiday.

Walking below a pale blue sky, snow gasped a satisfying crunch as my boots sank deep. Ahead, forests grew healthily and high, each pine surrounded by a delicate layer of frost and there, mere miles away, were the towering peaks of the Brüster mountains – the last stronghold before the bitter chill of the Icelands. We were at the northerly tip of the Snowlands, and the air certainly felt like it.

It was incredibly cold, yet the sun still had enough power to warm the cockles of this old Herder. I lifted my head, absorbing each facet of light.

A tug on the back of my coat. It was a little girl, standing shyly.

I smiled down her. "Well hello there."

Only four years of age, she was trying to hide a bashful smile, her eyes looking anywhere but me. With styled hair and clothes properly cleaned and trimmed, this little Aristocrat wanted to talk to me.

"You're pretty," she said, her voice so small and delicate.

From behind her back, she presented a small bouquet of pastel blue flowers. Most likely taken from a vase in the Manor. I would have to return them later.

"Why thank you," I said. "What's your name?"

"Maria." Her small shoulders hunched up as she rocked back and forth.

"That's a very pretty name."

"Thank you. What's your name?"

"Maya," I lied. It was also so difficult to lie to children.

"You speak funny."

"You like my accent?" I spoke some random words in Herdinese and beamed at her sweet giggle. "Do you like the snow, Maria?"

She nodded.

"Have you ever built a snowman?"

"What's a snowman?"

I gasped, hands upon my hips as I considered such outrage.

"You don't know what a snowman is? Well, we'll just have to do something about that, won't we?"

So, as the sun fell low in the sky, little Maria and I built a snowman.

"Maria!" hissed a woman with cropped brown hair and a face resembling the metal edges of a gate. "Come over here now!" she yelled, before disappearing back into the house.

"Oho," I said, looking down to Maria and sticking my lower lip out.

"Can we finish it?" Maria mumbled. "I want to finish the snowman."

She stared sadly at our creation, which still missed a head.

"I'm sorry," I said, then took one of the flowers from my pocket and held it between my fingertips. "But it's still cold – I'm sure our snowman will stay like this until next time."

Her smile was contagious, so beguiling. I bopped the flower against her freckled nose and her loud giggle melted my heart.

The music loudened.

"*Maria!*"

"You better go," I said, raising an eyebrow. "See you later, kiddo.'

"Bye, Maya!" she called behind her, eventually disappearing.

In her absence, I twirled the green stem between my fingers, the pastel blue petals shining against the bright white of the snow.

"You continue to intrigue me, Miss Doe," Mason said.

He seemed to appear out of nowhere. The snow crunched beneath his boots as he strolled towards me, hands in the pockets of his black coat, the snow bright against the red scarf around his neck.

I sighed out my frustration. "How on earth do I intrigue you now?"

Mason tilted his head to little Maria, happily skipping through the snow. "It's rather refreshing to see you have a heart."

I laughed in spite of myself. The last of my *heart* washed away with the blood of the fourth man I'd killed.

Snow crunched loudly as I wandered away from the snowman. Mason strolled by my side.

"Well, she's a child," I said, as if that explained everything.

"She's also an Aristocrat."

"Maybe so, but the innocence of a four-year-old clouds everything. When she looks at us, she just sees *people*. She doesn't see Slaves or Masonians, or even Aristocrats. It's like we're all the same."

"You truly believe you and I are the same?" Mason doubtfully raised his eyebrows.

"I don't mean *you*. I mean, c'mon – you're not even human."

"Well observed."

"I just mean that Maria doesn't see me as a Slave, or even a Herder. To her, I'm an equal. *That's* what's refreshing."

"Others do not share your views."

"You mean that woman in the window?" She reminded me of a growling Pitbull. "Who was that?"

"Maria's mother."

"Yikes," I remarked, spurring Mason's small titter. "Who's her father?"

"I'm certain it's Barnabas, though he has yet to admit it."

I recalled the sight of Barnabas that morning, with his red eyes unable to focus, and his skin pale and thin.

"Barnabas is a drug addict, isn't he?" I realised, gazing solemnly ahead.

"Yes, he is. Many of my Social Circle are."

"Of course," I grumbled, painfully aware of Mason's toothless grin.

"It's a rather lovely agreement. I provide drugs, they provide information and unwavering loyalty."

The sun gleamed above, making my head hurt. All these despicable arrangements, so many deplorable personalities. It was all getting too much.

"If you'll excuse me, Sir," I said, massaging my temple. "I have to prepare for tonight."

Mason sceptically raised his eyebrows. "Oh, is that so? Is that why you've been building snowmen?"

"Anya's indisposed, so I had to occupy myself somehow."

"Indisposed? Is she ill?"

"For his sake, I hope not."

Mason's amused little chuckle echoed around the space. In this conversational lull, I heard the music. It was so easy to hear the music when I was with him.

"What are you, exactly?"

"I beg your pardon?" His tone was not malicious, just surprised.

"You're not human, so, if I may, what are you?"

He did not answer. Instead, he simply smiled. "I am many things, but they are not meant for your ears."

"Why not?" His eyes were glorious. I kept seeing them in my vision: they were so bright, so tempting. My heart raced, my blood tingling with some unknown instinct.

Mason's heavy hands rested upon my shoulders, grounding me back to Frost Manor.

"Because you are not like me," he eventually replied. "You would not understand."

Heavy hands slid from my shoulders.

"I best not keep you, Maya," he said. Gracing me with one last smile, he wandered back to the Manor. Yet, he only managed a few lethargic paces before he turned with a salacious little smirk. "Of course, you're always welcome to spend the afternoon with me. I can think of many things we could do before dinner."

I smiled tightly. "I'd rather walk in on Anya deep-throating a polar bear, but thanks for the offer."

Mason's hearty laugh echoed up the trees.

* * *

The dinner party was in full swing.

Aristocrats had eaten their fill of six courses and escaped to a small reception room, containing two brown leather sofas, some paintings and a few ornamental cabinets. The fireplace was lit and sent a sticky warmth throughout the room. But it was plain and boring and hardly spread the Aristocratic magnificence I was accustomed to.

Nevertheless, there I was, roaming around in a tight halter-neck black dress with my shoulder blades on display. My hair was loose, flowing down my back so my tattoo was covered, yet I still felt on edge.

Other than Erik Doncaster, these people were strangers. Most were evidently druggies, for they possessed the same hazed, hectic expression as Barnabas Price, who was dressed in a tuxedo and, for all intents and purposes, seemed to polish up like a new penny. The constant sheen of dilated eyes did mock his addiction, however.

The Pretender was also present. Standing in the corner of the room, her fake eyes scanned everything, yet her very frame remained unmoved. The dress she wore, a bright scarlet garment with red diamantes, seemed a few sizes too big and I wondered how that woman could lose even more weight.

With a polished silver tray full of whiskey tumblers and cigars, I politely offered her a drink.

"Fuck off," she replied, bringing a glass of white wine to her scarlet lips. The bruise had faded during our stay at the Manor, but it still painted her eye with an ominous green tinge that even the most sublime of makeup could not conceal.

"What happened?" I asked, quietly.

She observed me from the corner of a shaded, opal eye. "What does it look like?"

"But why?"

She huffed bitterly beneath her breath, taking another sour mouthful of wine. "I provoked him. I told him he should pay more attention to me than shag all his Slaves. He's got his eye on you, *Maya*."

I sighed, despondently. "I know he does."

"I must say," she said, gracing me with a sideways glare, "you don't seem particularly concerned. Need I remind you of your *destiny*, sweetheart."

"Are you thinking of my destiny, or your longevity?" I spat back. "*Sweetheart.*"

She merely smiled: an exhausted, dejected smile that did little to portray her cosmetic beauty. "Just keep your fucking legs closed."

And with that, she stormed her way around the room.

In an effort to ignore my rising dread, I continued my duties and offered a drink to Barnabas Price.

"Thank you, Miss...?"

"Doe," I replied.

A slight startle when Barnabas pinched my elbow. "What's your first name again?"

"Sir, please," I said, my voice stern. I tried to edge away but he merely tightened his grip.

"Oh, but a Slave as lovely as you must have an equally lovely name." His discoloured teeth sent waves of revulsion down my skin.

I sharply pulled myself away, the tumblers clinking on the tray.

A warm had slid around my back, stopping just short of my hip.

"Barnabas, may I remind you that Miss Doe is my property." Mason's tone was harsh and stern. "You would do well to remember that in future."

If Barnabas was troubled by Mason's warning, it was impossible to tell beneath his drug-induced calm.

"Of course, Lord Mason." Barnabas smiled a horrific yellow grin and disappeared into the crowd, a lit cigar between his fingers.

Once out of sight, I hastily wriggled from Mason's touch. "With the greatest respect, I am *not* your property!"

"Hm, I have paperwork that says otherwise." He hid his grin beneath the tumbler of whiskey. "Regardless, you should know by now that I don't like to share."

"There's nothing *to* share!"

"Then why are you blushing?"

Breathe in... One... Two... Three...

"Excuse me, Sir," I glowered. "I need to continue my duties."

Ignoring Mason's penetrating stare, I continued around the room.

Exhale...one...two...three...

My entire body burned. A thin sheen of sweat formed at the base of my spine, concentrating into a single ball of radiating heat. The whiskey looked so refreshing, so calming. I wished to down the entire tray, for the tension in my muscles to flow out with each alcoholic breath.

The sooner that evening was over, the better.

A woman, pale and emaciated, burst into the room. The black dress flowed around her limbs, yet the chiffon fabric covered nothing more than two small breasts and her groin. Despite her brave attire, she rushed to Mason and gripped the lapels of his jacket with trembling hands.

"My dear Lord Mason," she gasped, her bloodshot eyes wide, cheeks sinking into her skull. "I know you've brought some and I can't wait, I need it now!"

Mason's expression soured. He ripped her hands from his jacket and called harshly to the crowd, "Control your pet, Barnabas!"

Barnabas Price rushed to the growing scene and held the woman back with two bony hands.

"Katherine, I've told you –"

"No, Barnabas! I need it now, I can't wait till tonight!"

She elbowed him hard in his abdomen. He grunted and Katherine slid from his hands like slick oil. "*Please!* I'm *desperate*. I'll do anything, absolutely *anything*."

"There is nothing you could give me," Mason spat with evident disdain.

Now her mannerisms turned lewd. She ran her hands up and down her bony body, emphasising her visible rib cage. "But, my good Sir, there must be something I can do for you..."

I watched, shocked and then troubled, as Katherine's long arms wrapped around Mason's neck, pushing her body close to his. Mason soon responded, slinking his hands up her body.

Katherine was oblivious as a hand sank into her long, black hair, but that lecherous expression soon twisted into fear as he squeezed her neck, hard.

"Look at me," he hissed.

Mason stared hard at her, *into* her. Blood pooled in her eyes, overtopped her lashes and streamed in great rivers down pale, gaunt cheeks. Her entire body infested with shakes and she tried to scream, but Mason's hold upon her larynx was too tight, too vicious. What erupted instead was worse than a scream: a guttural, pained hiss that originated somewhere deep in her throat, created by only the foulest of fear. It was an abhorrent noise.

Drops of blood dripped to her dress, and as the life disappeared from her entirely, Mason released her. She fell in a heap, those bloodied eyes still open.

Once it was done, Mason rubbed his eyes and marched from the room. A door slammed shut, propelling us into stunned silence.

* * *

We were in the dining hall.

It was the early hours, yet many of the guests refused to sleep. Barnabas Price was still in the reception room, cowering over Katharine's corpse and wondering how to explain her foolish actions to Mason the next morning. The Pretender had also retired for the night. No doubt a failed Connection was foremost on her mind.

The majority of the guests, however, did not want to retire for the evening. Instead, they consumed copious amounts of alcohol. It was obvious that their intoxication was the only thing that stayed their primordial fear. If they stopped drinking, they would fully understand what they saw. If they sobered up, that *noise* would carve into their nightmares, vibrating their eardrums from the inside out. No, for the sake of their own sanities, they had to keep drinking.

As the last of the clock's chime echoed around the room, Bentley found me.

"Maya," he said, his face both flushed and pale. "We've run out of whiskey. I've had permission from Barnabas Price to utilise his private whiskey collection from the drawing room. I need you to go and collect a bottle."

Nodding, I did as instructed. In a rush, I kicked off my shoes just outside the door and ran silently through the Manor.

I expected the drawing room to be empty as I burst inside.

Mason slouched in one of the armchairs. His bowtie was undone, the tails of which were falling down his shirt and the buttons open at the collar. He held a tumbler of whiskey limply in his left hand, and his right pinched the bridge of his nose. Both eyes were shut as I entered but his gaze quickly found me.

The door shut of its own accord, startling a Herdinese curse.

"Oh I-I'm so sorry…" I cursed again, glimpsed behind me and then back to Mason. "I-I didn't know anyone was in here – I'm so sorry, I – "

"What are you doing here, Maya?" His voice was quiet and gentle.

The ability to form words was a tedious task, so I cleared my throat.

"We've run out of whiskey," I quietly replied, unable to face him. "I've been asked to fetch another bottle from Master Price's private stash."

Mason placed his drink on a small table and stood to his feet. He lethargically strolled to the other side of the room, towards an antique drinks cabinet, full of bottles. There was a fireplace on the right side, though it was filthy, appearing as though it had not been used in some time. On the other side sat an old record player with a stack of records perched precariously beside it. Ignoring the drinks, Mason picked out a circular black disk from the collection.

I watched as Mason fitted the record player with the disk, and delicately set the needle against the grooves. Music erupted from the player. It was old music: soft and delicate, containing so much life.

Mason stood motionless, absorbing the music.

Finally, he turned to me.

"Dance with me," he said.

"What?" The contact lenses burned at his request. "N-No, I can't, I-I – "

"It's just a dance, Maya," he said, taking my left hand and placing it upon his shoulder.

"I know, b-but I don't know how to dance, I – "

"Then let me show you."

He positioned us: his left hand supporting my right, his right upon my waist. Then, he moved. Slow steps from side to side, pulsing softly with the beat. Panicking, I tried to keep the rhythm with appalling consequences.

"Don't concentrate too hard," Mason said. "Relax, and let the music do the rest."

I closed my eyes, forcing myself to ignore where I was or who he was, and let the music consume me. Could I hear a piano? No, I don't think I could, but the music was beautiful. I was entranced, moving my feet in tune with Mason's.

"Well I'll be damned." He smiled softly to himself. "Turns out, you're quite a good dancer."

We continued like that for a while, the music surrounding us. Warmth spread through the fabric of my dress, originating from Mason's hand as it lay, gently, upon my waist.

Any other day, I regretfully admitted that I might have enjoyed dancing with Mason, but that night, my thoughts were fixed upon Katherine... The blood dribbling from her eyes... So much blood...

I tried to concentrate on the music, desperate to let it wash away the memories of that smoky, suffocating room.

"Maya, are you alright? You seem troubled." Exhausted, a soft titter escaped him. "Well, more troubled than I would have expected."

"It's not my place to ask..."

With a tender touch, he lifted my chin. My eyes darted over his handsome, tired face, glimpsing anywhere but his eyes but even then, I could see them shining.

"You can ask me," he said.

Licking my lips, the fabric of my dress tightened through a tense sigh.

"How do you kill them?"

Mason aimlessly stared at a point over my shoulder, his mind wandering. "Eyes are windows into the soul. By looking into one's soul, you can see everything about them."

"I don't understand," I said, transfixed by his voice, the music, the warmth of his hand upon my waist.

"Souls are shaped by our experiences, deformed by both extreme ecstasy and unimaginable tragedy. I am able to see those souls, to see the shape of them, the experiences that define one's personality.

"Human souls are weak. Even the most meagre of experiences shape them, remould them into something far removed from its original form." His touch on my waist tightened; not much, but my attention was fixed. "Things that are easily formed can just as easily be warped and destroyed."

I exhaled a shaky sigh, securing my grip on Mason's shoulder, and noticed the thick veins streaking his eyes.

"Does it hurt you?"

"A little – a door works both ways. If I look into another's soul, I'm allowing them a look into mine. Although, unlike theirs, my soul is sturdy, and more than capable of surviving."

My mind wavered, however unwillingly, to my name – my *real* name. The Connection was so real then, so easy to form. Had I wanted to, all I needed to do was to look up and stare hard into Mason's soul.

"What do they see?" I said in a fearful, barely audible murmur.

"I do not know. One cannot see the contents of their own soul, even when looking into a mirror."

A small, frightened tear trickled down my cheek. The music – was it the piano or the record? – continued to sooth me as Mason wiped the tear with his thumb.

"Are you afraid you'll share the same fate?" he asked, his head tilting. "Why do you fear such a thing?"

"Because deep down, I will always be Campbell Anders's little Wild One. One of these days, you'll want nothing more than to stare into my soul."

Mason placed a cool finger beneath my chin, and lifted my teary face.

"Maya," he said, softly. "You know that staring into your soul is the last thing I want to do."

Mason brought me closer. Consumed by musical instruction, I did not fight. I let the music guide me, concentrating on Mason's warmth as he pulled me towards him.

Our lips were mere inches apart. I closed my eyes.

The door opened with a loud creak.

"Oh!" Bentley stumbled, stopping dead in the doorway. I snapped my head back into my own possession. "Please forgive my intrusion, Sir. I simply thought Miss Doe had–"

"It's no matter, Bentley," Mason said. I could not tell if he was angry or startled, but nevertheless I quickly exited his warm embrace. Everything shivered in his absence.

"Please excuse me," I said, unable to look at him. "I better get back to work."

Mason gave a subtle nod and collapsed into the armchair.

"Goodnight, Miss Doe," he said.

"Goodnight, Sir," I quietly replied, and quickly exited the room.

* * *

ANYA and I were the only ones in the dining hall when Mason arrived for breakfast.

"Good morning," he said, marching to the buffet table. We muttered a vague reply with bowed heads, refusing to even glimpse at him. Anya, I believe, was still shaken by Katherine's murder. She did not wish to look at Mason because she was afraid.

My reasons for avoiding him were somewhat different.

Why didn't I look at him? I honestly don't know. Was it fear, humility, disappointment? Forbidden desire? Could have been all of these things, or none of them. All I knew was that my brain was exploding with the incessant, furious drones of a piano. It was berating me for pulling myself away, angry for ignoring my destiny. If I looked at him, I was afraid the music would completely overwhelm me.

Mason sat down with his plate of toast, and only then did I see the stack of papers in his possession. I curiously eyed them, attempting to decipher the small print on the front. To my dismay, I was unsuccessful.

I jumped as Anya nudged me. I frowned at her, wondering what in Hel she wanted.

She mouthed, *"Coffee."*

"Oh!" My limbs sprung forwards, coffee pot ready.

Mason was still reading his letters. As I poured, I read the name of a town: *Ivy Clearing*. Then the name of a man, *Gunther Erinbold,* and someplace called *Fort Watson*.

"He's a conspirator who was captured," Mason suddenly said, casting me a sideways glance. Stunned, I held the coffee close as its hot heat punctured my blouse.

"I-I'm sorry?" I breathed.

"You were reading my letters." Mason glimpsed up with a smirk. My mouth fell limp, trying to form a believable lie that would explain my sly behaviour. "No use trying to deceive me. I could practically feel your breath as you peered down."

"That was the steam from the coffee," I brusquely replied, marching back to Anya's side with a straight spine.

"Of course it was." Still smiling, Mason continued to flick through the pages. "At any rate, you're evidently curious and so I shall elaborate.

"Gunther Erinbold was captured almost a week ago by a Masonian Patrol, not far from the small village of Ivy Clearing. As I am sure you have read, he is being held at a nearby Fort, and I must say, he is being rather cooperative. How considerate of him."

Mason continued, "I am paying Gunther a visit this afternoon. I am sure it will be most enlightening."

Anya stirred. "Excuse me, Sir."

"Go on, Miss Whittaker."

"Forgive me, but I was under the impression we would be going back today?" I do not know if she was afraid, or simply insincere, but her tone was filled with a gross disappointment that Mason was quick to notice.

Expressing a most judgmental glare, he smirked at her. "What? Have you become bored of all the men here?"

Anya's cheeks flushed an unattractive colour.

Mason's smirk persisted as he cast his gaze back to his letters. "In answer to your question, Miss Whittaker, you and the rest of my household will be returning to Fjord Territory this afternoon. I and a few others will return a few days later."

"Very good, Sir," Anya sheepishly mumbled.

Barnabas Price entered, still in his dressing gown, his hair unkempt and his bloodshot eyes covered by a dark pair of sunglasses.

"Oh dear, Barnabas," Mason said. "You are looking a little worse for wear this morning."

Gripping the back of the chair with both hands, Barnabas cleared his throat and put an icicle down his back – figuratively speaking, of course.

"My most *sincere* apologies for the behaviour of that...*woman* last night," he said, his hoarse voice shaking. Was it from drugs, alcohol or fear? Probably all three.

Mason waved his arm. "Sit down," he snapped.

Throwing his paperwork a short distance away, Mason's glare could cut the table in half. "I don't much care for the health of the whores you bring here, but first be sure they can handle whatever you give them. Next time, I will not be quite so apologetic to you, or the rest of your household. Are we clear?"

"Irrefutably."

"Good," Mason snapped, springing forwards and scraping butter on the toast. "Aside from grossly insulting me, her actions ruined what would have been an excellent evening.

"Still," he continued, glimpsing at me from the corner of his eye. "The evening wasn't a total loss."

High, screeching notes of a piano erupted inside my head. I shot my gaze to the floor, biting my tongue around the ache.

Before long, Barnabas ordered me to his aid with caffeine.

"Fill that one up as well," he said, sliding another cup towards me. "I'm going to need a lot this morning."

24

The Palace was surprisingly homey when we returned.

It was a strange feeling, stepping foot into the warm extravagance after the damp, wooden walls of Frost Manor.

What made it better was the obvious absence of Mason. The train journey was long and monotonous, and I spent the entirety of its two-day chug staring out the window, wondering what in Hel's name I was doing.

What happened to the revulsion I felt? The sickening fear of discovering what I was to Mason, what *Alira* was meant to do with him?

I do believe the music had squandered those emotions, rendering them meaningless behind the seduction Mason was well-practised in.

Because that's exactly what was happening. I was being seduced, and it was working.

I hated myself for it.

So, I relished that train-journey. It gave me time. Time to myself, time away from Mason. Time to think about what I was going to do, what steps I would take to rediscover my inner humanity, my inner sense. I could not give into Mason. One failed move, one lack of control, and he would discover my secret.

I would not swap one form of slavery for another.

That night, the piano made sleep difficult. It was restless, screaming at me. I squirmed beneath the bedsheets, the pillow pressed down against my skull as I desperately tried to drown out the noise.

But I couldn't. The music was in my head and it wouldn't let me go. *Why wouldn't it let me go?*

The Reading Room was cold as I entered, yet the piano was loud and insistent, willing me closer and closer until I was perched upon the stool. I lifted the keylid with a pounding heart, excitement brewing. A precious, calm moment as the soft pads of fingers stroked against the keys.

Music erupted. Familiar, intoxicating music that soothed my pounding skull. Completely absorbed, I sprinted after those notes as they whirled around the room.

The music became more forceful, more intense, before the last note quivered those strings. All was silent.

A heavy, relieved sigh. Hands caressed my invigorated, luscious hair as my head was *finally* quiet.

"Beautiful!"

The keylid slammed down, protecting the keys from the aqua stare of Jayson Montgomery.

I cursed loudly. "What in Hel's name are you doing? You scared the life out of me, Jayson!"

"I do apologise." His smile was fundamentally chilly as he moved closer. I noticed he still wore his uniform, complete with the weapons belt. The music in my head resurfaced – this time, as a warning.

"What are you doing here, Jayson?" I asked.

"I heard music. I wanted to see what was happening."

"Well, it's just me," I forced an awkward smile. My attention briefly flicked to the window as the first of the Fjordland snow fell from the sky. It sent a shiver across the room, my arms included. I rubbed my hands up and down, hiding a nervous swallow, and calmly wandered to the door.

"I had a hankering to play the piano," I said, avoiding his eye. "I'm not supposed to be here so I would appreciate it if you didn't say anything."

"Of course not." Jayson's smirk persisted. "But it'll cost you."

"What are you implying?" I asked, eyes narrowed.

He shrugged. "Oh, I dunno. A bit of this, a bit of that."

"Get to the point, Jayson."

Jayson merely smiled, his white teeth gleaming. "Don't worry, I'll keep your secret safe. It'd be a shame if Mason killed you."

Something dark and unsettling grew in the pit of my stomach. Forcing a smile, I opened the door to leave.

"Oh," he said. "I've heard about what happened at Frost Manor."

"What?" I squeaked.

"With you and those Masonians."

"Oh," I realised, exhaling. "Old news now. I'm over it."

"Damn shame though, innit?"

"I-I'm sorry?"

Jayson chuckled, a darkness falling. "I got my promotion."

"Congratulations, but what's that got to do with me?"

He smiled again – a great big beaming grin – and for the first time, I saw the sickness growing inside of him. It was black and grungy, like tar.

"That means, Maya, that I expect to see a lot more of you in the coming months."

I took a step back, towards the door. "Not sure Mason'll like that."

Jayson's grin merely widened. "Then it'll be our little secret, hey?"

I bolted from the room, Jayson at my heels. Masonian boots echoed against the marble.

Heart pounding, adrenaline *racing*, I traversed the Downstairs stairwell in two long leaps. I collapsed at the bottom with a sharp shriek and propelled myself down the corridor.

Without a backward glimpse, I found the room I shared with Anya and slammed the door shut behind me.

Anya startled awake, her hair matted and her eyes struggling to focus.

"Maya?" she croaked. "What's wrong?"

Energy dispersed. I collapsed onto my knees, cowering, and surrendered to the panic attack biting at my lungs.

* * *

A DAY LATER, I worked in my little kitchen, idly cleaning dishes while visions of Jayson Montgomery lingered. They were like odours, sticking to the membrane just inside my skull. As the snow kept on falling, I replayed what happened in that Reading Room. What *almost* happened was too hideous to even consider.

I'd told Anya everything. First, she was horrified. Then, disgusted.

She ordered me to inform Mason, to strike some sort of deal whereby I give my body in return for his protection.

In reply, I simply spat on the floor.

No, there were other means at my disposal, other methods whereby I could get Jayson off my back. Surely, I was not the only one to see the darker side of his personality, felt the fear he was an expert at striking?

A horrible little thought popped into my head. A wicked, impossible thought...

The Masonian who attacked Tia was a Captain, Anya had said.

Tallis being the only Captain I knew, I had assumed it was him. What if it wasn't?

No, it was impossible. Jayson Montgomery wasn't a Captain, for Odin's sake! And even if this supposed *promotion* would have pushed him up the ranks, he certainly was not a Captain when Tia was attacked two years previously.

Two years.

What did Jayson say? Elbow deep in scalding dish water, I thought to earlier conversations. One seemed to raise its foul head, that shrill voice convulsing in my memories: *"I expect to be getting a promotion soon... I've been a driver for almost two years now, so it'd be nice to do something else for a change."*

My stomach turned, my fists clenching around the dish cloth as I wondered, quite horrifically, if the only reason Jayson Montgomery was a driver was as a punishment.

A punishment grossly unbefitting the crime.

I licked the scar on my lip, glaring at the thick veil of snow as each trickle of disgust grew stronger and stronger...

A sharp knock on the door. I spun on the spot, a dirty wet teacup raised and ready to strike!

"Oh, Tia..." All air shot out in a relieved breath.

"Expecting someone else?" she asked, her bright blue eyes scanning me up and down.

Sighing, I hastily grabbed the towel. "You could say that."

This was the first time I had seen Tia since our return. I was unprepared for the uncomfortable silence.

"So..." I began, throwing the towel to the side. "What can I help you with?"

Tia crossed arms over small breasts and trudged her way into the room. Her tanned skin, though still flawless, had developed a pale sheen, yet only intensified the blueness of her eyes.

"I'd like to talk to you," she said.

"About what?"

"Mason."

My heart sank to the dishwater, fighting the urge to dive in and hide beneath the soap suds.

"Oh," I managed. Slowly, Tia and I met in the centre of the room and took residence on opposite table chairs.

"Okay, look..." She licked those pale lips, her mind carefully forming the words. "Firstly, I want to apologise for my behaviour. It was unfair of me to do that, I know it wasn't your fault.

"Secondly, I want to talk to you about Mason. Or, at least, your relationship with him."

"We don't *have* a relationship, Tia."

"I know..." She threw her hands across the table and grasped mine in a calming hold. "I've come to change your mind."

I jumped to my feet, ripping away from that treacherous woman, and stormed to the window. "Did he put you up to this?"

"No, of course not." Tia came beside me, her eyes wide and understanding. "I just know a lot of what you're going through. I struggled with the same inhibitions, the same reluctance as you have now."

My hands gripped the basin until the scars on my knuckles shone.

"I don't want to, Tia," I stated, absolute. "Simple as that."

"But *why?*"

"How can you ask me that?" I stared at her, my eyes dripping with judgement. "We both saw what he did to Hallie, we both know what he's done to all those other people! He caused Ragnarök, Tia, he's slaughtered *billions!*"

"He saved me..." She blinked once, and then twice. "Maybe not in the conventional way, but he offered me protection and not a day goes by where I don't thank all Gods how lucky I am that he did."

"I don't want to take that protection away from you, Tia."

"My situation with Mason was always going to be temporary," she said, sadly. "But I'll be okay. Don't fight his wishes if that's the only reason you're holding back."

"It's not the only reason."

"Then what is it?"

My real name, the music, my destiny...

I remained silent.

Tia rubbed her bare arms, trying to reduce the chill that had seeped into the room.

"There are many advantages to doing what he wants... A-And not just with protection, but other things as well. Little...*niceties*, that can make living in this place a bit more bearable."

"But he's already taken me to the Snowlands and we haven't done anything!"

"Because he thought he'd win you over there." Tia placed a hand upon my shoulder, as much patronising as it was gentle. "And something did almost happen, didn't it? I can see it in your face."

I quickly avoided her gaze. Tia sighed. "I know the sort of games he plays, how seductive he can be."

"I'm not doing it, Tia," I said, pushing myself away from the sink – away from *her* – and disappearing into the pantry. I scanned uninterested eyes across a hundred labelled jars as Tia lingered in the doorway.

"Are you afraid of the act itself? Because he's not rough, or cruel or into anything weird or–"

"Please stop talking..." I sighed my frustration to the jarred pickles.

"I'm just trying to understand why you're being so defiant about this."

"Isn't it obvious, Tia?" I said, exhausted. "After everything he's done, everything he's done to *me,* why can't it be enough to say that I simply don't want to?"

"Because he's obsessed with you, Maya." Tia raised two neatly plucked eyebrows and descended into the pantry. "You're right: he's an evil man. So, don't you think he'll take matters into his own hands if you don't start reciprocating his advances?"

"Don't make me fear him any more..." I leant my forehead against a jar of damson jam. The cold glass soothed my headache.

"Don't make me see him hurt you..." Tia's eyes glistened with unshed tears. With a hearty sniff, she said, "Besides, fear is good. It can make you stronger, more confident."

Patience could only go so far. I grabbed the first jar I saw, stormed into the kitchen, and slammed it on the counter so hard the glass cracked.

"You don't even have to acknowledge that it's Mason you're with!" Tia's frustration became evident. "Just close your eyes and think about someone else, o-or drink till you just don't care anymore! C'mon, Maya, you must know how to get through these things."

"But that's just it, Tia. I *don't* know. I-I don't know any of it..."

The words hung heavily in the air before they dropped to the floor with a defiant slam.

"Oh," Tia said, quietly. Slowly, she approached. "Then, now more than anything, you need to reconsider your position."

"Why?"

"Maya," she said, tenderly. "Don't you want your first time to be on *your* terms rather than his?"

Tears came, overwhelming my stony exterior. I slapped them away, quickly.

"I'll think about, okay? That's the best I'm prepared to do."

"I can live with that."

She forced a smile that, no matter how downhearted, was genuine enough to make her eyes sparkle. "I'll leave you alone now."

She clanked her way to the corridor. In her exit, the hands of greedy men came rushing back with thought after thought after thought... I licked my lips, dragging down any last inhibitions.

"Tia..." She stopped and looked at me with those doleful eyes, straddling the doorway with two red heels. "I need to ask you something, a-and I know it involves bringing back dark memories and I'm so, so sorry for doing this to you... But I wouldn't ask unless it was important."

Tia swallowed, her delicate throat convulsing. She accepted my question with a slow nod.

"The Masonian who attacked you..." I said, squeezing the counter hard. "What was his name?"

Tia's head bowed through the assault of horrific memories. It seemed an awfully long time before she met my eye.

"His name is Jayson," she replied. "Captain Jayson Montgomery."

25

WINTER

Winter arrived in the Fjordlands with more brutality than I thought possible. For two days, the Palace was inundated with blizzards reminiscent of the northern climes.

Hellish winds whipped down chimneys, howled down corridors, created sheens of white upon walls hidden from a fire's warm glow... Downstairs, where the walls were thin and insulation was weak, our little wood burners worked constantly, their supply of fuel not likely exhausted for fear our bed sheets would freeze together.

Outside, the surviving leaves had been removed completely, ripped from their mother's bare branches and cast off to an icy grave. Only emerald green needles and pinecones remained, encased in crusty white – their own private cocoons, so they might yet survive the harsh winter.

In my little kitchen, idly cutting vegetables, I gazed at the snow flurries. It was relentless: a constant sheet of moving white. That particular afternoon, only the bright lights of Mason's convoy could puncture the wintry wall.

I sighed out my trepidation, and tried to continue my work.

Tia and I had not spoken since that awful conversation, in that same kitchen. We simply continued about our business, neither avoiding nor confronting. We just existed, two very different sides of the same coin. That coin currently resided in Mason's pocket, just waiting to be thrown.

Had I thought about Tia's words? Of course I had; I couldn't stop thinking about them. I had lain awake for hours, listening to that *fucking* music inside my head, and debated how I would spend my remaining days as Maya Doe.

I just didn't know what to do. I was lost, aimlessly climbing up a mountain but knowing deep in my sinking heart that I would not emerge at the summit. How could I? How could I take those final, ginormous leaps only to fall off the edge on the other side?

All these thoughts whirled with the same intensity as the outside blizzard. It was early afternoon and yet the sun had already fallen to the horizon, dousing the land in a darkness the blizzard quickly to accentuated. The *Shortest Day* of the year would be in two weeks, the *Last Day* a week after that. Winter in the Fjordlands seemed quick to remind us of it.

Cleaning the kitchen table, the bulbs of garlic gently swaying above, my two neglected shoes lay scattered across the floor. Everything was normal.

The characteristic sounds of boots echoed up the corridor. I panicked and scurried to the sink just as Mason entered.

"Good afternoon, Maya," he said.

Mason removed his weapons belt and placed it delicately on the table. I could see it reflected in the window, each sapphire on his sword glittering in the artificial light.

"My, you're very quiet today." His boots took slow, authoritative steps and rested directly behind me. The heat from his body spread into my back, licking across Jörmungandr's black skin.

I tried to focus on the dirty dishes.

"Apologies, Sir," I said, brusquely. "I have a lot of work to do, is all."

Mason took a brief glimpse over my shoulder, and his warm breath fluttered across my cheek.

"Evidently," he said. "Yet, I'm sure your chores can wait."

"I'm really busy."

Only then, when Mason's hands came sliding around my waist, did I chance a look at his reflection. His eyes glowed back at me, his lips stroking the seven golden rings of my ear.

"Liar," he whispered.

Those arms tightened around my waist, fingers dipping into the gaps of my blouse, stroking the bare skin beneath. I softened at his touch, my head lulling onto his shoulder. My eyes closed of their own accord, strange and new sensations building somewhere deep inside of me...

Then I remembered where I was and what I was doing and stood up straight, removing Mason's touch with a smooth tilt of my hip.

"Don't touch me," I snapped.

In one quick movement, those arms curved tightly around my waist and pulled me into his hard contours.

"Why not?" He smiled against my ear. "After all, we were interrupted at Frost Manor. Surely we need to make up for lost time?"

He dug his fingers into my scalp, pushing the hair over my shoulder and placed small, delicious kisses against my jawline. I relaxed into him, completely, my head rolling against his shoulder. I was malleable, pliable beneath the tenderness of his lips and his holding arms tightened...

The buttons of my blouse were quickly undone. A shallow, audible breath as Mason's warm hand traced the smooth skin of my abdomen. His hand moved up, until a gentle squeeze of my breast.

"Mason, stop," I gasped, pulling myself away.

A low chuckle filled my ear as he removed his hand. "Why do you resist me? You're obviously enjoying this."

"Because you're you and I'm me, and this isn't right."

"I strongly disagree." I twitched at the sharp nip on my ear lobe.

"No, Mason..." I pulled myself forward. "S-Something about this isn't right – it feels *wrong*."

And it did. Somewhere, beneath the mounds of delicious tension inside my belly, there was something holding me back, something that was just...*off*. The music, perhaps? It was difficult to hear over the roaring of my blood.

A small shriek left my lips as Mason jerked me back, his smiling lips against my jawline, his hand slinking down across my belly button and into my skirt.

I did not register Mason's hand inside my underwear until it was already there. Until new and strange sensations assaulted every nerve and rendered my limbs like jelly. My hands crushed the basin, lifting myself higher on my tiptoes as my eyes squeezed shut. My jaw dropped with the sweet, agonising pleasure.

"Does this feel *wrong*, Maya?" he whispered in my ear, his voice calm and so different from my vocal, laboured breaths.

It became more intense, more *consuming*. The pressure was building up and up...

Then Mason removed his hand.

"I'll see you later, Miss Doe," he said. I shivered as he removed his warmth, my back and brow licked with sweat and all this pleasure coiled within me with nowhere to go.

Trembling, I looked at my reflection in the window. Two amber eyes gazed back. Two lying eyes that were playing a *very* dangerous game.

The scrape of metal on wood as Mason replaced his weapons belt. And there, just like that, the Destroyer of the Old World had returned. He had seduced me, again. I had let him.

I was *weak*.

The new pleasure that still lingered was squished and deformed into the familiar anger I knew all too well. I squeezed the basin tight, determined to keep my building *fury* under control...

But then I saw his gratified little smirk, and I just saw red.

"No," I said, loud and firm so he understood. "I won't see you later."

Mason formed a wide, egotistical smile. "My, you are a challenge!"

"I don't know what's happening," I said, hastily redoing those three open buttons. "I don't know what power you have over me, but it stops *now!*"

His amusement began to fall, slowly at first, and then accelerated.

"I am *not* Tia! I will *never* be her, so you can move on to someone else because as Freya is my witness, I will *never* be your lover."

Mason bowed his head, his tongue tightly pressed into his cheek, just *aching* to say something. Slowly, he walked around the table, hands safely concealed within the pockets of his coat.

"Bold words, Maya," he said. "Bold words indeed."

"I mean every one of them."

Mason came to rest against the counter, directly before me. "I could force myself on you," he said, glaring. "Don't think I wouldn't. Such things are hardly new to me."

"Then why don't you." I tried to keep my voice steady, but Mason saw the first trickles of fear and that sadistic smile reformed anew.

"Because you *want* me, and although every part of you is fighting it, you can't deny that little rush of excitement every time I touch you."

"The only thing I want is to be free of this place."

"Be careful, Maya. You're starting to sound like the late Hallie Osbourne."

"I sound like Campbell Anders." The smile dropped from his face. "And I'd listen to him over you any day."

Mason sprung forward. Hands dug into my arms. I struggled against his grip, but he was too strong, too vicious. The edge of the counter dug into my lower spine, and I was helpless but to lie there, pinned over it with both hands held with crushing force.

"I wonder what secrets lay hidden inside your soul, hm? Anger, fear, arousal?"

I shouted some Herdinese insult and his smile simply grew. "Oh, such language! Do you have any idea how much I would *long* to stare into your soul, Maya? To see what secrets you're hiding from me, to discover what part of you I need to pick apart before you give in to what I know you want?"

"Just choose someone else!"

"But I don't want someone else, Maya. I want *you*. I've wanted you since the moment I first saw you, on the stage of that empty Theatre." Very slowly, he leant down over me, until our noses were almost touching. Two diamond eyes *glared* as all essence of his handsome face disintegrated beneath pure, pitiless amusement.

"I don't want to force you, Maya. I feel it would endanger a rather lovely agreement by which we'd both mutually benefit."

"Go to Hell!"

"Oh, such fire!" He nuzzled into my jawline, inhaling my scent. A short, sharp whimper escaped my lips as a hard bulge pressed into my thigh. Mason saw my fear. His smile grew.

"So," he declared, suddenly standing upright, letting me slide, shocked and terrified, to the kitchen floor. He walked around the periphery and idly picked out an apple from the fruit bowl. "I will offer you a deal."

"I don't want your deal!"

"Nevertheless, we shall have one."

Apple still in hand, Mason walked to the kitchen table and leant both his elbows upon it, smirking at me. "I shall give you until the *Last Day* to give yourself to me freely. If, by the end of the year, you still refuse... Well, you remember dear Hallie."

Smiling, Mason pushed himself upright and took a hearty bite from the apple.

"The clock is ticking, Miss Doe," he said between the crunches. "I suggest you hurry."

* * *

STANDING in the Dining Room with the rest of the Slaves, the ticking of the clock was the one thing I noticed.

It was such a funny thing. The delicate, monotonous *tick tock, tick tock*. Always in the background, yet only audible when the threat of time was very much present. Many things could intensify the draw of that repetitive clock. It could be anticipation, panic, excitement. Or knowledge of the painfully inevitable.

Deep down, I always knew Mason was going to find me. I did not expect it to be like this.

Outside, the blizzard had ceased. In its absence, the Palace had been transformed.

The grounds were pristine, coated in an untouched layer of white. The moon had peeked its silver head from the clouds, dousing the white world with silver. Even the mountains, further away than ever, were coated in such a healthy layer of silvery white... I felt I might sink into them and never resurface.

The first light of the aurora trickled between the last remaining clouds. I longed to see it, to gaze up at the wondrous veil of pinks and blues, and feel my parents staring back from behind the heavenly colour.

I remember the first time I saw the dancing lights in the sky. I was very young – too young to realise how old I was – but I had stared up to the glorious waves of dancing colour. I had pointed it out to my Pa, who sat beside me with his coat made of reindeer hide, and asked what it was.

"*Your Mama's up there,*" he had said.

That was a long time ago. Now, I was in that Dining Room, berated by the ticking of that fucking clock, and all the while trying to calm my pounding heart.

When Mason did inevitably storm into the room, it felt like it might claw its way from my chest. The piano had also resurfaced at Mason's presence – of *course* it had – and was scratching at me from the inside, laughing and judging in equal measure.

Mason sank into his chair without a word, a pile of papers tucked beneath his arm. As he organised the letters across the table, I grudgingly filled his wineglass.

"Did you know, Miss Doe," he began, his angry eyes teasing, "that alcohol is a wonderful relaxant? One could even say it lowers inhibitions. It is an interesting notion, do you not agree?"

When I still did not answer, he glared. "I asked you a question, Maya."

"Yes, I will drink it," I spat, my eyes burning behind the lenses. "Is that what you want me to say?"

"I want you to come to your senses." His fists clenched tight. In fact, his whole persona reminded me of an angry little child who just wasn't getting his own way. "But not tonight. I daresay I just don't have the mental capacity to deal with you much longer."

"It's a good job you won't have to then."

The words were out before I could stop them. Four pairs of eyes found me in one singular, sliding motion. One was made of pure ice.

"I'm sorry, Sir," I gasped, the reality of my position – as a Slave – brutally catching up with me. "That was out of line."

Mason did not reply. He simply sat there, glowering at me for a few moments before he returned to his letters.

Beside me, Anya tried to catch my attention, nudging me delicately with her elbow. I ignored her entirely, choosing instead to focus on the ticking of that damned clock.

"There is a two-day meeting in Blackberry's Clearing at the end of the week," Mason said, his eyes quickly scanning the letters, clearly not absorbing their meaning. "Miss Whittaker, Miss Doe, you will be required to join me."

Anya's excitement was palpable. Mine was less so.

"Sir, please find someone else," I said, gazing mindlessly ahead.

The End of Everything

"But I don't want someone else," Mason snapped.

"I don't want to go."

"Did I give the impression that you had a choice?"

I remained rigid, closed off, and desperately tried to ignore the contents of that Dining Room.

Blackberry's Clearing. Where even *was* the place?

I inwardly groaned, feeling the growing sense of panic yet not having any inclination what to do with it. Beside me, Anya gently touched my arm.

She frowned at me, her concerned look only bubbling tears from the back of my eyes. I squeezed them shut, ignoring the scratch of the contact lenses, until I regained control. I returned my attention to that Dining Room with my very skin made of ice, impenetrable to even the most powerful glare.

Mason was halfway through a steak when he said, "Miss Kingsley, a word of warning that Captain Montgomery has been reinstated to his former status. As I'm sure you're aware, this means he is free to wander the Palace."

"Yessir," Tia whispered, her empty eyes fixed ahead.

"Good. Captain Tallis is still his superior so he is the first point of contact should there be any trouble."

"Yessir, thank you Sir."

And there, just like that, Mason's protection over Tia had ceased. Blown away, like leaves in the wind.

Tia remained unmoved, absorbing the reality of her new predicament with silent clarity. Even her eyes remained still. Wide and dull, they remained fixed ahead, staring at some unknown point in the empty air.

* * *

A FEW HOURS LATER, when the last of the dining plates had been cleaned, when Tia's sobs finished echoing in the Downstairs corridors, I stood before a door.

It was larger than I remembered. Veins of gold crisscrossed the surface, forming the vague picture of some magnificent stag. Its golden antlers etched the wood, eventually disappearing into the wooden frame.

Filling my lungs with air, I placed three determined knocks on the door to Mason's Office.

A call for me to enter.

The handle clicked loudly as it turned, and as the door screeched open, I daresay I was the last person he expected to see plodding in, heels dangling from her fingers.

"What the hell do you want, Maya?" He returned to writing his letter, the golden fountain pen frantically scribbling away.

I closed the door behind me and cautiously stepped closer. My eager eyes immediately found the violin, resting as patient as always next to the window. I strenuously ignored it.

"Is this a bad time, Sir?"

"That depends on why you're here." Harsh diamond eyes flicked to me, the golden pen dropping with a loud thud as he sat defiantly back in his chair.

"I want to discuss the deal with you," I said. My big toe was curled beneath my foot, pressed down to the point it was almost breaking. The pain seemed to help the growing anxiety in my chest.

Mason's ears perked up, his eyes sparkling with just a glimmer of carnal hope.

"I'm listening," he said.

"Before I start, I just want to say that me being here is not giving myself to you... I-I'm still not ready for that." Mason rolled his eyes. "But am I right in thinking there are certain...*perks* that befit someone in my position?"

"What *perks* exactly did you have in mind?"

"Protection." A gust of wind howled through the Palace, distant trees rustling in the icy breeze. "Am I right in thinking I have protection?"

"If that is what you wish," he said.

My lips parted on a deep, calming breath. "I'd like any protection I'd get to apply to Tia."

"I'm not protecting both of you."

"I know. That's why I'm only asking you to protect her."

Mason sat back in his chair, his brooding brow shadowing eyes swimming with intense contemplation. "You would give up your own protection for Tia? Why would you do that?"

"Because Jayson Montgomery is a pig," I snapped. "A-And for him to be freely wandering around the Palace is just...*sick*."

Mason thought for a moment.

"If I do this, I trust you realise that you will subsequently lose your own protection."

"I do."

"You're prepared for that?"

"I can take care of myself."

"That, I have no doubt." He chuckled quietly to himself, his eyes darting across the ornamental rug. "Alright, Tia will be protected."

"Thank you, Sir," I said on a relieved sigh.

"Our deal still applies, Maya."

"I know."

We remained staring at each other, the wind gently howling outside the window. As the silence grew awkward, I rocked back onto my heels.

"Goodnight, Sir."

I turned to leave his office.

"You're playing dangerously close to fire," Mason said. "Bargaining with me does not often work favourably."

"A girl's gotta try though, right?" My shaky attempt at humour did not go down well.

"Be careful," he said, glaring. "I am not known for my patience. I may decide to end our agreement sooner than the *Last Day*."

"Mason, I – "

"Begging does not bode well either," he snarled. "I strongly suggest you reconsider your foolish position and accept my generous offer."

Fear snaked up my gullet. I did not reply.

"Get out, Maya," he eventually spat. "Before I take matters into my own hands."

26

Anya and I were with Bentley and two other footmen, patiently waiting in the Dome Room.

It was early morning and the world was doused in a heavy cloud. It made everything dark and dismal, and more than fitting my mood.

Admittedly, I had warmed to the idea of Blackberry's Clearing. Hardly in brighter spirits, but I was more accepting of the circumstances I had been forced in. For now, I still had two weeks left until Mason would try and kill me. I owed what little sanity I had left to be as positive as possible, not least so I could try to formulate a plan. So far, all plans I envisaged ended with Mason's deadly stare.

I had developed a newfound respect with the other maids, Tia especially. As soon as she was told that I had forfeited my protection to save hers, she threw her arms around me. She had cried then, balling her eyes upon my shoulder. We sank into the middle of the kitchen, both of us on our knees, unable to release each other.

I had been her best friend ever since.

Mason had been decidedly chilly, which was an immense relief. But following the outburst in his office, he refrained from any more threats, stewed in his own mood, and simply let me...*get on*.

The clock in the Dining Room was louder than ever.

The music caused me great angst, teasing me with such fluctuating volume. One hour, it would be mellow, casually lingering at the back of my mind. Others, it would pound my skull with enough force to make me shriek and squeal. The switch between the two was just maddening.

Nevertheless, the trip to Blackberry's Clearing would be a welcome escape from that Dining Room clock, at least. Waiting for the luggage to be packed, I observed the selection of people joining us.

The Pretender paraded downstairs in, shockingly, her silk nightdress and matching gown. Her fake eyes, though free of bruises, were bordered with thick red lines.

"Ma'am," Anya remarked with a delicate frown. "Are you travelling like that?"

"God, Anya, do you hear yourself sometimes?" She rolled her eyes. "Of course I'm not going like this – I'm not going at all!"

"What?" I spluttered. "why not?"

The Pretender smiled at me: a horrible smile that spat despise. "Because he doesn't want *me* there, Miss Doe. He wants you. *All* of you."

And with that, she marched back to the upper levels of the Dome Room. Shaking away her comment, I reformed my icy exterior and followed Anya to the cars.

I noticed that Jayson Montgomery was not driving. He was present, however, and made sure to send me a knowing look up and down.

He smiled as I passed him. "Been playing music again, Maya?"

Panic rose. Mason was not yet present, yet I still frantically searched for that piercing diamond glare.

"Be careful around him," Anya said to me once the car doors clinked shut. "After you gave up your protection for Tia's, you're on his radar."

"Oh, I was on his bloody radar beforehand," I mumbled bitterly, my breath fogging up the window as I counted five, six, *seven* Masonians. All coming with us to Blackberry's Clearing.

Bloody fabulous.

* * *

THE JOURNEY to Blackberry's Clearing was over in a breath, especially as the piano dimmed beneath the noise of the engine. It was peaceful, in that car. I was even able to nap.

Soon, the late morning sun hung low in the sky as the convoy stopped.

Sunlight poured in through the window. I squinted, desperately trying to see past the light. I shuffled across to Anya, peering through her window, where the sun had yet to reach.

Mason shook hands with a large black man, already dressed in a tuxedo that a large fur coat was only just able to cover. As each hand flicked in the sun, glints of gold jewellery shone like small beacons. Indeed, the man was dripping in gold.

"Who the Hel is that fellow?" I muttered in Anya's ear.

"That's Thackeray, I think."

"And he is?"

"He *was* the proprietor of one of the largest drinking houses in the Fjordlands."

"And now?"

"Dunno, but judging by all that gold, I'd say he's pretty important."

We both jumped as the door burst open. Sunrays illuminated Captain Montgomery's blond hair, yet that grin was concealed in shadow.

"Come on, ladies," he said. "Wouldn't want to miss the view."

Gritting my teeth, I shuffled myself from the van.

"What're you doing here, Jayson?" I scowled.

One side of his lip curled. "Same as you. Wouldn't want to miss the view."

General Alden marched the Slaves together. The footmen were behind us, lugging the hefty trunks on their backs.

"This way, Sirs." Thackeray's sonorous voice echoed up the trees, propelling us on with a large wave of his hand.

He led us to some steps. Horrible structures – old and weathered, and appearing to have broken a fair few necks over the years. Anya clutched me with a tight grip as the dangerous path meandered through the trees.

One of the footmen paused to secure a slipped trunk back in position. We stopped, allowing time to bask in the beauty of the forest. The trees were far higher than those in the more northern Territories, puncturing an unblemished blue sky. The forest itself was dense and thick, allowing no more than a couple of metres to be seen in all directions. Once again, the thought of escape hit me like a train. Perhaps I could disappear inside those trees? After all, there were no dogs to eat me on my way out.

But the hillside was dangerous, with large boulders, ice and snow. The steep steps were the only part that was remotely accessible, and only because some poor sod had probably spent all night clearing them. There were no dogs because the physicality of the environment simply impeded any escape. No dogs were needed.

Eventually, the trees dispersed. Glimmers of sunlight fought to the snowy undergrowth, falling upon my skin. I absorbed as much as I could, craving its warm light. I looked down, carefully placing my feet, until I felt Anya nudge my arm. Having reached the end of the forest, I looked on, astounded.

Before us, the fjord bathed in rich, golden light. It was a large, magnificent structure: deep and wide, with steep cliffs dropping to turquoise waters, originating from the glacier at the far left. An enormous marvel, the glacier meandered its way down the steep mountain slopes, eventually meeting the fjordic waters. Deep cracks dug into the glacier, streaks of turquoise glowing from its icy depths. If one held their breath, the faint creaks of sliding ice echoed in the distance.

These fjordic waters spread through the rocky crevasse and emptied into a glittering, blue ocean dotted with icebergs and sailing ships. Sails opened and bulged, carried by the winds to other ports across the Territory.

Blackberry's Clearing was built on a manmade circular courtyard, stretching far over the fjord to boast the magnificent view. To the left: the glacier pure and unspoiled. To the right: a sparkling sea dotted only by icebergs, ships and small, gentle waves.

All of the town's one-hundred inhabitants resided in little stone houses, all with wooden doors, decorated with gold. A fountain proudly stood in the centre of the courtyard, its water frozen in some elaborate position, and the surrounding pool dusted with a fine layer of white, like icing sugar. By far the grandest structure, however, was a large grey-stone building, clinging to the cliff side. Red and blue fabric draped on either side of two wooden doors, intricately carved.

"Where are all the citizens?" I asked Anya, for the town itself seemed deserted.

"In the Town Hall," she replied, tilting her head to the grand building. "They usually have an enormous lunch whilst they discuss business, though I doubt –"

"Ladies, your presence is required in the Town Hall," Bentley suddenly said, parading towards us with a sullen, almost envious look upon his face.

"*Us?*" Anya frowned. "Our duties aren't required until the evening."

"There will be a change of plan this year."

"Why?"

"Because they're eager to get this party started, Miss Whittaker. So, if you both value your lives, I suggest you do as you're told."

* * *

TECHNICALLY SPEAKING, the *lunch* was more of a late-afternoon ordeal. The guests, including Anya and I, spent the next few hours changing into formal attire before the feast began at precisely 3:30pm. Once the food was consumed, the wine had been drunk and the petty conversation exhausted, the guests retired to the Overview.

The Overview was a large conservatory, protruding from the cliff side and allowing a pristine, unobstructed view of the entire fjord. Tall windows gleamed and sparkled on every wall; no doubt cleaned thoroughly for Mason's arrival. The Overview itself was more of a social hub, with small tables, sofas, armchairs, even a few chess and bridge tables. It also contained two bars, located on opposite sides of the room. Anya was in charge of one, and I the other.

An impressive fireplace was cut into a stone wall, currently home to a crackling fire. Thick logs fuelled this fire, occasionally splitting and allowing small, glowing sparks to race up the chimney. The room itself was crowded, stuffy, and stiflingly hot.

Of course, such heat only exacerbated the tight, sweaty monstrosities we were required to wear. Also black, the lower rim of the dress finished a few inches above my knee, the neckline low and boasting too much cleavage. The dress's long arms completely covered my wrists, and clung uncomfortably beneath both armpits, making its tight presence known every time I breathed.

Evening fell and the guests were drunk, giddy, and terribly noisy. Topics of conversation were limited to sex, conspiracy and murder.

A few familiar faces jumped out, including Emilia Eynesbury and, of course, the Ulster Woman. She acknowledged my presence, openly grimaced, and then stood with a skinny hip bone jutting out of a long, emerald green dress.

Joe Matheson was also present, dressed in a tuxedo and looking gaunter than ever. I smiled warmly when I saw him – an emotion he did not reciprocate.

"Maya, how are you?" he asked with a gentle pinch of my elbow.

"Stop acting like I'm some china doll about to break," I snapped back. But as the fabric of the dress stretched with a heavy sigh, I admitted that I could do with a friendly shoulder.

"Look," I said, finding those eyes the colour of seafoam. "There's been a...*development*, a-and I don't know what to do about it, and it's kind of freaking me out."

Joe's eyes immediately glazed with concern. "Has someone hurt you?"

"Huh? No, no, nothing like that... I-I mean, not really... But it's complicated."

Joe took a rushed look over narrow shoulders. "Meet me after breakfast tomorrow, we'll talk then."

Then, just like that, that funny man scurried back into the crowd of Aristocrats with whom he was desperately trying to socialise.

Sighing, I continued my whiskey rounds. Soon, I met the large man called Thackeray. He presented me with a gleaming white smile and rubbed the beads of perspiration from his bald head.

"Ah, you must be the new Slave. Miss Deer, was it?"

I barely hid a snort. "*Doe*, Sir."

Those golden rings gleamed as he took a tumbler from the tray. "Ah yes, my mistake. An associate of Campbell Anders, I hear."

"A friend, yes."

"You must know an awful lot about the Rebellion, then?"

"What? Oh, no, not at all." I smiled awkwardly.

"But, sweetheart..." He grinned at me. "Campbell was charged with conspiracy."

"We were framed," I replied, then spotted Joe's charismatic smile through the crowd. "Ask Mr Matheson, he was the one who sold us, who *lied* about us, simply to save his own skin."

Thackeray took a large gulp of whiskey, several chins wobbling as he swallowed. Replacing the tumbler on the tray, he looked down his nose.

"Your naivety is pitiful."

Then he disappeared into the crowd.

As the hours wore on, the animals grew hungry. Trays of freshly made sandwiches and other generic finger-food were brought up from the kitchens, swiftly demolished, but the Aristocrats wanted more. More food was consumed, yet the Aristocrats did not settle. The claustrophobia did not lessen.

The immense heat made my head fuzzy and my breathing weak. Frantically glimpsing at each happy, sad, ecstatic, giddy face, I knew I had to escape. There were too many people – *too many people!*

A door led to the outside balcony. I rushed to it, almost tripping over my own heeled feet.

The cold air hit me, wiping away the sweat and panic. I inhaled the clean air into my lungs, letting the cold consume me. Other than the muffled tones of drunken laughter, it was silent on the balcony. Wind howled as it gently travelled down the cliff side, and though it was faint, it was enough to blow the music away. For the first time in months, I was at peace.

I wandered to the edge of the balcony, leaning over the balustrade, casting my eyes upon the sights. The glacier was to the left, the sea to the right. The moon shone brightly: a pearl against a black sky, joining the billions of stars. Indeed, I had forgotten just how beautiful a proper night's sky could be.

Another gust of wind stroked cold fingers through my hair. I closed my eyes, imagining that I was free, that I would jump onto the nearest ship and escape the pompous, Aristocratic stock for the rest of my days. I wanted to explore the world: to climb a lonely mountain peak, to feel the crunch of snow beneath my boots, to gaze upon the unspoilt drama of the land below...

I was not meant to be confined.

The clink of the balcony door. I groaned, for it was either Aristocracy or Bentley's nagging tone, and I was in no mood for either. I wanted to remain in my safe solitude, with the wind stroking my face, brushing its fingers through my hair. Was that really too much to ask?

Bitterness returned as someone came up beside me, their hands resting upon the railing. I turned to them, about to snap that even a Slave deserved her privacy. Words whipped away as Mason's bright eyes gazed to the fjord below.

"Oh – excuse me, Sir," I spluttered. "I'll get back to my chores right away, I-I just needed some air."

"I'm not Bentley," he said, briefly casting his eyes towards me. "I understand the need for fresh air, so stay if you wish."

I thought about this for a long moment. The rational part of my brain told me to run back to that humid, stuffy Overview while I still could. Yet, as the glacier creaked and slinked its way down the mountainside, I admitted the draw of the outside world was simply too much. Sighing, I joined Mason's side. Music loudened inside my head, once again dissolving the anger and disgust, and turning it into something almost...*normal?* The thought was worrying and inherently unlikable, but at least on that Balcony I could lose myself in the view of a free world. Compared to that, Mason's presence was a manageable annoyance.

We remained in silence for a while, each of us absorbed in our thoughts, our own appreciation of our surroundings.

But Thackeray's smile kept encroaching from the back corner of my mind, mocking me, spoiling the view. Eventually, the anxiety became crippling.

"Sir," I asked, gripping the rail with both hands.

"Hm?"

"The Free People's Rebellion."

"What about it?"

"You don't think... I mean, you *know* that Campbell and I didn't have anything to do with that, don't you? We were arrested for conspiracy, but we were completely innocent."

Mason's bright eyes slid to me, a small frown marring his handsome features. "Yes, I know that."

"Truly?"

"Yes."

I sighed out a hidden breath, leaning both arms against the railing. The frost bit my skin through the thin material of my dress, but the cold discomfort was refreshing upon skin licked with sweat.

"Where's all this coming from?" Mason asked. "It's been months since you were captured. Surely such worries should have been washed from your mind long ago."

"Thackeray implied Campbell was part of the Rebellion all along. He called me naïve for thinking otherwise."

"Oh, pay no attention to Thackeray. I've only recently accepted him into my Social Circle, and I daresay he just wants to make his superiority over you known."

A feisty click of my tongue, hardly a stranger to such Aristocratic ways.

"Admittedly, however, I have often wondered that myself."

"What?" I startled. "That's ridiculous."

"Is it? Maya, you didn't know Campbell the way I did. Rebellion was in his blood."

Although unspoken, Gainstorn raised its foul head. I wondered, for what seemed to be the thousandth time, what unspeakable actions went on in that town. After all, if there was one thing both Mason and Campbell agreed upon, it was that the events of Gainstorn were so horrific, so unjust, they should never be uttered again.

"No, that's not true," I said. "I was with Campbell when we both learnt about the Free People's Rebellion."

"How did you find out?"

"Joe Matheson told us, just before Waterman's Quarry. On the way there, we found a conspirator you executed, a warning nailed in his foot, complete with a wanted poster for Mikael Ashworth. Only then did we know the full scale of the Rebellion – Campbell had no idea before then."

"Well, that's somewhat refreshing to hear." Mason sighed. But then that sadistic smile reappeared. He stood to his full height. "But seeing as the subject had been brought up, what do you know about the Rebellion?"

Still gripping the railing, I faced the sky and groaned. "See you *do* think I'm a part of it!"

He laughed softly. "No, I don't. I'm just curious as to what you've heard."

"Honestly, hardly anything at all. I know its name and that its leader is Mikael Ashworth, but that's it."

"Campbell never said anything?"

"How could he? He didn't even know about it." I huffed out a frustrated sigh. "Besides, even if he *did* know about it, he wouldn't have joined. He was a damaged man after what you did to him."

"Ah yes." Mason smiled, leaning upon the railing with cruel eyes glittering. "I enjoyed punishing him."

"Did he deserve it?" I asked, carefully, trying to conceal my spite.

"He deserved more. No punishment could avenge Gainstorn."

"Because he weakened you?"

"He didn't weaken me," Mason snapped, then gently added, "Not directly, at least."

His gaze focussed on the fjord below, silently absorbing each slope, each colour, each texture of the world he created with such loving, devoted care.

"Mason, what did he do?"

Mason sighed, lost in his thoughts as the icy wind caressed his features. His hair rippled, like streaks of black velvet.

"He did something evil, even by my standards."

Something winded me, pushing all air from my lungs, forming the mist between my lips. I bowed my head, contemplating his words and wondering just how *evil* he meant. Campbell Anders was a good man: a brave, honest, true man.

What *evil* could he have possibly committed for Mason – of all people – to judge him for it?

The words ached at the tip of my tongue, but as I saw Mason's thoughts swirl and convulse, I admitted that such things may be best left unspoken.

We remained leaning on that railing, just admiring the view.

"Why this?" I asked, some moments later.

"Hm?" Mason was slowly brought from his reverie.

"This." I gestured to the vista. "Why, when you created this world, did you choose all this when you had limitless choices?"

"How do you know my options were limitless? For all you know, mountains and ice could have been my only options."

"Not according to *Moonsilver*." I smiled. "There are all sorts of landscapes in that book."

"Ah, you've finished it?" Mason seemed proud. "So, now that you've read it properly, what do you think of it?"

"I've enjoyed it. It's had adventure, action, romance… It's been a nice escape over the past few months." A large creak from the glacier echoed up the fjord. "But still, why mountains? Why not beaches, or deserts?"

"It's my favourite, simple as that."

"You did a beautiful job," I said, sincerely.

"My, was that a compliment?"

"No."

"It sounded like one."

His attitude was prickling at my skin, like nettle rash. I ran my tongue over my teeth, my lips tightly shut as I glared at him from the corner of my eye.

"Oh," he remarked, grinning. "If looks could kill."

Ignoring him, I admired the glittering specks in the sky.

"Are you really prepared to leave all of this?" he eventually asked me. "You've told me how beautiful the world is, and by the way you look at it, I doubt you want to die just yet."

"I'm *not* dying just yet," I said, sharply. "Sixteen more days to go, Mason."

"And counting."

Wind blew my hair behind me, and I basked in its sensation. My eyes closed, my head inclined back as I let the freedom consume me.

"Don't have false hope, Maya."

"I'm not. I know the consequences of my actions."

"Then why do you persist with this immature jaunt?" He scowled at me, his eyes burning. "What are you trying to prove?"

"That I can't be controlled, for one. I am a Slave and I have been for many months now, but I am the only one in control of *my* body, and no threat or *deal* from you can possibly change that."

Mason laughed to the sky. "I have yet to decide if you're brave or foolish."

"Foolish," I said. "Definitely foolish."

A heavy sigh escaped me, the cold caressing the last specks of sweat upon my brow.

"Doesn't matter what happens to me anyways," I eventually muttered. "You'll just go back to Tia."

"Probably." Mason smirked. "You seem rather annoyed by that."

"Because it's disgusting. The way you throw us around, flicking from one of us to the other. It's sickening."

"Oh, is it? Tia had a very different view. She even thanked me for it."

"She thanked you because she was a very damaged woman and you took advantage of that."

"I think you'll find it was a mutual advantage."

"It wasn't mutual – Tia had no other choice but to agree! You could have picked any of them – *any* of them – and yet you decided on Tia only after she was attacked! What happened, she kept saying *no* to you before Jayson destroyed her?"

"I had little interest in her beforehand."

"Why, don't like undamaged goods?"

"Hardly." He smirked again. "I was with Verity Ulster."

A blast of icy wind, chilling me to the bone.

"Oh dear Maya, you've suddenly gone very pale."

"*Verity Ulster?*" The name was acid on my tongue. "You've got to be kidding me."

"I do believe, my dear, that your eyes are turning the same shade of green as Verity's." A wide smile formed that spoke salacious volumes. "Jealous, are we?"

"Absolutely not!"

"My, your cheeks are blushing."

I covered my face, feeling its radiating heat. Mason's presence suddenly turned the vast wilderness into the most claustrophobic space I'd ever entered. I had to escape from that balcony.

"Excuse me, *Sir*."

Glaring, I slid beyond his view and strolled back towards the Overview. Mason stayed still, gazing at the landscape he created many, many years ago.

Quite suddenly, I stopped. Light had appeared above me.

Glorious pastel blues and greens undulated across the sky as a single, flowing wave of light. Dull at first, they grew brighter and bolder, dancing in tune, strangely, with the piano inside my head.

Had Mason created the aurora, just at that very second? I pushed away the unsavoury thought: I did not want my moment of wonder tainted by a desperate man's attempts to attract me. Nevertheless, if it was him, then his efforts had paid off.

He looked at me when I reappeared at his side, leaning on the railing.

"If I stay out here for a little while longer," I said, gazing above, "will Bentley throw a fit?"

"Probably." Mason titled his head, admiring my wonder. "But I'm sure you can handle it."

* * *

THE NEXT MORNING, after I had served breakfast, I waited for Joe Matheson.

Sat cross-legged on the squeaky bed, I was in the Slave's Dormitories beneath the Town Hall. No windows, which was of great annoyance, but there was at least a small electric heater that did wonders for laundry. I was required to wear the black dress again that night, so I had scrubbed the scent of cigars and sweat from its tight fabric, and hoped it would dry quickly.

A small knock on the door.

The ground was freezing against my bare soles. I leapt back on the bed as soon as Joe Matheson entered, cradling my frozen feet.

"So, what's happened?" Joe asked. He pulled the arms of his jumper down and remained standing against the wall. It was all very domineering.

"Oh, sit down, for Odin's sake!" I snapped.

Irritated, he sank like a boulder on the bed next to me. "That better?"

"Much, thank you." I wiped the exasperation from my face and said, in a much calmer tone, "Thank you for coming."

"Don't mention it," he said, his mouth shadowed with stubble. "But you didn't half worry me last night. What's going on, girl?"

I exhaled a long breath. Where did I begin?

Ultimately, I started at the beginning: from my chat with the Pretender, to the music. Then to Jayson Montgomery, to Mason's initial infatuation with me, and then finally to his terrible deal, with even more terrible consequences.

Joe listened intently, his face growing paler with each syllable.

As I finished, Joe simply stared into mid-air, the sleeve of his jumper tucked tightly against his lip.

"I don't know what to do, Joe," I said. "If I try to escape, I'll die or he'll catch me. If I stay, he'll look into my eyes and then he'll also catch me. What do I do?"

"I don't know," he whispered. But then he jumped to his feet, pacing around the room with his grey loafers shuffling against the stone. "No, *no* – I will not accept this. There must be something we can do to get you out of this fuckup."

"Like what?'

"*I'm thinking!*"

"Oi, lose the attitude!"

Joe dropped to his knees and put two trembling hands upon mine.

"Maya," he said, forcing calm. "I'm sorry, girl, but you're the End of Everything and for the sake of all people in this world, we can't let Mason find you."

"*The End of Everything?*" I forced out a bitter chuckle. "I'm not sure I even believe that anymore."

"Does Mason strike you as the type of man who would believe rumours?"

No, he didn't. In fact, he was the exact opposite. Somehow, I *was* the End of Everything. That's what Mason wanted and according to him, that could only occur when I gave him a child.

I forced an anxious swallow. "I'm worried about Jayson Montgomery too."

"Yeah, I can't believe you gave up the only protection you had there, girl. What a stupid thing to do."

"If you've not got anything constructive to say, then just leave me alone. I-I can't be dealing with your bullshit right now."

Joe placed two angry hands upon his hips. "Do you think there's a real chance this Captain fella might attack you?"

"I-I dunno, maybe... I-I don't want to think about it."

"Right." Joe's entire persona shifted, returning to the charismatic Trader who always gave me a good deal. "Give me till tonight. I'll see if I can get something to help you."

"Thanks," I said, exhaling. "Now it's just Mason."

"Do you really think he'll go through with it?"

"What do you think?" I gave a sarcastic raise of my eyebrows.

If anything in that wretched world was certain, it was that Mason would look into my soul on the *Last Day* of the year. And if he looked into the eyes of Maya Doe, it would be the eyes of Alira that would stare inevitably back.

"Then you need to escape," he said, when all other options were exhausted.

"You don't understand, the place is impenetrable! They've got snipers everywhere and man-eating dogs if the bullets don't work." I shook my head, defeated. "Either he'll find me, or I'll die trying to escape that place."

"You have to try," Joe said, squeezing my knees. "Wait till the last minute – who knows, he might change his mind – then run for it. Run as fast as you can and don't look back. Use the trees, climb them to escape the dogs."

Quietly, I nodded, agreeing with his every word because at the end of the day, he was right. Truth be told, a bullet in the brain was better than my inevitable fate with Mason, should he ever discover who I truly was.

"I have to go," Joe Matheson said, standing to his full height. "I'll give you a signal later tonight if I've got the stuff."

"What *stuff*?"

"I dunno yet." He sighed, playing with the little dimple on his chin. "I'll see what I've got."

He marched to the door, his forehead marred with deep, concentrating lines.

"Oh, wait!" I said, just before he left. "A couple of names have popped up that are proving to be annoyingly mysterious."

"What names?"

"Svenja and Sebastian Svellec. I know the woman has golden teeth." I watched for any glimmer of realisation, but he remained annoyingly difficult to read. "You ever heard of them?"

Joe's tongue pressed tightly into his cheek. "Not the woman, but Sebastian Svellec... That name I've heard of before."

"When, from whom?"

"A Messenger in the middle of Bolton Square, many years ago now."

"What was he saying?"

"His obituary. Sebastian Svellec is dead."

The End of Everything

* * *

TEMPERATURES in the Overview had only increased. A healthy fire raged, spurting sticky heat all directions. Aristocrats coped by drinking to excess. Men removed their dinner jackets, women flapped napkins before their faces. The balcony was inundated with those who found the heat a little too overcoming. I was annoyed at this, for now I had nowhere to go. I was forced to carry on, to serve more drinks to drunk Aristocrats.

Somewhere in the mess of people, I spotted Joe Matheson. We locked eyes almost instantly. A sure wink of a seafoam eye, and I marched towards him with one hand supporting the tray, the other low at my side.

Joe deftly transferred a cool metallic object and disappeared from the room. I tucked it into my tight sleeve, making my innocent way back to the bar.

Gods, it was so hot in that room! A bottle of champagne winked at me, sitting in an ice bath. Desperate, I popped one of the smooth ice cubes into my mouth. The relief was instant, filling my mouth, and then my sore head, with numbing cold. Pure *bliss*.

"Miss Doe, I have a job for you." Bentley's sharp voice caught me by surprise, and I almost choked on the ice cube. Bentley studied me for a moment, watching as I tucked the cube into my cheek.

"I'm eating ice," I somehow mumbled, casually filling up tumblers.

"Yes," he said, brusquely. "Well, go to the cellar and collect two bottles of the house port that were bottled in *Year 166* and *Year 167*. That should do." And with that, he was off, meandering through the crowd as he wiped the sweat through his greased hair.

Chewing at ice cubes, I was swiftly on my way.

The cellar was dark — and cold, actually, so it was a welcoming reprieve. The steep steps, leading down into the cellar, boasted a frozen, pale sheen that glistened in the dim light. The thought of breaking my neck a little too worrisome, I removed the red heels and left them just outside the door. Slowly, I descended.

Wine racks filled almost every available space of that utter *labyrinth*, only leaving small aisles to walk through that could barely fit two people. Inside the racks, bottles filled every nook: wines, whiskeys, ports, meads... The vintages were endless.

I began the tedious search for the ports bottled in *Years 166* and *Year 167*. I ran my fingers over the labels, blowing off dust and being careful to note which way I was turning.

A bottle caught my attention. Swatting dust from the yellowed label, I squinted at the year: *1896*.

I frowned. That was a *none-date*. A relic from the Old World, perhaps? Shrugging, I accepted the typing mistake and swiftly continued my search.

A few minutes later, loud footsteps echoed on the frozen floor.

"Hello?" I breathed through pearly steam. "Who's there?"

My stomach acid curdled. I peered around the corner. No one.

Sighing, I turned to the next stack of bottles.

Jayson Montgomery stood proud ahead.

I screamed, curses rolling off my tongue. Laughing, Jayson steadied me by the arm but I shook away his touch.

"Jayson, you scared the life out of me!"

"Ha, it was worth it to see the look on your face!" Throwing his arms up, he did a pathetic – if not offensive – attempt at my Herdinese accent. Scowling, I continued to scour bottle labels.

"What are you doing down here?" he asked, following me like a lost puppy.

"I'm trying to find something for Bentley," I replied, still checking labels.

"You're going to be down here forever," he said, still following me with a smirk upon his face. I glimpsed behind my shoulder, noticing the silver revolver hanging from his hip.

A subtle check of the object Joe Matheson had given me, the one still concealed in the sleeve of my dress. It felt like a collapsible knife.

I quickened my pace. "I'm almost done. Besides, Bentley is expecting me in a few minutes."

"Liar." Jayson slithered up behind me.

I jumped away from him and rushed down the next aisle.

"What are you doing down here, Jayson?"

"You ran away from me in the Reading Room. I wasn't done with you."

"Yeah, well I was done with you!"

I needed to get out of that cellar. I needed to find Anya, Joe, *Mason!*

"Oh, Maya, you break my poor Masonian heart."

"I didn't realise Masonians had hearts." Each aisle I took ended in another, or a wine rack, or a wall...

"Oh we do, but we don't often use them." His voice echoed off the frosted stone walls. "We prefer to use other parts of our bodies. They're much more fun."

"I'm sure Tia Kingsley would disagree." I was running now, my wild heart beating with the music.

"Tia Kingsley is a slut." His voice rose up from somewhere in the mess of wine racks. "She was always strutting about, always flaunting her long legs and those plump tits, and then she gets a shock when I try to fuck her?" His sick laughter rumbled in my lungs. "She had it coming."

I rounded the first corner, then the second, then the third and was met with another wall. I threw my hands in my hair, stifling a fearful wail, unable to leave this labyrinth and the predator that lurked within.

"Well," I shouted, retracing my steps, "you can't touch her now, she's under Mason's protection!"

"Oh, I know. Quite a shock if you ask me, I didn't think the bastard would be so amiable to your requests. But, when one door closes, another one opens, hey Maya?"

"Wouldn't know about that, all my doors are firmly locked."

"Not for long, all they need is a little *bang!*" Something hard slammed against one of the wine racks, the bottles clinking and clanking in their beds. "Y'know, to get things moving."

I saw footprints on the stone floor. My bare feet had warmed the frost, creating a melted trail back to those stairs.

I ran, meandering my way around those wine racks. So close, only a little further!

Jayson Montgomery appeared from an aisle, directly in front of me.

I skidded to a halt, my bare feet slipping and I slammed against the frosted floor. Jayson marched forwards, his aqua eyes devoid of humanity, his cheeks red, his temple pulsing.

"C'mon, Maya," he said, smirking. "Be a slut for me."

Two hands came at me. I grabbed the neck of a wine bottle and slammed it into one of those arms. Jayson shrieked, recoiling. I scrambled to my feet. Fingers gripped my wrist, jerking me to him.

His look of pure carnal rage... The music in my head took a desperate note.

The knife... *Where was the knife?*

I shook it out into my hand, flipped the blade and sliced Jayson's face.

He screamed and fell into a wine rack. Blood oozed from the gaps between his fingers. Legs flailing wildly, wine bottles shattering, I turned my back to Captain Jayson Montgomery and ran, just as the metallic sounds of his revolver clinked throughout that wine cellar.

***

I leant against the wall, panting and shaking. I inhaled all the air I could, the stench of cigarettes and Jayson's sickening cologne still infesting my lungs. The music was soft against my head, caressing me, soothing me as I wiped a terrified tear from my cheek.

My mind was still in that cellar, still feeling his touch upon me. I clenched my fists, my fear deforming into an intense, burning anger. My mind now focussed on one person, I tucked the bloodied blade into my sleeve and marched into the Overview.

The heat hit me instantly. Bentley called my name, demanding to know where I had been. I scanned the room, pushing past everyone until I found my target.

Mason was laughing with one of his associates.

"Sir, may I have a word?" I snapped. He looked me up and down. "In private?"

"Of course." Gulping back the last of his champagne, he replaced the flute on the nearest table. Leading me from the room, he placed a hand between my shoulder blades.

"Had a change of heart?"

"You wish."

"Tick-tock, Miss Doe." Mason smirked beside me. "Tick-tock."

Mason led me to a small library. Dark and dingy, books lined each wall.

Although the room contained a chandelier, the light it produced was dim and merely allowed Mason to scrutinise my shaken demeanour.

"Something amiss?" Mason asked, marching to the other end of the room. He took the liberty of pouring himself a whiskey from the small bar that resided there.

I gently pushed the door closed, finding comfort in its resounding click and knowing that – out of everything – Jayson could not hurt me when I was with him.

But whilst basking in that security, the terror that lingered from that frosty maze twisted and deformed into rage. I threw my hands across my face, smudging away the last visions of Captain Jayson Montgomery. My hands fell to my side as I berated Mason with a glare that spoke volumes.

"You need to control your *fucking* men!"

Gulping down the whiskey, Mason fumbled with the glass in his hand and tried – unsuccessfully – to hide his smirk.

"Oh dear, you seem a little upset."

I paced in front of him: some feeble attempt to utilise the last drips of adrenaline in my blood. "By the Old Gods, you better not have put him up to it."

Mason scowled. "And why would I do that?"

"Oh, let me think – some perverse attempt to persuade me perhaps?"

"If I was going to persuade you, Miss Doe, I wouldn't ask for someone's help."

I stopped pacing and rested in the middle of the room, panting. Mason leant against the wooden wall, tugging at the collar of his shirt. He eventually gave into temptation, and removed his bowtie completely. He threw it lazily to the floor and unfastened the buttons of his collar with a few sharp tugs.

I still paced around the room. "I've given up my protection for Tia, and I accept that, but there has to be something said for disciplining your men!"

"What good would that do? My Masonians are hardly decent people."

Adrenaline seeped through the dirty soles of my feet. In its place, exhaustion rose. I supported myself with hands upon my knees, exhaling more air than I thought possible.

Before me, Mason moved steadily closer. "Did he hurt you?"

"No."

"Good." He smiled at me. "It's refreshing to know that I don't have to share."

"Yeah, well you might not be so lucky next time." I nastily scowled. Mason's smile grew wide as he closed the remainder of the space, both hands in his pockets.

"I'm sure we can come to another arrangement."

"Please, not another one of your fucking deals," I glared, exasperated.

"Oh…" He chuckled softly to himself. "I think you'll find this one more than agreeable. After all, I am feeling particularly magnanimous this evening."

"What in Hel's name does that mean?"

Mason's beautiful eyes shone as he stood directly before me. "It means I will offer you protection from Captain Montgomery. You, as well as Tia."

"Both of us? But why? You said to me the other day – "

"Call it a change of heart."

His smile was all it took. The piano rose up as a shooting pain behind my eyes, willing me on, wanting me to fall headfirst into his seduction.

Ever so gently, Mason placed a finger beneath my chin.

"So, what do you say?" He smiled at me again, and something inside me squirmed in excited anticipation.

"No, I-I'm not doing it," I forced myself to reply, but the music kept singing…

"But you want to."

"No, I-I don't…"

Mason ran the soft pad of his thumb across my lower lip. "I've told you, Maya. If you're going to lie to me, lie well."

The music disappeared as Mason touched his lips to mine.

For a moment I was stunned, unable to move as he kissed me. Then my body began to react to his touch. Closing my eyes, I kissed him back. His lips were warm and soft, utterly delicious.

He gently tugged my hair and ran soft lips across my neck. My hair soon flowed down in waves, and in the silence of the room, I felt free.

My arms wrapped around his neck, my breaths strained and quickened. With a fervent ferocity I never knew I possessed, I found his open mouth and licked the haunt of whiskey from his tongue. His lips curved into a pleased smile.

He pushed me to the wall of books, hands rushing up and down my body, and in one quick movement, he lifted me from the floor. My legs wrapped themselves around his hips as he pushed himself closer, locking me in place. My eyes closed, enjoying this moment of forbidden longing as he caressed the smooth skin of my legs. Hands moved further up my body. I didn't care: I was too engrossed in the moment, in *him*.

My dress was pushed up high around my waist. I inhaled his scent – the glorious smell of surrender and want and passion all rolled into countless, fast intakes of breath. Those warm hands found my abdomen, pushing their way higher, squeezing my bare breasts as my arms locked tighter around him.

Something hard was between us, pushing against my most intimate area, and for one brief moment, I wondered what in Hel's name I was doing. But then a single hand slipped beneath my underwear and I moaned my surrender to the ceiling.

The clinks of metal as Mason unbuckled his belt. I spread my eager legs wide.

But, as Mason's belt fell limp and his flies were opened, I heard something.

It was quiet at first, almost delicate. Piano notes floating listlessly around my skull.

But as our passion became more intense, more certain, the music grew louder and more powerful, so that when Mason freed himself in all of his glory, the music was obliterating everything else.

Not yet, Alira, it seemed to sing, *we require a Connection first.*

Placing both hands against his shoulders, I firmly – reluctantly – pushed him away.

Although hesitant at first, he eased me to the ground. Laughing softly to himself, he wandered to the opposite side of the room as the sounds of zips and belt buckles percolated the small space. My limbs trembling, I swiftly tugged my dress down.

Mason leant both hands against the wall, his breaths deep and slow as he regained control of himself. Afterwards, he hastily poured another tumbler of whiskey.

"You know," he eventually said, facing me with a glorious grin. "One of these days, you're not going to push me away."

I avoided his gaze, the longing within my body still so strong. My heart thumped wildly, and I was hot. It was suddenly very hot in that room.

"I told you, I don't want to."

"You could have fooled me."

His diamond eyes were so bright, so penetrating, as he sipped a little of the whiskey.

"Don't let your stubbornness be the end of all this," he said, raising a judging eyebrow. "You know you want to give in to me, you just won't let yourself."

"What's the point? We all have to die at some point."

"But not in sixteen days."

"Fifteen," I whispered, avoiding his gaze.

Mason came to me, sighing, as he held the tumbler low in his fingers.

"Why do you resist, Maya?" he said, cradling the side of my head. I closed my eyes, absorbing his touch.

"I have to," I said, allowing the remains of a sad smile to flick across my face.

The music had returned. It was eager – oh, so eager – as it practically dared me to look into his soul.

"Why?" he frowned at me, lightly tracing his thumb across my ringed ear. I didn't answer. Swallowing hard, ultimately, I did the only thing I could do.

"Goodnight, Sir," I muttered. Without another glimpse, I exited the room, closing the door behind me.

27

It was unusual for Mason to be so late for breakfast.

As Anya, Bentley and I waited patiently in the dining hall, I mindlessly filled coffee cups and gazed through the tall windows to the fjord below. The mid-morning sun bled across the sky, while glaciers glowed dirty orange in the fiery morning light.

A sharp click of Aristocratic fingers stole my attention.

There were only six Aristocrats that morning, caressing their hungover heads and gently feasting on meagre mouthfuls of dry toast. Joe Matheson was one of them, looking like death itself.

"Big night, Joe?" I muttered as I passed. He did not reply, but simply glowered into his glass of orange juice.

Despite my morning duties, my mind kept wandering to the events of the previous evening.

The attack from Jayson Montgomery was a sick memory, yes. But I had used the knife, and that simple fact calmed me more than anything. I was sure he'd think twice before cornering this *Wild One* again.

But what happened afterwards, with Mason and the music... The memories filled me with both intense excitement and crippling regret. For the life of me, I could not decide which emotion was more prevalent.

What *was* notably prevalent was the music inside my head, so fucking jovial that I wanted to slap the teasing notes from my skull.

I had not uttered a word to Anya about what happened, and certainly not what had *almost* happened. She would only scold and shout for my continued reluctance.

Like Hel was I going to tell Joe. The very thought made me cringe.

So, I remained alone – forever alone – idly fighting my own inner contrasts.

Heavy footsteps rang throughout the air, contracting my stomach. Wooden doors burst open and Mason stormed into the room, portraying pure, unfiltered rage.

"Where is it, Maya?"

All eyes flocked to me. I remained startled, wide-eyed, unable to move as Mason stood directly before me. Hot breath beat upon my forehead. Bright eyes glowed orange from the rising sun. "The knife you used on Captain Montgomery. Give it to me."

Tendrils of fear licked my skin. Mason's jaw clenched. "Do not make me search you."

Defeated, I reached into my bra and plucked out the collapsible knife. Such a small thing: slim and compact, and more than capable of producing a rather nasty cut.

Mason snatched it from my hand.

"Where did you get this?"

Joe Matheson turned ghostly white in my peripheral vision.

"Found it," I replied, quietly.

"Where?"

"The Overview."

Did he know I was lying? It was uncertain: his glare remained unchanged. The anger that seeped through his white shirt neither raised nor lessened with my explanation.

Finally, he sat down, twiddling the knife in his fingers for a few moments before securing it in his trouser pocket.

Silence commenced.

As the sun grew even higher, I thought of the previous evening. The feel of his lips, his hands... The desire I had for him in that one, priceless moment. It was like nothing I'd ever felt before. A warm rush at the memories, which I hastily pushed away.

Mason was calm then. He was gentle, *loving* even. A very different man to the one sipping his morning coffee.

Later on, as the last Aristocrat swayed from the room, Mason was the last at that table.

"See to it our belongings are packed for the return journey," he said. We dutifully bowed and made our way out. "Not you, Miss Doe."

Anya sent me a cautious, worried stare as the doors shut with an ominous bang.

Tension pulsed between us, so thick it could be cut with the knife Mason held up between his fingertips.

"Now, you and I both know that you did not simply find this lying about. Frankly, I don't much care where you got it, or who gave it to you, but I do take issue with the twenty-eight stitches in Montgomery's face!"

"With the greatest respect, Sir, but you weren't in that cellar. I had to protect myself."

"Protection or not, drawing Masonian blood is over the line!"

"What Jayson tried to do to me was over the *fucking* line! I'd do a lot more than spill a few drops of blood if I had to!"

Mason sprung to his feet, knockings chairs over. I tried to rush back, impeded by the wall he was quick to pin me against.

"You are a *Slave*, Maya! The whole purpose of your life is to make your Masters happy. To fulfil their wishes, to serve their desires and to *not*, under any circumstances, maim them or the men who serve them!"

"You'd rather the alternative?" My eyes burned with fresh tears. "Gods Mason, do you even know what he'd do to me?"

Mason smiled then: a calculating, sadistic smile that completely dissolved any *desire* or *excitement* I'd enjoyed mere hours beforehand.

"You wavered your right to protection last night, so I don't much care what happens to you anymore."

Something inside me hurt. Some deep, unknown ache that filled my chest and threatened to burst. I swallowed the hard lump pressing at my throat, helpless as a single tear escaped. Mason wiped it from my cheek.

"I wouldn't worry too much, my dear." A evil smirk formed. "At this rate, you'll be dead in two weeks regardless."

His smile widened. "Who knows, maybe Jayson will push you to reconsider my proposal. It's what happened with Tia, after all."

That evil bastard took a precious moment to see the hope drain from my face, lapping up each ounce of misery, sucking on my despair, feeding on each and every bit of my hurt until sufficiently satiated. With a final smile, he left.

I was alone.

Heels scraped against the wood as I collapsed to the floor, silently sobbing this strange pain into my hands.

Memories of the previous evening rushed. Of the excitement I felt, the *longing*... The taste of his lips, the warmth of his hands, the sparks of excitement as he smiled at me, *touched* me...

They all disintegrated, deforming beneath tainted light. I tried to find the anger, wanting – for the first time in months – to feel it rise up and consume this new, strange sense of hurt that felt so alien. This one surprise, unknown emotion was destroying me from the inside, mocking what Maya Doe had once felt.

Whether from the music or my own fucking weakness, I had wanted to give myself to Mason. But not anymore.

From the moment I'd been enslaved, I'd been waiting for an *opportunity*. An opportunity to escape, a glorious moment when I could run out onto those frosted grounds and be free of that hellhole forever. But such an opportunity was a dream, it would never arrive. I had been waiting nine months for a miracle that would never come to fruition.

But not now. Now, it was time to take control of my life, my destiny.

Before the *Last Day*, I would escape. Whatever happened, Maya Doe would be dead by the end of year. Too long had she controlled my actions. Too long had I allowed myself to be absorbed in *her* life.

I threw my hands down, my eyes burning against the sun, and embraced the powerful resolve within each facet of orange light.

For the first time, I accepted who I really was. I was not *Maya Doe*. I was not Mason's *toy*.

I am Alira. I am the End of Everything.

28

The *Shortest Day* was upon us.

I watched the clock tick by, for what seemed like hours, until the sun eventually peeked its shy, ruby head through the trees. Crimson light devoured the Palace: a bloody hue that turned the snow a deep, dark orange and tinted trees with black. The sky, though cloudless, was a dark, deep blue, accentuated by the low sun. It was ethereal, beautiful even.

Watching the world go by in the little kitchen, I had been chatting to Tia since breakfast. Just random things, nothing of any concern. It was the idle chit-chat one partook between duties, to fill the empty air and dull the sound of impatient piano notes.

It had been a few days since I told Tia about Blackberry's Clearing. About Jayson's attack, my passion with Mason, his anger... All of it.

Tia had listened with growing concern, then gently covered my cold hand with hers. She told me not to worry, that Mason would not stay mad forever, and there was still some time before the *Last Day*. Now, I had a week to save myself.

But I didn't want to save myself. At least, I didn't want to save Maya Doe.

I despised her. I despised the feelings she had, her *weakness*. I needed to rekindle my inner *fire*, the fervent desire to *run, escape,* to climb the tallest mountain and scream my lungs to the Old Gods themselves!

As the clock's dreaded tick went by, I started to remember why I was once called, *Wild One*.

Tia didn't know my true name was Alira. She didn't know that I had diamond eyes, or heard the most beautiful music, or had an inner rage that could destroy everything I loved in less than a heartbeat...

She did not understand why I couldn't just *give myself* to Mason. She had no idea at all.

So, we had settled on talking. Just talking. About everything, and nothing. Just to fill the empty air with words. A way to pass the time as I counted the hours to Maya Doe's demise.

One week left. One day until I would run.

I intended to run fast.

Boots and a coat were safely stored beneath my bed. A knapsack of baked bread and a couple of jars of preserved vegetables were the only things I could afford to take with me. The jars were heavy, after all, and the blankets took up space. I needed to be light, skipping across the snow without food weighing me down. Besides, I knew how to hunt. I would eat rats if I had to. No, just a loaf of bread and a couple of failsafe jars, should a blizzard decide to strike.

All I needed were clothes. A Slave's uniform was a ridiculous set of garments, and both my legs would be lost to the weather should I run in my current state. No, I would sneak into the Pretender's bedroom, when she was otherwise engaged, and do my best to find some fitting clothes. Jewellery would also be nice – something to sell for a hunting rifle. Then maybe I could shoot a stag, pretend it was Mason.

Yes, I was almost ready.

Just one more night.

Sitting below the bulbs of garlic and strings of herbs hanging from the ceiling, Tia and I chatted for the best part of an hour before a small boy tentatively knocked on the door.

It was Harry, the youngest footman. The youngest Slave in the Palace.

"Afternoon, mate." I smiled at the nine-year-old, yet it quickly dropped. Brown eyes covered in shadow, his round face pale and shocked. "Harry, what is it?"

"The Mistress has some news," he said, his voice high and raspy.

"News? What news?" Tia asked, sensing the same urgency.

Those dark brown eyes slid to me. They were so sullen, so sad, and resembled something far older than Harry's short nine years.

"She didn't say... But she asked for you by name and said you needed to see her immediately."

Mason. Had he discovered my secret? Had he discovered *hers?*

"Where is she?" I asked, panic swarming like bees.

"The Green Room. Please hurry Miss, she says it's urgent!"

Visions of those cruel, sadistic eyes matched the ferocity of the piano inside my head. Barely having time to think, I removed my scarlet shoes and left them dumped beneath the table.

"No, Maya, wait!" Tia leant across the table to the small, scared boy. "What did she say *exactly?*"

"There's no time, Tia," I said through frantic breaths. "I-I have to go, I have to see what she knows."

What *he* knows...

Ignoring Tia's shouts, I was out the door.

Bare feet pounded against wood, then marble. The Dome Room was silent and empty when I entered, all except for the sharp slams of feet as I ran to the Green Room.

I bounded inside, scanning each dark crevice.

"Ma'am?" I desperately called.

The chandelier cast a dark, dim light across the starkness of the Green Room, and across a black table, bare for all except a small fruit bowl, the contents inside browning with neglect. A fireplace, bordered with black and green marble, remained unlit and unused. The room itself was surprisingly cold and had not been entered in some time.

Footsteps arose behind me. I turned to the sneering, stitched face.

"Jayson!"

"Hello, Maya."

He hit me. A sudden, sharp whack across my cheek that threw me to the ground. My outer eyebrow slammed against the corner of the table. Pain consumed everything, a sharp ringing in both ears, my vision dizzy. The world spun and darkened with every passing second, my hands scrambled to push myself from the dark green rug beneath my fingers.

Jayson took a large handful of my hair and whacked my head against the table.

The pain was instant, unyielding. I rolled to my back, the light fading. Blood pooled against my hairline.

Somewhere, as music clung to my waning consciousness, I heard Jayson's sneering spit. "You *bitch!* Do you see what you did to me? *Do you?*"

He pointed to the large gash on his cheek, spreading from his ear all the way down to his jawline. The wound was swollen and still very fresh, only held together by those twenty-eight black, protruding stitches.

The room gradually came into focus. Specks of light danced across my eyes, matching the ferocity of those piano notes.

Get up, Alira, they desperately sang. *You need to get up!*

Pain sank to my stomach. I vomited on the rug.

Jayson laughed at me, a horrible shrill squeal of evil, and dragged me from the pool of vomit with a single tug of my leg.

"Does your head hurt, sweetheart?" Standing above me, he kicked my legs apart and sank to his knees. "I sure hope so."

Two fingers pressed hard into the bloody wound, sending sharp stings of pain across my eyes, my head, my entire face… The panic of the music matched my heart. I began to realise what was happening. I tried to scratch him, my arms flailing wildly, but my limbs were weak, my strength pathetic.

"Oh Maya," he said, his face flushed as he swatted my hands away, like black flies.

He pinched my nose, covered my mouth. I couldn't breathe.

"You see, I was willing to be gentle with you in that cellar. I would have made it good for you. But now…" Dry, chapped lips stroked each ring on my ear. "But now, sweetheart, you'll only wish we were back in that cellar…"

The world faded. Black encroached from all corners, my consciousness dangling by a fraying thread…

The door burst open. Arms flew around Jayson's neck, wrenching him back with a high squeal.

Air shot down my throat and filled my aching, gasping lungs.

Shouts – a woman's shouts – and then Jayson's strained groans as she pushed and punched him to his knees.

Bouncing blond locks came over me, as did Tia's frantic begs. She shook my shoulders, begging me to get up and *run*.

The metallic swoosh, the sickening sound of cutting flesh.

Tia's shocked eyes grew large as the tip of a sword erupted from her belly. I watched, stunned and horrified, as she fell to her knees, staring at each drop of blood as it fell from the blade thrust in from behind her.

The sword was quickly ripped out. Tia Kingsley collapsed to the floor, blood trickling from the corner of her mouth.

A horrible, strangled scream left me. I tried to crawl to her, to help her!

Jayson grabbed my legs, pulling me back. The stench of sweat and cigarettes as he held me down, bringing fresh bile to my throat.

"You should really learn just to give up." A hot hand found my breast and squeezed.

I tried to scream. Jayson snapped his hand across my mouth, my lungs bursting with the pressure. "Shh, we wouldn't want anybody to hear us now, would we?"

His hand was up my skirt, tugging my underwear. The sharp rip of material. Plump tears raced as he pressed his hot, excited body into me and as I tried to buck him off, the sick bastard only grew more aroused. My tears came harder.

"Don't worry, Maya," he said, panting. He reached for his belt buckle. "Who knows, you might even enjoy it."

He removed his hand from my mouth and swiftly pressed his lips to mine.

The music exploded.

A violin – *Mason's violin* – screeched at us from inside our heads: deafening and powerful and *infuriated*. Mason's eyes flashed before my retina, his enraged scream mixed with the angry, seething notes of our combined music.

The very Palace shook, ornaments trembled against their confines.

Jayson flung himself against the wall, shrieking, clutching his head as the music clawed, scraped, and scratched inside his skull.

Eventually, the pain diminished. Panting and breathless, Jayson just stared at me; his eyes bloodshot, his face twisting with the last remnants of pain.

"...Oh my God..." he breathed. "You're... You're *her?*"

I remained silent, unable to move.

"Shit..." Fear consumed him. He stumbled from the Green Room, supporting himself against the wall as he rushed down the corridor. The door slammed shut behind him. Tia and I were left alone.

The piano caressed me, trying to make me understand that I was safe from Jayson Montgomery, and that I was untouched, unviolated and that everything was going to be okay...

The violin, however, had a very different tone.

I heard Mason's unmitigated *fury* in the Dome Room just as Jayson entered.

"I-I'm sorry Sir, I didn't know it was her, I –"

The sickening thump of Jayson's head echoed as it rolled to the floor.

Mason's *rage* boomed throughout the entire Palace.

"Let me make one thing perfectly clear! If anyone *dares* to touch my mate again, *I will kill all of you!*"

Enraged footsteps, then the shaking slam of a door above. The Palace was left in still silence.

"Tia..." I breathed.

Groaning, blood dribbling from my jaw, I crawled my way to her. Her eyes were still open. Small tears trickled from her lashes, dribbling to a bloody mouth forming strained, audible breaths. A fearful look up and down her body, across a blouse was drenched in blood, and the spreading pool of crimson beneath her.

I pressed against her wound in a desperate attempt to stop the bleeding. She was cold, ever so cold...

"Tia, y-you're going to be okay," I whispered. "Please just hold on..."

Her lips trembled, the red lipstick unnaturally bright against her paling skin. Slowly, she brought a bloody hand to my cheek.

"Don't let him find you..." Those blue eyes stared hard, knowingly into my own. "You mustn't... let him..."

And then, finally, Tia Kingsley took her last breath.

* * *

I was in the Reading Room.

How did I get there? I do not remember.

The last thing I saw were Tia's eyes as I gently closed them, protecting the intensity of that blue stare. A small, tender kiss upon her forehead, then I stumbled to my feet.

Now, I stared at my reflection in the window. The sun had already descended, plunging the world into darkness.

Still, through this darkness, I could see the snow. It fell gracefully from the sky, soothed the aching in my head.

Artificial light plagued the Reading Room. I could see my reflection; the state of the damaged, lying woman staring back.

A thick cut decorated my eyebrow, spreading blood all the way down my face. It dripped onto my blouse, marring the spotless white fabric. A young bruise formed through the swelling, spreading through a head that throbbed. It matched the nausea in my belly and the ringing in my ears.

A small cut plagued my inner thigh. It stung as I moved.

I stared at the pale, damaged woman in the window and wondered if it was Maya Doe or Alira staring back at me.

At the end of the day, did it matter?

Oh... It had stopped snowing.

The door to the Reading Room opened with a resounding creak. Mason wandered in and shut the door behind him. My stomach lurched at his presence. I could not move.

I followed his reflection in the window, his blue coat swaying as he came to stand next to the piano. Slowly, he lifted the keylid.

"Coincidence is a funny thing." His tone was dark and sinister, matching the music's echo.

He ran his fingers along the smoothness of those keys and small, delicious tremors ached beneath my skin.

Mason pressed a single key. The note erupted from the strings, finding my ears immediately. My eyes closed of their own accord, absorbing the intoxicating sounds.

"I killed Jayson Montgomery today." He pressed another key. "I killed him because he assaulted my mate. A rather curious development, don't you agree?"

Another note pressed. A shaky breath exhaled from tight lungs.

Slowly, Mason walked to my side. "I asked you a question."

"Yes," I eventually breathed.

Mason's head tilted, ever so slightly. I felt his eyes scan my injuries, before he delicately placed a finger against my open wound. I winced.

"Montgomery tried to assault you in Blackberry's Clearing. You both told me this, and both in your own words. But he was a most stubborn, uncontrollable man, and certainly not the sorts to give up easily. Evidently, given the scene in the Green Room."

I remained silent, unable to speak as a small, lonely tear trickled down my cheek.

"Did Tia discover what was happening? Did she try to save you?"

A sharp intake of breath. My limbs shook noticeably, feverishly...

"Regardless, imagine my surprise when the foolish Captain suddenly switched his attention to my mate."

A wicked smile appeared. "You see, my mate and I are bound to one another, albeit the rules of such a binding are rather skewed in my favour. I can lay with any woman I choose, but she..." He began to laugh, softly shaking his head. "Oh, she can only lay with me, and I know when another man tries to force himself upon her."

I could feel Jayson's weight on top of me, his lips pressing hard on mine, then the furious notes of a violin screaming throughout our skulls.

"Of course, anyone who dared to lay with her would be severely punished, as the late Jayson Montgomery had thus shown. All my Masonians know this.

"Nevertheless, Montgomery did not strike me as a foolish man and despite my best efforts, I cannot see him attacking a woman when he knew it would lead to his own death."

Mason dropped the finger from my eyebrow and slowly traced it down my face, cutting through the blood and tears, and resting it vertically upon my lips.

"Attacking a woman with a secret, on the other hand, seems much more plausible."

Very slowly, the finger slid from my face. With a gentle hold, Mason took my chin and lifted my head to the light.

"Ah, yes..." he mumbled to himself. "I can see the lenses now. Almost imperceptible unless one actively searches for them."

I tugged my head from his touch, then stumbled. The world spun around me as I supported myself against the wall.

"Is that concussion? Or the music?"

"I... I don't know what — "

"Oh of course you don't. As I said, coincidence is a funny thing."

Mason gripped my upper arms and slowly manoeuvred me to the piano.

Sickening pain. Everything rocked back and forth, the entire world suspended on a moving pendulum. I stumbled, falling back into his hold.

Mason gently lowered me to the piano stool. Twenty-four keys loomed before me, each black and white block appearing to jump and switch places.

Hands squeezed my shoulders. "Play for me," he whispered.

When I did not move, he reached across and pressed the first note of the song. Air shot into my lungs, the lure of that piano suddenly so strong and powerful that I could think of nothing else. Mason pressed down the next key. The room was already smothered, suffocating...

"S-Stop," I breathed. "Y-You...can't play..."

"You're right," he said. Feigned tenderness as he pushed my long, matted hair from my shoulder. "This isn't my instrument. I'm not supposed to play it."

Mason took a hand from my lap, still caked in Tia's blood, and brought it to the keys. His hand was so large compared to mine, his fingers dominating my own. He positioned me and pressed.

The note captured me, digging its claws deep. I lost control. My other hand jumped to the keys, continuing the song with frightening intensity. Mason squeezed my shoulders as he listened, enraptured....

Fingers danced across the keys. I closed my eyes and surrendered to the beautiful, encapsulating music that consumed *everything*.

My wounds healed, flesh stitching back together, the notes blowing away the fog of concussion. Everything was bright, everything was clear. Bruises faded, cuts healed, blood rushed back to ashen skin, so that soon the only evidence of my trauma was the dried blood upon my hands, my face...

The music became more intense, *gratifying*, and as the last trickles of musical ecstasy filled the Reading Room, awareness crashed back with suffocating force.

No sooner had the last note been played than I jumped to my feet, shrieking, ripping myself away from Mason's hold – the *music's* hold – and slamming my back against the far wall of books.

"Feeling better?" Mason glared.

"What did you do to me?" My heart pounded like some wild animal, trying to escape from that room, escape from *him*.

"*I* didn't do anything. The music has the ability to heal us, revitalise us. Although, I'm sure you know that by now.

"How long since you first heard the music, hm? A week, a month?" I remained silent, my hands trying to claw through the books at my back. Mason took a step closer. "Judging by the look on your face, I'd say a lot longer than that.

"You know, this music is a funny thing." He smiled incredulously, almost disbelieving. "It's directly linked to our subconscious, yet it only knows what we know – nothing more, nothing less. I've heard complete silence in my head for months, and then as soon as I put the pieces together and realised who you really are…" He closed his eyes, consumed. "…Well, now I can't stop hearing it…"

Very slowly, those eyes slid open. "Tell me, how long have you heard the music?"

"I-I don't know what you're talking about."

"Oh really?" He took a step forward. "I can always just take a look into your soul and find out for myself. Though I'd appreciate it if I heard it from your mouth. A disclosure as it were, or a confession." The room was silent, the music deafening. *"How long?"*

Rage boiled behind those diamond eyes. I debated lying. I concocted many stories inside my head to explain the occurrence of the music. Each one was more ridiculous than the last.

"The Theatre," I whispered.

Mason lifted his head and chuckled darkly. "My, I have been played for a fool."

"I-I was scared. I was always told you were going to kill me, I never – "

"Tell me, were you *scared* in Blackberry's Clearing? When you were going to give yourself to me, when the music begged you to stop, were you *scared* of me then?"

Mason scowled, taking another step closer. "I've always thought you were incapable of lying, my dear. But I'm beginning to think you're one of the most talented liars I've ever known."

Another step forward. Then another. "It's a shame really. Had you come to me before, had you told me who you really were, I would be inclined to be nicer."

Fear, though ripe and thick within my blood, made room for a new emotion. In that one, startling moment, I remembered what sort of monster Mason was, what he had *always* been.

"Y-You expected me to just tell you?" I relished the fleeting feel of this anger, this *fury*, as it helped soothe away the intense shaking of my limbs. "T-To run to you with my eyes wide open and sparkling? Well f-forgive me if I refuse to apologise, that I refused to surrender to you after everything you've done and everything you *will* do!"

Before me, Mason's mouth widened into a sinister, spectacular grin.

"You really are a fool." He chuckled bitterly to himself. "I am too. I have been played remarkably, *embarrassingly* well."

That smile disintegrated. "Tell me, do you remember what I said to you, in this very room, when you first arrived at this Palace?"

He took another step closer. "I told you not to embarrass me. It was a warning, clearly. Well, my dear, you have certainly embarrassed me. Most certainly, indeed."

The door screamed in my peripheral vision.

Mason's eyes flicked to the door, then back again.

"I almost want you to run. I want to catch you, I want to feel your fear as I do so." Mason laughed horribly, sadistically. Lips puckering, he kissed the air between us.

I burst from the room, viscous fear inside my veins. That knapsack sprung into my mind, safely concealed beneath my bed. I moved to the Downstairs staircase but a Masonian blocked my way.

Fearful tears threatened. I saw the corridor of jade columns, my route to the grand Palace doors, to *freedom*...

Masonians littered the room, blocking all exits. Their coats clashed against the bright white of the marble, their eyes hard and unyielding...

Diamond eyes were the hardest of all. "Tell you what, I'm going to make you a deal."

My clammy hand found the handrail, a bare foot searching for the cold marble step as I slowly ascended.

"I'm going to let you run. I'm going to let you have that final chance at freedom. Because that's what you want, isn't it, *Maya Doe?*" He spat my false name through gritted teeth.

I wanted to scream, to beg him to be merciful. Fear had removed my voice, squishing it down, far away beneath layers of pure terror.

Before me, Mason seemed impatient. "Well, go on then. I'll even give you a head start."

Another step was found beneath my toe. Then another, and then another.

"Oh, and a word of warning, my dear." He smiled again, but hatred lingered. "Amber eyes do not become you. Do not make me pluck them out."

I ran with a horrid sense of newfound energy. I wanted to scratch that energy out, expel it from my body just like those contact lenses!

The reality of what happened – *Jayson, Mason* – caught up like a bullet in the back. I paused in the upstairs corridors, fighting the growing panic in my chest.

He knows who I am, he knows who I am!

Now, more than ever, I had to *run!*

But run where? To whom? An idea popped.

I rushed to the Pretender's bedroom and threw my shoulder at the gold-veined door.

Two bloodied eyes stared back at me.

I collapsed to my knees, staring at her lifeless body. Her red, opal eyes gazed out into nothingness, her lifeless expression so twisted and final...

Cautiously, I moved closer. Her neck was broken, malformed. Mason must have snapped it before the failed Connection could finish its job.

Time was not on my side. I scanned the room.

Clothes were laid neatly upon the bed: a pair of jeans, a jumper, and a suede coat. A pair of boots were poised by the window. Clearly she realised my attack – felt the very Palace shake at Mason's fury – and decided to get the Hel out of there. She was evidently too slow.

Mistakes were not meant to be made twice. I would not survive in those bloody clothes so I quickly changed. Then, I finally – *finally* – removed those contact lenses.

Mason knew who I was. He had warned me about them. That was one warning I was not prepared to ignore.

Movement from the corridor. Shouts, screams, the pounding of angry footsteps.

I heard the ticking of the clock.

A bitter gust of wind as I pushed the window open. Clouds cleared, allowing the stars to shine in sparkling glory. Mountains shone silver in the distance, the pass between the two highest peaks bathed in moonlight. That was my road to another Territory, the way out of the Fjordlands forever!

Deep, steady breaths as I found a foothold against a drainage pipe. The rough metal chilled my hands as I slowly climbed down. I dropped the last six feet, falling heavily in the snow, dusting my entire body with white. I peered around with my freed eyes, staring at the grounds bathed in silver moonlight.

I crouched low, my eyes darting everywhere for signs of movement. Nothing.

But something was happening at the Palace. Gunshots, shouts, dogs barking.

Dogs.

Without thinking, I ran. Panic was growing, wiping all rational sense. I was clumsy and foolish and a Masonian lunged into my side.

I fell into the snow, my breaths frantic and frightened as I scrambled back. A revolver pointed in my face, the barrel dark and waiting. The Masonian smirked at me, his fur hat speckled with white. He took his aim.

A gunshot ricocheted up the grounds. The Masonian fell with an opened head, speckling the snow with blood and bits of brain.

Sniper.

I startled, searching everywhere. My eyes scanned the roof for the dark hole of a gun, aiming. But there was nothing. No guns, no people...

Just the emptiness of the Palace grounds, the teasing hope of freedom...

That dropped revolver glinted bright in the snow. Cold and heavy to the touch, I secured it in my jeans, scrambled to my feet, and *ran*.

The trees were so close! Just a little farther and I could climb them.

Dogs were released behind me, their ferocious barks echoing through the icy air, their paws battling with the deep snow.

A strained wail, my legs burning as I forced them faster and further. Visions of those snarling muzzles, those sharp teeth, the ripping of my clothes, my flesh...

I heard the thundering of its feet, the heat of its breath...

Another gunshot. The dog yelped and retreated.

I cowered and shrieked, afraid the bullet was for me but knowing deep in my hammering, terrified heart that those snipers were the only reason I was still alive. Those dogs were released for amusement, nothing more.

A tree beckoned me with its skeletal branches, and I leapt my slender limbs into its structure. I made a foothold on the trunk, my arms clinging for dear life as another dog snarled at my feet.

A shot, a whimper and the dog fell dead in the snow.

I groaned out my fear and climbed. The trees were crowded, a route easily spotted. I jumped from one tree to another as they creaked and cracked beneath my weight.

Masonians were below me, scattered in the virgin snow.

The golden fence loomed through the trees. A steep drop – at least ten feet – to the other side. I hesitated.

A shot, a buried bullet in the neighbouring tree, splinters erupting from the collision.

With a great breath, I leapt.

A shriek as I landed in the deep snow, shock rippling up my bones. Masonians gained ground with more dogs barking through the fence, digging at the ground beneath...

I scrambled up, only to collapse. My limbs were straining, burning with heat and ice, but I groaned loudly through the pain and found a solid foothold. I bounced up like a hare and raced into the forest's protecting arms. A bullet whizzed by and buried in a tree. Splinters of wood exploded, scattering like drops of water.

"*Don't shoot her!*" Mason's voice barked. A shot vibrated the air: a prelude to the Masonian's body sinking heavily in the snow.

Mason stood before the golden fence and banged his hands against it. Then he stopped, looking in my direction. Could he see me? I did not wait to find out.

I turned my back to Mason's Palace and sprinted further into the icy wilderness.

29

How long had I been running? It must have been past midnight. The *Shortest Day* was no more.

Aching with exhaustion, my pace slowed to a walk. Limbs dragged behind me, gouging long tracks in the snow. The aurora had reappeared, dancing, its pale light fighting through the mass of pines and needles. Still, through all the colours and the movement and the sheer splendour of it all, the silver moonlight persisted. No doubt it had moved away from the mountains, but I remained hopeful as I followed its light. The snow was still deep, and it was cold.

Bitterly cold.

Wrapping my arms tightly around my chest, I remembered the revolver. How many bullets did I have?

I took the heavy instrument in my hands, admiring its polished surface. Cracking it open, there were three unspent bullets. It snapped back together with a satisfying click, and I replaced it in the waistband of my jeans.

I missed my hunting rifle. There were markets everywhere and I was well acquainted with them. Surely, I would be able to sell the revolver? As long as people didn't ask too many questions regarding how I acquired it, of course. How much did my old hunting rifle cost? Was it one hundred gold coins, or two hundred?

Pines rustled in the wind. Such a soothing sound, made ever more poignant as the piano had *finally* disappeared. For the first time in months, I was free of the music.

Perhaps it was my proximity to Mason? I pushed the thought from my mind, deciding it best not to consider why the music was the way it was. Mason was right: it was a funny thing.

Tia was on my mind. Was she content now? Now that she was finally rid of the nightmares of the last two years, could she finally sleep in peace?

I thought of Anya, and Heidi and Luna. I shed a tear for them all, wishing I could have brought them with me.

I did not shed a tear for the Pretender. It was not that I didn't want to, but simply that I had none left to spare. Tears were a valuable commodity.

My stomach rumbled ominously in the night. And I was thirsty – ever so thirsty.

I thought of the revolver again. With poor range and a precision that was dicey at best, it was hardly an ample weapon to hunt with. Still, needs must.

I narrowed my eyes, refining my vision to see through the trees. It did not take long to spot a lonely doe.

Pfft. Maya Doe. Ample prey, really.

She wandered quite happily, nuzzling the snow. I plucked out the revolver, and crouched low through the trees to get a clear shot. A steadied aim against a fallen log. Closing one eye, the doe was directly in my sight.

Sticks cracked upon frosted, snowy ground. We startled, straining our ears to the forest. Something spooked her. She leapt off through the trees and was out of sight in an instant. I sprung upright, my limbs supple and ready to dart after her. My eyes narrowed, searching every gap for signs of movement.

Music slammed into me.

It returned with a vengeance, yelling and screeching through my skull. Shrieking, I clutched my scalp, sinking deep into the snow as my limbs failed. Only when the pain and the *unbearable* noise subsided did I realise I was surrounded.

Masonians. They were everywhere, their swords poised and each long blade gleaming in the moonlight. There were so many, *too* many!

I held the revolver firm, pointing at each one of them. They were unfazed, their eyes unmoving.

The pound of Mason's boots as he stood on a tall rock, overlooking me.

Heidi was before him, held by him. Mason crushed one hand around her neck. The other held a revolver pushed into her temple.

My feared face met them. Mason had ample time to see the obvious sparkle in my diamond eyes, the way they usually glowed silver in the moonlight. That evil, sadistic grin worked across his jaw, stretching from one side to the other.

"Hello Alira," he said.

~THANK YOU FOR READING "THE END OF EVERYTHING"!~

Please leave a review on Amazon and/or Goodreads, as these are incredibly important for all authors, but especially for indie authors. Not only do reviews help more people find my books, but reviews also provide valuable feedback for me too!

For exclusive content and updates on my new releases, don't forget to sign up to my newsletter at:
    www.esmecarmichael.com

Thank you so much for your support!

ALSO BY ESME CARMICHAEL
THE CONNECTION SERIES

THE MOVER OF MOUNTAINS
Book Two

* * *

Can you feel the music?

Maya is gone. Now, imprisoned in the bowels of Mason's Palace, Alira must find the strength to survive. But as destiny sings louder with each passing day, Alira can't understand why Mason wants to destroy the world he so lovingly created. What secrets is he hiding about his past, about *her* future?

As unexpected alliances are formed and enemies lurk around every corner, Alira wonders if she will ever find happiness. And, most importantly, what part of her humanity is she prepared to sacrifice in exchange for a future?

ALSO BY ESME CARMICHAEL
THE CONNECTION SERIES

THE WALTZ OF WOLVES: PART 1
A New World Novella

* * *

Thirty-three years before The End of Everything, there was a waltz of wolves...

Campbell Anders wishes nothing more than to escape Maelstrom. Endlessly bullied by his cruel, Aristocratic family, Campbell's life is nothing short of miserable. But when the charmingly cocky Harrison Dagger is dragged into the Anders' family home, Campbell's life takes a dangerous, unexpected turn...

This is the story of how two very different boys, from two very different backgrounds, formed the unlikeliest of friendships, and started a Rebellion that would change the entire course of Mason's New World.

Filled with tension, suspense and dark foreboding, *The Waltz of Wolves* is a standalone prequel that will be released as 3 novellas between the main books in *The Connection Series.*

CONTENT WARNINGS

Please note, "The End of Everything" is a dark fantasy which includes the following themes:

- Sustained threat
- Foul language
- Violence
- Blackmail
- Prostitution (implied, not described)
- Assault
- Rape scenarios
- Grief
- Death
- Drug use (both usage and distribution; implied but not described)
- Alcohol use
- Suicidal thoughts
- Slavery
- Pregnancy
- Traumatic birth

ABOUT THE AUTHOR

Esme Carmichael is an independent author based in Liverpool (UK). She has been writing stories for as long as she can remember and published her debut novel — *The End of Everything* — in January 2021.

Esme enjoys putting a dark twist on familiar tropes, creates stories with vivid worlds and writes characters full of snark, body and life. She's currently working her way through editing and publishing her long list of stories, ranging from high fantasy tales to paranormal romances.

When not writing, Esme works full time as an ocean scientist and is gradually working her way through her ever growing TBR pile.

- facebook.com/esmecarmichaelauthor
- instagram.com/esmecarmichael_author
- goodreads.com/esmecarmichael

Printed in Great Britain
by Amazon